ROUGAROU

JUDITH ANN MCDOWELL

World Castle Publishing, LLC
Pensacola, Florida
Copyright © Judith Ann McDowell 2011
Paperback ISBN: 9781955086035
eBook ISBN: 9781955086042
Second Edition World Castle Publishing, LLC, May 3, 2021
http://www.worldcastlepublishing.com

Licensing Notes

Cover: Karen Fuller
Editor: Beth Price

There are those for whom the night Becries
A call they can't ignore.
To set them forth to walk this
Earth as many have before.
Would you send them back with pious words
To cleanse their evil souls?
Then hide beneath your cloak of white
While they wither in the throes of a living hell
They did not choose,
Yet are caught within its grasp
Too weak to break the chains that bind
Hence they have been cast.

CHAPTER ONE

Louisiana 2010

Jack Olivier' cut the motor of the small boat before it could bump the wet stilts of the old shack sitting atop its rotting timbers. Loud grunts from hunting gators echoed along the banks as lapping water slapped against the sides of the boat, breaking the stillness of the night

"Too late to turn back now," he murmured, tying the boat alongside the one already there.

Climbing the slippery ladder, he could see the faint glow of a candle moving from somewhere inside, and his heart picks up speed as the door is pushed open.

"Jack, what brings you to the bayous in the dark of night?" Her breathy voice with its Cajun accent flows over him.

"I need your help, Chandra."

For a brief moment, she watched him, her green eyes alert. Then, stepping to the side, pushed the door open wider.

A sharp odor of musk filled his senses as he walked past her. The smell did not offend him. He knew the scent well; knew it would remain, calling forth vivid images he wished to forget.

A glimmer of fear showed in her eyes as she set the candleholder down on a small kitchen table. "What is it you wish of me?"

Dropping into an overstuffed chair, he tried without success to hide his tension. "I think you can guess."

Her hand flew to her throat. "Someone has moved into the mansion."

"So much time has passed, I thought we'd moved beyond havin' to worry."

"Evil does not die, Jack." She stared through the weathered screen door at the gathering mist. "It only lies dormant. Waiting."

"You have to warn them, Chandra." He ran a tired hand through his thick, dark brown hair. "I don't know how. I mean, how does one warn others 'bout the likes of him and not come off soundin' like we're the ones they should be leery of?"

"What you ask of me, I am unable to give."

"Unable or unwillin'?" He gazed at her in the dim light. "You know as well as I, no one else will go up there. Christ! Even I haven't been in that house since..." He shoved his tall, lean body from the chair to push past her and onto the porch.

Close on his heels, she jerked him around to face her. "You, and others like you, think since I have the gift to see what others cannot, I am beyond his reach. The powers of darkness are very strong, Jack." Her slender arms twined around her body. "Only a fool would challenge their wrath."

"Chandra, I'm talkin' 'bout a flesh and blood man. You're talkin' as though he's some kinda demon. Yes, the man's dangerous, but he's still human."

A slight laugh bubbled up from her throat as she looked at him, shocked he could be so naïve. "Alright." He trailed a finger over her high cheekbones as the nostrils of her straight, well-defined nose flared with frustration. "I realize there are powers I can't explain. I know you can do things I would never have believed possible. Such as talkin' to spirits or healin' those who come to you when even the doctors have given up. But, Chandra, I'd be willin' to bet every cent I have, you can best him."

Her beautiful face, bathed in the glow of the full moon moving out from behind the clouds, relaxed for a moment before taking on the shadow of fear once more. "Then you will be a poor man, Jack, for I know his strength." She pushed his hand from her face. "Tell me of the people living in the mansion.

To keep himself from reaching for her again, he shoved his hands into the pockets of his jeans. "I don't know much, only what I overheard at the post office. A man, his wife, and three little girls moved in a few days ago."

"Of course." The words slid from her throat. "That is why it has been so long since anyone has occupied the mansion." Her long, bare nails bit into her arms as she stood trying to sort out her racing thoughts. "The others had no children, so they did not get offered a lease on the estate."

A slight shiver of fear passed over him. "Why do you say that?"

"The strength of evil is at its peak when the blood of the pure is spilled. What purer blood is there than that which is yet to be tainted or defiled?" She ignored the way his brows drew together; refused to look away as disgust replaced fear. "Would he not think it sweeter than the finest wine? They trust with their very souls, my naïve friend. It is this innocence which calls and tempts the evil to come for them."

His eyes grew wide as he realized the full impact of her words. "You're tellin' me not only is he psychotic, he enjoys killin' children?"

"These people are nothing to me! Yet you ask me to risk my very life to protect them!" She plopped herself into the nearest chair. At her cold indifference, he drew back as though seeing her for the first time. "You think me unfeeling." Her beautiful eyes rounded as she cocked her head to one side. "You feel that way because you do not know what you ask of me."

Stepping up behind her, he kneaded the taut muscles of her neck, smiling as she dropped her head forward in an open invitation for him to continue. "I'm askin' you to stop somethin' before it's too late. If you want, I'll go with you to talk to them."

"No," Chandra shrugged his hands away, "if I decide to put myself at risk, I will do what needs to be done alone." She left her chair, distancing the space between them.

His gaze slid over her tall form, noting how the hot, humid night molded the thin gown to her body. With a determined shake of his head, he continued. "What I don't understand is why you think he'll know if you go to them." Anger at her stubbornness, and the uncomfortable tightening in his groin, sharpened his words. "It isn't as though he can see what goes on at every moment of the day and night."

"His eyes can see what others cannot." Chandra slid a hand beneath her hair to lift it from clinging to the back of her neck. "Never doubt his ability to search me out to extract payment for what he would deem his just due."

"Chandra!" In two quick strides, he crossed the porch, taking her by the arm and spinning her around to face him. "The man is insane!" His fingers dug into her flesh as she tried to back away out of his reach. "The doctors who pronounced him cured were only after the old man's money! I think the best thing for all of us would be for me to go alone and tell them what they need to know."

"Will they listen?" Her eyes closed, sending out a silent plea.

"I'll do my best to see they do." His voice softened as he stared down at her. "At any rate, he won't look to you for revenge."

"It could work." She allowed herself to warm to the idea. "You are one of many, whereas I would be the first person he would come for."

"Then it's settled." He leaned forward, pressed his lips against her cheek. "I have two clients comin' to see me at different times tomorrow, but I should be free in the late afternoon."

Chandra gazed up at him, seeing the goodness in his dark brown eyes. His narrow, boyish face revealed his feelings, feelings she remembered all too well. "I know you think I am talking about things which have no real place in your world."

Blood-drenched walls and the sickening smell of bodies left to lie in the sweltering heat long after the pulse of life had stopped beating crawled into his mind. He pushed the disgusting thoughts away to brush her mass of ebony hair back over one dusky shoulder. "Chandra, I know bad things happen in this world. I also feel a lot of it can be avoided."

She pushed his hands away. "So many believe because they go to church and say their prayers each night, evil can never touch them. They are so wrong."

When he reached for her, she sidestepped him, putting

out her hands to ward off his embrace. "You see what is on the surface, Jack. So much more goes on in this life people do not know about."

"Chandra, I am a believer in God, don't try and tell me we ain't protected. The Lord don't work that way."

"Yes, we have protection, but right now, this earth is a battlefield. Even your Bible speaks of Satan's reign, and although I do not believe in Satan, I do believe there are dark spirits on this plane. Jack, listen to me. It is the dark side that is in control."

"Again, I get the feelin' we're talkin' 'bout two different things. I'm talkin' 'bout Lawrence Hindel, a deranged killer. Money bought his freedom and turned him loose on the people of this town. Everyone here has enough sense to stay away from that house, but these people ain't from here. They have no idea what danger they're in. I can't close my eyes and pretend somethin' can't happen!" He turned, striding towards the ladder.

***

Standing in the doorway a few moments later, she watched his boat disappear around the bend. Chandra felt her body grow cold with terror, for she knew what she had to do. But first, she would ascertain, beyond all doubt, danger did exist.

Storm clouds moved across the full moon, followed by low rumblings of thunder.

Seating herself in a chair beside the open window, Chandra concentrated on freeing her spirit from the confines of her body. Taking several deep breaths to relax her mind, she shut out all sound and movement. From the fluttering curtain blowing away from the window to the sounds of tree frogs making themselves heard below. Always before, she found this an easy task. Now knowing the danger to herself and others, her mind froze with fear, which thwarted her efforts to reach out to those in need.

Forcing the fear deep inside, she felt herself become weightless as her spirit soared from the flesh and blood shell sitting upright in the tattered old chair.

In no time at all, she found herself walking the sprawling grounds of the Hindel Mansion. Light streamed through high windows, pushing back the shadows reaching across spacious lawns as she moved up the wide stone steps to the front entrance.

Passing through the door, she halted just inside to watch three young girls, whose ages she guessed to be six, eight and maybe ten coming towards her down a wide staircase. Such beautiful children with their long blond hair parted in the middle and hanging well below their waists. Their large blue eyes shone with the innocence of youth. As she watched them, she felt an unusual sadness come over her at the thought of what may be waiting for them in the shadows.

***

An unnatural howling arose from beyond the sturdy walls, stopping each girl in mid-stride as they looked one to the other, trying to discern what caused it. Then, as if by some unspoken agreement, they ran as fast as their young legs would allow through the cavernous rooms to where a man of perhaps thirty-five and a woman somewhat younger sat in conversation.

"Mama! Did you hear that?" The oldest girl threw herself into the safety of her mother's arms.

"Yes, Margaret," her mother allowed, pushing the child from her, and smoothing the hem of her dress back down to cover her knees, "it sounded like a dog."

"But...it sounded hurt," Margaret's eight-year-old sister cried, her large eyes growing even larger.

"I don't think so, Rebecca," her father spoke up, trying to put the children at ease. "It's some neighbor's dog out hunting."

"I wish we could have a dog," she whined, settling herself on the floor at his feet.

"Now, we aren't going to start this again." He glanced at her over his wide-rimmed glasses.

Their mother entered into the conversation. "You both know what Mr. Quigly, the caretaker said when we leased this house. He said no pets!"

A long, deep-throated howl combined with echoing peals of thunder brought all five people up straight.

"Good god! That is unnerving, isn't it?" The tall, thin-bodied man, dressed in a long-sleeved white shirt and black slacks, laid his crossword book down on the table beside his chair. Rising to his feet, he walked over to the floor-to-ceiling window. Pulling back on the heavy drapery, he gazed out onto the shadowed grounds. "That's enough to make the hairs on the back of the neck stand up!" He shivered, dropping the drapery back into place before turning to face the ones watching him.

"Didn't make my hairs stand up," six-year-old Lisa whispered, trying to sound brave while at the same time inching closer to her mother, who reached out towards her.

"Roger," she glanced at her husband, "maybe it's some hungry stray." She inserted an embroidery needle into a pillowcase she had been stitching to set it aside. "Why don't I set some food out for it?"

"Janet, if we start doing that, before you know it, it'll be hanging around all the time." He withdrew a pipe from a carved wooden holder setting on the end table. "Mr. Quigly will assume it's ours and accuse us of breaking our lease. The man strikes me as the sort who would refuse to return our money, too." He popped the lid from a large can of tobacco and, taking a pinch between thumb and forefinger, placed it in the bowl of the pipe, tamping it down to a loose fit. "I think it goes without saying, we would be in a sorry mess if that happened."

"Roger, please!" She nodded to the girls.

"What? Oh yes...well...anyway," he glanced toward the three small girls whose trusting eyes watched him as he continued, "none of you are to feed that dog. His gaze swung to include his pretty, blond-haired wife. "He'll find his way back home."

"All right, girls, it's bedtime." Janet cut short the conversation before the children had a chance to begin their campaign for the dog's well-being. "You need to scoot upstairs and change into your gowns. Be sure and put your dirty clothes in the clothes hamper. Daddy and I will be up soon to tuck you in."

***

With a resigned sigh, Margaret herded her sisters ahead of her towards the staircase. Watching her parents over her shoulder, she lowered her voice to a conspiratorial whisper. "I think Mama and Daddy are mean not to let us have a dog. I don't care what they say," her small mouth settled into a determined pout, "after everyone's in bed tonight, I'm going to take some food out to that poor little dog. He must be so hungry to cry like that."

"I'll go with you." Rebecca placed a small arm around her sister's waist.

"Me too! Me too!" cried Lisa, determined not to be left out of anything discussed in a whisper.

Halfway up the stairs, they heard the strange howling erupt once more.

"Listen!" Margaret whispered.

"Yes! Listen!" Chandra cried, but they couldn't hear her. The children did not know what awaited them. If found on the grounds, they would not stand a chance. Evil does not hesitate when its prey is so near and available.

She must warn them. She had witnessed the love between this family. Now she could not turn her face from them. She had to return to her body. They could not see her vaporous spirit.

Outside, piercing howls split the night silence once more. Very close this time. So close she could smell the distinct odor of wet fur.

CHAPTER TWO

Chandra could see the old shack waiting atop the dark waters of the bayous. Her mind cried out with relief, then froze as she glimpsed a small orange glow through the open window. Knowing she had no choice, she reentered her body. When she opened her eyes, she saw him sitting in a chair, a thin cheroot held between his fingers and smiling.

"Chandra, did you think we wouldn't know?"

She opened her mouth to speak, but the cold gray eyes watching her stilled the words in her throat.

"Chandra," he echoed her name in his deep, husky voice, his piercing gaze refusing to release her, "think back to the night you placed your soul in my hands."

As though she had no will of her own, her mind led her back through time to her sixteenth year when her eager young body first felt the aching hunger and throbbing heat that comes with the awakening of womanhood. Hot sultry nights when the body is unable to relax, and the mind takes advantage of the blood fever.

The throbbing of the drums called to her, pulling her from her slumber in the late hours of the night. Sitting up, she felt the rough sheet brush against her budding nipples, making them ache with the strange raw hunger she had been experiencing of late. In a huff, she flung the stifling linen to the floor, her naked, sweat-slicked body relishing the slight breeze blowing in through the open window. The pounding continued its demanding call.

With a low moan, she picked up the thin, transparent gown from the foot of the bed to slip it over her head, uncaring of how the sheer fabric clung to her damp body. As though she no longer controlled her movements, she left her room, walking out into the night to answer a call she could not ignore. The full moon, casting a pale glow out over the dense foliage, aided her unclad feet in picking their way through the barbed vines winding their way across her path.

A strong stench of rotting flora, ever present in the swamp-infested bayous, hovered in the night air to fill her with a sense of foreboding. She tried to alert herself. Tried to shut out the sounds of the pounding drums calling her attention away from the danger lurking within these shadowed bogs, danger of stepping into one of the many bottomless tombs of quicksand. She could feel her heart thudding in her chest, feel her mind recoil with fear as she visualized the gaping mouth and sharp fangs of the lethal water moccasins swimming, perhaps, inches away in the brackish waters.

On and on she ran, until at last she came to a clearing. No sound greeted her, except those of the night creatures. Even the drums were silent. Dropping to her knees, she waited, trying to draw some much-needed air into her tortured lungs. She could smell her own stench wafting up to her as she knelt there in the wet grass. Pushing her damp hair back from her face, she looked around, trying to see into the darkness. Out of the corner of her eye, she saw a movement.

When she looked up, she saw a group of people gathering around her in a large circle. The flickering light from the many long-handled torches driven into the ground bathed their all but naked bodies in a soft, yellow-red glow. Her throat grew dry, and her pulse quickened as she watched them. The men wore baggy, white cotton trousers. The women wore full-flowing white cotton skirts and nothing else. She felt heat rise to her face as she saw their bared breasts jiggle each time they moved. Then, realizing her own lack of concealment, crossed her arms over her chest.

She tried to rise to her feet, but her tired body would not obey her commands. She sank back down on the sandy grass, trying to still the blood pounding in her ears.

He stood looking down at her, his black, high-top boots

planted far apart. Her eyes moved up his tall, muscular frame, noting the well-fitting black pants and white shirt stretched taut across wide shoulders. A cold chill passed over her as she glimpsed the sardonic smile pulling down the corners of his wide, full mouth.

She found herself staring at this handsome man, with his darkly tanned skin and thick, raven black hair hanging just below the wide collar of his shirt. She guessed his age to be in the late forties, middle fifties, but the deep-set, steel-gray eyes staring back at her showed a depth of living that far surpassed his outward appearance.

With her heart still fluttering in her chest, she accepted the hand he held out to pull her to her feet then against his broad chest. He stared down at her, placing one hand in her long, tightly curled black hair. When she would have turned away, he pulled her head back hard, forcing her to look at him.

She shivered as his cold, thick-lashed eyes kept her frightened gaze riveted to his. She breathed the smell of him into her mind relishing his clean, male scent. The smell made her feel giddy and, at the same time, made her own sharp scent become more pronounced. In her innocence, she feared her musky odor would offend him. She tried to pull away.

His dark head bent forward to lick the moisture from her skin. As her salty taste laved upon his tongue, a hunger so strong it made him tremble filled his body. With a low growl, he yanked her slim hips against his own, all the while keeping his wet mouth and tongue playing over the racing pulse of her throat.

Somewhere in the darkness, a deep throbbing filled the air. The repetitive rhythm matched the pounding in her loins. Never has she felt so alive, so filled with a need to give and to take as she is in the arms of this stranger who has stripped her so completely of her inhibitions. Meeting his lust, she yanked his hot mouth from her throat. Her greedy lips all but devouring him in her need. With the smell of him filling her senses and the taste of his hot mouth yet lingering upon her tongue, she moaned deep in her throat. Pushing her young body tight against his, she ground her well-rounded hips against him.

Without any warning, he set her away from him. It was so sudden her heightened needs refused to realize he no longer craved her touch. A cry tore from her throat as she sprang at him, trying to draw his mouth back to her own. With cold calm, he pulled her arms from around his neck, but she refused to be deterred from her hunger.

"No!" she panted. "I need you!"

This time his refusal is more brutal as one large hand lashes out, slapping her away from him. She lay on the damp ground whimpering like a small child. She could feel his cold eyes watching her. Then, to her astonishment, he walked away from her.

Pushing herself to her feet, she took a hesitant step in the same direction then stopped as he turned back to glare at her.

"You will not follow me," he demanded.

"I will follow you!" she screamed at him. "You cannot stop me!"

In two quick strides, he is beside her, grasping her shoulders and shaking her into compliance. "You will obey me!" A strange look covers his face as his hands drop back to his side.

"Am I so beneath you, you would throw me away like so much filth?" she lashed out at him. "Is it the color of my skin which repels you?"

Without touching her, the anger now gone from his voice, he replied, "Nothing about you repels me. Except, perhaps, your innocence."

Hope rekindles in her eyes as she reaches for him, but he stays her hands. "The passion burning within you now will fade with time."

"No! It will not!" she cried out her anger. "If you had no intentions of taking me, why in God's name did you fill my body with such hunger?"

"Do...not...bring...your...God...into what has passed here!" His eyes flashed with unleashed anger. "For believe me! He has no place anywhere near the likes of me!"

"I don't understand your words."

He simply gazed at her then turned to leave.

"No! Don't go!" She took a step forward, stopping as he turned back. "I don't want to beg," she held out her hands to him, "but I will if you take me with you."

"Does your young life mean so little to you?" A look of sadness falls over his face.

"What do you mean?"

"Forget this night," his deep voice beseeched her. "Forget me. You will survive none the worst for my having walked away from you."

"You are the one who called me here. Aren't you?"

"I thought I wanted you." He fought the urge to give in to her pleas. "I see now I was wrong."

She did not cry out this time or try to hold on to him. She stood where he left her, watching him go. But her gaze stayed fixed on his retreating back. When she could no longer catch sight of him, she began to run, her bare feet making no sound on the damp grass as she stayed far enough back so as not to alert him to her presence. His long strides made it difficult for her to keep him in her sights. She kept her eyes fixed on his white shirt, the one thing standing out in the darkness.

Hearing the loud squeaking of a gate, she stopped, crouching down to hide herself among the tall foliage. Over her harsh breathing, she heard a loud clanging sound. Moving ahead, she could see a tall gate of wrought iron. Quickening her pace, she saw him walking towards a large, three-story house. She waited until he disappeared inside then, holding a deep breath, she pulled on the gate. Nothing happened. The gate refused to budge.

In a panic, she looked around, searching for a way to get inside the vast grounds. She would have to climb over the well-defined bars with their sharp spears of ornamental iron atop the black fencing. For once, she welcomed her reed-thin stature as she pulled herself up and over with little trouble. She made her way through the grounds and up to the main entrance of the house.

Silence greeted her as she peered through the slightly opened drapes covering a large window. She could see him, his back turned to her, staring at something across the way.

Without giving herself time to think, she ran up the wide stone steps and opened the front door. Leaving the door ajar, she made her way through the house, searching for the man whose touch her hungry body still craved. A strange sound, not unlike someone in pain, came to her. She followed the sound until she found herself staring at his broad back through the open door of a library. She walked into the room, followed his line of vision up to a painting hanging over a large fireplace.

The portrait, done in oils, was that of a slender young woman of average height. Black hair fell in a natural flow down her naked back, and pink nipples stood erect on full breasts showing her strong arousal. Her full, sensuous mouth parted in a teasing smile showed even white teeth. She had a wild, untamed look about her. The nostrils of her small straight nose hinting at her European ancestry flared. But her eyes are what held one mesmerized. Deep emerald green and slanted upward at the outer edges, they cast a startling contrast to her light-brown skin. Chandra's eyes moved down further to the thick, dark triangle between the girl's thighs and felt a sharp stab of jealousy.

As though he sensed her presence, he turned, staring at her, his face filled with such suffering she felt her throat tighten on a sharp intake of breath. Without a word, he turned his attention back to the vision smiling down on him.

"She's very beautiful," Chandra said, and knew she meant it as she moved the rest of the way into the room to stand beside him.

He nodded, his gaze still fixed upon the painting.

"What is her name?"

"Angelia," he breathed the words. "My beautiful...dead... Angelia."

Euphoria filled her. Unable to stop herself, she asked, "What happened to her?"

With a strangled cry, he turned to face her. His damp eyes filled with anguish. "I happened to her!"

"I don't understand." She backed away from him.

"No, you don't, although I promise you will." He moved towards her, his steel-gray eyes filled now with an unholy light.

"I warned you not to follow me, but you did not listen. I promise you, Chandra, after this night, you will never wish to disobey me again."

Now, as she sat across from him in the old two-room shack above the bayous with the memory of all those years still burning through her mind, she waited. Waited for the horror to return.

CHAPTER THREE

Standing in the darkness, Rebecca held the door while Margaret looked around for a large rock with which to prop it open. At last, in a nearby flower bed, she found what she needed. Motioning Rebecca to come outside, she wedged the door open enough for them to get back inside.

"Here, doggy, doggy, doggy," Margaret called into the darkness. Except for the splashing rain, beating on the wide, circular, cobblestone driveway, all remained quiet in the rolling fog.

"Margaret, we're getting all wet!" Rebecca cried, trying to pull her sister towards the door.

"Oh, all right! Take Lisa's hand before she slips and falls," she told her, leading the way back up the steps. As they started to close the door, they heard a mournful howling coming from somewhere nearby. "There! Did you hear that?" Margaret turned back. "He's still here!"

"Margaret, I don't want to go back outside," Rebecca whimpered. "It's wet and cold, and I'm scared."

"Me too," Lisa spoke up, shivering, her wet gown plastered against her small body.

"Oh! You're both a couple of fraidy-cats." Margaret pushed her wet hair out of her eyes. "Go ahead then. I'll take the food to the poor little dog myself."

Rebecca took hold of her sister's arm. "Maybe it's not a little dog at all, Margaret." She looked around, trying to see into the rain. "Maybe it's a big wolf!"

Shaking the hand from her arm, Margaret laughed a

strangled laugh. "Wolves don't live in Louisiana, silly. They just live out west."

"I'm cold!" Lisa whined.

"Then go to bed!" Her sudden unease at Rebecca's warning making the tone of her voice much more biting than she had intended.

"You don't have to be mean to her, Margaret. She's just crying because she's still a baby."

At the sight of her younger siblings huddled together, Margaret dropped a kiss on Lisa's cold cheek. "I'm sorry." Smiling through her tears, Lisa continued to shiver. "Rebecca, take Lisa upstairs and get her dried off and into another gown. Be sure and hang the wet gown over the shower door to dry. I'll be up as soon as I take this food out to the dog."

"Why don't you just set the food on the step and come in?"

Holding a finger to her lips, Margaret cautioned her. "If I set it there, Mama and Daddy might find the bowl before I can take it back in the house in the morning. I'm going to take it out behind the big oak. The dog is sure to find it there."

"I wish we'd never heard that stupid old dog." Rebecca turned Lisa in the direction of the hallway. "He's just gonna get us in trouble."

Gathering the hem of her long gown in one hand, Margaret ran across the rolling lawn to the large oak, the one closest to the mansion. Making her way to the back of the huge old relic, she set the food bowl down within easy reach then turned toward the house. A loud rustling sound, from somewhere nearby, stopped her. "Here, doggy, doggy, doggy. Come on, I know you're hungry." She stared through the rain and fog, watching for the hungry stray to come to her. "Come get the food waiting for you." For long moments the loud drumming of the rain splashing against the gnarled and thick-leafed limbs drowned out all other sound.

Then, over the shrieking wind, a terrible howling split the silence. The eerie sound froze the young girl back against the trunk of the tree. Unable to move, she gazed into the pouring rain. Fear rushed blood through her veins until her pulse hammered inside her ears.

Knowing she is trapped with nowhere to run, she calls out to the two people she trusts more than anyone else in her short young life.

"Mama! Daddy! Help me!" she screamed over and over. The shrieking wind caught up her fevered pleas, and without mercy, tumbled them back to a throat already being devoured by the evil lurking within the shadows of the Hindel Mansion.

***

A surprised Janet walked into the room to find Rebecca and Lisa already seated at the table.

"My, this is a first." She withdrew a wide, bib-apron from a kitchen drawer. Placing the bib over her head, she adjusted it to cover her sleeveless, pink blouse and white shorts before tying it around her trim waist.

"We're hungry," Lisa informed her.

"What else is new?" Janet leaned into the refrigerator, taking bacon and eggs from the shelf.

"Is the coffee ready?" Roger hung his suit coat over the back of his chair before seating himself at the head of the table.

"Not yet." Janet turned at the sound of his voice. "I just came down myself.

"Janet, I told you," he glanced at her over the morning paper, "I have an appointment with Brummel this morning. He's going to go over my contract from the publishers." He snapped a page of the paper into place. "Do I have to do everything in this house in order to get things done?"

"Oh, Roger, calm down." Janet cracked first one egg then another into a bowl. "You're always in a hurry."

"Where's Margaret?" He closed the paper to lay it aside. "Still upstairs sleeping, I suppose. Well," he pulled the cup of coffee she set on the table towards him, "if she is, then you'll have to drive her to school this morning. I can't be late for this appointment."

"Rebecca," Janet said over her shoulder as she pushed the beaten eggs around the skillet, "run upstairs and tell your sister to get down here."

"She's not up there." Rebecca's fingers picked at a slight hole in the vinyl tablecloth.

"What do you mean she's not up there? And stop picking at that hole before you have it so big we'll have to throw the whole tablecloth away. Now get upstairs like I told you and call your sister."

"I told you, Mama. Margaret's not up there."

"Well, where else could she be at..." she glanced at the big clock hanging over the entryway, "6:30 in the morning?"

"I don't know, Mama." Rebecca dropped her eyes.

"What's going on here?" Roger demanded, watching Rebecca.

"Margaret went to feed the doggy," Lisa spoke up.

"Lisa, be quiet!" Rebecca yanked on the sleeve of her sister's nightgown.

"Rebecca, if you know something, you better tell us right now!" The tone of her father's voice brought her up straight in her chair.

"Margaret went outside to feed that little dog after you and Mama went to bed last night." She lifted one small hip then the other as she tugged her gown into a more comfortable place. "She just hasn't come back yet, is all."

"Good God!" Roger jumped up from his chair. "Do you mean to tell me your sister has been outside all night?" He saw tears well up in her eyes as she stared up at him. "Why didn't you come and tell us?"

"I don't know!" she cried, the stark fear in her father's face beginning to transfer itself to her. "I fell asleep."

In the unsettling atmosphere, Lisa began to whimper. Within moments the pressing appointment and everything else of any importance flew right out of his mind as Roger ran from the house in search of his eldest daughter.

Janet busied herself with making breakfast, trying to keep everything as normal as possible so as not to upset the girls still sitting at the table. Every few moments she would go to the door trying to catch a glimpse of Roger or, better yet, Margaret. As the minutes slipped by without any word, Janet turned off the stove and pulled her other two children towards the back door. "Come on," she told them. "we're going to find your sister."

But they didn't find her. Although they covered almost every square inch of the sprawling grounds looking for her until a distraught Roger admitted they needed help. "Go call the police, Janet! Tell them what's happened and how long she's been gone."

With one hand pressed against her throat, she nodded, then turned, running up the driveway to the house.

"I'm sorry, Daddy!" Rebecca whispered, taking Roger's large hand in hers.

Uncaring of the stains the wet grass would instill on his black slacks, he stooped to one knee to gather her against his chest. "I know you are, Rebecca. I shouldn't have yelled at you." He tried to still the pounding in his chest. "It's just...that..." his words became muffled as he buried his face in her hair.

"The police are on their way, Roger," Janet told him, coming across the lawn.

"Where in God's name could she have gone?" he asked of no one in particular as he pushed himself to his feet. "And in the middle of that storm?"

"We'll find her, Roger." Janet wrung her hands. "I know we will!"

In the distance high pitched wails of police sirens echoed through the still morning, growing louder as the cars veered off the main road and onto the wide lane leading up to the mansion. Four police cars, and one unmarked car, skidded to a stop outside the closed ornamental gate.

Roger ran towards the fence to let them in. As he threw open the gate, the cars drove forward up the drive. The lead car slowed as Roger walked towards the house. One of the officers talked to him through the open window. "We had a call about a missing girl. Are you Mr. Stewart?"

"Yes. My wife called." Roger's voice shook with his fear.

He put the car in park, grabbed his two-way radio on his way out the door. Standing in the driveway, he and two deputies saw the other officers spread out over the grounds. He brought his attention back to the harried man standing beside the car.

"Tell me what happened here last night."

"Nothing happened." Roger stared in confusion.

The officer glanced up as Janet and the girls made their way across the lawn. "Are you telling me your daughter took it upon herself to go wandering alone in the night? For no reason?"

"No. No, I don't mean that." Roger yanked on his knotted tie until it sagged around his neck. "Somebody's dog kept howling. I guess, according to my daughter Rebecca, Margaret felt sorry for the animal and took some food out for it."

The look passing between the deputies was not missed by either Janet or Roger.

"Is there a more private place we can talk?" The officer nodded to the children.

"Yes." Roger worked on unbuttoning the first three buttons of his shirt. "Rebecca, take Lisa and go play in your room. Your mother will come after you in a little while," her father added as he saw a look of concern cross her face.

The officer walked with the worried couple to the house, listening as they told him everything he needed to know about their missing daughter.

After everyone was seated at the kitchen table, the officer introduced himself as Lieutenant Detective Donavan Hays of the Saint Anthony Parish Sheriff's Department.

"How did you people come to find this house?"

Roger drew back, staring at the man. "What does this house have to do with finding Margaret? She's been missing for hours! We need to find her!"

"My men are already searching the grounds, Mr. Stewart," Hays told him in a calm voice. "The K.9 unit's on the way with their dogs. Trust me, everything that can be done will be done."

"Oh, God! I'm so scared!" Roger turned his head from side to side, kneading the back of his neck.

"I'm scared for you, Mr. Stewart," Hays said.

Roger's startled gaze collided with the focus of the man seated across from him. "Why do you say that, Lieutenant?"

Sidestepping the issue, he replied, "Now, tell me, how did you and your wife come to find this house?"

Roger slumped back in his chair. "We met the caretaker of the estate soon after we drove into town."

"How did you know he was the caretaker?" Hays lifted one brown eyebrow. "Had you already met him before coming here?"

"No," Janet spoke up. "A man, who introduced himself as Mr. Quigly, came over to the moving van. He asked about our moving into the parish."

"I told him we needed to find a house for rent, but until we found one, we'd be staying at the Inn," Roger took up the conversation. "Quigly said he might be able to help. He told us about the estate. That it's up for lease. When he told us the price, I thought I'd heard wrong."

Hays slipped out of his suit-coat, draped it over an empty chair, rolled up the sleeves of his white shirt, then reached inside his shirt pocket to withdraw a small notebook. "What price did he quote you?"

"Five hundred a month, utilities included. We drove right out here so he could show us around. I wanted the house the moment I laid eyes on it." Roger looked over at Janet, who nodded in agreement. "I wrote him out a check for the entire year right then and there."

"Hmmm, very interesting." Hays tapped the pen against the notepad. "Did he say why he asked such a low price?"

No." Roger paused in thought. "I wondered about it, but I didn't want to appear unappreciative, so I didn't say anything."

"How about any trouble that's happened here in the past? Did he mention anything about that?"

"No." Roger's gaze shifted over to Janet. "He never mentioned any trouble. The one time he made me a little nervous is when he asked about the girls."

"What about the girls?" Hays sat up straighter in his chair to lean forward.

"He asked if they belonged to us. I thought he'd call off the deal because the owner of the place didn't allow children. When I told him the girls are our daughters, he just smiled and wrote out a receipt for a one year lease."

"That *is* interesting." Hays straightened his light blue tie smoothing it down into place over his ponderous stomach, all the while continuing to write in the small black notepad he had before him on the table.

"Now, I've answered your questions." Roger pulled his chair in closer to the table. "What kind of trouble happened here?"

Reaching inside his shirt pocket, Hays withdrew a pack of cigarettes. "Do you mind?" he asked, already shaking a cigarette from the pack.

Roger pushed an ashtray across the table.

Hays inhaled the smoke into his lungs, waiting for the soothing effects of the nicotine to quiet his jangled nerves. "About five years ago, another family by the name of Rawlins lived here on the estate. They also had young girls. In fact, they looked to be about the same age as your girls." He tapped the cigarette against the rim of the ashtray. "They didn't live around here, either."

At the word "either," Roger started to ask what difference it could make, then decided to hear the man out.

"The first hint any of us had something may be amiss came when Bob Wilks, the paper boy's father, called telling us we might want to check out the estate. His son said no one picked up the papers anymore, and he didn't have any room to stuff them in the box. Since no one had called to cancel the subscription, he thought something could be wrong."

"Why didn't the boy come up to the house to check it out himself?" Janet asked, a puzzled frown creasing her brow.

"That's one I never thought I'd hear," Hays said. Then, realizing how his statement must have sounded to the couple watching him, he declared, "Since you aren't from around here, you would have no way of knowing the reputation of this house."

"No, Mr. Quigly never said anything," Janet replied.

"That doesn't surprise me," Hays growled.

"What kind of reputation are you talking about, Lieutenant?" Roger asked, anxious to get the conversation over and the man sitting at his table, wasting his time, back outside looking for Margaret.

Hays began snapping the tip of his pen in and out until

Roger reached over, removing it from his fingers to lay it down on the table. Hays retrieved the pen, attached it to his notepad. "Sorry about that. It's a nervous habit."

The Stewarts looked at him, waiting for him to continue.

Knowing he had no choice, Hays obliged them. "For years, people of the parish have talked about this place as being haunted."

Janet and Hays could actually hear the breath being expelled from Roger's lungs. "Haunted? Christ! I thought the way you were going on, this place might have been the scene of a blood bath!"

"A blood bath pretty well describes it," Hays stated.

"What the hell are you trying to tell us?" Roger shouted, the chair he had been sitting in falling backward as he jumped to his feet.

"As I said," Donavan grabbed the back of the chair, set it upright, "the talk concerning this place went on for years." He kept his voice low and steady as Roger pulled the chair back away from the table then sat down. "The kids around town kept it stirred up. The adults tried to ignore it. 'Course when the Rawlins family moved in…" his voice trailed off as he looked up to see one of his deputies standing in the doorway.

"Lieutenant Hays, could I speak to you for a moment?" The young deputy nodded to Roger and Janet.

"Excuse me." Hays pushed himself to his feet to follow the man outside.

"Roger, what is happening here?" Janet leaned across the table to her husband. "Why won't he let us go and search for Margaret?"

"They're trained deputies, Janet." His voice held his frustration at the seeming laxity in finding their daughter. "They know what they're doing. We have to trust them."

"Mr. and Mrs. Stewart, Mr. Quigly has just arrived. If it's agreeable with you, I'd like to bring him in," Hays said.

"Yes! Please!" Roger left his chair. "Maybe he knows something that will help us find Margaret!"

"We can always hope that will be the case." Hays motioned

the man inside. "Mr. Quigly, would you step in here, please?"

Making his way toward the couple waiting for any help he could offer them, the short, balding man, who appeared to be in his middle to late sixties, reached out for both their hands. "Mr. and Mrs. Stewart, I can't tell you how sorry I am to hear about Margaret's disappearance. When I looked out my window this morning and saw all the police cars up here, I got dressed and came right up."

"Have a seat, Mr. Quigly." Hays pulled a chair out from the end of the table. "Your coming here will save me a trip down to your cottage."

"That's quite all right." Quigly seated himself and reached out once more to take Janet's hand." I want to do everything in my power to help find that poor child."

"I'm sure you do." Hays watched him. His deep set, dark brown eyes hooded. "So why don't you begin by telling me where I can find Lawrence Hindel."

"Afraid I can't be of much help to you there, Lieutenant." Quigly withdrew his hand. "Mister Lawrence hasn't been on the estate for some months now. I would venture to guess he's in England with his father. In any case, he hasn't written telling me to get the house ready for his return."

"But," Roger spoke up, dropping into the chair beside Janet, "we just paid a year's lease on this house. Are you saying the owner could come back expecting to live here at any time?"

"Lands no, Mr. Stewart," Quigly crossed his thin legs at the knee, "Mister Lawrence would never do that," he laughed a nervous laugh, tracing a long fingernail over a dark blue spidery vein running beneath the pale skin. "Before he left, he told me to go ahead and lease the place if I could find suitable people."

"And your way of finding suitable people is by walking up to a family you've never laid eyes on before to offer them the estate." Hays flipped open the notepad once more.

"I consider myself to be a good judge of character, Lieutenant." He swung one foot, incased in an open-toed sandal, back and forth. "I knew right off the Stewarts'd fit this house just fine."

"Tell me, Mr. Quigly," Hays leaned back in his chair, keeping his eyes turned from the open-toed sandal, showing curling nails protruding from the man's toes like a deformed claw, "why did you inquire about the children before you decided to lease the Stewarts' the estate?"

A flicker of fear flashed in the watery blue eyes. "No reason. I like to know who will be living here," Quigly explained, running sweaty palms up and down his dark blue walking shorts. "The estate is my responsibility."

But Hays had registered the fear in the man's face at the mention of the children. Something to keep in mind, he told himself.

The sounds of slamming doors outside brought Hays to his feet. "Sounds like the K9s have arrived." He drew back the kitchen curtain for a quick look in the direction of the driveway. "Now we can get the search for your daughter underway in earnest. Hays picked up his notepad, putting it in his pocket. "I think it would be better if the two of you remained inside with your children." He placed a restraining hand on Roger's shoulder, curtailing any objections as Roger started to rise to his feet.

"Someone will be checking back to fill you in on what's happening with the search."

"I think I'll wait with the Stewarts," Quigly declared. "I don't want to be in the way."

"No, I would rather you come with me." Hays motioned the man forward with a wag of his fingers. "My men will be conducting a thorough search of your cottage. I'm sure you'll wish to be present." Hays turned as the man got to his feet. "You don't have any objections to them doing a search, do you, Mr. Quigly?"

"It wouldn't matter if I did, now would it?" Quigly lifted his head, his full-lipped mouth settling into a childish pout.

"No. Just a slight delay until we get a search warrant, is all."

"As I already said," he tugged the white sport shirt, plastered against his back, away from his skin, "I want to do everything I can to help in the finding of poor little Margaret."

"Right." Hays glowered at him, reached for the suit coat, then dropped his hand back to his side as he ushered Quigly outside.

Sitting alone at the table, Roger and Janet stared out the window as the deputies, and their dogs moved in different directions over the estate. Wrapped within their fear over their missing daughter, neither thought to question the bits and pieces they had been told about the very house they now called home.

CHAPTER FOUR

Images came unbidden, stealing into her mind like the flashes of a bad dream.

The sounds of ripping flesh and the loud slurping noises he had made while satisfying his fiendish hunger on the body of an innocent child repulsed her, yet she knew better than to look away. The cold anger washing over her, as she stood in the shadows not two feet away, watching, remained a very real part of her.

Jonathan Hindel the man, who in the heat of anger and grief, robbed her of her innocence. And Jonathan Hindel the epitome of evil, who had plucked her very soul from her body, making it an empty tomb in which to house another, had long since become one and the same.

Leaving her bed, she walked over to stand before a large mirror sitting atop an aged dresser. She pushed against the moveable oval frame. Moving closer, Chandra peered into the glass at the image reflected there. She marveled at the large, dark green eyes, still bright; honey colored skin still taut across high, well-defined cheekbones. The small straight nose above the full pink mouth flared now with wonder. After all the years she had lived upon this earth, her face still gave no hint as to the number of those years. She stood now, thinking back to that time when her life had changed forever.

He walked towards her. His cold gray eyes glittering with an unholy light, changing his handsome, middle-aged face into a mask of deathlike horror. He reached out, and with one quick jerk, pulled her trembling body up against his own. The scream bubbling up in her throat disappeared as he pulled her head back, forcing her to look at him.

"I gave you a chance to flee from this night and everything it held for you," he breathed the words down on her. "You chose not to listen. You allowed your hunger to overrule your sense of danger, Chandra." His dark gaze swept over her trembling mouth. "The right of free choice is a gift! I offered you that gift, but you refused it! Now, I will show you what you have chosen!" He brought up his hand to stroke her face. "As the years pass by, one after the other, remember you, not I, made the choice to live the life you will now live throughout all eternity."

"No!" Chandra screamed. "Let me go! I promise, if you let me go, I'll leave here and never come back!"

He lifted her into his arms to make his way up a wide staircase, all the while holding her against his broad chest and turning a deaf ear on her pleas to be set free. Up, up they climbed until they, at last, came to the room he wanted. Without letting her go, he continued striding across a wide spacious room. When he came to the foot of a large and heavy oak, four-poster bed sitting high off the floor and surrounded by white, gauze-thin draperies, he stopped. Standing her before him, he tipped her small face up to his. "After this night, you will know a hunger that can never be sated. The world as you know it, Chandra, will no longer exist. I will give you a new world. A world you never thought possible."

"I do not wish to know your world," she whimpered, her need to escape from him mounting by the moment.

"You will, Chandra." He yanked back a white, satin bedspread to reveal the matching sheets hidden beneath. "I promise you, you will."

Pulling her closer, he removed her thin gown, slipping it up and over her head to hold it between his strong hands. "When I saw you there in the clearing covered in this rag, I wanted to rip it from your body. You are a beautiful woman, Angelia… Chandra," he amended, shaking his head as if to clear his mind of an intrusive memory. "A beautiful woman should never go through life dressed in rags." A low growl left his throat as he shredded the thin material then threw it to the floor as though the very touch soiled his hands.

"I have nothing to wear now," her voice grew silent as he stared at her.

With a disgusted snarl, he pulled her across the room, yanking open the doors of a large armoire.

Her frightened eyes widened as she stepped forward to gaze upon the many gowns and dresses hanging before her. "They're beautiful," she whispered, her voice filled with awe. She touched the fine silks and satins, allowing their softness to slide through her hands. "Whose are they?"

"They are yours, Chandra."

The soft fabrics fell from her hand. "No. They are not mine. They are hers."

"Not anymore." He scooped her up in his arms to lay her down in the middle of the wide bed.

She watched him straighten, then disrobe. Her mind screamed a warning, but her heated flesh refused to heed its warning. His body bathed in the soft glow of moonlight shining through the tall window fed her hunger. In silence, she held out her arms to him. With a rush of breath, he came to her, wrapping her in his strong arms, devouring her hot mouth with his.

"You are mine, Chandra." His words all but stilled as he buried his face in her hair. "You will never leave my side for any reason."

At that moment, with the white-hot fire of lust burning between her legs, she told herself she would never wish to leave his side. She would never wish to be anywhere but here, wrapped within his arms with the flaming heat of their passion consuming them. He lifted his dark head, gazing down at her. Needing to see his own lust mirrored in her eyes. She did not disappoint him. With a vaunting growl, he slid his hungry mouth over her hot skin until he, at last, came to the place he most hungered for. Taking his time, he allowed her heated moisture to bathe his tongue, savoring the taste of her arousal.

Chandra could feel herself spinning out of control as her tortured body reached for a feeling, that in her innocence, she could not name yet, knew she had to have. Again and again, he brought her body to the brink of indescribable pleasure, then lifted his mouth, denying her the satisfaction she so craved.

"Beg me, Chandra!" His passion-filled eyes caught hers and held. "Beg me to end your suffering! Promise me everything you hold most dear in this world, including your very soul!"

"Yes!" she cried out. "I give you everything! Everything!"

"Say the words, Chandra!" He unwound her grasping fingers from his thick black hair. "Say, I give you my soul, Jonathan, to end my suffering!"

"I give you my soul, Jonathan! End this suffering! Now!" She grabbed hold of his dark head, once more, to shove him back where she so needed him to be.

He fought her groping hands then pulled her withering body beneath him. With one sharp lunge, he stripped her forever of her innocence. With a strength born of overpowering need, she rolled her body atop his, stealing, at last, the control she needed to hold him imprisoned within her hot tightness. Throwing back her head, she rode him without mercy until she felt the first hot spasms begin to rack her body.

All through the long, passion-filled night, she turned to him. Demanding, and taking, and satisfying the deep hungers he had awakened within her body. At last, as the first rays of dawn crept into the room, she rolled her sated body from his to fall into a deep sleep. Her tired mind forgetting the dark promises she had made in the heat of her passion.

Much later, when the realization of what she had done returned to haunt her with all the clarity of an unending nightmare, she would, at last, see the evil she had traded her very soul to be with.

Shaking the memory from her mind, she stepped back from the mirror, unable to deny the truth staring back at her. Eternal life. That's what he had promised her. And he had kept his promise. As each year followed the one before, she noted little change in her appearance. Her parents, her friends, everyone she had known, and traded to be near him, had gone on to their eternal resting-place. For her, there would be no eternal rest.

For a brief moment, she wondered at the women of this world and what they would be willing to give to stay young and beautiful. Would they leap at the chance to live forever, untouched by the horrible diseases running rampant over the face of the earth? What would they trade to forego that day when they would look into the face of a loved one and not be able to recall his name because the cells in the brain had already decayed from age. Would they also trade *their* souls? She shuddered, remembering her agony of the night before.

At first, she refused, when Jonathan told her, she must accompany him back to the mansion. She knew why he wanted her there. They had stood in the shadows waiting for the children to appear. She had heard his intake of breath when they had gone back inside the house. Felt the tautness in his large body as he tried to leash his anger. Then, her heart froze as she saw the one child returning, running through the rain to the big oak.

She knew he had seen her too. She wanted to call out, to warn the child to go back but knew she could not. The girl never had a chance as he leaped upon her, driving her small body to the ground. The horror lasted but a few short moments. She watched from her hiding place among the trees as he picked up the lifeless body to carry it off.

Knowledge he had not just bitten the child but ripped her body until it lay in a defenseless heap, making it impossible for her to return as one of them, stood out as the one good thing she could glean out of the sickening scene she had been forced to witness.

Her punishment over, for the time being, she turned to leave when she caught sight of a movement. Hiding herself behind a tall tree, she waited to see who could be watching. It had been but a matter of moments before she saw a man of short stature running toward the big oak. She watched as he ran around the tree as though checking to make sure no sign of the child could be detected. When at last he seemed satisfied, he left, making his way in the direction of the small cottage set back amongst the trees, and situated several yards down the lane from the mansion.

CHAPTER FIVE

Lieutenant Hays tapped on the back screen door then walked into the house. Janet finished pouring coffee for herself and Roger. As she saw Hays standing in the doorway, she reached for another cup, telling herself not to be too hopeful.

"Have you found her yet, Lieutenant?" Roger asked, already rising to his feet.

"No. Not yet." He swiped a weary hand over the sweat beads collecting atop his head, smoothed the thick, dark brown hair on each side and down the back into place. "The dogs picked up her scent at the back door and followed it to that big oak, then lost it." He walked to the kitchen table. "With all the rain, I'm surprised they got that much, but I think your daughter has been abducted."

The startled look passing over Janet's face had Roger on his feet now and moving towards her. Knowing his words could not be tempered, he told them the rest of what he suspected, "From the way the dogs carried on, it'd be my guess somebody hid out there and carried her off."

"Oh my God!" Janet felt the cups, filled with steaming hot coffee, slip from her hands, spewing scalding liquid across her feet and into the air before shattering onto the floor.

"Janet!" Roger wrapped her in his arms. "We have to stay strong now. God won't let anything happen to our little girl. The police will find her!" He clutched her body tighter against him. "You know they will!"

"Why her?" Janet sobbed into his shirt. "She's just a baby!"

"Mr. Stewart, why don't you and your wife come sit

down?" He brushed at the coffee stains dotting his dark blue suit pants. "I realize this is hard on the both of you. But if we're going to have any chance of finding Margaret, we all need to keep a clear head."

"The Lieutenant's right." His voice shook with the frightening visions running through his mind. "You come sit down." Roger guided her over to the table, pulling out a chair and easing her into it. "I'll clean up the mess."

"Mrs. Stewart," Hays waited until she sat down before trying to enlist her help. "Have you noticed any strangers on the grounds? Any salesmen, or anyone coming to the house you don't know?"

"No," Janet sniffed, wiping shaking fingers beneath her nose. "Roger's a real stickler for keeping the gate closed and locked. No one could get in. That is," her stricken gaze hastened to her husband, "except Mr. Quigly. I'm sure he must have a key to the gate."

"I see." He sipped from the cup of coffee, Roger sat before him. The strong brew helped to wet his dry throat. "One of you mentioned something about a howling dog. What can you tell me about that?"

"There's nothing to tell." Roger set his and Janet's coffee down on the table, allowing his hand to linger for a moment on her wrist.

"You could be right," Hays shrugged his rounded shoulders, "but what did the dog sound like? Did it sound like a big dog? A small dog? A wolf?"

"Come to think of it," Roger's brows knitted in thought, "it did sound like a wolf. But that's impossible. There aren't any wolves in Louisiana. Are there?"

Hays felt his stomach plunge, and he lifted the cup of coffee to his mouth. "Maybe a few straying out of Texas. They wouldn't come close to a house, though."

"Then why did you ask about a wolf?" Roger glanced at him.

"There's something I think I should tell you. This morning, before one of my deputies came to the door, we talked about another family who lived here?"

"Yes," Roger pushed away a sandwich, left sitting on the table since noon, to lean forward in his chair, "I think you said their name was Rawlins."

"That's right." The ulcers gnawing at his stomach screamed out in agony, only to be ignored as Hays took another long swallow of coffee. "I said they had children about the same age as your two girls. They also had another girl; a ten-year-old."

Without thinking, Roger reached for Janet's hand.

"She disappeared pretty much the same way your daughter has."

Janet looked at him, then whispered, "What are you trying to say?"

"The Rawlins family also reported hearing what they thought to be a wolf, howling outside the mansion the night their daughter came up missing. I'd venture to guess she did the same thing Margaret did. She went out to feed what she thought to be a dog, and that's the last anyone ever heard from her.

"Oh my God! My God! My God!" Roger gathered Janet into his arms, rocking them back and forth.

"That's not all," Hays said, cursing himself for what he knew he had to do.

"No!" Roger drew away from Janet, throwing up his hands. "I don't want to hear any more! It doesn't concern us! Please," he cried.

"I'm sorry, Mr. Stewart." Hays ignored the man's plea for silence. "It does concern you. It concerns everyone living in this house."

Shaking his head, Roger beseeched him to wait. "Janet, why don't you go up and check on the children? I'm sure they must be frightened by all the goings on here."

"Yes, Roger." She pushed herself from the table, anxious to be away from the gruesome story. "I'll go up right now."

"Thank you. Janet doesn't need to hear anything more that will upset her."

"I disagree." Hays fixed him with a serious gaze. "I think she needs to be aware of the danger surrounding this house as much as you do. And, I feel it's imperative for all of you to leave here as soon as possible."

"You can't be serious!" Roger crossed his arms on the table. "I told you we paid a full year's lease on this damn house! We're all but broke."

"What is more important to you, Mr. Stewart? This house or your family?"

"My family, of course!" Roger shouted, then lowered his voice. "But where the hell are we going to go? I just told you," he breathed through clenched teeth, "we don't have any fuckin' money!"

"Calm down, Mr. Stewart. I can get you a room at the Cedar's Inn for tonight. We'll also see about getting your money back from Quigly. Son of a bitch knew better than to rent out this goddamn house!"

"And, what about all our furniture? Our belongings?" Roger began to pace the floor. "We can't just walk off and leave everything here! We just can't!"

"Mr. Stewart," Hays nudged him back to his chair, "right now, all I care about is the safety of you and your family. We'll come back in a few days for your belongings. What I want you to do, right this minute, is go upstairs and pack enough clothes to get you through tonight."

"I refuse to leave this house until my Margaret is found, safe and sound!" Janet told them, coming to stand by the table.

"Mrs. Stewart," He glanced up, berating himself for not hearing her walk into the room, "I apologize for my language, but I meant what I said about the need for all of you to get out of here." She shook her head, her knuckles turning white as she gripped the back of a kitchen chair. "Mrs. Stewart, I'm asking you to trust me on this. For the sake of the children you have left, trust me! Please!"

"What do you mean, the children I have left?" she voiced the words in a shaky whisper, lowering herself into the chair.

"I didn't mean to put it that way." With thumb and forefinger, he brushed his thin mustache into place. "I'm sorry. I meant that time is of the essence here!" In his need to make them understand, his voice took on a harsher tone. "I can't, and won't, allow you and your family to spend another night here!"

"Unless you intend to carry me out of here, I'm not leaving until Margaret is found safe and alive," she told him, fear giving her added courage.

"If that's how it has to be," Hays got to his feet, his patience at an end, "then I guess that's the way it will have to be."

"Lieutenant Hays," Roger stood up, "we don't mean to tell you how to do your job." He licked dry lips, trying to force the words he wanted to say past his throat. "You have to look at this situation from our perspective, too. What if Margaret comes back and finds no one here?" He prayed to God she was able to answer that wish. "I have to agree with my wife. We're staying!"

Hays knew any further argument, right at that moment, would be useless. "Then would you at least think of the safety of your other children and allow me to remove them? My wife, Barbara, will be glad to keep them until we can get everyone out of here and into a suitable place."

"Roger?" Janet looked to her husband.

"I still don't understand why all this is necessary." He ran a nervous hand through his thinning hair. "Although I guess you have your reasons. All right, yes. If your wife will take the children, then I guess it will be okay."

Hays reached for his cell phone then remembered he had left it in the jeep. "Do you mind if I use your phone? I want to let my wife know to expect the girls."

Janet pointed him in the direction of the living room. "The phone is sitting on the end table."

As Hays left to make his call, Janet turned. "Roger, what is going on? Why are we being asked to leave?"

"I don't know." He gave her cold hand a quick squeeze. "I do know, I've had enough of standing around here doing nothing while our daughter is out there somewhere alone." Roger turned in the direction of the backdoor.

"Where are you going, Mr. Stewart?" Hays asked him, coming back into the room.

"I'm going where I should have been all along!" Roger told

him over his shoulder. "I'm going to try and find my daughter!"

"My men are already searching for your daughter, Mr. Stewart. I would prefer if you stayed inside." Hays moved to stand in front of him.

"I don't give a damn what you prefer! I am a free citizen!" Roger poked a finger against his own chest. "This is my daughter we're talking about. Now please, step out of my way!" Roger ordered, trying to walk around the robust officer.

"I can't let you do that, Mr. Stewart." Hays planted his feet into place.

"Are you telling us we are prisoners in our own home?" Janet strode across the floor.

"What I am telling you is you are all in danger here! But you refuse to listen to me!" As he talked, he placed a hand on each of their shoulders, turning them back toward the table. "My wife is willing to keep the girls tonight, so I would appreciate it if you'd get them ready to go. One of my deputies will drive them over."

"I don't like being without the girls." Janet crossed her arms in front of her.

"I agree with you, Janet." Roger placed an arm around her frail shoulders. "I don't think it's necessary.

"Well, I do!" Hays fought to keep his temper under control. "If the two of you are determined to stay, then all I can do is stay with you! I'll also have some of my men stand guard outside. I want you to understand something, though," a determined scowl settled over his face, "by refusing to leave here, you're putting every damn one of our lives in danger!"

"No one is asking you to stay!" Roger squared his lean shoulders, refusing to look away. "If you feel you're in danger, then take your men and get the hell out! We'll find our daughter on our own!"

"Listen!" Hays told him, breathing hard against his anger. "I realize how upset you are, but you'd better pull in your horns and calm down. As soon as those kids," he nodded toward the stairs, "are out of here, I'm going to tell you just what the hell we're up against here!"

Janet leaned into the safe arms of her husband, all the fight gone out of her.

After he had seen the children on their way, he sat with their parents in the living room, and with as much calm as he could bring forth, tried to explain what they needed to know about the house they had thought themselves so lucky to find.

"I want you folks to listen to what I'm about to tell you."

"Yes, we'll listen," Roger told him, still determined to search out Margaret on his own. "But hear this. If I feel your reasons for keeping us sitting in this house instead of out looking for Margaret are unfounded, nothing you can say is going to change my mind about going to find her myself."

"Fair enough," Hays replied, sure in his belief that after they heard what he had to tell them, they would beat him out the door.

"Then let's hear what you have to say." Janet settled herself close to Roger.

"The Rawlins girl's disappearance sparked a nightmare." He leaned forward to pick up the ashtray from the coffee table. "A nightmare none of us will forget for the rest of our lives."

The air in the big house turned cooler as Roger and his wife sat waiting to hear the reason Hays wanted them to leave. "This happened in the middle of August with a steady climb in the humidity." Hays withdrew his pack of cigarettes. "As I recall, it must have been a couple of weeks after the girl disappeared when I get this call from the paper boy's father, asking if I'll drive out and check on the family."

Janet stared out the window focusing her attention on the gathering storm and trying to still the droning voice of the man seated across from them. She could see men scurrying to roll up their car windows. Their actions, right at that moment, seemed so natural she struggled against her mounting fears to surround herself with their movements. Telling herself, when it rains, people roll up their windows. When it grows dark, people turn on their lamps. And, when your child disappears, you go out of your mind. The thoughts raced through her brain until she fought to silence them. With mental effort, she forced her attention back inside the room.

"Along with two of my deputies and Jack Olivier', a good friend of mine, I agreed to come out and have a look. I don't mind telling you I don't like this place. I never have. And I don't scare easy." Donavan tapped a cigarette against his lighter. "Anyway, when we drove up in front of the house, we could see the Rawlins' Land Rover parked up ahead. The minute we stepped out of the car, we could smell the stench."

Roger's head jerked upward. "Hays, I don't think my wife needs to hear this."

"Whether she needs to or not, she's going to," Hays refused to drop his gaze. "You're both going to hear why I want you out of here."

With a look of disgust tinged with more than a little fear, Roger settled back against the couch. "Jack and I led the way up the front steps. The door stood partway open, and the closer we got to the inside, the stronger the stench became. I think we already knew what had happened. There's no mistaking that smell. I pushed open the door, and we stepped into a slaughterhouse."

"Good Christ!" Roger breathed.

"Christ had nothing to do with what we found in this house that day." Hays heaved himself to his feet. "Come on, I want to show you something."

With arms entwined, Roger and Janet followed him from the room. When they stood in the foyer, Hays told them to wait as he opened the door, then walked into the family room to pull the drapes. The gathering storm plunged the room into total darkness.

"We didn't have enough furniture for this room, so we kept it closed off," Roger explained, standing in the darkness. "Just what is it we're supposed to be looking at?"

"Be patient. You'll see in a moment."

The darkened room, including the ceiling, walls, and carpet, seemed to come alive with splashes of a light, eerie green.

"What...the...hell...is...that?" Roger exclaimed, his voice taking on a breathless tone as his hold on Janet tightened.

"It's a spray called Luminol," Hays said.

"Why would someone coat a room with green spray?" Roger stared into the gloom, unable to turn away.

"They didn't. I want you to both fix what you're seeing in your mind, then we'll go back to the living room, and I'll explain what happened here." He yanked on the drapery cord, anxious to return the room to its former setting.

As they sat in the living room with the overhead light and all the lamps turned on high, Hays, in a calm manner, explained what they had just witnessed.

"When Jack, myself, and the other deputies walked into this house, I thought we'd just stepped into a horror movie." For a brief moment, he closed his eyes on the chilling memories. "The entire family, except for the missing girl, lay dead in that room." Even after all these years, he could still recall the smell. "From the decomposition of the bodies and the stench, I'd guess they'd been dead about a week."

Thick green liquid pooling beneath the bodies, as the men lifted them into body bags for their removal to the morgue, flashed into his mind. He swallowed against the bile, trying to fight its way upward from his stomach.

"I don't think a spot in that room remained untouched by blood. What you saw was blood."

"How the hell could it be blood?" Roger leaned forward, anxious to punch a hole in Hays' absurd story. "Blood isn't green!"

Hays continued, ignoring Roger's interruption and taking some morbid satisfaction in the man's ignorance of investigative technique. "After the crime lab and everyone else assigned to the case finished up, the owner's son, Lawrence Hindel, showed up demanding everyone leave." The picture of a wild-eyed Hindel, his high-pitched, girlish voice screaming out threats of a lawsuit, his thin arms flailing the air as he ran nonstop around the room, remained burned into his mind.

"Jason Rogers, the Prosecuting Attorney, decided he wanted more than just pictures depicting what had happened. So, after we were through with the house, he sent us back. Of course, by then, Hindel had already had a cleaning crew in here to clean up all the blood and gore, but even so, we went ahead and sprayed the entire room with Luminol."

"What's that?" Janet asked, her cold hand curling around Rogers.

"Luminol is a special spray used to detect blood." Hays lifted the ashtray from the coffee table. "Even after a room has been scrubbed down, Luminol can show where the blood has been." Now, if they just had a spray that could wipe blood from a person's mind, they would have something. The thought skipped through his mind, but he kept it to himself. "You spray Luminol over a suspected area," he withdrew his pack of cigarettes from his pocket, "turn out the lights, and in a few moments, you have your answer." He flicked the lighter, holding it beneath the third cigarette out of the second pack he had opened in less than six hours. "Course we already had our answers. They lay sprawled all over the room."

Leaping to her feet, Janet stumbled over Roger's legs as she made her way down the hall to the bathroom, arriving just in time to empty the contents of her stomach.

Ignoring the sounds coming from the nearby room, Hays went on with his story. "We arrested Lawrence Hindel for the murders. He went on trial, and after a little less than two weeks, the jury found him not guilty by reason of insanity."

Roger threw his hands wide, searching his mind for a plausible explanation. "That can't be! I heard Mr. Quigly say, just this morning, he's residing in England with his father. If he's insane, why isn't he in a sanatorium somewhere?"

"Because his father, Jonathan Hindel, bought his way out of the sanatorium." Hays tapped the ash from the cigarette into the ashtray he held on his knee as Roger stared at him in disbelief. "After spending one year locked away from society, the doctors proclaimed him cured and turned him loose. Now you see why I say it is imperative you get yourself and your family the hell out of this house!"

"How?!" Roger inched his way forward. "If Margaret comes back," his voice cracked with frustration, "we have to be here!"

Hays stared into the brown eyes begging him to understand, and he sighed, "Mr. Stewart, I don't think your daughter will be coming back. And if you're honest with yourself, I don't think you do either."

When a pale and shaken Janet returned to the room, Roger left the couch to go to her. "Janet, I think it *would* be best if we did as Lieutenant Hays has suggested. I'll go pack us an overnight bag. Why don't you stay here with the Lieutenant?" He slipped his arms from around her waist. "I won't be long."

"No!" The word fought its way upward from her throat as she backed away from him. "I am not leaving here until we find Margaret."

"Ma'am, I hate to be the one to say this, but as I just told your husband, I don't think Margaret will be coming back."

"No? Well I do, Lieutenant Hays." She held one hand against her mouth, the other pressed against her churning stomach as she stared out the window into the gathering darkness.

At that moment, a loud howling echoed through the stillness, freezing the attention of all three people in the room.

"That's the same howling we heard last night." Roger glanced at Hays, pulling Janet back into his arms.

At the sound of footsteps pounding through the house, Hays called out, "We're in here."

Following the sound of Hays' voice, an ashen-faced young deputy slowed down through the hall to enter the living room. "Sir, you're needed outside. The dogs are on to something. Jamison sent me to tell you."

"Yeah, Adamson, I'll be right there. You two are coming with me." He held out a hand, motioning them forward. "I'm not about to leave you alone in this house."

CHAPTER SIX

As the three walked outside, Adamson waited for them on the top step.

"Where's Jamison now?" Hays asked.

"I don't know, Sir. He heard something rustling in the bushes out there," he pointed across the lawn, "so he took off with the dogs in that direction."

"Simple son of a bitch should have waited," Hays flicked his cigarette into a high arch. "No telling what he'll run into out there."

The deputy nodded in agreement. "I tried to tell him to wait for you, but you know Jamison when he thinks he's on to something."

"Jamison!" Hays yelled into the darkness. "Jamison, get your ass back here!"

"Do you want me to go after him, Sir?" Adamson stepped forward.

"No, I don't want you to go after him," Hays growled, throwing a restraining arm in front of him. "I want everyone to stay together." He made his way down the wide steps. "Where are the other men?"

"Still out searching for the little girl."

"What did they turn up at Quigly's place?"

With a slight shake of his head, the young man glanced away. The next instant, a loud yipping and whining came to them from the direction of the large maples lining both sides of the vast lane leading up to the mansion.

"They got something cornered!" the deputy grinned.

"Yeah. Now the question is what?" Hays unsnapped his holster. "Come on," he waved them all forward. "I don't make a habit of taking civilians with me, but it's safer than leaving you here."

"I don't want to see your dogs fighting with some poor animal," Janet frowned, backing away.

"If we're lucky, that's all they'll be fighting with." He motioned Roger to bring her with them.

Walking to his jeep, he unlocked the door and, reaching in, withdrew a large flashlight. "Stay close," he cautioned them, "I just have this one flashlight."

"Roger," Janet pulled back away from him. "I don't want to go!"

"Mrs. Stewart, I didn't ask you." He clicked the flashlight on high beam. "I'm ordering you! Now come on!"

In the bright glare of the light, they made their way across the lawn. When they reached the trees, Hays called out, "What is it? Can you see?"

"They got something trapped in the bushes down here!" came a deputy's nervous answer.

Drawing his gun, Hays turned to Janet, "Cover your ears. I'm going to signal the rest of the men to come in."

With that said, he fired two shots into the air.

The silence came alive with loud howls and high-pitched yips. "Whatever it is, it's got the K9s!" Adamson said. Running forward, they could see two deputies standing hip-deep in tall foliage. One of them turned, looking up to where they stood.

"I don't think you want the woman to see this, Lieutenant," he cautioned.

"Yes, I do." Hays grabbed Janet's arm, pulling her with him.

When he smelled the blood, Hays flashed a beam of light down into the weeds. "Still want to stay here now, Mrs. Stewart?"

Her pulse pounding, Janet stared down at what had once been a beautiful Doberman Pincher, but no longer. Now the dog's head lay inches from its neck while the stomach gaped open, its entrails scattered amongst the weeds.

"Oh God!" she gulped in air, her stomach convulsing.

The men's faces reflected their shock as they looked at each other, trying to think what could have made their leader do such a cold and callous thing to a woman whose own child remained missing and, who may have already met with the same horrible end as the dead and mutilated dog lying at their feet.

"Sorry I had to do that, Mrs. Stewart." He yanked a handkerchief from his back pocket, held it out to her. "Maybe now you'll see how imperative it is for you and your husband to get away from here."

Unable to speak, she held the handkerchief to her mouth, nodding her compliance as Roger gave her a hand back up the hill.

"Adamson, take a couple of the men and get Shadow ready for transport." He nodded in the direction of the slain dog. "I want him taken to the morgue. When you get there, tell Perkins I want him to check for saliva or anything else that might help us identify what killed him. And one more thing." Hays stopped him as the deputy began to walk away.

"Yes, Sir?" Adamson turned, waiting for the rest of his instructions.

"Tell him I said if he tries to pawn this off on a Student Medical Examiner, I'll have his ass up on report by tomorrow morning!"

"I'll tell him!" Adamson moved away before Hays had a chance to give him any more unwanted messages.

"Mr. and Mrs. Stewart, let's get you back up to the house to get ready to leave. Drummins," he turned his attention on a burly officer standing nearby, "I want you to take the Stewarts and three other deputies back to the house and wait there while they pack some clothes. When they're ready to leave, they can follow you to the Cedar's Inn. Tell whoever is on duty, the sheriff's department will cover the bill."

"Yes sir, Lieutenant." The officer directed the couple ahead of him.

For a moment, his gaze lingered on the backs of the three people as they made their way back across the lawn towards the house. He turned his attention on the men busily wrapping the dog in a large sheet of plastic. "Did any of you get a look at what Shadow tangled with?" Hays made his way deeper into the weeds shining his light around the surrounding area.

"Yeah, I did." Paulson, one of the men, stood up.

"What did you see?"

"You ain't gonna believe it, but what I saw, or at least think I saw, looked like a large-sized wolf. But, Lieutenant." Paulson stopped him as he turned to leave.

"Yeah?"

"That ain't all."

"I'm waiting," Hays gave the man his full attention.

"I could have sworn whatever killed Shadow walked upright."

"Oh, I believe it." Hays withdrew a cigarette from his shirt pocket. "Probably something sired by Hindel, goofy as that fucker is."

"I know whatever it is, it's big!"

"It might be big," Hays flicked his lighter, eyeing Paulson over the flame, "but it ain't too big it can't be brought down with a bullet!"

"Are you gonna want a few of us to stay out here tonight?" He pushed the words past a throat dry with apprehension: "'Case it comes back?"

"No." Hays blew a stream of smoke into the air. "No way in hell do I want any of you staying out here or coming back on your own when you're off duty. This place is off limits to everybody unless they got a lot of backup!" Hays grinned as he heard Paulson's sigh of relief.

"What about continuing the search for the girl?" Paulson hated the way his muscles tensed in hopes this question, too, would be rejected.

"We'll continue looking for her just to keep the press off our asses. We all know we're never going to find her. Not alive."

"You know, Lieutenant, I just had a hell of a thought." Paulson relaxed somewhat, now that he knew they would be leaving soon. "What if all those stories we used to spread, about something being up here, turn out to be true?" A slight smile pulled at the corners of his mouth as he saw the other two deputies straighten up to stare at him.

"I remember all the shit my buddies and I used to pull." He removed a black cap emblazoned across the front with the initials S.A.S.D. to run the back of his hand across his forehead. "How we'd come up here on a full moon and try to scare the Be-Jesus out of whatever family lived here at the time."

"Yeah," Hays nodded, thinking back. "I went on more than a few of those raids myself. It's a wonder, after what we saw here tonight, a few of us didn't end up dead."

"I know one thing for damn sure," he replaced his hat, reached out, as one of the deputies handed the wrapped body of the slain dog over to him, "I better never hear of my kids coming here. When I get home tonight, they're gonna hear all about what I saw down here."

Placing one hand beneath Paulson's elbow, Hays helped him climb the steep hill. "No, they're not," Hays told him as Paulson placed the heavy carcass on the ground. "I don't want anyone out of the department to know about this." He stood for a moment, both hands on his hips stretching backward, allowing his breathing to slow back down to normal. As he watched the much-younger Paulson heft the heavy burden up in his arms, then with little effort over his shoulder, he cursed himself for his laziness at keeping in shape.

"If word gets out we got some kind of monster running around loose. The damn phone won't stop ringing." Hays quickened his steps to stay even with Paulson. "If you want to tell your kids anything, tell them about the missing Stewart girl. That in itself should be enough to scare the piss out of them."

"Do you think the same thing that got Shadow, got the girl?" Paulson slowed his steps in an attempt to give Hays a chance to catch his breath.

"Wouldn't surprise me."

"Could I ask you a question?"

"Why I treated the Stewart woman the way I did?" Hays asked, already seeing the question coming.

"Yeah. That ain't like you."

"All damn day, I've been trying to get her and her family out of that house to no avail. She kept insisting she wouldn't leave until we found her daughter. When I saw Shadow all ripped to hell," he swallowed hard against the memory, "I knew I'd found a way to make her leave."

"You did what you had to." Paulson waited as Hays lifted the trunk of the squad car, anxious to relieve himself of his burden.

"Well," Hays glanced towards the house, "looks like they're ready to leave. At least that will be one less thing to worry about."

"Lieutenant Hays," Roger called out, coming down the driveway, "I'm going to leave the front door key with you in case you or any of your men need to get back inside. All I ask is that before you leave, please be sure and lock up." With a shaking hand, he held out the key as Hays walked towards him. "Everything I own is in that house."

He pocketed the key. "I'll be at the Inn about noon tomorrow to pick you up. I'm sure I can get enough of the men in the department to bring their pickups so we can get your furniture into storage. After we get your money back from Quigly, I think an offer of gas money will take care of their trouble."

"I appreciate all your help, Lieutenant."

"No problem. I'm just glad you and Mrs. Stewart have decided to leave."

"After seeing that poor dog, you couldn't force us to stay here!"

"I hated to do that to her, but I had no choice."

"I know you didn't," Roger gulped, the strange buzzing in his ears escalating. "I guess I better go. Looks like they're ready to leave. See you at noon." He forced his feet to carry him back up the driveway.

As Deputy Drummins drove away with the Stewarts following in their own car, Hays breathed a sigh of relief. "I better go back inside and make sure everything is secure."

"Hold up," Paulson fell in beside him. "I've always wanted

to see this house. Peekin' in the windows is the closest I came," he admitted, a sheepish grin splitting the corners of his generous mouth.

Hays laughed, feeling some of the tautness in his large body relax. "Who woulda thought a peeping-tom would grow up to be on the sheriff's department?"

Letting themselves in through the front door, they continued down the hall until they came to a large, well-set-up kitchen. Paulson gazed around him. "Goddamn," he whistled through his teeth, "would my wife ever love to cook a Thanksgiving dinner in a room like this!" He pulled open the oven door of a built-in range, stooping to look inside. "She could cook a twenty-five-pounder in there with plenty of room for her pies all at the same time." He pulled open another door. "Man, it's even got another oven on top! How the hell do people afford luxuries like this?" Paulson wiped away the smudges his fingers had left on the shiny, silver-chromed handles with the sleeve of his shirt. "Old man Hindel must be well-heeled to afford a setup like this!"

"A woman could be a regular chef with little effort, that's for damn sure." Hays admired the expensive appliances. "But I wouldn't want to live here." He walked through the kitchen to the living room, switching off lights as he went. "All the misery that's taken place inside these walls? Shit!" He pulled his hand back, deciding to leave the one lamp burning. "You couldn't give me this goddamn house!"

"I guess when you put it like that, I wouldn't want it either," Paulson admitted, his enthusiasm dwindling.

Hays stopped, anger at his own uneasiness pushing him to stand firm. "Hey, Paulson, how'd you like to see the room where we found the Rawlins family?"

Not wanting to appear weak, yet at the same time not sure how he would react, he mumbled, "Yeah, I guess so."

"Come on, I'll show you."

Following close behind, as Hays made his way down the hallway, Paulson could feel a slight tingling beginning at the base of his spine. "Turn on some damn lights; I can't see where the hell I'm going."

"Stay close. It has to be dark in order to get the full effect."

"All right, but if I run into you, don't bitch, I warned you beforehand." Paulson kept up a steady stream of chatter to relieve his mounting tension.

"Now stop," Hays put out a hand halting him; laughed when Paulson flinched at his touch. "Look right in that room." Hays turned him in the direction of the family room.

At the sight meeting his eyes, Paulson felt his frayed nerves freeze. "Good Christ Almighty! I've heard what Luminol can do. This is the first time I've seen it with my own eyes, though!"

"Pretty spooky, huh?"

"Can you imagine waking up hung-over to see something like this? Be enough to make you take the pledge!"

"Or pick up the bottle and start all over."

A loud rapping on the front door, inches away from where they stood, had both men backing up.

"Who is it?" Hays called out, his pulse kicking into high gear.

"It's me, Ramey, Lieutenant," came his answer.

"Go around to the back. I'll meet you there," he declared, then murmured, "Soon as I shake the shit out of my shorts!"

"You and me both," Paulson agreed, with no trace of humor. "Let's lock up and get the hell out of here."

Nodding, Hays motioned him back the way they had come. Walking down the hall, they could see, through the gold ornamental window in the large oak door, the officer standing on the back step waiting to be let in. Unlocking the door, Hays pulled it wide then stood talking to the officer through the screen door. "What is it, Ramey?"

"We found the little girl, Lieutenant," the officer reported.

"You gotta be shittin' me!" Hays pushed his way outside.

"No, Sir! She's laying out near where Shadow got killed."

"Are you sure it's the Stewart girl?" Donavan glanced over at Paulson as he heard his sharp intake of breath.

"No," Ramey admitted, "but whatever it is, it's wearing a nightgown."

Without saying anything more, all three men hurried their steps across the lawn.

As Ramey shone his flashlight out over the area, Hays stared down at the mutilated body half-hidden in the weeds. He felt his stomach recoil. "Get the coroner out here," he told Ramey. "Use your cell phone; I don't want this going out over the airways." He handed Ramey his car keys. "On your way back, grab my camera off the front seat and bring an evidence bag. Be sure and lock my rig back up!" He turned to Paulson. "Soon as I get some pictures, I'll let you help me get her gown off. I'll take it to the Stewarts for identification. They don't need to see what's left of their daughter."

"You know Perkins is gonna be pissed if we disturb the body before he gets here," Paulson warned.

"Perkins can get fucked! The Stewarts are going to identify her nightgown, and that's it!"

"Coroner's on the way, Lieutenant," Ramey told him, holding out the camera by the strap.

"Thanks, Ramey. We can handle it from here." Together they made their way down the bank.

"What in the hell could have ripped her apart like that?" Paulson asked as Donavan snapped pictures of the gruesome scene.

Donavan slung the camera around his neck. "Okay, let's get her gown off."

"Christ, she looks like a pack of wild dogs got at her." He held up the torn body so Hays could slip the grown over her head.

"You saw what got her." Hays finished the disagreeable task as fast as he could. "It makes my insides crawl to think what this poor kid went through before she died."

"I don't envy you having to go to her parents with this news." Paulson laid Margaret's body back down on the cold ground. "Do you want me to go with you?"

"No. I'll handle it," Hays slipped the gown into the evidence bag. "It's all part of the job."

"I guess this changes our idea about getting out of here

tonight," Paulson said, already knowing his answer.

"Yep," Hays straightened up, "I want at least ten men securing the scene, and I'm afraid you're going to be one of them."

"Like you said, Lieutenant," Paulson followed behind as Hays made his way up the bank. "It's all part of the job."

***

As he pulled the Jeep-Comanche into a parking space at the Cedar's Inn, he hesitated a moment before switching off the ignition. Then, knowing he couldn't put it off any longer, he turned the key, silencing the motor. All too soon, he stood in front of the door the woman at the motel desk said was being occupied by the Stewarts. Tapping on the door, he waited.

Roger answered his knock almost at once. "Lieutenant. You didn't need to bring the key tonight." He motioned the officer inside. "You could have given it to me tomorrow."

"I didn't come about the key, Mr. Stewart." His stomach plummeted as he saw fear leap into the man's eyes. Anxious to get his business over with, he looked around the small room for a place to sit.

"Come on, Lieutenant, have a seat over here." Roger hurried to empty a chair. "Just let me move this stuff. These rooms are so small there's no place to put anything."

Hays could see Janet propped up in the bed. He withdrew from his pocket the evidence bag he had brought with Margaret's gown stuffed inside.

"I'm sorry to have to tell you this, but we think we may have found the body of your daughter earlier this evening." He heard air whistle into Roger's lungs. "I brought her gown for you to identify rather than have you view her body."

With a shaking hand, Roger reached out for the brown paper bag, pulling it open and peering inside. "I can't see it well enough to say if it's Margaret's."

Taking the bag from Roger's hands, Hays reached inside to remove the gown. Caked in dirt and other debris, the gown, saturated with blood, looked like a soiled paint rag.

Roger stared at the gown still in the officer's hand, turning his head this way and that. When Hays made to hand it to him, he shook his head, backing away. A sob pushed its way to the surface to erupt from his throat. Roger clamped both hands over his mouth, trying to stop the sobs before they could escalate into screams.

"Please look at it," Hays pleaded with the man, knowing the other alternative would be so much harder.

"Hand the gown to me," Janet said, above the loud sobbing filling up the room. She slid off the bed, giving Roger a brief glance as he stood as though frozen, trying to get himself under some kind of control.

When she held the gown in her hands, she shook it out as best she could, then held it beneath the bedside lamp, looking for a spot not soiled or smudged. "It's Margaret's." She handed the gown back to Hays.

"I'm sorry, but are you sure?"

"No." She locked her hands together, trying to stop their trembling. "It looks like one I bought for her, but I can't be sure. We can compare it with the ones I have of the girl's back at the mansion, though."

"Then before you sign the papers stating you gave a positive identification, why don't we compare them?"

"We can do that," she exhaled the words on a shaky breath, walking back over to stand beside her husband.

"Thank you, Lieutenant, for coming to tell us. How soon will we be able to see our daughter?"

The request took Hays off guard, making it difficult to still the tremor in his voice as he replied, "I suggest you don't."

"She's our daughter." Janet pulled Roger to her side. "In order to get on with our lives, we have to be sure it's her."

Hays looked to Roger, who by now had gathered some of his composure, and found the same determination in his eyes as he saw in his wife's.

"We'll want to get an autopsy done, but after that, you'll be able to claim the body for burial."

"I don't mean to be rude, Lieutenant, and I know it's getting late, but would it be asking too much for you to bring our girls here tonight?" Janet whispered her strength, at last, beginning to waver. "We need them with us now."

"I understand." Hays squeezed her shoulder. "I'll go gather them up right away."

As the door closed on their grief, he remained standing for a moment allowing the humid night air to settle over him. He could smell the scent of fallen rain. Then another smell crept over him. The unmistakable smell of fear. Walking to his vehicle, he tried to still the terror threatening to overpower him. Within moments he sped out of the parking lot on his way home, his need, right at that moment, to hold his own little girl close, pushing everything else from his mind. Everything, that is, except the evil that once again reared its ugly head against the small town of Saint Anthony Parish and the people he had taken an oath to protect.

CHAPTER SEVEN

Chandra heard the deep throbbing of the drums beginning just after sundown. Their incessant rhythm heralding the most sacred of all nights, the night of All-Hallows Eve. That one night a year when the spirits of the dead walked upon the earth to take their rightful place among the living.

She donned a long white robe then wrapped her shoulder-length dark hair in white linen, making sure to tuck each strand beneath the soft fabric. Earlier, bathing in the waters of the bayou, she had scrubbed her body with soap-lathered moss until her skin tingled. When she finished, she left the waters to walk naked back to her shack. Her body would remain clean. She would not defile it on this sacred night with any garment other than the white robe.

Workmen, readying their fishing boats across the channel, stopped their work to stare at the tall, naked woman striding up the planked walkway. Hungry eyes feasted on high breasts and rounded hips. Chandra ignored them. When next she appeared, dressed in her long white robe with her dark hair wrapped tight, they no longer found her of any interest. Although she would have been of great interest to each and every one of them had they known who they watched and lusted over. But they didn't know, and very few would have believed had they been told.

As Voodoo Priestess, Chandra belonged to the bayou people. That mixed breed of French-Creole who never missed a Christian sermon each and every Sunday morning, yet at the same time continued to embrace their age-old African beliefs. Even in a world fraught with a never-ending cry against them, they held their rituals deep in the bayous, away from the prying eyes of the town's people and those same self-proclaimed moralists who delivered their Sunday services.

Uneducated whites, who had no choice but to house themselves and their families in the old shacks lining the banks, chose to turn a deaf ear on the strange rituals practiced in secret by their black neighbors. Though try as they may, they couldn't ignore the drums. The pounding rhythm called to them in the darkness. Reaching through the thin walls with a dire reminder of how vulnerable they could be to the far reaches of the unknown.

As Chandra entered the clearing, a loud cry went up from the waiting crowd. The tempo of the drums changed to that of a stronger, deeper rhythm heralding her arrival. As she stepped into a large circle, drawn in white powder on the ground, the drums ceased and all around her became still.

She could feel their dark eyes watching her, feel their growing need to know which one from among them she would choose to bestow her most coveted gift. The gift of sharing the touch of Angelia. The breathtaking voodoo priestess whose powers did not die but continued on in the spirit housed within the body of Chandra to rival that of every other priestess.

Chandra's dark eyes scanned the multitude of black faces milling around her. At the very back of the assembly, almost obscured because of her short stature, she glimpsed a young female of perhaps seventeen years of age. Without hesitation, Chandra began making her way through the crowd. When she came within arm's reach, she stretched out her hand. The girl moved forward. The deep throbbing of the drums filled the silence as the people made a pathway for their priestess and her chosen one. Moving through the throng of people, Chandra could hear the girl's breath rush from her lungs in her excitement; her brown eyes shining as she saw all the people watching her, their own eyes filled with awe, respect, and more than a little envy.

Stepping into the white circle with the girl at her side, Chandra lifted her arms for silence. All sound ceased. The men in the white baggy pants lifted the drums, suspended from their necks by a long bright red strap, up and over their heads to lay them aside. Then they waited for Chandra to begin the ceremony.

With the girl standing before her, Chandra chanted deep in her throat. The words coming out of her mouth made no sense to the people standing around them. They sounded disjointed. High pitched one moment, then low, almost like a moan the next, as she swayed back and forth. Her hands reached out but did not touch the girl who gazed at her as she danced and chanted the strange, hypnotic words passing from her lips. The watching crowd waited to see the transformation from the young female to Angelia as Chandra invoked Angelia's spirit to come forth. They gazed at the girl's round face waiting for it to change to a small heart-shaped face, waited for the full mouth to take on a more sensuous softness.

Sharp intakes of breath filtered through the crowd as the girl began to change. Eyes that moments earlier had been a deep, chocolate brown now stared through glittering orbs of emerald green, a strange contrast against her now, light brown skin. Small breasts, unconfined beneath the fabric of a thin pullover dress, swelled and jiggled as she swayed back and forth, caught up in the rhythm of Chandra's melodic chanting.

He walked from the trees, his footfalls making little sound, as he made his way across the sandy grass toward the circle.

Chandra grew silent, stepping back from the young girl swaying to a sound she alone could hear as she watched him approach. Taking the young woman by her shoulders, he peered into her face, searching for the one who still possessed his every waking moment. Angelia gazed at him through the eyes of the child standing before him. Jonathan's breath became ragged as he pulled her against him.

Chandra witnessed the change in his stern features transfiguring from anger to complete adoration as he stared down into the face of the woman he held.

Jonathan picked her up in his arms and, without a word, turned in the direction of the mansion. Chandra watched him walk away and closed her mind to yet another sin against her soul. She tried to tell herself she had no choice, but the truth of her actions would remain to haunt her. Just as they had with all the others, she had chosen for him.

The drums beat a slow deep rhythm, but Chandra remained unmoved by their calling. Her mind strayed to another time. A time when she still craved the feelings she believed no one but Jonathan could bring to her lust-starved body.

By now, she lived in the mansion with Jonathan, shunning her parents, friends, and anyone who spoke against him. With Jonathan, she could set aside her childish ignorance and allow the terrible throbbing in her young loins to burn out of control. Her trust in his abilities, as a capable lover, never disappointed her. Night after night, he fed the wild cravings holding her in their grasp and satisfying her needs until she could slip into the dreamless sleep of the innocent, content in Jonathan's mastery of her needs. As her body grew accustomed to these relaxed feelings, she noticed a lack of urgency in her need to be with him every night, as she had in the beginning of their relationship. Before long, she found herself turning her back to him, her body still satisfied from the night before.

At first, Jonathan made no demands on her, telling her, as with all things new, sooner or later, the attraction would wane. His understanding of her feelings made her turn to him more. Strengthening her belief, she had made the right decision in turning a deaf ear on her family and friends when they tried to warn her about Jonathan. Had it not been Jonathan who came to her family's defense when they railed against him? Telling her they did this out of love and worry for her? Soon she cut herself off from everyone but Jonathan. Now when they made love, they made love with the utmost of feeling. If she did not desire to make love, he would not force her, but he did insist on holding her while she slept each night. Then little by little, she began to notice a change in her desires. It was like when they first came together. Back when she could not get enough of him. The tender nights of sleeping in his arms became a thing of the past, as she turned to him, not for loving comfort, but out and out lust! Jonathan met her in her lust to try different things. Things she never dreamed she could ever want, let alone crave, with an insatiable wanton hunger. Chandra found herself unable to think of anything or anyone but Jonathan. As days passed into weeks and then months, she found herself slipping ever deeper into the dark nothingness that made up Jonathan's world.

Shaken from her reverie of years past, Chandra concentrated on the waiting people around her. With a determined effort, she held out her hand to a small woman who came forward.

"Whom do you wish to speak to?" Chandra asked her.

The woman pulled a thin white shawl up and over her sagging breasts. "My son," she replied.

"A tall young man with deep-set eyes is standing to your left side," Chandra told her. Her words brought a toothless smile to the lined and withered face. "He says to tell you he is safe and well on the other side, and you are not to worry about him. He also says to tell you that when you feel a strong presence in your room at night, not to be afraid, for it is him sitting beside you telling you he still loves and watches over you."

The old woman reached up, wiping a tear from her sunken cheek, then squeezed Chandra's hand in gratitude before placing a handful of change in a tall bottle sitting on the ground.

One by one, they stepped forward to receive a loving touch and to hear an endearing message from those who had passed beyond the veil. Chandra stood and watched as smiles, tears, and sometimes even laughter replaced fear as the spirit of a loved one recounted through her a fond memory no one but he or she could know.

A movement in the trees caught her eye. Without waiting, Chandra brought the night's festivities to a close. When everyone had gone, she waited for the girl she had chosen to come to her. Instead, she saw Jonathan approaching alone.

"Where is she?"

"She will not be coming back." A look of defiance crossed his handsome face.

"What? She has to come back! Otherwise, I will not be able to remove Angelia's spirit from her body."

"That is the reason she will remain with me." Jonathan smiled down at her.

"Why are you doing this? You know as well as I, the longer

Angelia has possession of her body, the harder it will be for me to remove her spirit."

"The girl does not need to be removed." He started to turn away.

"I will not allow you to do this!" Chandra said, uncaring of his anger.

He turned back, an angry scowl covering his face. "You will not allow? You…will…not…allow!" His steps punctuated each word as he hastened back to her. In one swift move, he yanked her to him. "It is for me to say what happens to this person. She pleases me; therefore, she will remain with me for as long as I say." One hand slid down the side of her face. "It won't be that bad. Think back to when you laid by my side. I can still hear your cries of hunger. Remember, Chandra?"

With a repulsive shudder, she drew back. "It is your choice, Jonathan; the girl means nothing to me."

His deep baritone laugh disrupted the quiet of the night. "After all these long years, could it be jealousy I hear in your voice, Chandra? Such a childish waste of emotion in one so strong." He turned her back to face him, tipped her chin upward to smile down at her. "You know you are always welcome to join me in my frolic."

Chandra felt her blood freeze as she mentally tried to push his hand from her face and at the same time not let her feelings speak aloud how much she loathed him. Without a word, he dropped his hand, and turning on his heel, walked away from her.

Chandra remained where he left her, trying to quiet her breathing and not let her anger consume her. She knew him to be a man without feeling, an entity of darkest evil that could destroy her if he chose. She remembered how it had been with him. The uncontrollable lust, and later the depravity she had entered into of her own free choice and her heart froze with self-hatred.

Jonathan introduced her to his dark needs bit by bit. Letting her believe her own lust called out to be satisfied in such vile ways while he remained close to take away her pain. Much later, she found why she behaved the way she did, but by then, she didn't care.

CHAPTER EIGHT

The shrill ringing of the telephone jerked him from his slumber. With an impatient curse, he reached out, snatching the receiver from its cradle. "Hello!" Jack Olivier' barked, uncaring of his tone.

"Didn't wake you, did I?" A familiar voice came to him on the other end of the line.

"No, hell, I'm always up at..." he squinted at the small bedside clock, "a quarter to seven on my day off."

"I'm sorry, Jack," Donavan Hays laughed.

"What's up?" His anger receded, and he reached for the pack of cigarettes lying on the nightstand.

"You sure you want to know?" Donavan said, all trace of humor now gone from his voice.

"Well, hell yes." He placed a cigarette between his lips, reached for his lighter. "If you didn't plan on tellin' me, what the hell did you wake me...." his voice slid to a stop, and his stomach coiled into a hard knot. "Oh fuck! Don't tell me! This is about Hindel bein' on another rampage, ain't it?" Jack sat up straighter in the bed. "One of my clients said they heard on the scanner shit was comin' down out at the mansion again."

"I don't know if it's Hindel, but somebody or I should say something, sure is."

"What happened?" Holding the phone close to his ear, Jack tossed the cigarette into the ashtray then threw back the covers to get to his feet.

"We got a call about a missing little girl yesterday morning out at the mansion. M.O. sounded pretty much the same as with the Rawlins' kid. But in this case, we found a big difference."

"Hindel came into the station and gave himself up?" Jack looked around for the pair of jeans he had taken off the night before.

"No." Silence lulled on the line as Hays closed his eyes against the sickening pictures running through his mind of Margaret's mangled body lying half-hidden in the weeds.

"I'm waitin'." Jack found the jeans thrown over a chair, and bracing the phone beneath his chin, balanced his weight on one foot to begin pulling them on.

"This time, we found a body, Jack."

Jack swallowed, trying to push the words past his throat as memories of another time flashed into his mind. "What kinda shape did you find her in?"

"Picture the scene we walked into with the Rawlins family, then step it up about ten notches." Hays rubbed his aching temples, trying to ease the pain before it had a chance to crawl upward into his skull.

"Ah, shit!" Jack blew out his breath. "Any sign of Hindel?"

"Nope. According to Quigly, he's in England with his father."

"Yeah," he snorted a derisive laugh, "and I got a twelve-inch dick." Jack stretched the neck of a black T-shirt over his head. "You don't believe that do you?"

"What, Hindel being in England or your ego having a growing spurt again?" Hays chuckled, relieving some of the tension.

Stuffing his wallet into his back pocket, he grinned, "I'll ignore that. So, what time are you pickin' me up?"

"Can you be ready in about fifteen minutes? I want to be out there before the next shift comes on. If I leave right now, that will give me just enough time to swing by for you."

"Other than putting on my socks and shoes, I'm ready to go now, so stop and pick me up some coffee. I can make it on an empty stomach, but I'll be damned if I'll do it with no caffeine."

"Yeah, I can do that and Jack?"

"I'm here." He tucked his shirt into his pants, zipped.

"Bring your gun." With that said, he hung up the phone, leaving the man on the other line to wonder what danger lay ahead this time.

Jack remained standing inside the lobby of his apartment house until he saw Donavan pull up to the curb then walked outside. As he climbed into the jeep, Hays gave him a sideways glance before pulling out into traffic.

"You couldn't find a clean, long-tailed shirt?"

"Yeah, but why bother? I got a permit to carry a gun. 'Sides, it's too damn hot for a button-up." Leaning forward, he reached behind him to pull a snub-nosed .38 from his belt. "Think we're gonna need this, huh?"

"I don't know about you, but I ain't about to go out there unarmed." Donavan nodded to the coffee sitting in a holder between the seats, "I hope you still drink it black cause that's how you got it."

"That's the way I like it." Holding the cup away from his lap, he lifted off the top, blowing on the steaming liquid before venturing a small sip. "There's no better pick-me-up in the world than a cup of strong black coffee first thing in the morning. Want some?"

Donavan's stomach flip-flopped as the smell of the coffee wafted across the seat. "I'll pass. My kidneys are already screaming."

"Pulled another all-nighter, didn't you?" Jack took another drink of his coffee, letting the caffeine chase the cobwebs from his mind.

"I hadn't planned on it. When I got the call about a missing kid out at the mansion, I knew I had to get everyone out of that house before we had another nightmare on our hands like the Rawlins family."

Jack swallowed the last of his coffee, dropping the empty cup into a trash bag hanging from the cigarette lighter. "I know you're gonna find this hard to believe, but sittin' here talkin' 'bout them, I swear I can still smell the stench of that day."

"No, I know you can." Donavan pushed in the clutch, shifting the rig into low as they turned off the main road and onto the lane leading up to the mansion. "You need to smell it once, and it will stay with you the rest of your life. I remember my parents taking me to the hospital to see my grandma when she had cancer. We walked into her room, and I almost puked right there on the floor. It smelled so bad. Being a kid, I thought the nurses just neglected her. Mom did too. Later in the day, when the doctor got there, Mom asked him about the foul smell, and he told her what she smelled is the smell of death."

"You serious?"

"Yes, I'm serious. When a person is near death, their organs shut down, and the body starts to decay from the inside out." Donavan switched off the air-conditioner, rolled down the window, grateful for the clean scent of rain-swept earth. "I'm not saying it smelled as bad as it did when we found the Rawlins family, but it still reeked.

Needing to get off the subject of foul odors with just a cup of black coffee on his growling stomach, Jack brought the train of thought back to the Stewarts.

"Did they give you a hard time 'bout leavin'?"

Donavan snorted, keeping a wary eye on the tree line. "I thought Mrs. Stewart would have to be hog-tied and carried to get her out of there. She kept insisting she wouldn't leave until we found her daughter safe and alive. I tried to look at the situation from her line of reasoning, but the closer it got to sundown, the edgier my nerves got, until I lost all patience with her."

"How did you get them to leave?" Jack withdrew a cigarette from his shirt pocket, handing one to Donavan.

"One of the K9s tangled with something on the estate and lost. I made her look at what we had left."

Jack glanced over at him as Donavan tapped one end of the cigarette on the dash. "She didn't leave me any choice, goddamn it!" He lit the cigarette, inhaled. "She wouldn't leave until we found her daughter, and from past experience, I thought we could forget about that, so I did what I had to." He tossed the lighter back on the dash with more force than necessary.

Jack fished in the front pocket of his jeans, pulled out a handful of bullets. Opening the cylinder of his .38, he began loading them one by one. "I notice you're back to smokin' a lot again."

Donavan dropped his eyes to the full ashtray he had neglected to empty the day before, and his voice became gruff. "As I recall, you used to smoke them one after another right along with me."

"Yeah," Jack snapped the chamber closed, "then I got smart and got out."

"You got off the force, but you never got out," Donavan corrected him. "You like the chase too damn much!"

"There's a big difference here, Donavan. It ain't my ass on the line anymore. You don't get this solved and solved quick, the heads of the department are gonna start breathin' down your neck. You know it, and I know it."

"If they want it done any faster, they can get up off their lazy asses and come out here with me!" He took one last drag off the cigarette and reached for the ashtray, then swearing under his breath, flicked it out the window instead. "I don't want this going any further, but I think what's going on out here has been going on a lot longer than any of us think."

"Meaning?" Jack settled back in his seat.

"Meaning, I think all those stories being bantered around about this place being strange ain't so far off."

"Are you sayin' you don't think it's Hindel doin' these killin's?" Jack eyed him over his sunglasses.

"Maybe." His hand moved toward his shirt pocket, but this time he forced it away. "One of the men thought he saw something last night."

"I'm listenin'." Jack turned in the seat when the conversation lulled to a halt.

Donavan cleared his throat, wishing he had thought to bring some juice. "He saw what got the K9."

"And, it was?" Jack motioned him with one hand to continue.

"A large wolf."

Unable to control himself any longer, Jack sat back in his seat laughing. "And it wore a red and blue checked shirt and knee-patch jeans. Right?" His mirth filled the interior of the Jeep. "Oh, and don't forget the frayed rope strung through the belt-loops and tied around the waist.

"Paulson didn't say anything about clothing; he just said it walked upright." Donavan brought his attention back to his driving, looking straight ahead and scanning the trees.

The smirk on Jack's face vanished. "Ah, Christ! You ain't tellin' me you believe this horseshit!"

Pursing his lips into a thin line, Hays continued gazing out the window, eyeing their surroundings. "You didn't see the Stewart girl. If you think back, you'll recall how we found the Rawlins girl all mauled. We'll never know if the same thing happened to the rest of the family because, by the time we got to them, we just had bloated bodies."

"Donavan, for shit sake, Hindel went in there and just started slashin'."

"Maybe, but the autopsy couldn't say how they had been killed. We just took it for granted that's what happened. Which reminds me, I need to get hold of Perkins. I want to see what he turned up." He punched a number into his cell phone.

"Be sure'n ask if he found any animal hairs stickin' to her." He turned before Donavan could see the smile forming on his lips.

"Good idea," Donavan replied in all seriousness.

"Lord Jesus! And I thought I was teeterin' on the edge before I quit," he declared, trying to ignore the conversation going on beside him.

Placing the phone back in its holder on the dash, Donavan cursed the man he had been talking to. "The son of a bitch still don't have anything.

Jack turned sideways in his seat, all trace of humor gone from his voice. "You know I didn't mean it 'bout the animal hairs."

"I know, but you came up with a good idea anyway. And, I already told them to check for saliva."

"Donavan, I think this job's gettin' to you. Hindel's nuts, I grant you that, but I don't think even *he* has taken to chewin' on his victims."

"Something sure as hell is." Hays looked at him, his gaze refusing to waver. For a long moment, they continued to stare at each other until Jack reached out, taking hold of Donavan's arm.

"Listen, buddy, this is a hard case. It involves another child, and I don't care what anyone says. The ones involving a kid are always the hardest to deal with. Why don't you let someone else handle this one? You and Barb could take that vacation you've been talkin' 'bout for the last five years."

"Is that what you'd do?" Jack dropped his eyes, and Donavan growled, "That's what I thought."

As they pulled up in front of the mansion, Donavan switched off the engine. "Here comes Paulson. He can tell us how the night went."

Jack opened the door on his side, sliding his feet to the cobblestone driveway. "Okay, how many werewolves did you see durin' the night?" he called out as Paulson walked toward them.

"Shut up, Jack. We got enough problems without that."

"Just tryin' to lighten the mood's all."

"Yeah, well, this ain't the place to be spoutin' jokes," Donavan shifted his attention to Paulson. "How did things go during the night, any problems?"

"Passed without a hitch." One thing did 'cause some unease, though. We heard someone beatin' drums and chantin' most of the night."

"What do you mean?" Hays walked around the jeep to where Paulson stood.

"Sounded like people havin' a party out there in the swamp." He nodded straight ahead, where the lawn sloped down into high foliage. "Drums, chantin', people moanin', downright eerie."

"Just a bunch of kids. They like to do weird stuff on Halloween. I'd rather have them out in the swamp stompin' on palmettos than in town where they can tear shit up."

"No, we're not talkin' 'bout kids." Paulson glanced towards Donavan, then looked away.

"Why not?"

"Sounded like that mulatto woman who lives in the bayous. You know, the one all the blacks go to for their healin's and such."

"Why her?" Donavan saw Jack moving towards them out of the corner of his eye.

"I went to her for a readin' one time at a psychic fair," he admitted in a sheepish manner. "It was my wife who wanted to go; I just went along to humor her. Although, in all fairness, I gotta admit, the woman's pretty damn good. Everything she told me would happen did. Anyway, that night, we heard a lot of singin', dancin', and melodic chantin'. I know she's the one I heard last night, 'cause I recognized the sound of her voice."

"That far away coulda been anybody," Jack spoke up.

"Coulda been," Paulson agreed. "'Cept, I don't think so. Tell you one damn thing though," he lowered his voice to just above a whisper, "even if she is black, I wouldn't mind being alone with her. She's got to be one of the best lookin' women I've seen in my life. And, get this," he looked around to be sure no one else could hear him, "the men workin' the fishin' boats; say they see her walkin' naked."

Without being obvious, Donavan moved his large body between the two men. "Then everything else stayed calm during the night?"

"Yeah," Paulson said, "although one of the men did think he saw someone or somethin' movin' around."

"How did the K9s react?" Jack zeroed in on the conversation.

"K9s had already been removed by then." Paulson braced for what he knew would follow.

"What the hell do you mean the K9s had already been removed?" Donavan could feel the back of his neck already beginning to tighten. "I gave you explicit orders to keep them here. Right?"

"Yes, but...." Paulson tried to explain.

"I don't want to hear any "buts!" Hays interrupted him. "When I give a goddamn order, I expect it to be carried out!"

"Jesus Christ! Hear the man out!" Jack stepped forward as Hays slammed a fist down hard on the hood of the jeep.

"I'll listen, but it better be good," Hays replied, one hand going to the back of his neck.

"Captain Sinclair called on the radio to tell me he'd be sendin' someone to pick up the dogs. I tried to tell him you gave us orders to keep them here, but he said that after what happened to Shadow, he wants the dogs here just in the daytime," Paulson summed up the problem, hating the fact he had to be the one to relay the message.

"That spineless prick!" Hays growled. "What the hell is the good of having K9s if some bleeding heart won't let them do their job?"

"I'm sorry, Lieutenant," Paulson said.

"Not your fault." Hays dismissed the apology with a flick of his hand. "Who told you about seeing something out here last night?"

"Jamison. Said he saw some movement down towards the lake. Bein' alone and all, he didn't check it out."

"I can't blame him there. Could be one of the few times he showed good sense." Hays reached through the window of the jeep to grab his radio. "Jamison, this is Lieutenant Hays. Meet me down at the water behind the house before you take off. I need to talk to you."

"Yes sir, Lieutenant." Jamison's voice crackled over the airway.

Hays clicked off the radio, tossed it back on the seat. "Did you hear any more sounds that might have been out of place last night?"

"No, just the chantin' and the drums."

"No howlin'?" Jack grinned, turning away as Donavan shot him a sour look.

"Nope, and speaking of that, here comes the K9s."

"Yeah, now that we don't need them," Jack laughed.

"That remains to be seen." Donavan opened the door to the jeep, turned the latch on the glove compartment to withdraw a loaded .44 Magnum. "Paulson, go tell Blain to bring his dog over here. I want to see if he can pick up a scent down where Jamison said he saw movement."

"'Course he'll pick up a scent. He'll pick up the scent leadin' back to Quigly's place," Jack said. "You can bet your ass that little fuck didn't stay in last night."

"You're wrong there, 'cause we kept a close eye on him," Paulson spoke up. "He never ventured out of his cottage all night."

"Go get Blain and his dog, and we'll see what we can find out," Hays told him.

As Paulson walked away, Jack edged close. "You don't believe he heard Chandra out there last night, do you?"

"He could have." Hays placed his .44 in the shoulder holster. "You said yourself she's into that kind of shit."

"I said she's into healin' and fortune tellin'," Jack shot back, an angry scowl covering his face. "We both know what Paulson heard last night. Voodoo!"

"Who's to say she ain't into that, too?" He worked on adjusting the shoulder strap to a more comfortable position. "You gotta admit she's a weird lady."

"She ain't into that shit, though."

"How the hell do you know what she's into? It's been months since you've seen her." When Jack remained silent, Donavan shot him a disgusted glance. "You don't mean to tell me you're seeing her again?"

"No... well... not like... no," Jack hastened to explain. But Donavan could see Jack was holding back on the truth.

"Oh, Christ!" His shoulders drooped in disbelief. "After all the pain she put you through?"

"I told you I ain't seein' her!" Jack lowered his voice as he saw Paulson, Blain, and a large German Shepherd headed their way. "I went out there to talk to her."

"About what?" Hays didn't bother to hide his anger. "Climbing into the rack for old time's sake."

"Goddamn it, Donavan! When I heard someone had moved into the mansion, I went out there to see if she'd be willin' to warn them 'bout what they could be gettin' themselves into! Fact is, I was plannin' on comin' out here yesterday, but then I heard 'bout somethin' goin' down and decided to wait."

"Instead of going to her, why didn't you tell me?" He slapped a hand against his chest. "I'm the one whose job it is to take care of shit like that."

"Because I thought she could…." he shut off his words as Paulson and Blain walked up to them.

"Ready when you are, Lieutenant," Paulson said.

"We'll finish this conversation later," Hays promised before turning away.

They could see Jamison waiting for them down by the water's edge. When he spied them walking his way, he came forward.

"What do you want to talk to me about, Lieutenant?"

"Paulson tells me you saw someone moving around down here last night."

"Yeah. It looked like someone heading towards the trees."

"Do you think he saw you?"

"No, sir," Jamison scratched the K9 behind the ears. "I squatted down to keep outta sight."

"Smart move. Could it have been Quigly?" Hays kept his eyes trained on the trees. 'five-' five-' five-'-four-' maybe?"

"Nope, I saw a figure a lot taller than that. I'd say at least six' six"." Jamison led the way down a small hill. As they got to the bottom, a set of footprints showed in the wet sand.

"Get the dog over here!" Hays ordered. "Let's see where they lead."

The K9 stepped into the prints, sniffed, then took off with his nose to the ground through the trees.

"He's for sure onto somethin'." Blain grinned, giving the dog its lead.

"I sure as hell hope so since he just stepped all over the goddamn prints!" Donavan growled.

"Good news is, can't be a werewolf." Jack pulled his gun from the back of his belt, hastening his steps to keep pace with the track dog. "Sun's still too high in the sky."

"Shut up, Jack. Now ain't the time," Hays warned, his breath coming in short pants.

The dog left the shore, splashing into the water, whining and turning in circles.

"What the hell's he doin'?" Hays watched as the dog ran up on land then back into the water.

"Footprints end right at the water's edge," Blain observed. "They must have had a boat anchored here."

"Son...of...a...bitch!" Hays sent a foot-length of sand flying into the water. "Now we can't get a cast of the prints, 'cause the dog's got them fucked up at both ends!"

"Sorry, Lieutenant." Blain pulled his dog to shore.

"Ain't his fault. All he can do is what you trained him to do." Hays jumped back as the dog shook the excess water from his coat.

Jack shoved the loaded .38 back in his belt as the men looked around to make sure they hadn't missed anything. Although his focus stayed on the men, his thoughts strayed to a tall, dusky woman who still reached into his mind, calling forth memories of nights long passed.

He thought back to a night, almost three years ago, when he and Donavan had received a call about a young, thirteen-year-old black girl who had disappeared down in the bayous. Arriving late in the evening at the old clapboard house sitting on the banks, they had already been talking with the girl's parents when Jack looked up to see the most beautiful woman he had ever laid eyes on standing just inside a rickety screen door. He thought how out of place she looked standing in such a hovel. He recalled being so entranced with her he couldn't look away until Donavan nudged him back to reality. As he stood there, thinking about that time, his mind bypassed all the years in between.

A sharp jab in his ribs brought his wayward thoughts to an abrupt end as Donavan leaned in close, "You need to get your hormones in check, son. We're supposed to be professionals, remember?"

"She's gotta be the best lookin' woman I've ever seen in my life!" Jack whispered, feeling the heat of his arousal spread throughout his lean body.

"Maybe she's one of them voodoo women," Donavan

said, taking in the woman's reed-thin stature, her long, flowing white dress and matching turban. Although a woman of color, he could see her white ancestry in her fine chiseled nose and slanted emerald-green eyes with just a hint of yellow showing in the pupils. "Looks like a damn cat with those eyes!"

"Yeah, a luscious little pussy I wouldn't mind makin' purr," Jack murmured, already moving across the floor.

"You better leave that voodoo bitch alone before she has you walking on all fours!" Donavan hissed as Jack walked away, a roguish smile covering his face.

The missing girl's mother spied the strange woman standing in the doorway, and she hastened towards her. "Miz Chandra!" She reached out, taking the woman's small hand in hers. "Ah's so happy you is come."

The woman glanced at Jack, who stood watching her as she walked the rest of the way inside the house. "You sent for me. I am here."

"Mah chile, Lucinda's missin'. We be needin' yo' he'p in findin' her," the distraught mother said before her composure snapped, and she lapsed into a fit of hysterical weeping.

Chandra remained calm, letting the woman get all the hysterics out of her system before leading her to a chair across the room. Chandra knelt down in front of her, taking both of her hands in hers.

"You must be quiet now so I can hear the spirits tell me what I need to know."

The girl's mother grew silent. The soft tone of the other woman's voice and the energy flowing from her touch seemed to lull her into a state of tranquility.

Chandra closed her eyes, breathing in deep breaths, allowing her body to relax back on her heels.

Jack watched her, unable to look away.

Donavan came up beside him. "What the hell kind of witch shit is this?"

"Shhhh!" the girl's father hushed him from across the room.

"Your daughter's spirit has already passed to the other

side," Chandra told them in a calm and quiet voice. "The man who took her life lives three houses down from you. Do not go after him on your own, for he is a dark spirit and will not hesitate to harm you. You will find your daughter's body buried behind his house four feet in front of the tallest tree."

The girl's father rushed across the floor, taking his wife into his arms and sobbing.

Chandra rose to her feet in one fluid motion. As she walked to the door, Donavan reached out, halting her.

"How do you know the girl's dead?" His voice took on a biting tone. "Did you see the one who did it?" Chandra glanced down at his hand on her arm then brought her gaze back up, her green eyes flashing fire. As she stared straight into his eyes, Donavan felt fear shoot through his mind before he dropped his arm. "How do you know the girl is dead?" he asked again, pushing a calmness he didn't feel into his voice.

"The spirits told me." A slight knitting of his brow brought her proud head upward. "The spirits do not lie. Nor do I."

The way she watched him warned him to back off, but he came here to do a job, and by god, he meant to get all the information he could. He forced himself to take a step closer to her. "I just have a few more questions for you." Donavan almost smiled as he saw her lean back away from him. "What did you mean when you said the man who killed her is a dark spirit?"

Chandra looked at him, her dark gaze holding his as she studied him. Then with complete ease, she explained, "A dark spirit is one who comes into this life without a conscience. What you would call a psychopath. He neither cares about anything or anyone. He cares about himself and what life can bring to him. He looked on the girl as someone he could use, then throw away."

"I never believed in the theory of people being born without a conscience, but if you do, I guess we can go with that for the moment." He held her gaze a second longer, then reached in his shirt pocket for a small notepad. "I'll need your name and address so we can reach you later. You know, in case it turns out you're right, about where we can find the girl.

A slight smile formed on her lips. "My name is Chandra.

I live a mile due north of here off the banks of the bayous. My house is on stilts out in the water. It is the one you will need a boat to reach. Goodnight to you, Donavan Hays." With that, she turned to leave.

"Wait. He reached out to take her arm, then thought better of it. "You never told me your last name."

"My name is Chandra. That is all you need to know." She pushed open the screen door as Jack came forward.

"I'll walk out with you." He placed a hand on the small of her back as she continued out of the house. "I would be remiss in my job if I let you wander alone at night with a deranged killer close by."

The bare bulb covered with dirt cast a dim glow out over the small porch; Chandra walked down the steps with no problem.

"I want to apologize for my partner back there." Jack felt his way off the porch, trying to see into the darkness.

Chandra remained silent, walking toward a small boat she had earlier pulled up on shore.

"So tell me," Jack wished she would slow down and give him a chance to talk to her, "where's the killer's house?"

Chandra stopped without warning, making Jack reach out to keep her from pitching forward as he ran into her. Her scent filled the air between them as he held her, one arm placed around her waist. "Sorry." He leaned forward, breathing the smell of her into his senses. "I didn't expect you to stop like that."

"The house is the one without a light burning." She remained still, allowing him to hold her and trying to think why.

Afraid she would bolt and run if he didn't say something, he turned the conversation to the subject at hand. "How'd he kill her?"

"He waited until her family had gone, then sneaked into the house. He raped her, then slit her throat." Chandra pushed herself away from him.

"Sounds like a real sicko."

"All dark spirits are sick," she whispered. "They are sick in their souls. They take great pleasure in hurting others. The earth is their playground."

She said her words with such conviction Jack drew back, staring at her. "With any luck, we can get him in for help. We have some pretty good psychiatrists in the department."

"Your doctors can not help him. No one can help him." Chandra didn't need to see the disbelief in his face. She could feel it. "He enjoys the pain he inflicts. Pain is what he lives for."

"Then I guess all we can hope for is that he gets the death penalty, and they carry it out." Jack tried to humor her as they moved on.

"That would be but a temporary cure." She leaned down to shove the boat into the water, then stepped back as Jack pushed the boat out for her. "He would come back to grow up and begin the evil all over again."

This time she knew he would voice his opinion. "Chandra," her name flowed from his lips, "if the man's dead, he can't come back."

She turned to look at him. "The dark ones are born dead. They have nothing inside. They are born, spread as much evil as they can, then, when their spirit leaves their body, they are but reborn to start over."

For a moment, Jack released his hold on the boat to cup her small face in his hands. She did not move away. "Chandra, I'm not going to argue against your beliefs, although I find them hard to fathom. I just think this man is a sick individual who needs to be put away for his own good and for the good of the rest of us."

Chandra backed away without taking her eyes from his. "Don't you see? For the dark ones, there is no death." She stepped into the boat, seated herself, then pulled the rope bringing the motor to life.

Jack stood watching her leave, trying to make sense of all she had said and telling himself not to get mixed up with a woman who had to be crazy to believe the things she did. But his mind kept returning to the fact he had forgotten to even tell her his name.

"Are you going to stand here all day, or are you coming

with us?" Donavan nudged him, shaking him from his reverie.

"No, I'm comin'. Just thinkin' 'bout somethin'."

"Yeah, and I bet I can guess her name."

Without a backward glance, Jack walked up the bank ahead of the others, wishing he could tell Donavan he had it all wrong, and all the while cursing the fact that, as usual, Donavan had guessed the truth.

CHAPTER NINE

Chandra walked out onto the porch, settling herself with care against the rickety banister to listen for the sound of his boat. Gathering up her long hair, she turned her back to the slight breeze blowing in off the water. But the caressing wind, moving over the back of her neck, felt too familiar, and she dropped her hands back to her sides. When the spirits told her Jack would be coming to see her tonight, she toyed with the idea of not being here, but she couldn't force herself to leave. Besides, this time, his visit would be altogether different. Not like before when they looked forward to being together. When the throbbing in her loins became too strong to ignore, and she had accepted him into her arms and life, kidding herself into believing it would just be for a little while and refusing to see the feelings growing between them. He had no idea how much he brought to her life. How just hearing his laugh could reach inside her to blanket all the ugliness she had known for so long. But it couldn't last, not with Jonathan so near. Jonathan had tricked her. Tricked her into believing she could have dreams like any other woman. When he knew how much she had given of herself to another, how much she had let her heart be lulled into believing their lives to be over, he pulled her back to the sordid world she had chosen all those years ago.

A sob welled up inside her throat, and she fought to stifle it, to push it down deep where it could lay hidden. How pleased Jonathan would be if he could see her. How sweet his revenge to know the man she had chosen over him had hurt her far more than he, just by bringing her soul back into the light, breathing life into her frozen emotions and making her care about those around her. When the heart is cold and dead, it's easy to place another's life into the hands of evil. For you cannot feel what you do not know. When the spirit has turned its face from God, it is no longer white and pure. Without another caring soul to come forth to pull that soul back into the light, it begins to take on the murky color of gray, then all too soon, slips into the void, shrouding itself with darkness and rendering the heart incapable of human feelings. Little by little, Jack had pulled her soul back, shown her what it feels like to love and be loved. Like a warm hand reaching inside her chest to hold her heart in its palm: thawing its coldness and bringing warmth and light where before bitterness and negativity had dwelled. He also taught her about pain. Now, as she stood alone in the dark waiting for him to come to her, she felt the tears of that pain slip down her face. She reached up, brushing them away as she heard his boat coming around the bend. The searchlight, shining the way through the dark waters, threw its beam across the porch. Without thought, she stepped back out of its path, preferring the shadows.

The boat slowed, turning in the water, heading for the pier. The music coming from a portable radio died out as he moved closer. She heard the boat bump against one of the stilts as he swung out before pulling up alongside the dock.

Chandra listened as he cut the motor, then jumped to the walkway. Her heart picked up beats at the sound of his footsteps resounding on the planks, his footfalls climbing the ladder until at last he stood on the porch facing her.

"I knew you would come." She walked out of the shadows.

"Good, then my coming won't be a surprise." He reached out his hand to her. "Let's go inside. I need to talk to you."

"No!' She stepped back, unwilling to let him see her face wet with tears. "We can stay out here. It's much cooler."

"Fine with me." He shrugged his shoulders, dropped into one of the chairs to prop his feet up on the banister and wait for her to join him.

Knowing she had no choice, she walked over, seating herself in the chair beside him. "When I called, you refused to see me, saying to leave everything as before." Her eyes closed against the shame she had felt when in a moment of weakness, she had reached out to him to be rebuffed for her efforts. "Why are you here now, Jack?"

If only she had known how hard it had been for him to turn her away when he heard her voice on the phone, asking him to come to her. He gave his mind a mental shake, forcing the thoughts away, refusing to be caught up in her games again. "The last time I came, we talked 'bout one of us goin' to warn the people livin' at the Hindel Mansion to get the hell outta there. Remember?" He tried to see her face in the darkness, but she kept it turned away from him.

"Yes, I remember." She heard the weakness in her voice and cursed its betrayal of her.

"Good!" Jack dropped his feet to the porch and, taking her by her shoulders, turned her around to face him. "If you remember that, you should also remember tellin' me 'bout the man who had you so frightened 'bout goin' to warn the Stewarts."

"You're hurting me," she whispered, trying to move out of his reach.

"Chandra," he refused to release his hold on her, "tell me who this man is!"

"It's no one!" With strength born of fear, she wrenched herself away from him to get to her feet. Jack stepped in front of the door when she tried to open it.

"Then why the hell did you bring him up?" He jerked his face back just in time to keep from feeling the brunt of her long sharp nails. "Settle down, goddamn it!"

Jack flipped her around, holding her around her waist. "I'm not leavin' here 'till you tell me what I want to know!" His breath came in short pants.

She went limp, sagging back against him. "Lawrence Hindel. Who else would I be talking about?" Chandra felt his hold on her relax. Seeing her chance, she stepped forward away from him. Keeping her back turned to him, she rubbed her arms, trying to ease away the pain his strong hands had inflicted.

"Do you know somethin' the rest of us don't?" He pulled

her around to face him. "Like where Hindel might have been last night?"

"How would I know?" She kept her eyes cast downward.

The cop in him said loud and clear that she lied. Now all he needed to try and find out is why. "Ain't you the one who said his eyes can see what others can't?"

Her mind raced to correct the damage speaking her thoughts aloud may have already caused her. "Lawrence Hindel is not a normal man." She brought her head up, looked into his eyes. "You said yourself he is a deranged killer."

"I did, and you countered with the belief he'd look to you for revenge if you warned the Stewarts. Why did you say that?"

"Isn't it obvious? He knows I am psychic." Her voice quivered as she searched her mind for an answer he would accept. "Whenever anything happens in the bayous, everyone looks to me for the answer."

"Includin' Hindel?" Jack watched her.

"Yes," she admitted. "I have talked with everyone in the bayous at one time or another."

"All right," he kept his voice low so as not to warn her of his next question, "as you have already said, you're psychic, and you've talked with Lawrence Hindel. Now, what I want to know, is did you talk to him before or after the Rawlins family murder?"

Chandra looked up, her dark eyes refusing to drop their hold. "Did I talk with Lawrence Hindel before or after the Rawlins' family murder?"

"Chandra, don't play games with me. You heard my question! Did you talk to Lawrence Hindel before or after the Rawlins family was murdered?"

With complete honesty, Chandra answered his question. "It has been months since I have talked with or even seen Lawrence Hindel."

Jack continued to watch her, waiting for her to look away. When she didn't, he scratched his head, flopped back in his chair. "Woman, you are enough to make even the most patient man lose his grip on sanity!"

"I am trying to answer your questions with complete

honesty."

"All right, goddamn it! If you haven't seen Hindel in years, then why all the fear?"

"Just because I haven't seen him doesn't mean he can't be around." Taking pity on him, she ran a gentle hand through his wind-blown hair. "The police looked to Lawrence as their prime suspect, so I guess they have reason to think he is someone to stay clear of. Should I be any less cautious than the police?" She forced a laugh, trying to put him at ease and at the same time get him onto another subject.

"I guess it's true what they say, 'you can take the cop off the force, but…well…you know what I mean."

She didn't know how long she could keep the ridiculous smile pasted on her face and the kidding words falling from her lips when her mind screamed in fear he would trip her up. As if it had a will of its own, her hand began to move over his face. Silencing the little voice in the back of his mind that warned him of the danger, his own hand moved to cover hers. The warmness spread up her arm, jolting her from her deep thoughts. Without thinking, she jerked her hand away.

"You started it." His deep voice flowed over her, making her want to throw herself into his arms to take up where they had left off.

"I'm sorry," she whispered, her trembling hands gripping the banister to keep from reaching for him again.

"There's no reason to apologize, Chandra." She felt him move up behind her. He moved closer until she knew if she turned, she would be in his arms where she so longed to be. Instead, she kept her back turned away from him.

"If that's all you came to talk to me about, then I think you should leave. It's late, and I'm tired."

"Then why don't we go to bed, Chandra?" He left the invitation suspended between them.

Chandra felt her insides melt into liquid lava. Spreading downward through her loins as the old familiar throbbing pounded between her thighs. She gripped the banister tighter, trying to keep herself from reaching for him. Her body betrayed her in its selfish need.

"Don't you ever think about how it used to be with us?" He leaned in closer, his warm tongue caressing her ear and sending shivers over her heated flesh. "I know I do. The woman smell of you is still so strong in my mind it wakes me up at night."

A deep moan crept upward to spill from her throat as she turned in his arms, her hot mouth covering his.

His hands pressed her slim hips against him as he fed on her lush mouth, his tongue forcing its way inside to taste her sweetness. He picked her up in his arms to carry her, unresisting, inside the house. Chandra had missed him so much, fought her needs for so long, she had no defenses left to call on.

"Undress me, Chandra. I need to know how much you want me," he panted, unable to keep his hands off her.

She pulled the thin shirt up and over his head, leaning forward to draw her tongue over his erect nipples, bringing a shudder from his lips. Without taking her mouth from his hot flesh, Chandra fought to unbuckle his wide belt. When she felt the buckle come undone, she unzipped his jeans, unfastening the snap, and pulling her mouth away from him, rolled the jeans down his lean hips. Jack kicked the pants from his feet then started to remove the last of his clothing, but she pushed his hands away to remove them herself. Chandra filled her hands with him, her mind refreshing itself with the silken feel of him. She smiled, sinking to her knees before him as his fingers entwined themselves in her thick hair to pull her face closer.

Great waves of pleasure rolled over him as Chandra brought him to the peak of indescribable pleasure. She rubbed her face against him, looking up at him, her eyes filled with all the love her heart could hold, then jerked away, her eyes filling with horror. Fighting to stifle the scream moving up her throat, she stumbled to her feet.

"What the hell!" Jack turned, but he couldn't see anything. "Chandra, what's wrong? Did you see somethin'?"

"Leave, Jack!" she cried out, her hand pressed to her throat, "No! Don't touch me!" She struggled away as he tried to draw her against him.

"What in the hell's goin' on?" Jack growled, still trying to reach her.

"Jack, I'm begging you!" she sobbed deep in her throat. "Get dressed and leave here!"

"I'm not goin' anywhere 'til you tell me what's wrong!" he yelled, yanking her against him.

Breathing against her terror, Chandra tried to bring herself under control. "Jack, I want you to leave here. Please, do as I ask."

Male vanity came rushing to the forefront, pushing everything from fear to common sense out of its way as he stepped back. "Is this some kinda sick joke, Chandra? Your way of gettin' even with me because I didn't come crawlin' back when you called?"

His words knifed deep into her very soul, but she had no time to dwell on her own pain. She had to get him away from her. "I don't want your hands on me, can't you accept that?" She dropped her eyes, unable to watch the raw pain covering his face.

He glared at her as he jerked up his clothes. "I guess you got your thrills at my expense. Don't worry, I won't be back." He tried to keep the pain from his voice, all the while trying to ignore the ache in his groin.

Chandra stood back, watching as he yanked on his clothes, and with all the strength she could call on, laughed.

At the sound, Jack's head snapped up. "Chandra, I've never hit a woman in my life, but you could just be the first." He grabbed up his shirt. "Get the hell outta my way!" He brushed past her in his haste to leave.

As Chandra heard the slamming of the screen door, she twined her arms around her body. "Hurry, Jack! Hurry!" she whimpered as the images continued to run rampant through her mind. Images of a large wolf, his sharp fangs dripping blood as he loped behind Jack. Although she knew Jonathan placed this warning in her mind to let her see what could lie ahead if she continued to defy him, she couldn't stop shaking. Walking to the door, Chandra stared out into the darkness, watching as Jack's boat disappeared back around the bend. This time, she didn't bother to wipe away the tears sliding down her face.

***

The anger, boiling up inside him, refused to be cooled by the winds blowing across the waters. The elements had always been such a strong part of his psyche, able to lift him from whatever problems he experienced at the moment. Not this time. This time Chandra's laughing face taunting him and rushing him to get dressed and leave loomed before his eyes. In all his thirty-eight years of living, he had never met a woman who could reach inside his mind and twist his thoughts. Why had he taken a chance on being alone with her again? True he wanted to find out if Lawrence Hindel may be at the core of her fear, but he could have asked Donavan to come with him. He wanted to be alone with her.

The boat skimmed over the water in a smooth, straight-ahead path enabling him to see what lay ahead and on both sides as he continued on his way out of the bayous. A woman called out to him, waving him inland. Jack ignored her, admitting to himself there could be but one woman who could cool the fires still raging in his loins. Why couldn't he get her out of his mind? He slapped his hand hard against the boat's tiller. He knew the hell he had gone through the last time he allowed her to get too close. The long nights of lying awake, staring at the ceiling as he waited for dawn so he could leave her behind to go out and solve the county's problems.

He thought back to that time, telling himself he could think about it now. That the memories could no longer hold him in their icy grip because he controlled what he would and would not allow to come seeping into his thoughts. Still on the force and working beside Donavan on everything from vice, to narcotics, to homicide, his life had been a lot easier back then. He could go home at night and put most of the cases behind him. Then they had been called out about a young girl missing in the bayous. It seemed predestined for them to meet that night. He had walked her to her boat, and the next night, he had gone to the little shack she called home. Jack couldn't say when Chandra had stopped fighting and given in to the all-consuming attraction between them. Within weeks they spent all their nights together. That is, except on those nights he couldn't find her. His heart became strangled with fear on those nights, and his imagination ran wild as he pictured her in the arms of another. When she returned in the wee hours of the morning, she would always refuse to tell him where she had been, although he had used every tactic at his disposal to find out.

Then came the night she told him they were through. No explanation, just "it's over!" Jack felt as though a thousand volts of killing electricity had ricocheted throughout his body, bouncing from his heart to his brain, to begin all over again. Before long, the nights of no sleep and the normal stress of the job came together to take its toll on his sanity. He had opted to quit the force on his own before they asked him to leave, citing burnout on the resignation. The one to know the real reason had been Donavan, who helped him pick up the pieces of his life and went the extra mile by loaning him the money to open his own business.

"Well fuck her!" he yelled aloud into the quiet, jerking his thoughts back to the present. "I don't need her. I can find another woman, and a sane one at that." He switched on the radio to hear the haunting voice of Phil Collins, lead singer of Genesis, in the throes of "In Too Deep" and felt the knife slide in a little further. With an anguished snarl, he reached for the knob, then pulled his hand away as the DJ broke in with news of a body found out along the freeway.

The ringing of his cell phone called his attention away from the broadcast, and he clicked off the radio. Grabbing the phone from off the seat, he barked into the mouthpiece. "Yeah!"

"About time you answered this damn thing!" Donavan's voice came back to him on the other end.

"What's up?"

"Get over to mile-marker sixty-three! We got a body."

"Yeah, I just heard about it on the radio."

"How long will it take you to get here?"

"I'm in the boat, so it's gonna take at least twenty or thirty minutes."

"Oh Christ, don't tell me! You're in the bayous. Right?"

"Don't worry 'bout where I am, just look for me when you see me comin'!" With that, he shut off the phone. "Son of a bitch's worse than a bloodhound." He could feel the hot flush of shame rising to his face. Now that Donavan knew where he had been, he could look forward to a lecture.

Chapter Ten

He didn't need to see the mile-marker to know he was in the right place. The police had the entire area blocked off, with traffic backed up for almost a mile. Jack pulled off the road as far as he dared, trying to work his way past the line of vehicles. A State Trooper signaled him back in line with a wave of his flashlight. Jack ignored him. Instead, he leaned down, grabbing a portable red flasher off the floor to plop it on the roof of his pickup. The Trooper motioned him forward. Up ahead, he could see Donavan standing outside his rig parked crossways off the road. Maneuvering his way up beside it, he switched off the engine.

"You made it, I see." Donavan glanced at him, a cell phone held in his hand.

"Yep."

"We got a bad one!" He punched a number into the phone. "I'd say it's right up there with the others."

"What others?" Jack slid out of the truck, grabbing his raincoat on the way.

"Soon as I get off this damn thing, I'll take you over to see for yourself."

Donavan turned away, speaking into the phone. "What the hell's the hold up on that plaster cast I called for over an hour ago? It's going to be raining any minute out here, and I need to get a cast of the tire tracks beside the body before they're washed away."

While Donavan listened to what the person on the other line had to say, Jack shook out his coat, cursing under his breath as he spied a long rip trailing the length of the waterproof garment. Shoving his arms into the sleeves of the all but useless coat, he waited.

"He's on the way," Donavan spoke up. "I just hope he makes it in time." He dropped the phone inside his coat pocket. "Come on, I want you to see this!"

The body, covered with a plastic sheet, lay sprawled in the road. Jack moved in close as Donavan bent over. "Take a deep breath. You're gonna need it," he warned, then lifted the sheet.

Jack stared down at the nude and mutilated body of a slim teenage boy. As Donavan moved the flashlight upward over the body, Jack could see the damage to the top of what had once been a head. From the forehead back, everything had been scooped out. With nothing to hold it up, it looked as though someone had positioned the face, intact, on the ground above the shoulders. The eyes stared up at him in frozen horror.

"My sweet Jesus!" Jack felt his stomach lurch, and he turned away.

"Took a real sicko to do this one," Donavan said, rolling the sheet back into place.

"What the hell's goin' on 'round here?" Jack drew the back of his hand across his mouth. "First the Rawlins family, then the Stewart kid, now this. We need to find this son of a bitch, Donavan, and fast!"

"No, we're not just looking for one son of a bitch; we're looking for at least two! And I'll tell you something else." He straightened up, reached into his shirt pocket for his pack of cigarettes. "This one may be a distance from the Hindel Mansion, but I'm willing to bet it's Lawrence Hindel involved in this one, too."

"I don't know. This is different." Jack cocked his head, going over the wounds in his mind. "Somebody used a knife here. The others looked like they got ripped and mauled by a large dog or wolf." Jack reached for a cigarette before Donavan could put them back in his pocket.

"Gotcha, didn't he?" Donavan grinned.

Jack tapped the cigarette atop his lighter, his brows

knitting in confusion. "I don't get your point."

"Seven murders? Alike but different? And the last some distance away from the other six?" Donavan took a long draw on his cigarette, watching Jack's reaction. "Almost like someone wants to draw attention in another direction."

"You could be right," he nodded. "Be interestin' to see what forensics turns up."

"That reminds me if you're not working on anything in the morning. We got a date with Perkins at eight sharp to observe the autopsy on the Stewart girl."

"No, I got nothin' planned." Jack wished he could have said different. "My phone hasn't been ringin' off the hook."

"How are you fixed for money?" Donavan reached into his back pocket for his billfold, "You know if things get tight, I can always stand you to a few bucks."

"I'm fine," Jack nudged his hand away from his wallet. "Rent and utilities are up to date, and I got enough food, but thanks anyway."

Donavan shoved his billfold back inside his pocket then turned away, calling out as a sheriff's truck pulled up alongside them. "About damn time. Another few minutes and that sky's going to open up with enough rain to wash away any chance of getting those impressions saved."

"If you'd take an inventory of your supplies once in a while, you'd already have what you need to take them yourself." A burly man stepped from the truck, slamming the door behind him. "So, what we got, hit and run?"

"You're not even close." Donavan reached in the back of the truck for the sack of Plaster of Paris and any tools he might need to take a cast of the prints. "Grab the forms and the water."

Jack remained standing by the truck, thankful Donavan didn't need him at the moment. The sickening sight of the murdered teenager, coupled with all he had endured with Chandra, more than filled what he could handle right then. With any luck, Donavan would be too busy gathering evidence to think about his being in the bayous when the call came through about another body.

Had it been anyone else, Jack would tell him to back off and mind his own business, but no way could he do that with Donavan. Without Donavan there to pull him out of the dark world he had allowed himself to slip into, Jack knew he would have crawled over the edge without a care. Up until that time, he had never realized how fragile the human mind is and how easy it is for it to curl in on itself. Almost as though without hope, it has no reason to be, except to replay the same image over and over inside the mind. Why couldn't she see how much she had brought to his life? How good they had been for each other? He couldn't have been alone in these feelings. He had glimpsed the happiness in her eyes when they had been together, the complete surrender of emotions when they made love. What had gone wrong? When had these feelings changed? How could a person be so caught up in someone that when it ended, they didn't realize they no longer mattered?

He walked over to his truck and, opening the door, slid into the driver's seat. He sat watching the rain splatter on the windshield, trying to understand why he had thought he could be alone with her again and not touch her. For the first time in a year, he wanted a drink. He didn't glance over as Donavan got into the truck beside him. He just continued to stare straight ahead. The lengthening silence became too much. "Go ahead and say it," he breathed.

"Jack, there isn't anything to say."

"You don't even wanna know why I went out there?"

"Not unless you want to tell me." Donavan reached beneath his rain slicker to pull a handkerchief from his back pocket.

"I went out there just to talk to her." He flicked the lighter beneath the cigarette he held between his fingers. "As God is my witness, that's all I had in mind."

"Hold it." Donavan leaned over to pull the lighter forward before Jack could snap it shut. An orange glow lit up the interior of the cab as he drew the nicotine into his lungs. "What did you want to talk to her about?" he breathed the words on a stream of blue smoke.

"She told me some things last time I went out there that started me thinkin'."

"About what?" He tried to keep the anger out of his voice.

"Like I told you before, I wanted her to try and talk the people livin' at the mansion into leavin' before somethin' happened."

"What did she say?"

"Said they didn't matter to her. So she wouldn't risk her life goin' out there. "

"Can't blame her for that." Donavan sneezed into the handkerchief, blew his nose.

"I *don't* blame her for not wantin' to go out there. What stuck in my mind is *why* she didn't want to go."

Donavan turned in the seat, eyeing Jack as he continued to stare straight ahead through the windshield. "Are you gonna tell me what she said or leave me hanging?'

"She said if she tried to warn them, he'd look to her for revenge."

"Who's he?" Jack had his full attention now.

"That's what I went back to find out. She tried to make me believe she meant Lawrence Hindel. I don't buy it."

"Why not? He did the Rawlins family!" He rolled down the window, ignoring the rain to allow smoke to escape from the cab.

"Did he, or did he come in handy when we needed a suspect?"

"You stood right there!" Hays drew back in amazement. "You saw him running around the room like a goddamn lunatic, screechin' and screamin' at everyone in his path, just like I did!"

"That's true, I did, but that don't prove he did it." Jack stubbed out his cigarette in the ashtray. "Something in her actions didn't ring true."

"All right then, who do you think did it? We don't have a lot of options, remember. Jonathan Hindel was supposedly in England at the time of the murders and supposedly carried out all the legal ins and outs with the police and medical staff from there. So, without looking to Lawrence Hindel, that just leaves

Quigly, and there's no way in hell you're going to convince me that frail little fuck is strong enough to overpower a whole family!"

"The courts and the psychiatrists think Lawrence did it, so that's good enough for me. At least for the moment. Now, let's jump into the present and try and figure out who killed the Stewart girl and this teenager we just found."

"Your guess is as good as mine on that one. But I am willing to bet it is someone from the Hindel Mansion. Now, all we have to do is figure out who it could be besides Jonathan or Lawrence."

"What proof do you have Jonathan Hindel's in England?" Jack asked, drumming his fingers on the steering wheel.

"Quigly said that's where he..." his head whipped around, his voice trailed off into shocked silence.

"So you don't know if Hindel's in England, still at the mansion, or where the hell he is. Correct?"

"Well...he couldn't be at the mansion... or the Stewarts would have seen him."

"That's a pretty big house, Donavan. Who can say how many rooms are there that no one knows 'bout? And keep in mind, we never could pinpoint where Lawrence was livin' at the time the Rawlins family was murdered."

Donavan rolled up the window then reached for the door handle. "I'll take my truck. You can follow behind."

"Are you sayin' we're goin' out there without backup?" Jack grabbed hold of his arm before he could get the door opened. "I don't mean to sound like a complete chickenshit, but there's no way in hell I'm goin' out there with just the two of us."

"I'll radio ahead and let dispatch know where we're goin'. They can give us twenty minutes. Then, if I haven't radioed back, they can come lookin' for us. Does that make you feel better?" When Jack nodded, Donavan scooted out of the truck, shutting the door behind him.

Jack turned the key in the ignition, bringing the truck to life as he watched Donavan walk over to his jeep.

They drove through the rain on their way to a house

steeped in mystery and shadowed by evil in hopes they could unearth some of its secrets.

Donavan switched off the lights before rolling to a stop outside the locked ornamental gate, smiling as he glanced into the rearview mirror to see darkness behind him. As Jack pulled up beside him, he grabbed his handheld radio, opened the door to slide out quickly before the dome light could call attention to their being there. No sound greeted him as he stood there trying to ignore the warnings of danger already creeping their way up the back of his neck. Taking a deep breath, he held it for a moment, breathed out as he withdrew a key from his pant's pocket, then stepped forward to unlock the gate.

"Hold it!" Jack grabbed his sleeve. "What the hell is that?" He pointed at an upstairs window where the dim glow of a candle moved across the room.

"Somebody's inside the house." The words rushed from Donavan's throat in one quick breath. Without giving himself time to think about what they could be walking into, he inserted the key in the lock, grabbing the end of the chain before it had a chance to bang against the wrought iron gate. "We'll go in on foot." He keyed the radio, ordered back up, then pulled the.44 Magnum from its shoulder holster.

"I'll tell you one thing right now." Jack checked the cylinder on his small, snub-nosed .38. "If it is Lawrence Hindel sneakin' 'round up there, he better hope they have a good psychiatrist in hell, cause if he comes flyin' at me this time, he ain't gonna need one here."

"Just keep cool. It could be a bunch of kids for all we know."

"It ain't kids! I'll bet your left nut on that!"

Donavan walked forward. "You ready?"

"Hold on!" Jack stood looking at him. "Back up ain't got here yet."

"By the time we get to the house, they will be." The gruffness in his voice spelled out his uneasiness. "I don't want whoever's in there to disappear."

"Oh, hell no, we'll go chargin' in like rookies and meet it

head-on!"

"Spoken like a true cop!" Donavan laughed. "Shit-load of balls and an ass-full of brains! Right?"

"What the hell do you find humorous in this?" Jack peered into the darkness as they made their way up the shadowed driveway.

Both men put out their hand, stopping the other in mid-stride as a mournful howling split the silence; the eerie cry getting louder and more intense with each moment that passed.

"Oh...fuck!" Jack breathed each word with feeling. "Now I know we're in trouble!"

"Yeah? Well, so is whatever's out there!" Donavan vowed. The weight of the .44 held in his grip, giving him some much-needed courage.

"Where the hell's backup?" Jack tried to see through the thick fog.

"They'll be here. Just stay calm."

"Calm!" Jack spun around to stare at him. "Every time that howlin' starts, somebody dies a bloody, body-rippin' death!

"Backup's here!" He watched the vehicles, lights off, moving towards them up the driveway.

"Took them long enough!" Jack stepped out of the way of the oncoming patrol cars. "Another few minutes, and we'd be leavin' here in a body bag!"

"Surround the house!" Donavan ordered, leaning into the open window of each car as they rolled up beside him. "Somebody's inside! And go in pairs!"

As the deputies took off in the direction of the house, the howling began again.

"Sounds like it's coming from the mansion, but how? No animal could get inside; I locked all the doors myself!" Donavan's breath labored as he hastened towards the front of the house.

"Give me the key." Jack held out his hand, then ran up the front porch steps ahead of Donavan. Soon as the door swung open, Jack reached inside to turn on the light. "What the hell? The goddamn lights are off!" He continued to flip the switch up and down.

"I don't suppose you remembered to bring a flashlight, either." Donavan tried to see into the darkness.

"No, but I have this." Jack fished a small key-chain flashlight out of his pants pocket to hand it over. "Got any idea where the fuse box'd be in this shithole?"

"My guess would be in the basement. So, while I go check it out, I want you to stand at the top of the stairs."

"Be careful. That howlin' came from inside, not outside," Jack warned, staying close as they walked towards the basement, trying to see in the dim light.

"Yeah, I know. Thanks for reminding me."

As Donavan made his way down the steps, he tried not to think about what could be waiting just beyond the small beam of light. The carnage they walked into the night they found the Rawlins family crept into his mind, making it all but impossible to keep going down into the darkness. Sliding his foot to the end of each step, he was relieved when he found a solid floor beneath his feet. He stood for a moment trying to calm his jagged nerves, then shuffled forward, shining the beam at his feet, then around the area as far as the scope of light would reach, trying to locate the fuse box. At last, on a far wall, he saw it. With quick steps, he moved closer, pushing up on the metal handle. With a sigh of relief, he retraced his steps, looking for the light switch. "Damn thing must be at the top of the stairs," he spoke his words aloud, the sound of his own voice giving him a small modicum of comfort. He jumped, his heart pumping with fear, as Jack called out to him in a loud whisper.

"You doin' okay down there?"

"Yes, goddamn it!" he growled. "Flip the switch! It's right at the top."

He heard a click and hastened to the stairs as the basement lit up, drowning out the shadows with a rush of nerve-calming light. When he got to the top of the stairs, he moved through the door, turning on every light he could find, waiting for the eerie feeling of darkness to leave him. "It's almost as spooky in here with the lights on as it is with them off!"

"Yeah, I know what you mean." Jack looked around,

trying to throw off the distinct feeling of being watched. "I guess now we start going room to room."

"That's what we're going to do. Stay close." He turned in the direction of the family room. "I happen to be a firm believer in that old saying two guns are better'n one."

Jack forced his dragging feet down the hall. "I don't relish going back here." His heart pumped with dread as Donavan turned the knob then pushed open the door.

He could see the bloated bodies lying around the room, see the blood-drenched walls and smell the stench of rotting flesh, and he quickly retraced his steps.

"Close your eyes for a moment! Your mind is flashing back on you."

Without thinking, Jack did as Donavan suggested and soon saw the room in its normal setting. "No one's in the basement or on the first floor," he gulped in air, "so that leaves the upstairs."

"I guess we can't put it off any longer." Donavan pulled the door to the family room closed, then turned towards the stairs.

"Whoever or whatever is up there knows we're here. We're not going to turn on any more lights, so try to keep a level head 'case it is some kids trying to scare the hell out of Quigly by howling like a wolf."

"I don't know what you heard, Donavan, but what I heard *was* the howling of a wolf!" Jack gave him a sideways glance as they climbed the stairs."

Being as silent as they could, they made their way up the winding staircase, checking each room, including closets and under beds, to find them empty. At last, they came to a set of steps leading up to the attic.

"This is it. Whoever it is has got to be up there." Stepping back, Jack spread his feet wide and, gripping the .38 in both hands, stretched his arms in an upward position. "Open the door while I cover you."

Donavan held up his hand. "Wait a minute."

Relaxing his arms, Jack stared at him. "Now what?"

"This is Lieutenant Hays of the Saint Anthony Parish Sheriff's Department," he called out in a loud voice. "We know you're up here. Up 'til now, you're in violation of trespassing, but if you make us come in after you, you're going to add a felony charge, and you don't want to do that!" He glanced back at Jack, who gave him a look of "what-the-hell-are-you-talking-about?"

The door to the attic remained closed.

"That's it then, you had your chance, we're coming up!" Donavan yelled, then nodded to Jack. "Let's go."

"Are you sure this time?" Jack growled, cursing under his breath.

Ignoring him, Donavan climbed the steep stairs knowing Jack would follow. "On the count of three!"

Jack took a deep breath, then whispered, "I'm ready."

Donavan turned the knob then jerked open the door, staring into total darkness. Sliding his hand, he fumbled for the light switch. "Where the hell's the switch?"

"Maybe it's one of the old-fashioned kinds with a chain. That case, it should be in the middle of the room."

Flicking on the small flashlight, Donavan peered inside. "I can't see well enough, in this light, to know if the floor is solid or part beams. I don't want to get halfway across and fall through the son of a bitch!"

"Get behind me and give me the light." Jack maneuvered his body out of the way. Squatting down on his heels, he shone the light on the floor. "The floor's intact. They wouldn't have bothered to carpet it if they were gonna half-ass it." He stood upright, inching his way inside. In the middle of the room, he found the light. When he pulled on a chain dangling in front of his face, a bare bulb lit up, filling the large area with enough light to see their surroundings.

"It's empty!" Donavan said, his deep voice filled with disbelief. "Not a goddamn stick of furniture or boxes anywhere!"

"I gotta admit, this is a first!"

"They've got to be here somewhere." He looked around. "Where the fuck could they have disappeared to?"

"I don't know. Unless there's a secret passage here somewhere, and as old as this house is, that's not so far-fetched."

"All I know is we both saw a light in one of these upstairs

windows!"

"That's right, we did!" Jack declared. "Too bad Hindel didn't leave the floors bare, or we might have been able to find footprints in the dust. Let's go back to the bedroom where we saw the light."

"What the hell is that going to show?"

"A secret panel if we're lucky."

Shrugging his shoulders, Donavan yanked on the chain returning the room to its former darkness. Making their way back down the hall, they opened the bedroom door where they thought they had seen the light. "Smell that?" Jack sniffed. "It's the smell of a candle after it's been blown out. I thought I smelled it when we were in here a few minutes ago, but I didn't say anything." He walked over to peer out the window. "This window looks out onto the driveway. This is where we saw the light."

"Get over here and start pushing on walls. There's gotta be a false panel here someplace." Jack moved around the room, tapping on walls, listening for a hollow sound.

"You're not going to find anything here." Donavan stood watching him, his neat brown mustache inching outward. "Whoever was up here hauled ass out the back as we came up the stairs."

"All the doors and windows were locked, remember? Not to mention, the place is surrounded by cops?" He wondered at what age a person could begin the long decline into dementia, then back-peddled that thought to recall all his own less than intelligent moves of late.

"Oh yeah, I forgot." The smile left his face, his brow knitted in confusion.

The laughter, fighting its way upward at Donavan's baffled expression, disappeared as both men spun around, their guns cocked and aimed at the open bedroom door as someone cleared their throat coming down the hall.

"I didn't mean to startle anyone." Quigly stood in the open doorway. "I saw the lights on downstairs and thought I'd better get up here and check things out."

"Why didn't you get curious when someone walked

around up here with a candle or when you heard a goddamn wolf howlin'?" Jack eased the hammer of the gun forward and placed it back in his belt.

"I didn't hear any wolf howling," Quigly responded, his eyes wide with innocence. "And I for sure didn't know about someone in the house until I saw all the lights on."

"Either you're deaf, or the rest of us are hallucinating," Donavan told him, his upper lip curling with disgust.

"I can assure you, Lieutenant Hays, I did not hear a wolf or even a dog howling anywhere near here."

"You disgustin' little perv!" Jack took a menacing step towards him.

"Jack!" Donavan stepped between the two, "Mr. Quigly can't say he heard something if he didn't." He watched the man out of the corner of his eye, noting the slight smile lighting up the washed out blue eyes and tried to keep his own anger at bay. "I don't think he would have any reason to lie to us."

Swallowing his contempt, Jack moved across the room to continue thumping and pushing on the thick walls. To his surprise, Quigly walked over to stand beside him, almost as though he were baiting him. Jack ignored him, moving around him when needed to continue his search.

"What is it you're looking for, Jack?" Quigly asked, his voice taking on a parent-to-child tone. "Perhaps if I knew, I could help you."

The familiar usage of his first name, by someone as loathsome as the man following him around the room, set Jack's teeth on edge, but he fought the urge to respond in a heated manner. Instead, he smiled, taking some perverted pleasure in the man's reaction, as he continued to examine the walls.

"If you're looking for a secret room, you're wasting your time," Quigly snarled, unable to abide the man's ignoring of him any longer.

"Mr. Quigly!" Jack whirled, his eyes wide and unblinking. "Whatever gave you the idea I'm lookin' for a secret room?"

Donavan stood back, watching this mocking exchange with a good deal of interest and urging Jack with a subtle shake of his head to keep it up on the off chance Quigly would say something useful.

"The thought of findin' a secret room never entered my mind. I was just testin' the fine structure of this magnificent house." He spun around, his arms outstretched. "But," all traces of humor disappeared as Jack took a step closer to the man glaring at him, "if you want to talk 'bout Jonathan Hindel puttin' in secret passageways and hidden rooms, I'll be *more* than glad to discuss it with you."

Quigly gulped a drool of spittle, knowing he had said too much. "I never said Mr. Hindel had secret rooms here. I never said anything of the sort!" he stammered, wiping at his mouth and trying in desperation to recoup his words. "You're the one banging on walls. I didn't want you wasting your time, is all." He whipped a handkerchief from the back pocket of his walking shorts, mopped his mouth. "I for sure never said Mr. Hindel had a secret room!"

Sure now they were on the right track, Donavan stepped forward. "We know you didn't, Mr. Quigly. Jack here," he nodded across the room, "just wants to get a rise out of you." Pushing his true feelings beneath the surface, he draped an arm around the man's narrow shoulders, forcing himself to breathe through the mouth as the foul odor of rancid sweat drifted up to him.

Relaxing, Quigly allowed himself to be humored. "As I've told you before, Lieutenant, I take my responsibilities very serious. So, I guess I could have overreacted." A nervous laugh escaped his throat as he ran a shaky hand through his sparse, white hair.

"No harm done, Mr. Quigly." With a jerk of his head, Donavan motioned Jack forward. "I guess we've got all we can hope for here." He almost felt sorry for the man as he glimpsed a look of pure relief spread over his face. "The thing is, I can't ignore that howling."

"You heard somebody's dog, Lieutenant. I'm sure it's nothing to get alarmed about." Quigly felt tension trickle back in as he moved towards the door in hopes they would follow. "Dogs run through the swamps all the time hunting for rabbits and such."

"Still," Donavan hesitated, reached for his handheld radio, "I think to be on the safe side, we should get the K9s out here for a look."

"I don't think that's a good idea!" Quigly screeched, stopping just inside the room. "You never know. It could be the same thing that got your last police dog."

"That's a very valid point, Quigly." Jack walked up beside him.

"Well, sure." He reached to turn out the light. "I mean, you don't want the same thing happening all over again."

"You're right, of course." Donavan dangled a bit more hope, then jerked it back with no gaps in between. "Except, loss of life is the chance a K9 takes." With that, he keyed the radio, requesting backup complete with dogs.

"I'm afraid I'm going to have to refuse your dog's entrance onto this property, Lieutenant," Quigly announced, spreading his small feet wide and trying to affix a determined stance.

Jack cocked his head, wiggled a finger inside his ear. "Would you mind repeatin' what you just said? 'Cause I know I couldn't have heard you right!"

"I said, I'm refusing you permission to bring your dogs onto this property." His dull eyes widened with self-importance. "Since Mr. Hindel left me in complete charge here, I think I have that right."

"Then you better think again, Quigly!" Jack laughed, moving within an inch of the man's face and taking great satisfaction at the pure rage staring back at him. "This is a murder investigation! Which means we don't give a rippin' fuck what you say. We're comin' in with any and all help at our disposal!"

"We'll just see about that!" Quigly whirled, taking a few determined steps through the door, then stopped, an eerie smile deepening the sagging folds around his mouth. "You know, Jack, you could always go to your nigger whore with all your nosey little questions. You would be surprised what she could tell you."

Before Donavan could move, Jack's hand shot out, jerking the scrawny man off his feet. "You droolin'...sweat-stinkin'...

evil...little son of a bitch!" he snarled between clenched teeth. "Don't you ever talk 'bout her like that!" Jack shook the man back and forth until Donavan stepped forward, and with some effort, broke his grip on the man's throat.

With a loud thud, Quigly dropped to the floor. Jack glared down at him.

"You tried to kill me." Quigly fought for breath.

"Wrong," Jack grabbed the back of Quigly's shirt to haul him to his feet, "if I'd been tryin', I would've done it."

"Get all your men and get out of here, Lieutenant Hays," Quigly whined, rubbing his aching throat where a bruise formed in the shape of a handprint.

"Not that easy, Quigly." Jack smiled down at him. "We're gonna be here a while."

"I'm going to press charges against you for attempted murder!"

With a straight face, Donavan withdrew his notepad and pen from his shirt pocket. "Jack, do you wish to make a statement?"

"Yep! I sure do!" Jack stepped forward. "While in the midst of doin' my duty, I got attacked by this scruffy little prick here." He slapped Quigly on the back, almost knocking the man off his feet. "I retaliated by grabbing him by the throat when he reached for my balls with a wicked look in his eye, and that's when you came to my aid and saved me."

"Sounds right to me." Donavan folded his notebook, flicked the pen closed. As he placed the pen in his pocket, they heard three shots ring out in quick succession from somewhere near the house.

Shoving Quigly ahead of them, they raced out of the room, whispering a silent prayer for the safety of the men they had left outside to stand guard.

Chapter Eleven

"Over here, Lieutenant," one of the men called out as they came into view.

"What the hell's goin' on?" Donavan yelled, his gun already in his hand.

"Paulson got attacked! He had Jansen with him when it happened," Douglas, one of the deputies on guard, told him. "He fired at what had him down."

"Did he hit anything?" Jack stepped up to the man.

"I think so, but maybe you better talk to him. He's over here with Paulson."

Donavan withdrew his handheld. "Do you think it's bad enough for an ambulance?

"I don't know, I ain't had a chance to check him out yet. I heard somebody scream, then I heard shots. Jansen yelled out that Paulson had been attacked and that he'd fired."

Donavan grabbed one of the officer's flashlights, flicked the beam over the man lying in the grass. "How bad are you wounded?"

Paulson struggled to sit up, but Donavan pushed him back down. "I'm not sure. All I know is I feel like shit."

"Did you get a look at who or what you were fighting with?" Donavan continued to shine the light over Paulson's body.

"Yeah," he nodded. "It looked like a big wolf, but it walked upright."

Donavan shot a quick look at Jack, brought his attention back to the man on the ground. "Was it the same thing that got Shadow?"

"Yeah, and this time I know it's for real, 'cause I got the wounds to prove it!" Paulson attempted a laugh but couldn't quite summon the strength.

Donavan passed the handheld to Jack. "Get an ambulance out here! Pronto!"

Out of the corner of his eye, Jack saw Quigly try to inch away. Without interrupting his conversation with dispatch, he swiped one leg beneath Quigly's feet, bringing him down hard on the ground. Lifting the radio away from his mouth for a moment, he warned the man staring up at him. "Don't even think 'bout runnin', asshole! I can't miss at this range."

"Jansen, where are you?" Donavan called out.

"Right here, Sir!" Jansen stepped up.

Do you think you hit what Paulson tangled with?"

"I'm pretty sure I did! I heard the bullet impact, then something scream. I shot at it two more times before it ran off towards the swamp, but I didn't go after it 'cause I didn't want to leave Paulson."

"Ambulance is on the way." Jack dropped the handheld into Donavan's pocket, knelt down on one knee. "Damn, son!" He clasped one of Paulson's hands in a firm grasp. "You might get to dress up and go to an all-you-can-eat, for this one!"

"Right now, I couldn't care less. Can somebody cover me up? I'm gettin' mighty cold." His breath labored as he tried once more to sit up. "I can't breathe in this position."

"Get behind him, Jack, and raise his head up a little." Donavan stripped off his suit-coat to lay it over Paulson.

Jack moved, sliding all the way to the ground and lifting Paulson's head to a more comfortable position. "There you go, partner. Does that help you breathe a little easier?"

"Yeah, but I feel like I'm about to pass out." His head lulled to the side.

"Oh shit!" Jack shouted, all his CPR training flying right out of his mind. "Somebody check his pulse, quick!"

Donavan placed the tips of his fingers below Paulson's jawbone. "It's weak, but at least, thank god, he's got one. He's going into shock. That ambulance needs to get its ass here, now!"

The sight and sound of vehicles moving up the driveway brought Donavan to his feet. "That would be the K9 Unit. With any luck, they'll be able to track what we're looking for. Even more so if he's leavin' a trail of blood! Don't suppose you have any input on what that something is, do you, Mr. Quigly?" Donavan glanced down at the man still sitting on the ground.

"I'm sorry, Lieutenant Hays." A slight chuckle bubbled up in his throat. With regret, he pushed it back down. "I wouldn't have the foggiest idea, other than it's somebody's dog. Except now, it seems the poor little thing must be rabid, or it wouldn't have attacked your officer." He raised his soft voice to be heard by the other men standing nearby. "I hope I'm wrong because, from what I've heard about the treatment of rabies, it can be quite painful."

"Somebody...please...shoot...that...little...fucker!" Jack looked to the other deputies standing around and wishing he could be the one to pull the trigger. This time Quigly gave in to his urge to laugh, knowing the detectives could do nothing to stop him.

Donavan glared at him for a moment, then leaned over. "If I were you, Mr. Quigly, I'd think twice about this perverse need you seem to have of pushing Detective Olivier' past his limit. Otherwise, the next time he comes after you, I just might let him have you."

"We got here as fast as we could, Lieutenant." Officer Bailey walked over to stand beside Donavan, patting the large German Shepherd he kept leashed close to his side as the dog growled low in his throat at Quigly. "Captain Sinclair tried to stop us from comin' out here. He wanted us to wait 'til dawn, but I told him you said you wanted us here now."

"You did right, Bailey, and in the long run perhaps saved Sinclair an ass kickin' next time I come into contact with him."

"Yes, sir," Bailey grinned, then became serious. "We heard Paulson's down. How bad is it?"

"Yeah. We're not sure what attacked him, but one of the other men fired off three shots and feels pretty sure at least one of them connected.

"Do you have *any* idea what attacked him?"

"You realize what goes on in the department is, without exception, confidential. Right?" Donavan fixed him with a grim stare.

"Yes, I do."

"Alright. According to Paulson, he saw a large wolf that walked upright."

"Paulson's a good friend of mine, and I don't mean no disrespect toward the guy, but he's known to be quite a kidder at times," he laughed. "Are you sure he's serious?"

"I'll tell you, Bailey. Right now, he's lying over in the grass, maybe dying from being attacked by what he said he saw. Now you tell me, do you think he's serious?"

Bailey swallowed his laughter. "Sorry."

Donavan gave him a curious glance, then turned to the men standing a short distance away. "Jansen, we need you over here."

"Yes sir!" Jansen called out.

"I want everyone to stay together on this. I already got one man down. I don't want anymore."

Jansen walked up to where they were standing, giving Baily a brief nod.

"I want you to take all but four of the deputies to where you saw what attacked Paulson. Also, I don't want the guard dogs off their leashes. You are to stay with them at all times. Maybe that way we can prevent losing another one. Okay, get going!" he told them, pulling the handheld from his pocket to walk a short distance away.

"This is Hays! What the hell's the holdup on that ambulance I ordered about fifteen minutes ago?"

"It's en route, Lieutenant. Approximate E.T.A. is three minutes."

"Never mind, I hear it." He cocked his head as the shrill wailing died out in mid-chirp. After clicking off the radio, he walked over to check on Paulson. "How's he doing?"

"Still out," Jack said. "At least the ambulance is almost here." His attention shifted over to Quigly. "I'd like about an hour with that worthless slime. I guarantee you we'd come up with some different answers 'bout what's goin' on 'round here."

"I don't doubt you're right. He knows a lot more than he's letting on." Donavan took a few deep puffs off a cigarette, then bent over to pass the cigarette to Jack.

"Thanks. I didn't want to move him to light one."

"One thing he said did pique my interest, though." He leaned in close, lowered his voice.

"What's that?"

"What he said about Chandra. That is if she's the one he meant, and I think she is."

"I wanted to rip his goddamn head off when he said that!" Jack's voice deepened with his anger.

"You almost did!" Donavan grinned. "He's going to have one hell of a bruise where you grabbed him up by the throat."

"Good! Maybe he'll think 'fore he opens his filthy mouth next time, although I doubt it. Scum like him never learn!"

"Why do you think he singled her out?" He watched Jack. "Come to think about it. He ain't alone in bringing her name up."

"To answer your first question, I don't have any idea, and as to your hearin' someone else bring her name up, I don't know who the hell you're even talkin' 'bout."

Donavan nodded to Paulson. "He said he thought Chandra's the one out in the swamp the other night."

"Oh yeah, he did, didn't he?" Jack felt his stomach knot up as all the nights she wouldn't account for shot through his mind.

"It's all speculation. Quigly would throw anyone's name out if he thought it'd get him off the hook. He knows we're startin' to look to him for what's happening around here."

"Except that don't make any sense either." Jack inhaled a deep breath, blew a long stream of smoke into the air. "If you had somethin' this dangerous runnin' 'round your house, would you try to protect it? Hell no, you wouldn't! He says he didn't even hear the goddamn thing! We heard it, and if we heard it, he had to." Jack's eyes narrowed, raking over the man sitting cross-legged a short distance away. "Hell, what is it ...maybe five ...six hundred yards from the house to the cottage? There's no way he didn't hear a howl that loud. Lyin' shit!" Then Jack's anger switched from Quigly to Chandra. Why would she be out in the swamp taking part in voodoo? It just didn't add up! Could he have been that wrong about her? All the nights they had spent together in each other's arms, could it be he never knew her at all?

"So what do you think?"

"What?" Jack dragged his mind back from his wandering thoughts.

"I said, I guess what we need to do is run him in for questioning. Maybe we can get more out of him down at the station."

"Sounds good to me, but on what grounds?" Jack mashed the finished butt into the wet earth, rubbed his fingers down the pant leg of his jeans. "Sayin' you didn't hear a wolf howl ain't a reason to arrest someone."

"You're right, but assault is."

Puzzled, Jack looked up. "Who'd he assault?"

"Why you, of course!" Donavan replied with a somber face, then straightened up as two men came forward with a stretcher.

"We think he's gone into shock." Jack shifted his position, laying Paulson's head down on the ground.

"What happened?" A paramedic knelt down beside Paulson and, withdrawing a small flashlight from his shirt pocket, flicked the light over each eye.

"We believe he got attacked by some animal, a dog maybe. We're not quite sure at this point," Donavan spoke up.

Grabbing a pair of thin latex gloves from a large first-aid-chest, he pulled them over his hands then lifted away Paulson's torn shirt, shining a light over his bloody chest. "He's got some pretty deep lacerations. Must have been one hell of a good-size dog to lay him open this bad." The man pushed himself to his feet, lingering for a moment to stare down at Paulson. "Let's get him loaded up. The sooner we get him started on I.V., the sooner he can tell us what got hold of him."

Donavan shot a quick look at Jack, knowing they were

in trouble. "This man is not to be questioned without one of us being present."

"You got to be kidding!" The paramedic scoffed, pulling off his gloves to drop them into a plastic bag. "The first question we're going to hear, when we get him to the ER, is what he tangled with in case they need to start treating him for rabies."

"A wolf attacked your patient, young man," Quigly spoke up, his soft, effeminate voice taking on a breathless tone. "A wolf that walked upright. At least," he fluttered a small hand in the direction of the detectives, "that is what these two...gentlemen... believe."

"You have to excuse our friend here." Jack clamped a strong hand on Quigly's shoulder, making the man wince with pain. "We were just waitin' for you to get here so we could run him in."

Donavan stepped forward, and before Quigly could move, grabbed both wrists behind his back. "These rummies will say anything." He forced a light chuckle as he snapped a pair of handcuffs into place. "This one's one of the worst I've seen."

The man nodded in agreement, having seen his own share of the debilitating effects alcohol can have on the human psyche.

"How dare you!" Quigly screeched in alarm. "You will remove these handcuffs, or I will sue you for false arrest!"

"Come along, Mr. Quigly. You don't want us to have to borrow a straightjacket from the nice paramedics," Jack told him, keeping his voice low and gentle until they were out of hearing of the men working on Paulson. Then his voice changed. "Shut up, you little turd, or I'll shoot you right here and claim you tried to attack me again!"

"That's all right, Jack." Quigly's tone became compliant. "As soon as we get to the station, I will call my lawyer and then we will see who shoots down who."

"Whom Quigly! Who shoots down whom! You ignorant retch!" Jack shoved him into one of the police cars.

The driver of the car walked over to get his instructions.

"Take him to the station and book him for simple assault. He is not to have any phone calls or visitors. And I want him in a padded cell. Alone," Donavan ordered. "I'll be along as soon as I know what's going on with the search and after I check on Paulson."

"Yes sir! I'll see to it." He got in the car, motioning his partner to do the same.

As they drove away, Jack turned to see how Quigly handled being cuffed and placed in the back of a police car. Quigly looked at him, then threw back his head, laughing maniacally. "Nutty as a pan of granny's fudge."

Donavan stood off to the side, watching Jack and trying to piece together in his mind how, after all she had put him through, he could have allowed Chandra back into his life. The woman had all but destroyed him, for god's sake! What kind of woman would take a man to her bed, with all the feelings of a deep and caring lover, then drop him into a pit of utter despair without any explanation? Donavan didn't understand any of it, but he knew he wouldn't get his answers by standing around thinking about them. Walking over, he draped an arm around Jack's shoulders. "Let's go see how the search is coming along."

As they headed off toward the swamp, two deputies, who had stayed behind, fell in beside them. Enclosed within a curtain of rolling fog and rain, each man tried not to think about their surroundings, or worse, what could be waiting for them up ahead in the shadows when one of the deputies halted his steps.

"Hold it!" The man's voice, coming as it did, quick and unexpected, stopped everyone in their steps.

"What's wrong?" Jack cocked the lever of his .38, looking around.

"I saw movement over there by that big tree." He pointed towards a large oak.

In silence, they gazed into the fog. "Could be the men coming back," Donavan whispered.

"Not from that direction," Jack told him.

"Then it's some low-hanging moss."

They continued moving forward when, without warning, Jack's hand shot out, halting them. "Moss hell! Someone's walkin' this way!"

"Stop right there!" With his feet spread wide and griping his .44 Magnum in both hands, Donavan, along with each man standing beside him, cocked his weapon as he stared into the darkness, trying to see who or what could be walking alone on the fog-surrounded grounds of the mansion.

CHAPTER TWELVE

Chandra dove beneath the dark waters, again and again, trying to erase Jack's scent from her skin while the images Jonathan had forced her to look at kept replaying over and over in her head. The stark terror she felt at that moment did not feel like anything she had ever encountered in her many years of living on this earth. Even the night she traded her soul to be with Jonathan held no equal. Jack could no longer be a part of her life. The unmistakable pain and anger crisscrossing his face as she stood laughing at him tore at her without mercy. But, in the turmoil of that moment, she could think of no other way to get him to leave.

"How he must hate me," she murmured aloud, her breath catching on a sob.

In her mind's eye, scenes appeared much like a home movie running through an old-time slide projector. Unwilling to turn away, just yet, she allowed the memories, being shown to her frame by frame and click by click, to wash over her. She saw herself on the night Jack first came into her life. Cold, cynical, with a complete lack of feeling for all the innocent souls she led into evil. She saw the fresh, young faces of the girls she had chosen for Jonathan's lust, being led away, their souls forever touched by the darkness of his foul appetites. A feeling of shame crept over her, making her want to shut out the images, but she didn't, knowing there had to be a reason for her to see these glimpses of her life. The theme shifted. As she watched, she noted how little by little the main character, in the story unfolding before her, changed. The empty eyes staring out at her took on a spark of life, and the full mouth relaxed into a natural softness. Chandra watched these changes in amazement. She realized for the first time how much Jack had brought to her life. How day by day, he had pulled her soul a bit more into the light. She saw herself in his arms and glimpsed none of the wild frenzy always present with Jonathan. With Jack, her body and heart reached heights she never dreamed possible, and when she woke, her body still wrapped in a warm glow of total contentment, Jack remained by her side, his hand entwined with hers. For a moment longer, she continued to surround herself with these feelings. Then, unable to abide their cruel reminders any longer, she lay back in the water, eased her body out straight. Taking three deep breaths, she focused her mind on a pulsating light of emerald green. Her mind calmed as she brought the light closer. She visualized its warmth entering through the top of her head and down through her crown chakra. She remained still, allowing the light to filter into each of the other six chakras of her body until, at last, she felt herself relax as the healing warmth flowed through her soul to cleanse away all the negativity draining her of her peace of mind.

Her eyes snapped open as she splashed in the dark waters, trying to slow her pounding heart. With her mind surrounded with fear and silencing any chance she had of fighting this unknown threat, she swam towards the ladder, knowing she had to get out of the water. As her feet touched the walkway, she took off running to the house, the one refuge she could think of in a world gone mad with nonstop terror. As soon as the door closed behind her, the terrible visions leaped into her mind. Visions of Jonathan lying on the floor of a cave, his hands soaked with blood as he pressed them against his chest.

As she watched, his yellow eyes opened wide, staring straight at her as he screamed out her name. For an instant, she tried to ignore his demand, telling herself he could not force her to come to him. In desperation, she tried to fill her mind with other thoughts, but Jonathan persisted, keeping the image clear and focused.

The scene inside her mind changed to a sickening sight. She saw a body lying almost in the road covered by a green plastic sheet. Chandra tried to shut out the disturbing scene, but it became sharper, more intense. A man, whom she recognized as the detective who had questioned her about a murdered child in the bayous, leaned over the body to peel back the sheet. As the face came into view, Chandra screamed! The face, frozen in horror, belonged to Jack. Unaware of the tears falling down her face, she continued to stare in abject terror at the image in her mind. As she stood there, her mind flooded with terror, the image freeze-framed then split in half. At first, both scenes were the same, but as she watched, the face in the scene on the left changed to that of a complete stranger.

The relief, rushing through her body at that moment, remained so strong Chandra felt her legs give way beneath her. Sliding to the floor, she allowed the emotions running rampant throughout her spirit to drain from her body.

"Thank god, it wasn't you, Jack," she moaned the words, twining her arms around her body as she rocked back and forth.

"CHANDRA!" Her name exploded inside her head, snapping her from her euphoric ramblings and bringing her to her feet.

Knowing she had no choice, she readied what supplies she would need. As soon as she finished dressing, she left the house to go to Jonathan.

She made her way through the bayous, maneuvering the small one-man boat through the dark waters, the sound of the motor making little noise. She could see people on the banks of the swamp going about their normal activities; heard them call out to each other; heard the laughter of neighbor greeting neighbor, and her heart cried out with envy. She wondered what it would be like to be one of them. To have a family to take care of instead of living each day alone. Knowing, at any given moment, Jonathan could decide he no longer needed her. She continued, forcing her own pain deep inside. Jonathan waited for her. She must not disappoint him. With a determined flick of her wrist, she shut off the motor and, taking up the oars, one at a time, positioned them into the oarlocks situated on each side of the boat.

Through the fog, Chandra could make out the large house silhouetted in the darkness off to her right as she moved past the wrought iron fence skirting the banks.

The sound of barking dogs came to her out of the darkness. As soon as she could, she moved the boat further out into the water, away from the bank, and deeper into the fog.

The animals, sensing her presence, ran to the shoreline. She could hear men calling them back as they splashed into the water.

"Oh my god!" Her nerves froze as she realized what was happening. "Those are K9 dogs! They must be looking for Jonathan." She sat as still as she could, hoping they would give up and move in another direction.

"Can you see anything?" she heard one of the men call out.

"Naw, I can't see shit in this fog!" came another's frustrated answer.

"Then pull them back on land. We'll see if they can pick up the scent back down over the hill."

"They don't seem to wanna back off." The same voice came to her over the loud whining of the dogs.

"Unless you're ready to swim out there with them, I suggest you pull them back!"

Loud splashing accompanied by low growls and angry curses split the silence. Chandra remained quiet as the sounds of the dogs and their handlers disappeared back into the darkness.

A mental picture of Jonathan lying on the cave floor flashed once more in vivid detail as she waited for the chance to move on. Clearing her mind of the chaos happening around her, she reached out to him, transferring her thoughts to his. "It is not safe for me to come to you now. Police with their dogs are on the grounds looking for you. I dare not go to the house until they have gone."

His angry words resounded inside her head. "You must not wait! Go to the entrance! Now!"

Chandra knew better than to refuse. Taking up the oars once more, she rowed the boat further down-shore. Knowing she couldn't chance going all the way inland, she anchored the boat about two hundred yards out. From her medical supplies, she withdrew a large, zip-lock bag into which she placed everything she thought she would need to tend to Jonathan's wounds. When ready, she slipped over the side of the boat, then beneath the water.

She swam in the murky darkness, trying to find the entrance to the cave. Always before, when she had needed to use the outside entrance, she had done so during the morning hours when she could see where to dive beneath the water. Now, with darkness and the swirling fog surrounding her, she became disoriented, making her attempts to get to Jonathan more difficult.

With no choice, Chandra cleared the surface. Her need for air, pushing everything else to the side. She listened for any sound coming from the shore. When all remained quiet, she moved inland, looking for anything familiar to tell her where she needed to be.

Jonathan called to her, forcing her back beneath the water to try again. Instinct, more than anything, aided her in finding the entrance. Once inside, she stood for a moment, giving herself time to catch her breath. Then knowing she had to keep going, she walked deeper into the cave.

Up ahead, she could see the many lit torches lining each side of the entrance. Jonathan lay on a pile of blankets thrown over the floor, his deformed body trembling in pain.

She knelt down beside him to lift a misshapen hand away from his chest. When she did, she saw a large gaping hole. The wound matted with blood made it difficult for her to see how much damage had been done. Chandra could feel his large yellow eyes watching her as she spread the opening, trying to gage the angle of the bullet's entry.

Jonathan snatched her hand away from him.

"I have to see how bad it is," she told him as she reached out once more. This time he remained still as she pressed her fingers around the wound, trying to find the bullet. "All right, I can feel it." Her eyes connected with his then slid away.

Trying to appear calm, she withdrew her hand. "I brought everything I'll need to take care of you." She opened the bag to begin laying out her supplies. Knowing she would need to keep everything as clean as possible in order to eliminate the chance of infection setting in later, Chandra withdrew a square sterile pad to place over Jonathan's stomach.

"In your present state, I do not have anything that is strong enough to deaden the pain when I cut out the bullet, so you will need to lay as still as possible. It is up near the surface of the skin, but any sudden movement could make me injure you more than necessary." She glanced up to make sure he understood. An involuntary shiver passed over her as she looked at the grotesque form before her. His body looked to be that of a large man, but covered with short, thick black hair, almost like the fur of a wolf, but more course.

"Does my appearance frighten you, Chandra?" The words came into her mind as he watched her. "Remember those nights you spent in these arms?" She felt his long, claw-like nails move down the length of her arm. Her startled gaze clashed with his, then moved downward as his thick lips drew back to expose a row of sharp, yellowed fangs.

"Those days are long-passed, Jonathan," she told him, surprised at the strength sounding in her voice. "We must concentrate on now." She picked up a scalpel holding it at arm's length to pour a liberal amount of rubbing alcohol over the razor-sharp instrument. "I am ready to begin."

Without a word, he watched her.

Chandra stared back at him, forcing herself not to turn away and, in her own small way, refused him the control he so desired. The thick hair, still damp from his escape to the underwater cave and matted with blood, assaulted the air around her making her wrinkle her nose with distaste. She allowed her eyes to move over the contours of his face, noting the yellow, almond-shaped eyes beneath a broad, protruding forehead. The high and humped bridge of the nose with nostrils black and thick-skinned like the stunted muzzle of a wolf.

She spread the wound, then stopped. "It would be better

to wait until you change back. If I remove the bullet now and suture the wound closed, I could miss any hair carried inward from the force of the bullet. If that happens, you could get a bad infection. Also, in your normal state, I can give you something to deaden the pain."

Jonathan remained still thinking about what she said. As she waited, she saw his hand move back up to cover his chest. The hand, covered with the same thick, black hair as the rest of his body, looked very much like the paw of a large dog whose nails are left overlong without trimming and splay.

Chandra shivered, recalling the many scars she had carried on her body over the years as Jonathan, in the throes of passion, raked his nails down her back and buttocks leaving long bloody streaks.

"It will be light soon. We will wait," he told her, jerking her back from her thoughts.

Chandra rose to her feet, moving some distance away from him. She wondered if Jack could be among the men searching the grounds for Jonathan, then pushed the idea away in case Jonathan listened to her thoughts. She turned, looking at him and saw the thick lips curl into a feral grin then disappear as he arched his back, rising almost all the way off the blankets.

Chandra stood transfixed, staring in horror as Jonathan started to change back to human form. She had never witnessed a transformation before.

Either he would leave before the change began, or he would always send her away. Now he had nowhere to go, and he needed her here with him. He demanded that she turn around and not watch him as he changed back, but she couldn't.

Jonathan glared at her but could do nothing to make her obey him. For the first time in all the years since they had been together, Jonathan could not control her. Far back in the recesses of her mind, a small sliver of power began to take seed.

With morbid fascination, she watched him change from a foul-smelling thing of evil to his deceiving persona of a handsome, middle-aged human being.

A horrible stench rose up, filling the space around her

until she had to cover her nose to keep from vomiting. As she stood still, her eyes taking in the scene unfolding before her, her mind fought against what she witnessed.

The thick hair and skin covering Jonathan's body decomposed. Liquefying into a thick, green slime that oozed from every pore of his body. Chandra fought to keep her mind from splintering off in a thousand different directions as she saw Jonathan's features begin to materialize and his naked body return to that of a normal-looking man.

"Chandra, come here!" Jonathan murmured.

Still in a daze, Chandra forced her feet to carry her forward until she stood beside him.

"I must get into the water and cleanse myself. You will help me do this. You will find soap, clean towels and blankets in a chest over by that far wall." He nodded across the cave.

"Yes, Jonathan," she allowed the words to slip from her dry throat as she helped him to his feet, all the while trying not to be sick.

Although she lathered and scrubbed his body again and again from head to foot, the putrid smell continued to linger. "We must get you back so I can remove the bullet."

Weak now from his bath, Jonathan nodded, leaning on her as they made their way further back inside the cave. She left him leaning against one wall while she spread clean blankets over a large, oak, four-poster bed.

"You will not give me anything for the pain." Jonathan stretched his long body out straight on the bed, unwilling to give up any more control than he already had.

"It would be easier on you, Jonathan."

For a brief moment, he looked at her, then his face took on the angry scowl of someone out of patience. "You watched what happened to me! Do you think after what I went through, the mere removal of a bullet could hurt me?"

Chandra remained silent as she laid out everything she would need. When she finished, she watched him take a deep breath then nod for her to proceed.

Jonathan did not move one time as she removed the bullet,

nor when she sutured the wound closed. He but gazed at her, his dark eyes daring her to make his discomfort more torturous than necessary.

When she finished, she sat up straight on the side of the bed, letting herself relax for a moment before broaching a subject she felt loath to bring up. "Jonathan, will you be sending the girl back to me soon?"

For the first time, he smiled. "No. I realize, in my weakened condition, I must be content to simply look at my beautiful Angelia. However, for now, that is enough."

Chandra drew in her breath. "Jonathan, it is dangerous for this girl to remain, overlong, possessed by the spirit of Angelia."

"Do you think I care about her? My concern is for Angelia. How long the worthless one houses her spirit is of no concern to me."

"Where is the girl now? If she is still at the mansion, I can go later tonight and release Angelia from her body." Jonathan continued to smile at her. "What aren't you telling me, Jonathan?" Anger boiling up in her at his coldness toward an innocent human being, a mere child, silenced her fear of him.

"The little girl you are so concerned with is, right at this moment, being consoled by an old friend of yours." He laughed outright as he saw confusion moving across her face.

"I don't understand," she whispered, trying to shake off an eerie coldness creeping over her.

"Come now, Chandra! I am sure you can guess the name of the one you've been rutting with of late!"

Chandra's stricken gaze collided with his, and her breath became her enemy. "What are you saying, Jonathan?" Real fear clutched her mind as she struggled to get through to him. "If he talks to her, she could tell him all about me! You can't allow this to happen!"

Jonathan enjoyed her terror of the situation, a small punishment for defying him earlier. He continued his cruel sport, the sick fear on her face numbing his pain. "The girl will not be able to tell him anything. Her mind dwells in the same black nothingness as her soul."

"You would condemn Angelia to the nether-world of darkness?" she screamed the words at him! Then drew back, as she saw something change in his eyes. "You did not stop to think that when you damned the girl, you were also damning Angelia along with her."

The scream erupting from his throat almost touched Chandra's heart, for she knew all too well of his love for the woman he had lost all those many years ago.

"I did not think! I did not think!" he cried out. "You must bring the girl back! My beloved Angelia! I have made her suffer the torments of darkness!"

"Alright, Jonathan. Alright." She tried to soothe him, knowing how dangerous he could be to her in his present state. "If the girl can't talk or seems to be in some type of catatonic state, they will have to send her to a hospital. I'll find out where she is and remove Angelia from her body. Everything will be all right," she told him, hoping against hope her words were true.

As she left him, she tried not to think about Jack, knowing to do so would upset her more. Jack had walked out of her life, and she could not say or do anything to bring him back. Within moments she returned to the boat to prepare herself to find the girl Jonathan had thrown away.

CHAPTER THIRTEEN

Jack pulled the lever on the candy machine, then bent over as a Hershey bar with almonds, dropped down into the tray. As far back as he could remember, chocolate had always been a sure pick-me-up, right behind alcohol. Since he could not enjoy a good stiff drink at the moment, his choice this morning would have to be the ever-reliable chocolate bar. Ripping off the wrapper, he looked up to see Donavan walking towards him down the hall of the hospital.

"They got her settled into the psych ward." Donavan glanced at Jack's candy, then reached into his pocket for some change. "They're giving her some medication to relax her."

"Relax her? Good Christ! Isn't she pretty well zonked on her own?!"

"The doctor said she's in deep shock." Donavan popped half of an Almond Joy into his mouth as he headed over to the coffee machine.

"What the hell would a young black girl be doin' on the Hindel Estate anyway? It just don't make no goddamn sense!" He finished off his candy throwing the wrapper in the trashcan.

"No, it doesn't." Donavan tore the top off a packet of low-cal cream, dumping its contents into a Styrofoam cup filled with coffee, then reached for one of the many packages of fake sugar. "And I'll tell you something else," he stirred the concoction with a small, plastic swizzle-stick waiting for the strong brew to lighten up, "if the girl had been white, I wouldn't have been concerned about her other than her condition, but she isn't white, she's black."

"Black, white, what the hell difference does it make? She's just some hooker Quigly hired for the night. He sure as hell couldn't get it any other way." Jack pulled a pack of cigarettes from his shirt pocket then, with a curse, pushed them back inside. "The thing that shocks me is the fact she walks upright!"

"Whites don't practice voodoo." Donavan took a long swallow of his coffee then walked over to throw the rest of the cup in the trash.

"Oh, Christ! Here we go again!" Jack threw up his hands in frustration.

"We find a girl walking alone on the grounds of the Hindel Mansion. She's in some kind of trance… shock…or whatever, and by chance the men guarding the crime-scene just happen… just happen…mind you, to hear some kind of voodoo ritual going on out in the swamps a night or so earlier." Donavan left the snack bar in search of the cafeteria. "Now you tell me, don't you find that a wee bit coincidental?"

"No!" Jack fell into step beside him. "It's like I said, Quigly hired a hooker for the night, and she just stayed a while longer."

"I don't think so. This girl doesn't look like a hooker. She looks like a lost, pathetic kid."

"Is that right?" Jack drew back, his brows lifted in wonder. "Then what the hell do you call all those lost, pathetic kids we busted for bein' hookers?"

Donavan turned right, following the red arrow painted on the side of the wall and pointing the way to the cafeteria. "This one's different.

"How so?" Jack pulled out his wallet, thumbing through the few bills, most of them ones, lined up inside.

"You saw her dress. Would a hooker be wearing a raggedy, pull-over made from a dollar's worth of material?" Donavan watched Jack counting his money out of the corner of his eye. "Besides, if Quigly ordered up a piece of ass, it sure wouldn't be a split-tail."

Jack folded his wallet as Donavan lifted a tray from the stack sitting on the counter. "I'm going to have some bacon and eggs. Want some? My treat." He withdrew two sets of napkin-

ROUGAROU   131

rolled utensils and two heavy mugs, placing them on the tray he pushed ahead of him on the wide counter. "I figure it's the least I can do after waking you up at the crack of dawn on your day off."

"Well hell," Jack grinned, stuffing his billfold into his back pocket, "since you put it that way, how can I refuse?"

When a woman, standing behind a large, stainless-steel container filled to the top with scrambled eggs, looked up, Donavan held up two fingers. "Don't drop any bows. I got an ulterior motive." He pointed to the tray of steaming bacon.

"What might that be?" Jack snagged four pieces of buttered toast, dropping two each on the plates before the woman behind the counter could smack him with her pair of tongs.

Donavan paid the cashier, then headed toward a vacant table over by the window as Jack filled their mugs with coffee.

"We've always been a good team. I think it goes without saying I need all the help I can get in solving this one."

"Then I guess I'm your man." Jack pulled the plate of food over in front of him. "It seems, in this economy, no one can afford to get a divorce, so they don't need a spy." He unscrewed the cap on a bottle of ketchup, turned it upside down over his plate, smacked the palm of his hand down hard on the bottom.

"How long you been without a case?" Donavan glanced at Jack's plate, pushed the bottle of ketchup away. "I thought you were doing pretty good."

"I was for a while. The die-hards still needed me. Now even they need money more than their freedom." Jack sprinkled salt and pepper over his food, pushed the shakers across the table. "I think since they can't buy a piece of ass, they're willin' to settle for what they can get at home."

"Makes sense."

"Which brings us to your theory on what's happenin' out at the Hindel Estate." Jack forked up a mouthful of eggs.

"What theory is that?"

"That we got a werewolf runnin' loose 'round the parish?" He ignored the woman staring at him from the next table, her coffee cup poised halfway to her mouth.

"Jesus Christ!" Donavan laid down his knife and fork. "Will you lower your voice?"

"Sorry."

As Donavan leaned across the aisle, the woman pushed back her chair, grabbed her purse, and without a backward glance, hastened from the table. Donavan picked up his fork with a disgruntled shake of his head. "With any luck, she'll think you've just wandered out of your room. All the ketchup you got smeared across your mouth, it shouldn't be a far reach."

Jack wiped his mouth on a napkin, picked up a piece of crisp bacon to begin eating again. "You can't believe there's some kind of half-human, half-wolf runnin' loose out there."

"Paulson saw it twice. What reason would he have to make up something like that? No, I think he saw something." He bit into a piece of buttered toast slathered with jelly. "He strikes me as a pretty together guy. Besides, no one except a complete idiot would say they saw something that would make others question their sanity."

"I'm not sayin' he's makin' all this up. I'm sayin' he has to be mistaken. No, hear me out before you jump to Paulson's defense." Jack held up a hand for silence as Donavan swallowed his food.

"I can't wait to hear this!"

"What I'm suggestin' is maybe Paulson just thought he saw a wolf that walked upright. I mean, we gotta dark night, rainy, maybe what he thought he saw could turn out to be a…a… large…"

"Wolf that walked upright?" Donavan finished his thought for him.

"Goddamit, Donavan! There's no such thing as a werewolf!"

"Tell that to Paulson!" Donavan wiped his mouth threw the soiled napkin down on his plate. "If you're finished, I want to go up and check on him."

Jack glanced at a large clock hanging above the cash register. "It's almost eight o'clock. Thought you wanted to observe the autopsy on the Stewart girl."

"Shit!" He pushed back his chair. "I forgot all about that. Let's go!"

As the elevator doors swung open on the hospital's basement floor, the strong odor of disinfectants wafted down the constricted hallway. "I hate this goddamn place."

"Just remember to breathe through the mouth, not through the nose."

"It's not just the smell. It's the whole atmosphere. The air's so dry you can't breathe, and these hallways are so damn narrow you feel like they're closin' in on you."

"Get a grip on yourself." Donavan noted the thin layer of sweat covering his forehead. "Would you rather wait out here?"

"No, I'll come in with you. I just hope you didn't waste your money buyin' me breakfast."

Donavan laughed, then pushed on the swinging doors of the morgue. "You'll be fine. It isn't like it's your first time."

"In a matter of speakin', it is. I've never observed an autopsy on a kid before."

"Oh great. Maybe he got a head start, and you'll miss most of it. In any case, breathe deep, and if you feel yourself getting faint, step outside."

"Hays, Olivier'." A short, squat man with a healthy thatch of white hair looked up as they walked through the doors.

"Perkins," Donavan acknowledged him. "What have you got for me so far?"

"I don't have anything for you yet." Perkins finished tying a leather apron around his thick waist. "I just got her on the table."

"Ah fuck!" Jack whispered, his stomach doing an instant turnover as Perkins whipped off the sheet covering Margaret's body.

"What's the matter, Jack? You don't look good. Thought you'd be an old hand at this by now," Perkins grinned.

"Go easy on him," Donavan advised, his voice taking on a warning tone. "He's never observed a postmortem on a child before."

"No different than on an adult." Perkins reached into a steel tray, picked up a scalpel. "Just a lot less cuttin'."

Donavan moved over to stand beside Jack. "Ignore him," he murmured. "He's one hell of a Medical Examiner, and who's to say we wouldn't be a little jaded, too, working a job like this."

Jack stood looking at the small, nude body lying atop the cold, stainless steel table. The pathetic remains looked grotesque beneath the glaring overhead light and yet very vulnerable. "We gotta find out what did this, Donavan."

"Yeah, what did get hold of her?" Perkins entered into the conversation. "Somebody said a large dog, but goddamn!" He stood for a moment, the bloody knife poised in his hand. "He had to be a big one!"

"Why do you say that?" Donavan moved over to the table, keeping his eyes turned away from the mutilated form lying in front of him.

"You see this wound here?" He pointed with the scalpel to a gaping hole as he pushed Margaret's head up and back. "Whatever made that, took out the entire throat in one bite." He positioned her head forward again. "A dog, when attacking the throat, has to make more than one swipe to almost decapitate someone, even when that someone is a ten-year-old kid."

"Coulda been a German Shepherd or a Rott," Jack spoke up.

"Nope." Perkins shook his head. "Width of the wound is still too broad. Not to mention the fact her head would have had to be positioned upward at the time of the attack. Almost like something grabbed her by the hair and yanked her head backward just before it zeroed in on her."

"What did you find out from the lab on the saliva and hair samples I requested on Shadow?" Donavan changed the subject.

"Nothing definite yet." Perkins went back to work.

"What do you mean nothing definite?" Donavan felt queasiness low in his belly as he saw Perkins turn, letting a handful of the child's entrails slip from his gloved hand into a stainless steel container. He tried to close his ears against the wet "plop" as the viscous organs hit the bottom of the pan. "Either you know, or you don't." The gruffness in his voice echoed his feelings.

"I mean just what I said. We got conflicting results, so I ordered them done over."

"What kind of conflicting results?" Jack stepped forward.

Perkins stopped for a moment, dropped the scalpel into a tray. "The report came back saying the saliva found on Shadow could be human saliva. Since we know that can't be right, I ordered the tests to be done again."

Donavan held up his hand, cautioning Jack to silence. "Let me know when the results come back again, and if we still don't have any plausible answers, you might think about sending them off to another lab. Or, do what I ordered done in the first place."

"Yeah, I got your message about doing the tests myself. I got behind, so I let the lab do what they're trained to do. Guess I should have listened to you," Perkins said. "The rest of this is just routine." He picked up the scalpel again. "If you got something to do, go ahead."

"We want to go check on Paulson, but be sure and let me know what you find out with the results, not just on Shadow, but I want saliva and hair samples done on her, too." He gave the body one more glance before turning away, then stopped. "Did they find any saliva or hair on Paulson?"

"Not that I'm aware of. No one ordered a check for anything like that. Information I got is that a dog attacked him. ER did a blood work-up for rabies, found him to be clean." He shrugged his round shoulders. "I guess that's the extent of any tests."

"And now I guess it's too late to do anything about it."

Perkins nodded, leaving no doubt he had guessed right.

"Damn it!" Donavan kicked open the swinging door.

"I'll let you know just as soon as I get something, though," Perkins called after them.

Donavan ignored him, unsure of what he might say right then. He walked up, punched the button on the elevator.

"All Perkins can do is what he has orders for."

"That's true, but don't you think some initiative is called for here? I mean, he's got a kid lying in the morgue, with some of the same wounds as one of our own men! Granted, Paulson got mauled, not bitten as far as we know, but he suffered some deep cuts by being clawed. And, they were both attacked on the same damn estate, for Christ's sake!"

The elevator doors opened, and they stepped inside. "I get your meaning, but if all he was told is Paulson got attacked by a dog, we can't fault him for not thinkin' to check for any drool or hair." Jack tried to remain patient. "All they're concerned with is did...the... dog... that... attacked...Paulson...have rabies."

"Communication! That's what's lacking around here." Donavan pushed the button for the fourth floor. "If they were told *not* to talk about it, it would be all over the goddamn hospital!"

"You better hope you're wrong there."

"I trust Paulson. He knows enough to keep quiet about what attacked him."

Donavan opened the door to Paulson's room, staring into the semidarkness. He noticed the closed blinds on the window and the drawn curtain surrounding Paulson's bed. They could hear the steady beep of the heart monitor and what sounded like the hum of a blood pressure cup being inflated. The light over the bed cast a moving shadow onto the curtain.

Donavan cleared his throat, reached out to pull the curtain open enough to peek around it, and came face to face with a wide-eyed young nurse.

"No one is supposed to be in here!" She backed towards the bed. "Didn't you see the sign on the door?"

"Yes, I saw the sign." He pulled a wallet-like piece of tanned leather from his shirt pocket, flipped it open to display a badge. "I'm Detective Lieutenant Hays, from the Saint Anthony Parish Sheriff's department here to see Deputy Paulson.

The woman pulled the curtain open enough to step out, her movement backing Donavan out of her way. "Mr. Paulson is still unconscious." She became silent, writing on a piece of paper attached to a small clipboard.

Donavan waited until she had finished logging Paulson's vitals before trying to enlist more information. "What time will his doctor be doing his rounds today?"

She looked at her watch. "I would say in about an hour,

but it can vary an hour, either way, depending on how soon he can get away from his office." She motioned them ahead of her into the hall, pulling the door closed behind her. "Mr. Paulson has sustained some very deep lacerations. I know this will sound strange, but right now, his being unconscious is the best thing for him. Otherwise, we would have him on strong doses of Morphine."

"Morphine's a hallucinogen, isn't it?" Jack spoke up.

"Yes, it is." The young woman smiled, giving him her full attention.

"Well," Jack lowered his gaze to the small pin attached to her floral-colored scrub coat, "R.N. Lyons, don't you think he should be gettin', at least, a little of it now, 'stead of waitin' 'til he wakes up in a state of full-blown pain?"

Donavan looked skyward as Jack continued to turn on the charm, leaning in close as he talked.

"He's already receiving small doses in his I.V..." She curled her silky, collar-length blond hair back behind her ears. "His doctor wants him to be awake and talking before he administers larger doses."

"Why?" Jack lowered his voice, using all the allure he could call on to keep her talking.

"When a person has received a severe trauma, severe enough to render them unconscious, from loss of blood, shock, an attack, or, like Mr. Paulson who suffered from all three, they will sometimes dream about what caused the trauma becoming disoriented." Her voice took on a more professional tone, anxious to impress this rugged man, gazing down at her with such obvious interest. "It's quite common for them to get their dreams and reality tangled up in their minds. That's why it's important they not have any high levels of drugs in their system when they wake up.

"So, if Paulson wakes up ranting about something other than a dog attacking him, you'll know it's not a drug-induced hallucination, but say…more like a dream brought on by trauma." With caressing fingers, Jack replaced the soft hair that had worked its way forward, back behind her small ear.

"Maybe," she licked her lips, making the soft pink shade of lipstick glisten, "but I'm just his nurse. To understand everything, you'll need to talk to his doctor." With that said, she turned away, walking behind the large desk to seat herself at the nurse's station.

Donavan pulled Jack down the hall. "We're in trouble, Romeo. If Paulson wakes up yelling about being attacked by a large wolf that walks upright, they're going to listen."

"Maybe not." Jack leaned his head back, keeping the alluring nurse in his sights. "He's been unconscious, so they'll have to take that into consideration."

"I wish that damn doctor would hurry up and get his ass here. I'd like to know when he thinks Paulson will be waking up."

He had no sooner voiced the words than beepers started going off in the nurse's station, followed by an ear-splitting scream.

"Paulson!" They said at the same time, turning back to the room they had just vacated.

"You will both need to stay out here!" The nurse Jack had been finessing so well, brushed past them.

"No chance, lady!" Donavan grabbed the door before she could shut it. "Something attacked one of our men, and we're going to be here when he wakes up so we can find out what the hell happened to him!"

"All right, but you're going to need to stay out of the way!" She yanked on the curtain surrounding his bed. "Oh my god!" She pressed a button, spoke into the intercom. "Room 42 code red! Room 42 code red!"

Donavan and Jack rushed forward, one on each side of the bed, to grab hold of Paulson's arms and force him down on a bed soaked with blood.

"He's ripped out his stitches!" Jack said. "What a goddamn mess!"

"Do you think you can hold him down long enough for me to get some medication into him?" The nurse asked, already filling a syringe.

"Yeah, but you better make it fast," Jack told her. "He's got the strength of a pissed-off bull!"

As the men held him down, the nurse pulled up the sleeve of his hospital gown, rubbing the exposed arm with a cotton ball dipped in alcohol.

"Hurry up, goddamn it!" Donavan panted. "I can't pin him down much longer!"

"Hold on." She jabbed the needle into Paulson's arm, pushing the slender plunger in until all the medication in the see-through syringe had been injected. "He'll be fine in a moment." She ejected the used needle into a disposable container, dropped the syringe into the wastebasket.

They relaxed their hold, straightening up as two burly interns, dressed in dark green scrubs, rushed into the room.

"What have we got?" one of the men panted, moving towards the bed.

"Everything's under control now, thanks to these two detectives," she told them. "They were able to restrain him until I could get some diazepam into him. I think he'll be easier to handle now."

"I thought you said you weren't gonna give him a heavy drug," Jack reminded her.

"Diazepam works like Valium," she told him. "All it will do is relax him and keep him from being combative."

"Miss Lyons, do we have a problem here?" asked a tall, middle-aged man standing at the foot of Paulson's bed.

"I'm afraid Mr. Paulson has torn out most of his stitches, Doctor Rayford."

"Yes, I can see that." A disapproving frown pinched his brow.

"I had just stepped out of the room when he woke. These two gentlemen," she nodded to Donavan and Jack, "helped restrain him while I administered his medication."

The doctor spared them a brief glance, pulled free the medical chart clipped to the end of the bed. "The sign on Mr. Paulson's door says he is to have no visitors, Miss Lyons. Would you like to explain why my rules were ignored?"

Before she could speak up, Jack stepped forward. "Miss Lyons is not to blame here. In fact, we interrupted her. She asked us to leave, and we told her the same thing I'm going to tell you."

"And what is that?" He continued to read the chart.

Jack jerked his badge from his shirt pocket to slap it down in the middle of the medical chart. "That, I'm Detective Olivier' and this gentleman," he gestured towards Donavan, "is Lieutenant Hays of the Saint Anthony Parish Sheriff's Department!"

In the same tone he had used with his nurse, he replied, handing Jack his badge. "Why are the police here to visit Mr. Paulson?"

"Because, goddamn it! Paulson is one of our men, and he got attacked!" Jack ignored the warning look Donavan aimed his way.

"It is my understanding a dog attacked him. Although I find that hard to believe, given the severity of his wounds. But in any case, my question still remains. Why are the police here to see this patient when the sign on his door states he is not to receive any visitors?"

"Jack, I'll take it from here," Donavan interrupted, holding out his hand. "Doctor Rayford, I think we've gotten off to a bad start here." He shook the doctor's hand. "Detective Olivier' and I are here hoping to ask Paulson some questions about what attacked him. I realize, as his doctor, you're thinking of his wellbeing, but we have to look out for the wellbeing of everyone in the parish. If there's a mad dog running loose, we need to find him and quarantine him before he harms someone else."

"The test results came back negative for rabies. And, like I already said, his wounds were too deep and elongated to have been caused by a dog. I understand the attack took place on the Hindel Estate. Is that correct?"

Knowing he had no choice, Donavan answered, "Yes."

"I find that quite interesting, given we have another patient brought in and found wandering in a state of shock on the same estate."

Jack thought quickly. "Now you can understand why we are investigating not just Paulson but also the girl. We're not trying to step on anyone's toes here. Like you, we have a job to do."

Doctor Rayford looked at him for a moment, then smiled. "I guess I *was* a little pompous."

"Maybe a little," Jack agreed. "Paulson's not just one of our men. He's also a friend."

"Yes, well, we'll let you know as soon as he wakes up so you can question him." He walked over to Paulson's bedside. "Nurse, I'm going to need to redo these sutures." He tried to gage how much damage had been done, but with the amount of blood, he couldn't make a clear assessment. "Get someone in here to help you clean him up. After that, we can determine what size sutures it's going to take to put him back together again."

"I'll see to it right away, Doctor Rayford." She smiled at Jack as she walked out the door.

"Do you have any idea when he might be coming around? We're going to be here pretty much all day," Donavan said, trying to silence the anxiousness in his voice.

"I couldn't say for sure, of course. Since you're going to be here, I can leave word at the nurse's station that you are to be paged as soon as he wakes up."

"We would appreciate that. Now, we'll get out of your way and let you get back to work." Donavan ushered Jack to the door.

"I guess since we're going to be here, we might as well go all the way and check on the girl," Jack said as they walked down the hall.

CHAPTER FOURTEEN

They were stepping out of the elevator when Donavan reached out to pull Jack back inside, grabbing the sliding door before it had a chance to close. "Is this a damn coincidence or what?"

Jack looked up, following his line of vision down the hall. "What the hell is she doin' here?"

"I don't know, but I sure as hell intend to find out!" He kept his sights trained on the tall, dark woman as she turned to walk into one of the rooms.

"Hold on, Donavan!" Jack halted him as he began walking in the same direction.

"What?"

"Let her have a few moments before we go bargin' in. Could be she's been asked to visit someone."

"Maybe, but keep an eye on her. If she comes back out, follow her."

"Where are you goin'?"

"I'm going to find out what room they have the girl in. They said they would be moving her out of the ward and into a private room so they could monitor her better. I'll be back in a minute. Just don't let your *friend* out of your sight."

Jack stepped away from the elevator as some people walked up to stand, waiting for the doors to open. As he kept an eye on the room down the hall, he tried not to let his imagination get the better of him.

She has as much right to be here as anyone else. He tried to tell himself. A lot of black people believe she's a healer. It's some old person who thinks Chandra can do what the doctors can't. Yeah, he told himself. That's it. But his gut told him he didn't have a clue.

"Has she come out yet?" Donavan walked up to him.

"Am I still standin' here?" Jack replied, not bothering to hide the irritation in his voice.

"Come on then." Donavan ignored the sarcasm. "I got the girl's room number."

They made their way down the narrow hallway looking at each number above the door. When Donavan stopped in front of the door, they had seen Chandra go into Jack felt his stomach plummet.

Donavan motioned him back up the hall. "Don't even try talking her way out of this one," he warned, his voice low and threatening.

"Let's not say anything we might both regret, Donavan," Jack warned, all the while searching his mind for a reasonable explanation for Chandra's being there.

"All I'm saying is put two and two together. Paulson heard her out in the swamp the other night taking part in voodoo. We find a girl walking the grounds in a stupor, and now who shows up at her door? Pull your head out of your ass, Jack! This is more than a coincidence!"

Unable to stop himself, Jack smacked a fist hard against the wall.

"This ain't the place to fall apart." Donavan leaned in close, keeping his voice low and glancing around to make sure no one watched them. "We got a job to do, so let's get it done. Later, I'll take you anywhere you want to let all this out, but right now, let's go."

Jack straightened up, not bothering to wipe the blood from his busted knuckles. "Let's get it over with."

The door to the girl's room remained closed. Donavan turned the knob, trying to be as quiet as possible, hoping against hope to catch Chandra in some kind of ritual. Holding his breath, he pushed open the door to walk into the room, followed by Jack.

"Lieutenant Hays." Chandra looked up from her chair.

"How nice to see you again."

Donavan walked over to stand beside the bed staring in open-mouth disbelief at the young black girl, who, hours earlier, had been flat on her back, unable to speak. Now, she sat on the side of the bed sipping liquid from a straw in a Styrofoam glass, her dark eyes clear and focused.

Jack waited for Chandra to acknowledge him with a nervous apology.

"Jack," she held out her hand to him, "I didn't expect to see you here. Do you know Darcy?" She nodded to the girl holding Donavan's attention.

To keep himself from taking the hand she offered him, he stuffed both hands in his pockets, wincing as the material of his jeans brushed across his bruised knuckles. "No, Chandra, I've never met her." He kept a pleasant smile pasted on his face as he walked over to her." And, I'd be willin' to bet you haven't known her long either. Am I right?"

Chandra refused to be baited. "Of course I know her. She has lived in the bayous all her life." Realizing the danger she courted with Jack, she turned her attention back to Donavan. "Lieutenant Hays, is there some reason the two of you are here to visit with Darcy? While I find your concern charming, I also find it a bit odd."

Donavan swung around, staring at her with open confusion. Then, gathering his wits, he exploded, "I want to know how the hell you changed her from a walking empty shell to a normal healthy young girl."

"I'm afraid I don't understand what you are trying to say, Lieutenant Hays." Chandra's soft voice betrayed none of the fear trying to push its way into her mind.

"Bull shit!" Donavan slammed a chair down hard in front of her then straddled it. "When we found her, early this morning, she couldn't speak. Wandering around like a goddamn zombie! She couldn't talk, hear, or see! Nothing!" He threw up his hands, trying to make sense of everything. "Now, we walk in here a few hours later, and it's like nothing ever happened to her! You can't make me believe this is all just a goddamn fluke!"

"Mist' Hays," Darcy spoke up from across the room, "Miz Chandra din' do nuthin'. Ya kin talks ter mah docta. He'll tells ya, Miz Chandra din' hahm me none!"

"That's a real good idea, but first, I want *you* to tell me what happened." Donavan left his chair to stand beside her bed.

"Ah doan knows whut happened! Ah jes' woke up hyah dis mawnin'!"

"That don't make any sense! What happened to you last night? And why were you walking alone on the Hindel Estate?" Donavan fired the questions at her in rapid succession.

"Ah tole ya!" she cried. "Ah doan knows!"

"What is going on in here?" demanded a hefty, gray-haired nurse walking into the room.

"That's what we're trying to find out!" Donavan turned to face her.

"This patient is not to be disturbed. She has been through enough!"

"Just what is the "enough" you're referrin' to?" Jack entered into the conversation.

"That's between her and her doctor!" she snapped, lifting a blood pressure cuff down from where it hung on the wall.

Chandra tried moving unnoticed towards the door, but Jack stepped in front of her. "I don't think Lieutenant Hays is finished with you yet," he told her. "And even if he is, I sure as hell ain't!"

"No!" Donavan whirled, eyeing Chandra as she stood there looking at the girl watching her from across the room. "I'm no way near finished with her yet, but this ain't the place to say what I want, so I guess we'll continue this conversation someplace other than here."

Chandra glanced at the large clock hanging on the wall opposite Darcy's bed. "I can give you a few moments, then I have to leave."

Jack couldn't believe what he heard. "I don't think she understands what's happenin' here, Donavan."

"I know she doesn't, but that's not a problem because I intend to enlighten her real quick!"

"After you." Jack smiled, opening the door for her.

Chandra ignored him, brushing past him on her way out the door.

"Follow me." Donavan walked in front of her. He remained silent until they were seated in the visitor's lounge. Thankful, for the moment, they were alone.

Jack forced himself to sit in silence as he waited for Donavan to begin questioning her.

"Now, Miss Chandra, or Miz Chandra, or whatever it is people call you..." his voice slid to a stop as she turned in her chair, her dark green eyes daring him to continue his disrespect.

"My name is Chandra." Her voice held a chilled and low tone.

Donavan drew back, staring at her. "Lady, I don't give a good goddamn what your name is or what you *think* you are. To me, you're another so-called psychic con-artist, out to prey on the misfortunes of others and take them for all you can get!"

"Donavan," Jack spoke up in defense of the woman he still loved.

"Stay out of this, Jack. If you can't put your feelings aside long enough to do your job, then leave."

With every ounce of willpower he could summon, Jack sat back in his chair to allow Donavan to continue.

He bent forward in his chair, leaning an elbow on one knee. "Chandra," his voice dripped with respect, "tell me where you were on Halloween night."

"Where I go is no concern of yours." She fought to keep her voice even.

"Oh, but it is." Donavan smiled into her face. "Since you won't volunteer the information, I'll go ahead and tell *you* where you were." Donavan poked a finger into the air.

"If that is your wish." She bowed her head in his direction.

Donavan could not believe how calm she seemed. "I think you were in the swamps near the Hindel Mansion practicing voodoo that night." He watched her, waiting for her to drop her glance. To his surprise, her keen gaze remained fixed on his.

"Why do you say that?" Her voice stayed soft and

controlled.

Jack could feel his teeth clench. He wanted to reach across Donavan and shake the truth from her. At the same time, he prayed she could say something to convince him of her innocence.

"I say that because someone, who recognized your voice, heard you chanting and performing a voodoo ritual that night. Are you going to tell me this "someone" imagined what he heard?"

Chandra felt her pulse escalate, and her insides begin to quiver. She couldn't see around Donavan to glimpse Jack's face, but she could feel the tension building around her. She forced herself to relax, breathing in deep breaths until she felt her fear subside. Then she answered him, "The person, who said he recognized my voice the night of All-Hallows Eve, did not lie."

For a brief moment, Jack felt the room go out of focus, then swim back in. "Just what the hell did you do out there?" He leaned forward in his chair to look at her. "And don't lie to me, goddamn it!"

Donavan leaned back in his chair, folding his arms across his protruding stomach.

"I did what I do every full moon and sacred night, Jack," she told him, her voice sounding calm. "As Voodoo Priestess, I administered to my people."

Jack leaped to his feet, his hands balled into fists as he glared at her. "You tell me, and you tell me now!" he demanded through clenched teeth. "Is that where you disappeared to all those nights you left me?"

"Yes!" she spat, her own anger rising to the surface. "The bayou people depend on me! I heal them!" She jumped to her feet to stand nose to nose with him. "Do you think the white doctors care what happens to them? I can tell you, they don't! If they couldn't call on me, many of them would die!"

"If you're so proud of what you do, then why all the lies, Chandra? There's got to be more here than you're sayin'! Answer me!" He reached out, grabbing her by her arms, trying to shake the truth from her.

Donavan remained seated, recalling all the hell she had

visited upon Jack, and he welcomed the situation with an almost sadistic fascination.

Jack felt a sharp pain shoot through his shoulders, spreading a strange tingling down his arms all the way into his hands. His useless limbs released their hold to hang at his sides. He stood there staring at her.

Donavan jumped up, coming forward. "What the hell's wrong?" He grabbed Jack by his shoulders. When he received no response, he drew back, slapping him across his face.

Jack shook his head, regaining his senses, and felt the pain in his shoulders subside. A strange coldness settled over him. "You evil bitch!" he breathed, staring straight into her eyes, his voice filled with all the loathing he felt for her. "If you ever…use your dark powers on me again, I swear to Christ, with my last breath, I'll…break…your…fuckin' neck!"

The anger drained from her to be replaced with pain so strong, her mind screamed against its strength. With sheer effort, she silenced her suffering, showing him a face devoid of any outward discomfort. Feeling her control beginning to dwindle, she turned to walk out of the room.

Donavan remained, letting her go.

Jack waited, giving her enough time to leave the floor, then he walked over to where Donavan stood watching him. "For the first time in all the years I've known her," he nodded, giving emphasis to his words, "I can say in all honesty, it's over."

Donavan sent up a silent prayer draping an arm over Jack's shoulders and giving him a quick squeeze. "And for the first time in all the years I've heard you say that, *I* can say in all honesty, I believe you."

"So now what?" Jack said, anxious to be out in the fresh air and away from any chance of running into Chandra again. "Do we wait for Paulson to come 'round or just call it a day?"

"I don't know about you, but I'm ready to get the hell out of here." He grinned as he saw color flood back into Jack's face.

As they ran to the jeep, the skies opened up, drenching them to the skin before they could get inside. "I got an idea. Why don't you come home and have dinner with us tonight?"

"Any other time, I'd turn you down, but right now, I feel like bein' with family, so you're on!"

"Great! I won't even tell Barb you're coming. We'll stop by the market on the way and pick up some steaks and all the fixings. Hell, I'll even grab a bottle of good wine!"

"And I'll make you a promise, right here and now. I'll help you drink it."

The smile disappeared from Donavan's face. "Jack, I just remembered. Maybe getting some wine isn't such a good idea."

"You don't need to worry, Donavan." Jack felt touched at his caring. "I drank before to kill the pain. Today, I booted that pain in the ass and right out of my life."

"Then what's it going to be, partner, red or white?"

Jack laughed, liking the feel it gave him. "How 'bout both? One for you and one for me."

"Tonight, nothing can stand in the way of our celebrating!" Donavan felt almost giddy. Ignoring the rain, he rolled down the window to stick his head outside, and as they passed the large sign with the words 'Hospital Zone! Quiet!' gave out with the best wolf howl he could summon.

As the jeep's tail-lights twinkled in the gathering fog, a woman stood watching them leave, and her heart cried out with her anguish.

Chapter Fifteen

"Mama. Ma…ma." Margaret stood, surrounded by a swirling mist, her arms outstretched, her long blond hair blowing back from her face, calling out to her mother.

Janet walked towards her, her feet laden and slow. "Margaret? Is it you?" Her breath labored in her lungs as she started to run. "Oh, Margaret! You're alive!" She reached out her arms to gather her little girl close to her. Margaret backed away just out of her reach. "No, Margaret, don't go! Mama loves you!" Janet cajoled her. "Come back. Oh please, Margaret, come back," she sobbed, her heart racked with pain.

"You left me, Mama," Margaret cried out. "I came back, but I couldn't find you. Why did you leave me, Mama? I thought you loved me."

"No! No, listen to me, Margaret." She held out her arms, trying to coax the child to come to her, but Margaret backed further away. "You have to listen to me!" she pleaded with her. "They told me you were dead! Oh, Margaret, they told me you were dead!"

"You have to come back to me, Mama. I need you. Need you…need you…" her words echoed over and over, getting further and further away until Janet could no longer hear her. Until just the swirling mist remained.

"Margaret!" Janet screamed, bolting upright in bed, her face wet with tears.

"Janet." Roger sat up, switching on the small bedside lamp, then reached out, taking her into his arms and rocking her. "Honey, what is it? Did you have a dream about Margaret? I heard you call her name."

"Oh, Roger." She pushed herself back away from him to look into his face. "Margaret came to me. She accused me of abandoning her. Oh my god! She looked so frightened."

"Honey!" He rubbed shaking hands over her back, trying to soothe her. "It had to be a bad dream. Margaret is dead. She can't come to you. The mind can be very cruel at times, darling, but you had a bad, bad dream."

"No, Roger!" She shoved him back. "Margaret came to me for a reason. She wants us to come back to the mansion so she can be with us again. No!" She batted his hands away when he reached for her. "Margaret wants us to come back, and that's what we're going to do!"

"Janet, goddamn it!" He threw back the covers, slid his feet to the floor. "We can't go back and live in that house. Margaret's not there." He hated to add to her pain, but he had to shock her out of her need to return to a house that could end up getting them all killed. "Margaret is in the morgue." He walked around the bed to take her into his arms once more. "Do you hear me, Janet? Our daughter's body is lying in the morgue!"

"No!" Janet jerked away from him. "No! No! No!" She shook her head back and forth, punctuating each denial with a pounding fist against his chest. "She is not in a morgue! She is in that house!"

"Janet, you need to get hold of yourself." His voice softened as he tried to reason with her.

"Roger, I'm going back there. If you want to stay here with the girls you can! I'm going back where my daughter needs me to be."

His mind raced to think of a way to keep her with him. "Of course, yes, of course, but first, go take a shower and freshen up," he said each word as it came to his mind. "It will make you feel better. You want to look your best for Margaret, don't you?"

"Oh, Roger, thank you!" She threw her arms around his neck, raining kisses over his face. "Should we wake the girls so they can get ready?"

"No, not yet. Let them sleep for a while. We can wake

them when you're ready."

Janet left the bed, walking across the room to the small dresser sitting in a corner. She chose each piece of clothing she planned to wear. She straightened up, the clothes pressed against her chest. "I won't be long, Roger." She smiled, then walked into the bathroom.

Roger returned the smile as best he could. As she closed the door, he jumped up, going to where he had left his shirt the night before draped over the back of a chair. Trying to still his shaking hands, he reached into the pocket, hoping this is where he had put it. With a sigh of relief, he withdrew the card Lieutenant Hays had given him with his phone number printed across the bottom. Without giving himself time to think, he punched in the number on the telephone.

***

Donavan could hear the wailing of the wind as it raced down a dark road towards him. He hunched down in the tall trees trying to hide himself from something or someone he couldn't remember which because nothing made any sense here. He just knew danger surrounded him, and he had to get away. Someone grabbed hold of him, and he screamed, flailing his arms in an attempt to push them away. He tried to run, but his legs wouldn't move no matter how hard he tried. From far away, he could hear Barbara calling to him. He had to reach her! Had to save her! "Barbara!!!" His scream split the silence, jerked him from his nightmare.

"Donavan." Barbara shook him. "Wake up. You're having a bad dream, and someone is on the phone for you. He says his name is Roger Stewart."

Donavan rubbed a shaky hand over his sweating face then reached for the phone. "Hello."

"Lieutenant Hays?"

"Yeah," Donavan tried to clear his mind of the wine-induced fog settling like a shroud inside his pounding head.

"I'm sorry to bother you at this early hour, but I need your help."

"Who the hell is this?" Donavan pushed himself upright

in the bed, reached over on the bedside table to shake a cigarette out of an almost empty pack.

"Roger Stewart, Lieutenant. I told your wife my name. I guess she didn't hear me."

"What's up, Mr. Stewart?" His stomach recoiled as the odor from the lit cigarette merged with the stagnant air already surrounding him.

"It's Janet, Lieutenant, she had a bad dream about Margaret, and now she says she's going back to that house. I've done everything I can to talk her out of it, but she won't listen to me. I didn't know where else to turn!"

"Calm down." Donavan fought to keep the anger out of his voice.

"What am I going to do?!"

"Well, it's for damn sure you can't let her go back there! Take her car keys."

"I already did that! But, in the state she's in, she'll walk if that's how she has to get there. You got to do something, Lieutenant!"

I guess knocking her out is out of the question too! The thought flipped through his mind, but he didn't voice it. "Fuck!" He covered the mouthpiece.

"I'm sorry, Lieutenant, I couldn't hear you."

"Never mind. What is it you want me to do, Mr. Stewart?" he asked, afraid he already knew the answer.

"Could you come over here and talk to her? Maybe she'll listen to you."

"She hasn't before, but I guess if that's the one way to keep her away from that house, then I better."

"Thank you, Lieutenant, and again, I'm sorry to have to call on you like this."

"It goes with the territory. I'll be there as soon as I can. In the meantime, don't let her out of that room. I don't want to call out anyone else to go looking for her."

"No, I'll make sure and keep her here."

Donavan hung up the phone and, throwing back the covers, swung his legs off the side of the bed. Lingering for a moment as he tried to gather his wits.

A light tapping on the bedroom door drew his attention. "Yeah?" he called out.

Jack opened the door. "What's goin' on? I heard the phone ring."

"I just heard from Stewart. His wife had a bad dream. Now she's hell-bent on going back to the house."

"The Hindel Estate?" Jack walked the rest of the way into the room. "Is she out of her fuckin" mind?" He glanced behind Donavan as Barbara sat up in bed, pulling the neckline of her green satin, pajama top away from her throat, pushing a mop of blond hair out of her eyes. "Sorry, Barb."

"No, that's fine," she told him, yawning behind her hand. "I wondered the same thing."

"You're going with me, aren't you?"

"Soon as I finish gettin' dressed." He turned, heading back to the other room.

"I shouldn't be long, hon." Donavan leaned over, dropped a kiss on her bare shoulder.

"Take your time. I'll be right here when you get back," she laughed, already scooting back down beneath the covers.

"That's one of the things I love about you. I always know where to find you." He smiled over at her, but her even breathing told him she had already drifted back to sleep.

Tugging the seat of his red silk boxers to a more comfortable position, Donavan walked into the bathroom. Turning the faucet on cold, he cupped his hands, dousing his face with the chilling water again and again in an attempt to quell the sledgehammer beating a repetitive rhythm inside his skull. With a painful shake of his head, he reached for a towel, then the medicine cabinet. He pressed down hard on the top of the aspirin bottle, trying to unscrew the lid. "Jesus Christ!" he breathed aloud as the cap refused to budge. "Don't they make anything anymore that ain't kid-proof? Hell! The only one who *can* open the goddamn thing *is* a kid!" As if to prove him wrong, the lid gave up the struggle, dropping into his hand. "About damn time!" he growled, shaking out six pills, popping three of them into his mouth to wash them down with a handful of water.

Jack looked up as Donavan walked into the front room. "You don't think this woman's serious 'bout going back there, do you?"

"Here." He held out the aspirins. "I thought you might need these."

Jack took the pills putting all three into his mouth, then headed toward the kitchen for a glass of water. "I wouldn't put any bets on what that lady is liable to do," Donavan answered his question. "I already told you about the hard time I had getting them out of there. If she's that flipped out, I might as well attack her myself and save whatever's out there the trouble!"

"Sounds like she's a real handful." Jack walked back into the room.

"Pain in the ass is what she is! I'll tell you one goddamn thing! I won't put my men in danger because of her. If she's determined to get her and her family killed, then I can't stop her."

"Are you ready to go?"

"Yeah, let's get it over with," Donavan growled, jerking open the door.

***

Janet walked out of the bathroom, buttoning the last button on her blouse. "Why haven't you woken the girls yet, Roger?" She stopped just outside the door.

"I thought we would wait until it gets light before we go," he tried to pacify her.

"Roger, what difference does it make? The sooner we get back, the sooner we can find Margaret." She made her way over to where the girls still slept, blissful of the chaos unfolding around them.

"Janet, please." He held out a hand to her. "Let them sleep a while longer." When she turned to look at him, he could see the confusion flitting across her face. "Why don't you come over here and sit down with me?" He patted the space beside him, breathing a sigh of relief when she moved towards him. "Sweetheart," he pulled her down beside him on the bed, "you've got to stop and think about what you're saying. Margaret is gone. She's not coming back."

"You're wrong, Roger." Janet moved away as he tried to draw her near. "This time, I know you're wrong! Margaret came to me. She came to me, and she told me I have to come back so she will have me there to come home to." Her head bobbed back and forth, convincing herself of her words.

"Janet," he enfolded her in his arms, "I love you with all my heart, and I can't stand to see you in this much pain."

"I won't be in pain much longer, Roger, and neither will you. Don't you see? When we get back home, Margaret will come back to us, then all our pain and grief will go away."

"Janet!" Roger hugged her to him. "Margaret is not coming back. You had a bad dream. When a person is filled with grief, their mind plays tricks on them. Can't you see that?"

"You're not a doctor, Roger, so stop trying to pretend you are. Our daughter is coming home where she belongs. She'll be back with her sisters and her mama and daddy, and we'll be our old happy family again." She pulled away from him. "Just watch. You'll see I'm right."

Without being obvious, Roger reached up, pulling back the curtain to peer outside.

"What are you doing?" Janet gave him an impatient glance.

"Looking to see if it's raining. It sounded like it might be." Roger allowed the words to flow without thinking about them.

A light tapping on the door had Roger on his feet and walking across the floor. "Come in, Lieutenant." He stepped back out of the way, nodding to the man following Hays inside.

"Mr. Stewart," Hays held out his hand, "this is Detective Olivier', a good friend of mine."

"Glad to meet you, Mr. Stewart." Jack acknowledged him.

"Lieutenant Hays." Janet stepped forward. "What in the world are you doing here?"

"I called him, Janet," Roger spoke up.

"Whatever for? We don't have time to visit now, Roger. We need to get ready to leave."

"Mrs. Stewart, your husband tells me you're planning on going back to the mansion."

"That's right, we are." Janet crossed her arms over her chest.

"Do you think that's a good idea, given what you saw out there?"

"Please, Lieutenant, I don't wish to be reminded of that."

"I'm not trying to upset you. I'm trying to keep you from making a terrible mistake."

She raised a hand, glancing to the side. "I've already made up my mind."

"Why don't you come sit down and tell me why you want to return to a house that has already been the site of six murders."

Jack stood back, taking in everything being said and wondered if perhaps her grief had pushed her over the edge. Her next words all but confirmed his fear.

"I have to go back to that house." Her voice took on a lilting, singsong tone. "Margaret has come back home."

"I see," Donavan nodded, "and how do you know this?"

"Margaret told me."

"Margaret is dead. Remember? You identified her nightgown the night we found her body. I took that nightgown off her body and brought it for you to look at. Margaret is dead, Mrs. Stewart."

"No, she isn't. I saw her. I talked to her."

"How did you do this? Given the fact, we both know she is dead."

"Please stop saying that!" she cried.

"I am just saying what we both know to be the truth, Mrs. Stewart."

"I'm telling you she isn't dead! I talked to her. She told me I have to go back because she's there, waiting for me."

"Will you tell me in what way you talked to her? I mean, did she come here to the motel?" Donavan kept the frustration he felt out of his voice.

"No, she came to me in a dream."

"Did you hear what you just said, Mrs. Stewart?" The sadness in her voice tugged at him, but he knew he couldn't back off. "You said she came to you in a dream, and we know dreams aren't real, don't we?"

"This dream seemed different." She refused to be deterred from what she believed to be the truth. "This dream made me feel like she came to be with me. No, Margaret came here. I know she did."

Donavan reached out, taking her cold hand in his. "Mrs. Stewart, you are in extreme pain. I would venture to bet that right now, just getting out of bed in the morning is a chore. You have to work through this. I can't tell you when it will get easier, or even if it ever will. One thing I do know is that going back to that house is out of the question."

Janet withdrew her hand. "Thank you for your concern, Lieutenant Hays."

"Then it's settled." Donavan rose to his feet, motioning Jack to the door with a slight nod of his head. "Mr. Stewart, could I talk to you outside for a moment?"

"Of course." Roger pulled Janet to him for a moment before following both men outside.

Donavan breathed in the early-morning air trying to chase away the last of his headache. "Mr. Stewart, I don't want to alarm you, but I think your wife is on the verge of a breakdown. I think it would be a good idea to take her to the hospital. They'll want to keep her for a few days. If they begin treating her now, they can help her before it gets too serious."

"I'm scared to death for her. Last night, when we went to bed, she acted fine. Then she had a dream about Margaret calling her back to that house, and now she's actin' like a different person. How can someone change that fast?"

"It happens, Mr. Stewart," Jack said, placing a hand on his shoulder. "Believe me, it happens."

"I'm glad we didn't go to view Margaret's body. If Janet's this bad now, something like that could just push her over the edge with no way back."

"Would you like us to take the girls so you can run her up to the hospital? It wouldn't be a problem, I assure you. Why don't you go back inside and talk to your wife? If she's in agreement, as soon as you get them dressed, we'll take them to my house."

Donavan turned him in the direction of the door.

"I'll try, but I don't think she'll go for it."

"At least talk to her about it. If she says no, then we'll try another avenue."

As the door closed behind him, Jack expelled a breath. "My God, those poor people."

"I agree." Donavan pushed a hand against the back of his neck and rotated his head until he heard a loud pop. "I hope I'm wrong, but I'm afraid it's just going to get worse."

"How the hell could it get any worse? They've lost their daughter. Now, she could be havin' a nervous breakdown."

"I got an idea what kind of therapy the doctors might want to try. It's a terrible thing to have to go through, but it could shock her out of her denial."

"Make her view her daughter's remains? I thought they were plannin' on doin' that anyway."

"They were, except Perkins had a talk with them, and they agreed it wouldn't be a smart idea. Now, ugly as it would be, it could just be the ticket."

"Or it could be like Stewart said, push her all the way over the edge with no idea how to fight her way back."

"Lieutenant," Roger walked up to them, his voice sounding high-pitched and scared, "Janet said the girls aren't going anywhere, but back to that house with her."

"You can't be serious!" Donavan flipped his cigarette into the air. "I thought we had all that settled!"

"So did I, but she's still determined to go back. Lieutenant, I can't let my girls go back there, and I sure as hell don't want to!"

"No one is going back to that house, and that's final! The one thing you can do now is call an ambulance and have her transported to the hospital. You can use my phone, or I can make the call for you."

"Oh, Lord!" He wrapped both arms around his body, rocking back and forth. "I don't know what to do! The girls will be terrified if their mother isn't here to take care of them."

"Mr. Stewart, you don't have a choice at this time. Your wife is in danger of losing her mind. You have to make sure that doesn't happen."

"Donavan, why don't you go ahead and make the call?" Jack said, coming forward. "He's in no shape to make any decisions, and maybe havin' her looked after will relieve some of his stress."

"Good idea." He walked over to his jeep and, opening the door, slid inside.

"Our life is falling apart!" Roger sobbed. "I don't know how to stop it! Tell me how to stop it! Please!"

"You're gonna survive this, Stewart." Jack placed an arm around his shoulders, forcing himself not to back away. As Roger threw his arms around his neck, his sobs escalating.

"They'll be here in a few minutes," Donavan told Jack, walking back to where the two men stood. "Mr. Stewart, do you think you can pull yourself together long enough to get your daughters ready for us to take them back to my house?" Donavan rubbed a consoling hand over Roger's back.

"Janet said they can't go with you." His breath caught on a sob.

"That's all changed now. I've already called an ambulance. They'll be here in a few minutes.

"Come on, Stewart." Jack untwined Roger's arms from around his neck. "By the way, what's your first name?"

"Roger." He gulped the name on a shaky breath.

"Do you mind if I call you Roger?"

"No, I don't mind." He shook his head back and forth. "What's your first name?"

"My name's Jack, but you can call me anything you want. Everyone else does." He forced a slight laugh, trying to keep Roger's mind off the situation at hand.

"You seem like a nice guy, Jack." He rubbed the side of his hand beneath his nose. "I'm sorry for falling apart on you."

"Hey, don't worry 'bout it. I've been known to fall apart a few times in my life. Right now, we need to get you inside and wake your little ones. Mrs. Hays is plannin' a fun-filled day for them, so we need to get them up and ready. Do you think you can do that for me, Roger?"

"I'll do my best." He swiped at his nose once more, his movements jerky and unnatural as he tried to force himself to stand up straight.

Jack put his arm around Roger's waist. "Come on, pal, lean on me." He tightened his hold as he felt Roger relax against him. "I got you. You and me...we're gonna get through this. You believe me don't you?"

Donavan stood for a moment, watching Jack doing his best to hold the other man together. In silence, he cursed the woman responsible for losing him the best partner he ever had and the department a man they needed. Then he reminded himself she no longer wielded that power and felt his spirits lift. He looked up as an ambulance pulled up alongside of him.

"Hey, Simms," Donavan smiled, recognizing the man behind the wheel, "got you doing night-duty, huh?"

"Yeah, shit." Simms reached out his hand to Donavan. "You know how it is. You do what you gotta."

"Tell me about it. You know what time it is, and you see where I'm at."

"So, what's da story here? All we got is we're transportin' a white female on da verge of a mental breakdown."

"Yeah, a woman named Stewart. We found her daughter murdered on the Hindel Estate, and needless to say, she's not handling it well. Also, things have changed since I called in." Donavan gave him a sheepish hate-to-do-this-to-you look.

"Oh! Now we got a surprise comin'!" His dark eyes widened as he swung his head in the direction of his partner.

"Afraid so. You're going to be transporting the husband, too."

"You mean da're both slippin' over da edge? Man, dis is what Ah hate 'bout dis job!" He slammed a dark hand hard against the steering wheel. "I hate gettin' a psycho call, 'cause you never know which way dem mother-fuckers is gonna fly!"

"I don't like to admit it, but you're right." Donavan grinned, then became serious. "I want you to do me a favor if you can."

"You know all you gotta do's name it, Hays."

"I need you to cut the lights and move to the other exit. They have two more kids, which I'll be taking to my place as soon as you leave, and I don't want them to see all this."

"Hey man, no problem." Simms flicked a switch, stilling the bright, red and blue flashes of light whirling out over the parking lot. "Have des people been told dey're goin' to the hospital?"

"Not yet."

"So, what are we lookin' at here?" Simms' tone took on an air of impatience. "'Stead of one white female, we now got a male and a female, and both are goin' off their nut. And neither one knows dey're 'bout to take a ride! Zat 'bout sum it up?"

Donavan thought for a moment, then replied, "I'd say that pretty well covers it."

"You gettin' all dis shit, Rainey?" He smacked his partner against his leg. "You better be, 'cause 'member, I ain't in dis alone."

Rainy nodded his blond head in compliance, then turned away, his attention riveted on the motel door as someone pulled it open then pushed it closed. "I think we need to move up." He sat up straighter in his seat. "Someone started to come out of the room then went back inside.

"Yeah, that would be Jack," Donavan breathed.

"You got Olivier' with ya?" Simms grinned. "How's dat wild sombitch doin'?"

"He's coming along. He spent the night at my place." Donavan cut short the conversation, knowing they needed to get moving on what they had come for. "After we get the kids loaded up, I'm going to have him drive them around, giving us enough time to get the parents ready for transport. If you will, hit the siren two short blasts as you pull out, that can be his signal to swing back around for me."

"You got it, man." Simms pushed up on the gearshift, drove forward.

As they pulled away, Jack stepped out of the motel. "What the fuck were you doin' out here?"

"Simms is on duty tonight, and he's not looking forward

to dealing with the Stewarts. I tried to get him calmed down," Donavan hastened to explain.

"Well, Jesus Christ! He's a Paramedic! That's his job! 'Sides, you think he's got problems, wait 'til you get inside!" Jack told him as they made their way to the door. "You talk 'bout a cluster-fuck, this one takes it! I thought I was gonna have to tie her to the bed to keep her from killin' Stewart!"

Donavan reached out, halting him. "What do you mean?"

"I'm sayin' he has taken a flyin' leap right over the edge." He dove a hand downward, blew a whistling breath. "What amazes me is why he didn't do it a long time ago! That woman ain't stopped talkin' since you been out here! I mean, I know the woman's in pain, but goddamn!" He tried to drudge up some sympathy, but the sad face of Roger Stewart kept pushing it away. "On top of that, she says she *is* goin' back to that house, and every time Stewart gets his shit together long enough to try and talk her out of it, she hauls off and smacks him upside the head, tryin' to make *him* come to *his* senses! 'Bout all the poor bastard can do is try and dodge the blows!" Jack lit a cigarette, took two quick puffs, then flicked the fireball into the air to stuff the cigarette in his pocket. "In the meantime, I'm runnin' between them and two terrified kids!"

"Shit! Are the kids ready to go?" The dull ache in his head galloped back with all intentions of settling in.

"Hell yes, they're ready to go!" Jack gave him a wide-eyed glance. "No thanks to you!"

Donavan signaled Simms to come back. "Now, here's what we're going to do. You get both kids and put them in the jeep. Just drive around close until you hear Simms give two short blasts on the siren, then come back here and pick me up."

"And what the hell are you gonna be doin' all the time I'm drivin' 'round in circles with two squallin' kids?"

"I'm going to be helping Simms and his partner get the Stewarts ready for transport." The sour look on Jack's face had him rethinking his plan. "What? Would you rather I take the kids, and you stay here?"

"Hell no!" Jack's head snapped up at the idea. "That

woman could piss off the angels enough to kill her! You already know the length of my fuse!"

"Last time I heard it measured twelve inches, but we don't have time to argue it now 'cause here comes Simms!" Donavan took off running to open the door on the driver's side of his vehicle

The ambulance pulled forward then backed up, stopping a short distance from the Stewart's door. As both men bailed out, Jack ran outside, a child on each side of him, heading to the jeep.

"Now I want you girls to set down and get your seat belts fastened." He scooted into the seat beside them.

"We don't want to go with you!" Rebecca wailed. "We want to stay here with Mama and Daddy!"

"I know you do, sweetheart." Jack reached for the ignition key, his hand coming away empty. "What? Where the fu…" He cut off the word, jerked down the visor, searching for the needed key. "You girls stay right here! And…don't…get…out…of…the…car!" he told them. "I'll be right back!" He threw open the door and, as soon as his feet hit the concrete, took off running toward the motel.

"Mrs. Stewart, you need to calm down." Donavan tried to reason with her.

"I am not going to any hospital! I already told you that, but you refuse to listen to me!"

An idea flashed into Donavan's mind. "Mrs. Stewart," he held up both hands, trying to placate her, "if you won't think of yourself, then think of your husband. He's sick, and he needs your help." Donavan put every ounce of empathy he could call on into his voice. "At least ride along to comfort him!"

"He's not sick!" Janet's thin lips curled as she gazed at her husband. "He's just feeling sorry for himself, that's all! He's angry because he knows I'm going to leave him here and take the girls back with me to be with Margaret." Janet delivered a stinging slap across her husband's face. "Snap out of it, Roger!" she yelled at him. "So these men will get out of here and leave us alone!"

"Mrs. Stewart!" Donavan's hand shot out, grabbing her

by the arm as she drew back to deliver another blow. "Either you stop abusing your husband, or I'm going to arrest you for assault!"

"Donavan!" Jack called out. "Where the hell are your car keys?"

Without taking his eyes from Janet, he reached his other hand inside his pants pocket to pull out the missing keys. "Catch!" he yelled, tossing the keys over his head.

Jack snagged them in mid-air, turned to leave and tripped over Rebecca as she came running into the room, dragging a sobbing Lisa behind her. "I thought I told you to stay in the car!" Jack righted himself and swept a kid up under each arm on his way back out the door.

"Well, don't just stand there!" Donavan yelled at Simms. "You and Rainy get Stewart out to the ambulance, then come back!" He jabbed a finger above Janet's head.

"Now you see why I said what I did 'bout des kinds of calls," Simms murmured, lifting Roger to his feet as Rainy supported him on his other side. "Come on, Mr. Stewart; let's get you outta hahm's way."

"Mrs. Stewart, you're going to sit down over here and behave yourself." Donavan pushed her none too gently down on the bed.

"You can't force me to go with you. I have my rights!"

"Yes, you do!" Donavan inhaled a deep breath, wishing he could take a chance on sitting on the bed beside her but not willing to risk it in case she tried to bolt for the door. "And your rights, as of this moment, are to shut up and stay seated!"

"I'm going to report you to your superiors for treating me this way!"

"You do that!" Hays tried to slow down his breathing. "For what it's worth, I don't treat people this way, but, lady, you have exhausted the last ounce of my patience! Why can't you get it through your head the last place you need to be is back in that house?"

"My baby is in that house, Lieutenant Hays. Why can't you get *that* through *your* head?"

"Because your daughter is not there, Mrs. Stewart." Lord Jesus!" his mind pleaded. Please! Lend me some strength here! "Your daughter is lying, right now as we speak, in the morgue. I'm sorry, but that's just how it is, and if you want to hang onto your sanity, you better face that fact!"

"I don't believe you," she whispered, not bothering with the tears streaming down her face.

"Hays." Simms walked into the room. "We're ready."

"Come on, Mrs. Stewart." Donavan placed a gentle hand beneath her arm to lift her to her feet as Simms walked towards them. "Let's go get some of this pain put to sleep for a while."

CHAPTER SIXTEEN

Twilight lingered above deep waters, shrouding the entrance to a world known only to a select few. Eerie shadows moved over rocky walls, merging with shimmers of flickering light from blazing torches.

Jonathan walked through this shadowed world, a world of his own making. The one place he knew he could be alone without outside interference.

The discomfort in his chest, where Chandra had removed the bullet, became unbearable, making him long for the presence of another human being. He thought of sending for Chandra but knew the danger remained too great. His eyes lingered on the bottle of painkillers she had left, then looked away, afraid to chance the effects they might have on him.

In his need, he called out to the one woman able to lift the anger and desolation from his soul. "Angelia, I need you!" he cried into the stillness. Echoes of his own voice returned to taunt him.

"You cannot hear me. Even after all these years, you still cannot come to me when I need you."

Walking over to a long couch set back against the wall, he lowered himself down onto the soft cushions. Stretching his long legs out straight, he tried to relax his mind the way Chandra had taught him. But it didn't work. The pain refused to subside. He could see the face of the woman he needed in his life right at that moment. So clear in his mind, he knuckled his eyes, trying to blot out her image.

"You still have the power to haunt me! No matter how

hard I've tried to get you out of my heart, you're still there," Jonathan moaned the words, and hearing the depth of feeling in his voice, gripped both sides of his head in desperation of his shame. "I cannot allow you to control me any longer!" He leaped to his feet, uncaring of the pain his sudden movement brought to his wounds. In self-defilement, he slapped his hand hard against his injured chest, relishing the searing agony in a vain attempt to silence, for a brief moment, the throbbing pain cutting through his heart.

Blood seeped between his fingers, bringing a long, deep-throated groan into the silence. Jonathan allowed the pain to surround him, floating in its red haze until he felt the floor of the cave begin to move beneath his feet. Pulling air deep into his lungs against the rolling fog threatening to envelop him, he walked across the cave. Picking up one of the folded towels stacked on a nearby table, he pressed it into place against his wound.

"Chandra! You will come to me! Now!" he called out, uncaring of the danger to her and to him if she answered his call. He bent forward from the sheer force of his pain and, keeping his eyes focused straight ahead, made his way, step by slow step, to the couch. With the stained towel pressed tight against his chest, he eased his body down into a sitting position. Bracing against the pain, he fought to remain conscious. The bottle of painkillers and glass of water Chandra had left for him on the small coffee table in front of the couch swam into his line of vision. Gritting his teeth, he leaned forward to pick up the bottle. Unscrewing the cap, he shook out two of the pills popping them into his mouth to wash them down with a few gulps of water. At last, he leaned back against the thick cushions of the couch to wait for the pills to numb his pain.

As he waited, he focused on taking deep breaths to relax his mind and push the pain deep inside to a place of tolerable endurance.

Chandra would be here soon, he told himself, for she knew better than to refuse him when he called her. The thought shot through his mind bringing him upright, the sudden movement taking the dull edge off his pain. With real effort, he forced himself to relax, to send the pain back to a safe distance. Chandra did not know he needed her. She could not hear him when he called to her except when he called to her in his mind. In his weakened state, he could not afford a confrontation.

The medicine made him feel relaxed and a little sleepy. He leaned back against the cushions relieving his mind of all the worries plaguing him, and closing his eyes allowed a memory to slip, unhindered, from the recesses of his mind.

Dressed in a long white dress made from the finest silk money could buy and holding out her slender arms, Angelia walked towards him. The stark whiteness of the dress complimented her light brown skin and the inky-black hair tumbling down her back. A smile covered her beautiful, heart-shaped face as her emerald-green eyes locked with his in anticipation of being lifted into his arms.

Jonathan did not disappoint her. With a playful growl, he scooped her against his chest, holding her against him for a moment. All but weightless in his strong embrace, he smiled as the fragrance of her dark hair blew against his face. Jonathan laughed aloud, so happy to be with her again. He knelt, placing her on a blanket he had spread on the ground for them to sit on.

She glanced at a basket setting on the ground nearby. "I see we are to dine." She rose up and, lifting the white linen, peeked inside. A pleased squeal escaped her young throat, and she clapped her hands with glee. "You know what wine does to me." She plucked the sleeve of his white shirt.

"Yes, I do." Jonathan turned, hanging his black suit-coat on a long tree branch, before stretching his large body out straight beside her. Leaning forward, he cupped her small face between his hands. "However, that is not the reason I brought it." His face betrayed none of the anxious feelings running unstilted through his mind.

"Jonathan, you look so serious." The bright smile left her face as her brows lifted in question.

"Angelia, I have something to ask you, and I don't quite know how to go about it."

In a demure manner, her thick, dark lashes lowered,

hiding her green gaze from his. "You have never been shy with me before," she told him, her heart beginning to flutter inside her chest.

"I have never been afraid of losing you before," he whispered, drinking in the sweetness of her full mouth, his warm tongue savoring its heady nectar. Jonathan lifted his mouth, waiting for his breathing to return to normal.

"Jonathan," she reached up, running the back of her hand down the side of his face, "you could never lose me. Don't you know that?"

"Yes, Angelia, I could. Your father is a very influential man in New Orleans. His world is made up of the two strongest components known to man. Power and wealth!"

"My father loves me, Jonathan." She wiggled out of his arms. "He would do anything to make me happy."

"Your father does love you. I will not argue that. But even he cannot give me your hand in marriage."

"Marriage?" The word rushed forward from her throat. Angelia looked around, even though she knew they were quite alone. "Jonathan, what are you saying? The law forbids us to even think about such a thing as marriage."

Jonathan tried to leash the anger he felt pushing its way upward into his skull. "I will not have you any other way!" He gave in to the battle raging inside of him. "The law will allow me to buy you. However, it will never afford you the respect you deserve in being my wife!"

"My father would never sell me!" She drew back away from him, fearful of his sudden outburst of anger. "And my mother would never let me go away from her. I am too important to my people. Without me, they would have no one to heal them."

"Don't bring voodoo into this, Angelia," he warned her, his voice taking on a tone of complete command. "Your mother *has* failed you in not teaching you about the darkness of this world."

"My mother has taught me the wisdom of caring for those who need me. I am all they have. The spirits would never lead me wrong." She got to her feet, backing away from him.

"Your mother *has* failed you, Angelia!" He walked towards her, the fear in her eyes making the rage in him even more volatile. "She taught you about the white part of your beliefs. She cannot do that! If you are going to be a Voodoo Priestess, then you need to learn it all! The white and the dark! And believe me, there is a dark side!"

"Why are you behaving like this? My mother would never dabble in evil. She is a good and caring woman. She loves me!"

"So do I, Angelia," he breathed. "So do I!" He stopped a mere arm's length away from her. "I will never lie to you. I will show you both sides of what you are being reared for."

"I do not wish to remain here any longer," she told him. "You will return me to my mother."

Jonathan could not stand to see the fear stealing into her damp eyes. "All right, Angelia, I will take you home, but we are not finished with this conversation. The time will come when you will have to make a decision.

The time came in the afternoon of the fourth day after Jonathan had returned Angelia to her mother's small but impressive house in the French Quarter. The loud clacking of the doorknocker brought him to his feet, trying to think who could be calling since he had not received a calling card announcing a visit. Going to the door himself, Jonathan spied Angelia's father standing, hat in hand, on his front stoop.

"Monsieur Devereaux," Jonathan stepped back, surprise showing upon his face then, remembering his manners, he replied, "won't you come in?"

He handed the servant, who came forward, his hat and cane. "Monsieur Hindel, please forgive my coming to your home unannounced, but I feel this matter cannot wait until tomorrow."

It was apparent the man standing before him was a man of prestige. He was dressed in a long, black coat and pants tailored to fit his tall, robust build. The white silk shirt was plain with none of the frilled ruffles so popular among men living in New Orleans, and Jonathan found himself admiring the man's obvious taste in wardrobe.

"No, it is all right. Let's go into my study. We'll be more

comfortable there, I believe."

As Devereaux seated himself in a chair beside the hearth, he tried to quiet his racing pulse as best he could under the circumstances. He accepted the glass of port Jonathan handed to him.

Jonathan set the decanter of wine down on the small table beside his chair. As he settled back, he tried to think why the man could be here. He did not have to wait long.

"I am sure you are wondering why I have come and why I have chosen to come unannounced. I will come right to the point. I am here because of my daughter, Angelia."

"I see." Jonathan's heart raced at the mere mention of her name. Had Angelia told him of their secret meetings? He could not fathom her being so reckless, but then, her youth could make her very impetuous. He picked up his glass, taking a sip of the aged wine in hopes of calming some of the tension trickling in around him. "What is it about your daughter that involves me, Monsieur?" Jonathan did not mention her name.

Thick white brows lifted. "Are you saying you do not know my daughter, Monsieur?"

"Perhaps you will be kind enough to share with me the reason why you are here." The sharp tone of Jonathan's voice brought the man up straighter in his chair.

"How dare you speak to me in such a disrespectful tone of voice?" Devereaux's own voice dropped to a low tone making his anger very clear.

"I believe you to be a guest in my home, Monsieur Devereaux; therefore, you will conduct yourself as such." Jonathan set his wineglass down on the small table, rested his arms on the armrests of the chair, and turned his full attention on the man seated across from him.

Devereaux leaped to his feet, no longer able to leash the anger for this man looking at him with such arrogance. "I came here to talk to you about my daughter and your plans concerning her, but now, I will have none of your offers!" His dark green eyes, so like Angelia's, Jonathan felt his heart constrict, flashed with fury. "You have offended me, and you have offended the good name of Devereaux!"

"I think you would be wise to sit back down and discuss with me what you had planned to accept concerning your daughter, Monsieur." Jonathan smiled as he watched the man's eyes dart towards the door, then back to the cold steel confronting him.

"Am I to understand you are threatening me, Monsieur Hindel?" His voice remained strong and firm with none of the fear the man watching him had hoped for.

Jonathan poured them both more wine, then returned the decanter to the table. "What *is* the asking price for your daughter, Monsieur?" Jonathan picked up his full glass of wine, watching the other man over the rim of his glass. The thought of trading money for the girl he loved, the girl who would someday bear his sons, like he had when purchasing his servants and field hands, or the blooded horses in his stables, snapped the last thread of Jonathan's patience. "Keep in mind, at least I am being led to assume, we are discussing a young girl of color."

Devereaux walked to the door of the study. "That is something you need not concern yourself with, Monsieur Hindel." He turned, his dark gaze refusing to look away as Jonathan watched him. "For even if you offered me every cent you have and everything you own, it still would not be enough."

Jonathan remained seated as he heard the door open then close with a quiet click, secure in the belief the man would return with an offer befitting both their needs.

Days turned into weeks and weeks into months, but no word came from the house of Devereaux.

Jonathan missed her terribly, but he refused to be the one to make the first move. He forced himself to stay away from their meeting place in the flowered woodland beside the small lake. As a quadroon, Angelia would never be able to marry out of her color. To Jonathan, her one-fourth percentage of black blood made little difference. But Jonathan found himself bound to the laws of the land in as strict a bond as every other white man. When he realized how much Angelia meant to him, he had toyed with the idea of going abroad, knowing their alliance would be accepted there. Except he knew, leaving the south could never be an option for him. His home, roots, and a dark, dark secret kept him bound to the soil of his ancestors.

The day came when he knew he would have to make a stand if he ever hoped to have Angelia for his own. Swallowing his pride, he went to the home of Monsieur Devereaux, with all intentions of apologizing and mending their differences. He learned neither his expressions of regret nor his vast wealth could repair the damage already done.

Jonathan's anger, at being turned away from the Devereaux door, took on a life of its own. As each day followed the next, his fury increased until he could no longer contain the rage pounding within his mind. His pride cried out for revenge. Revenge, not just against the man who spurned him, but the girl whose beauty and unavailability combined to render him half a man.

A full moon cast its glow on the vast green lawns surrounding the Devereaux estate. Its silver beam aided him in making his way up the wide steps and into the house, as yet, undetected. No light shone in the large house, telling him everyone had already tuned in for the night. The winding staircase stretched before him. In silence, he moved up the stairs, his sharp sense of smell alerting him to the one he sought. He would not harm anyone except the one who had scorned him. The bedroom door stood open. Moonlight shining through the high windows, and his own keen sight, aided him in the darkness. He could smell him much stronger now. He moved closer to the bed, standing for a moment staring down at him.

As if he sensed another presence there in the room with him, the man woke, his eyes trying to see in the inky darkness. The figure moved, casting a shadow across the bed. Too late, the man drew in a breath to scream.

Jonathan took his revenge, feasting on the blood and body of Angelia's father and enjoying the look of frozen horror staring back at him.

Jonathan waited out the days with complete calm. He knew Angelia would be his. He saw no need for haste. This time when he went to ask for her, there would be no one there to tell him no, or, to turn him away.

Almost a month had passed when Jonathan decided the time had come for him to fetch his bride. Of course, after she belonged to him, they would move to his large old home near the bayous. Far enough away to insure their anonymity yet close to his family. There, he would marry his cherished one, and no one would ever be the wiser.

Dressed in his finest, Jonathan set out for the Devereaux Estate in a carriage polished to a bright sheen and pulled by two matching white horses. It never hurt to make the best impression when the situation called for it. The carriage turned onto the wide lane leading up to the mansion, passing the well-manicured trees and flowers abundant over the sweeping lawns.

The death of "old man Devereaux" and the way he died remained *the* topic on everyone's lips. Jonathan's card of condolence had been one of the first to reach the grieving family.

The carriage pulled up to the front entrance. Jonathan waited until the door opened and the ladder of steps dropped into place before he moved forward to step from the carriage.

Standing on the well-scrubbed stone driveway, Jonathan looked up to see someone standing at the window. Before he could catch a glimpse of the observer, the heavy drapery had been dropped back into place. Jonathan walked up the steps and, without any reserve, banged the heavy door knocker.

A comely servant-girl, who smiled a wanton invitation when she saw Jonathan, answered his knock.

Jonathan made a mental note to remember the enticing young girl for those nights when his appetite raged out of control, and his blood lust refused to be denied.

The girl led Jonathan into a large parlor, bidding him to make himself comfortable while she summoned her mistress. He smiled his most beguiling smile, chuckling when she fluttered her dark lashes flushing with pleasure at his obvious interest in her girlish charms.

On a small portable bar, Jonathan took it upon himself to remove the stopper from a crystal decanter. He poured a glass of brandy, moved it in a practiced motion beneath his nose, allowed the alluring aroma to bathe his senses. He lifted the glass to his lips, sipped, then smiled as he raised the glass again in a salute to the man staring out at him from a large oil painting hanging on a wall across from him.

"Monsieur Hindel."

He turned to see a tall, slender woman dressed in silver satin with black lace at the throat standing just inside the door, and he bowed slightly in her direction.

"My girl told me you were here." She walked the rest of the way into the room.

Her demeanor was that of a woman used to being in control. Jonathan felt a subtle twinge of unease as her dark blue eyes slid over him.

"Do I need to ask why you are here? Or do I rely on the words of my late husband?"

Direct and to the point, Jonathan admired that. Such a rarity in a woman. "I guess that would depend on what you have been told about me, Madame Devereaux."

"Coyness in a man is not a trait I find admirable." She lifted the decanter of brandy. "Now, Monsieur Hindel, I feel we can stop wasting each other's time and get down to the top price you are willing to pay for my late husband's bastard whelp." She brought the glass of brandy to her lips.

Jonathan threw back his dark head, allowed his laughter to spill forth. "Spoken like a true lady. A lady with the deed tucked away in a safe place amongst her valuables."

"Your price, Monsieur Hindel." She finished her brandy, set the glass down on the table. "And you are wrong. I have the ownership papers on Angelia right here." She patted a well-manicured hand against the pocket of her dress.

"I would have thought Monsieur Devereaux would have tried to find a way to free his daughter, given the deep feelings he held for her." Jonathan watched her, trying to determine how far he could go in bringing the hatred she felt for the girl he wanted to the surface.

"You can save your breath, Monsieur. My personal feelings do not enter in here. Also, I feel I must warn you, your offer is but one of many I have received for her."

A jolt of pure rage shot through his body. The dark glare he turned on her brought a smile to her beautiful face, changing her demeanor from a quiet, dignified lady to a free-spirited woman with a strong mind of her own.

"No other man will ever put his hands on Angelia," Jonathan spoke his words in a calm and quiet tone, but she could see the raw anger simmering just below the surface.

Forcing herself to remain calm, she sought to end their transaction as soon as possible. "I am still waiting to hear your offer, Monsieur Hindel."

"I have already signed a draft for the transference of $10,000 dollars into your account." The tone of his voice dared her to refuse.

"I have already filled out and signed the papers, giving you complete ownership of Angelia." She withdrew the paper from her pocket to hand it over. As their hands touched, she felt an icy chill creep over her body, making her jerk her hand away from him.

Jonathan smiled, taking great satisfaction in her unease.

Madame Devereaux turned, pouring them both a glass of brandy. Jonathan accepted the glass from her hand. He smiled, then held his glass high in a toast to their finished transaction. His lips brushed the rim before he set the glass down on the small table. Without a word, he walked from the room, leaving her to stare after his retreating back with a faint, nagging fear for the girl she had loathed since the day of her unfortunate birth, but now, could almost feel pity for.

That night, Jonathan left his home to go to the small house in the French Quarter. Anxious to have Angelia safe behind his sturdy walls, away from the admiring glances of other men. She belonged to him, now and always.

The man, who answered his knock at the little, off-white house with the surrounding terrace, had to be the biggest man Jonathan had ever seen. Well-over six-foot-six, and not an ounce of fat anywhere on his black, rock-solid body.

"Yes, Monsieur?" the man said, his body blocking the

entire entrance.

"Monsieur Hindel, here to see Mademoiselle Angelia," Jonathan said.

"Is Mademoiselle expecting you, Monsieur?" His deep voice held both respect and authority.

"No, she isn't. However, I am sure if you tell her I am here, she will reward you with a nice "thank you." He could feel his anger at being kept waiting, rising to the surface.

"Please come in, Monsieur. I will tell Mademoiselle you are here." He stepped back out of the way as the man brushed past him. "Please be seated." He indicated three chairs placed against the wall.

Jonathan declined, moving instead around the small but tastefully furnished house. He looked up as she came down the staircase, dressed in a gown of pale green satin. He could not take his eyes from her. The moment her gaze caught his, all thought of revenge left his mind and heart. If possible, Angelia looked more beautiful than he remembered. When she came close, he could see smudges of dark shadows beneath her green eyes and knew a moment of regret, knowing he bore the blame for their being there.

"Jonathan, what are you doing here?" Her sweet voice sounded as soft and melodic as he remembered.

He reached out, taking her cold hands in his, smiled when she did not pull away. "I have come to take you home, Angelia," he whispered, his senses drinking in the smell of her. "I have come to claim you as my bride."

Her beautiful eyes grew wide with alarm at his ill-chosen words. "Jonathan, what are you saying? Why do you insist on causing us both such heartache?"

"Angelia, I but say what is true. You belong to me now. I have the paper proving my words." He drew her soft body against him for a brief moment, then drew back, not trusting himself to be so close to her.

A small scream fought its way upward from her throat, and she jerked a hand up to stifle its escape. "You bought me?" Tears swam in her sad eyes, and she let them fall. "How? I mean…who…would do such a terrible…evil thing to me?" She tried to make sense of the horror happening to her world. Then she knew, and her legs refused to support her any longer.

Jonathan caught her as she swayed, scooping her up in his arms and carrying her to a sofa, he could see through the open door of the parlor.

"Mon, Petite'!" a woman shrieked, running forward and falling to her knees, amid the rustle of silk. "What has happened to her?" She drew one small hand to her lips, kissing its softness.

"I think she has but fainted." Jonathan looked at the woman kneeling beside Angelia. Now he understood where Angelia got her striking beauty. The woman who knelt on the floor looked very beautiful with her black, cascading curls caught up in a wide, loose hairnet. Her brown skin, a mere shade darker than Angelia's, remained smooth, showing no signs of aging. Her light, green eyes fell on him now, and in their depths, he saw fear. Fear for her daughter and herself.

"Why are you here, Monsieur?" Her voice trembled as she waited to hear his answer.

He withdrew the ownership paper from his coat pocket. With a deliberate calmness, he placed it in her hand.

She unfolded the paper, letting her eyes skim over the writing. A small scream erupted from her throat as the words leapt off the document.

Jonathan caught the paper as it slipped from her fingers, placed it back in his coat pocket.

"I did not realize she could hate my Angelia so."

Jonathan rose to his feet, stood looking at the beautiful girl lying on the sofa. He watched as her thick lashes fluttered open, then, upon seeing him, closed on a single tear escaping down her cheek. Jonathan skimmed a hand down her face waiting for her to acknowledge him. When her eyes remained shuttered against him, he withdrew his hand. "She will remain with you for now. When I return in the morning, I expect her to be ready to leave."

Angelia's mother stayed seated, her mind racing with ways to protect her child against the man who held both their lives in his hands. "Of course, Monsieur." She gave Angelia's hand a small squeeze.

Jonathan walked away, then stopped, and turning, faced the women watching him. "If upon my return to collect my property, I should find her gone, I will not hesitate to come after her or…stay my hand against the ones who have stolen her from me."

"You need not worry, Monsieur, Angelia and I have nowhere else to go. This is our home." Her voice dropped to a whisper. "This is *my* home." She corrected herself. "I will have her ready and waiting when you arrive."

For a long moment, Jonathan held the gaze of the woman who remained sitting on the floor beside Angelia. Then, with a slight nod, he walked from the room.

***

Moonlight shone out over the small garden enclosed within the black wrought iron fence. As he stood hidden within the shadows, he saw a horse and carriage pull up to the small house he had left earlier that evening. Within moments of the carriage's arrival, he glimpsed three figures emerge from the house. Two of the figures were quite small, the third large and hulking. Jonathan allowed them to leave, knowing it would be better to wait until they were on the road and away from the city.

The thrill of the chase coursed through his blood as he kept the carriage well within his sight. His feet, pounding on the grass skirting the road, never stumbled as the miles slipped away.

The carriage slowed then veered off the road turning into a grove of trees. Jonathan hastened his steps. He could see a coach a short way up ahead. Hiding himself back among the trees, he waited to see what would happen next. His harsh breath labored from his lungs as he watched.

One small figure emerged from the carriage, her feet making no sound as she ran to the waiting coach. Jonathan could feel his anger rising at Angelia's betrayal. He forced himself to stand motionless until the coach, with its lone occupant, moved ahead.

The small carriage did not move, thus giving the coach enough time to be well out of sight before it, too, pulled back onto the road.

The horse pawed the ground snorting its fear at what its acute senses warned lurked nearby in the darkness. A loud howling erupted into the stillness, and for a brief moment, the frightened horse reared its eyes bulging with terror.

Jonathan left the horse lying on the ground and, ignoring the driver as he took off running into the darkness, walked to open the carriage door.

The hulking presence waited until the door opened, then sprang, meeting the one who dared threaten his mistress. He had but a fleeting glimpse of victory before being flung through the air, the blood spewing from his throat already spraying the ground beneath him.

Angelia's mother felt herself being yanked from the carriage and thrown to the ground with killing force. When she could, she lifted her head and stared straight into the face of evil.

Jonathan grabbed her to him and, with one quick flick of his huge wrists, snapped her neck. As her body slumped to the ground, Jonathan could feel his body already beginning the change. The putrid smell surrounding him made it hard for him to breathe. As he turned to walk the short distance to where a small lake lay hidden beyond the trees, he felt his breath catch in his throat as he saw the one standing a short distance away, watching him. Of her own free will, Angelia chose to be returned, only to find him standing over her mother's lifeless body.

The memory washed over him with chilling clarity bringing with it the agony he fought to keep buried. With a cry wrenched from the very depths of his soul, Jonathan forced the memory back down into the darkness, the one place he allowed it to live. His wound throbbed with pain now, but as his hand reached once more for the bottle of pain medicine, he drew it back, unwilling to risk unleashing the even greater pain in his mind.

CHAPTER SEVENTEEN

"Come on, girls, it's time for dinner," Barbara called out, setting a platter of fried chicken down in the middle of the table.

"Isn't Donavan going to be here to eat?" Rebecca asked, looking around.

"Yes, he'll be here." She moved Lisa's small hand back away from the hot food.

"I'm hungry." Lisa rested her chin in her hands, her elbows propped up on the table.

"We all are, Lisa, but in this house, we don't start eating until everyone is seated." Barbara blew a strand of damp hair back from her face. "Rebecca, will you get a cube of butter from the refrigerator while I pour the ice tea?"

"All right," she replied, happy to be of help.

"Me too." Lisa hopped down from her chair to follow her sister.

"Well, okay," Barbara smiled as the little girl ran across the kitchen. "Rebecca, you take the butter out of the fridge, then Lisa, you can carry it to the table."

"Jenny, look. I'm gettin' dinner!"

"You're a good girl, Lisa," Jenny told her, then turned her attention to the window as she heard car doors slam outside. "Daddy's home!"

Lisa plopped the cube of butter down on the edge of the table to run after the other girls as they went to the door.

"Wow! What's this? Our own greeting committee!" Donovan laughed, pulling all three girls close in a bear hug.

"Mom!" Jenny called out, slipping her small hand in Jack's

to pull him the rest of the way into the house. "You better set another plate; Daddy brought Uncle Jack home, again." Her adoring blue eyes stayed focused on the handsome man grinning down at her.

"Hope you're hungry for fried chicken, Jack." She withdrew another plate from the cupboard.

"Only when it's yours, Barb." Jack came up beside her to brush a light kiss across her cheek. "Sorry 'bout droppin' in on you like this, again. Donavan insisted I come home with him." He shrugged his shoulders.

"You're always welcome here, Jack. You know that." Barbara returned his affection. "Besides, what's one more?" She laughed.

"Spoken like a true wife of the luckiest man on the sheriff's department." Donavan wrapped his arms around Barbara's trim waist to pull her in close.

Jack stood back watching their closeness and felt his heart pitch with envy, then jump as he overheard a conversation going on nearby.

"How come your mom lets your dad hug her like that?" Rebecca asked, wrinkling her nose with distaste.

Jenny stared at her in surprise. "Because she loves him, dingus. Don't your mom and dad hug each other?"

"Not anymore." Rebecca turned away, sadness covering her face. "They just yell at each other."

"I'm sorry, Rebecca." Jenny gave her arm a quick squeeze.

"All right, everybody get to the table," Barbara told them, grinning as Donavan scooped up Lisa to plop her down on a chair.

As everyone bowed their head, Donavan said grace, adding a special request for the health and safe return home of Rebecca and Lisa's parents.

"Why did you ask God to bring my mom and dad home, Donavan?" Rebecca spooned a helping of mashed potatoes onto Lisa's plate then her own.

Donavan looked at her. "Don't you want your parents to come home, sweetheart?" He forked a crispy breast of chicken onto his plate, then handed the platter to Rebecca.

Still deep in thought, she set the platter down on the table. "I don't know."

Barbara reached out, sliding pieces of the chicken on the plates of all three of the girls, then busied herself with dishing up the salad.

"Why don't you want your parents to come home, Rebecca?" Jack fashioned a neat dent in his potatoes with the back of his spoon, reached for the bowl of gravy.

"If they come home, that means we have to go home, too." Rebecca pushed peas around her plate with her fork.

"That's right, you would," Donavan said. "Isn't that what you want?"

"There's an ugly girl there, and she scares me," Lisa spoke up, her eyes wide with fear.

"Lisa, be quiet!" Rebecca hissed at her.

An icy chill skittered up Donavan's spine. He cleared his throat, trying to dispel it. "What ugly girl are you talking about, Lisa?" His tone stayed matter-of-fact.

"There's no girl. She's just making up a story." Rebecca shot Lisa a warning glance.

"I don't think so, Rebecca." Donavan held up his hand to quiet her as she made ready to argue with him. "Lisa, tell me about the ugly girl."

"She scares me when she cries," Lisa talked around her mouthful of chicken.

"Donavan, I think this can wait until after dinner. Don't you?" Barbara gave him a pointed look.

Grasping her meaning, Donavan picked up his fork. "You're right. Yeah...of course, it can wait. Besides, I got some big news!" He pasted a smile on his face, looked around the table. "Who wants to ask me what it is?"

The subject of the "ugly girl" was forgotten for the moment, as all three children raised their hands, calling out for Donovan to tell them his news.

"Jenny, remember some months ago I told you about Deputy Sandler's dog going to have puppies?" Donavan buttered a large biscuit.

"Yes." Jenny's ten-year-old face lit up with hope.

"They're old enough to be taken away from their mother now. So I put in our order for a male. We can go pick him up anytime."

"Oh!" she squealed, leaving her chair and running around the table to hug her father. "Do you mean right after dinner we can go get him?"

"If your mother says it's all right," he told her, laughing over at Barbara as she sat staring at him.

"Just what we need around here." She shook her head, trying to look displeased. "A dog! And a six-hundred-dollar dog at that!"

"Registered German Shepherds don't come cheap, hon," Donavan told her, slathering a spoonful of strawberry jelly over the biscuit. "Besides, the sire's the best K9 in the department."

"Oh…well! Now we gotta have him!" Barbara said, her eyes wide with the importance of the moment.

"Please, Mom!" Jenny cried, leaving her father and going where she could do her best we-can't-live-without-him act.

"You know, if we get him, you're going to have to help take care of him. That means potty training and the whole bit!"

"Can Lisa and I go too, Donovan?" Rebecca asked, her small face alive with excitement.

"Wouldn't have it any other way." Donavan drew back, staring at her as though her going along made all the difference to him. "When picking out a puppy, you need all the help you can get."

"We'll all go, but first, everyone needs to clean up their plates." Barbara chuckled as she saw Jack take another helping of everything on the table.

"What?" He looked over at her, a lopsided grin on his face. "You said you wanted everyone to clean up their plate. I just figured you meant the bowls and platter, too."

As soon as they were finished eating, the girls ran off to get ready to pick out the puppy. Donavan took advantage of their absence to talk to Jack.

"I hope you know you're staying the night."

"I am?" He sopped up the last of the gravy with his biscuit, popped the soggy concoction into his mouth, chewed, then washed it down with his last swallow of milk. "Why?"

"I'll tell you why!" Donavan said, as Jack got to his feet to walk over to the sink with his plate and silverware. "You're going to help me find out what Lisa meant."

Jack rinsed the plate putting it in the dishwasher, then washed off the knife and fork to drop them into the small silverware container. "You heard Rebecca. Lisa made up a story. What's so mysterious 'bout that?"

"Story my ass!" he whispered. "Did you catch the look on Lisa's face?"

"No. I still had food on my plate."

"Well, I did! And I can tell you right now she didn't make up any story. I think she saw something out there."

"Oh, Christ!" Jack finished drying his hands, hung the small dish towel back on the handle of the stove. "Here we go again!"

"Listen, hotshot." Donavan came across the room with his own plate and utensils. "Let me give you a little insight into six-year-olds. They don't make up stories. They listen to them."

"Maybe Lisa's the exception."

"Or maybe she did see something!"

"Now you're gonna tell me there's a ghost or some ugly girl scarin' the hell outta Rebecca and Lisa. For piss sake, Donavan, come on!"

"I'm not saying that goddamn it! I'm telling you I want you here to help me find out what's going on!" Donavan lowered his voice as he heard the kids coming down the stairs.

At the same time, Barbara closed the door on the dishwasher and punched the start button, Jack caved. "Oh, what the hell. You did feed me. I guess I owe you one."

"Damn right you do!" Donavan laughed, glad he didn't have to beg anymore. "I don't invite just anybody to eat Barb's cooking."

On the way over to pick out the pup, Donavan tried to

keep up a steady stream of conversation, all the while thinking of yet another curious incident involving the Hindel Mansion. When they arrived, everyone bailed out of the jeep. Donavan halted Jack as he started to walk off with the others.

"When we get back to the house, I'm going to ask Barb to take Jenny and Lisa outside with the pup. Then you and I are going to try and find out from Rebecca what's going on at the mansion. What do you think? Good plan?"

"All you're gonna find out is that Lisa's a good storyteller. But...," he threw up his hands, "if you're hell-bent on interrogatin' an eight-year-old, then I guess I'm in."

"Hey there, you two," a tall, skinny man with a mop of dark red hair walked down the driveway towards them, "see ya come to make an investment in a good dog."

"Sandler." Donavan nodded a greeting. "I brought the family. Hope you don't mind."

"I don't care who you brought, long as you brought your checkbook!" Sandler held out his hand to the detectives. "Freda's a little skittish around strangers, though. You might wanna wait 'til I get her in the other kennel before you bring everybody in to see the pups."

"That's fine," Donavan agreed. "Barb, girls, you need to wait until he takes care of the mother before we go to the kennels," he called out.

Barbara turned the girls back towards the jeep. "We'll wait with you."

Donavan chuckled as Barbara stood close to him, her arms surrounding the girls. "You can't blame a mother for being protective of her babies."

"We asked Mama and Daddy if we could have a dog, but they said no. All because Mr. Quigly don't allow dogs on the property," Rebecca spoke up, her voice becoming singsong as she mimicked Quigly. "I bet if we had had a dog, he woulda saved Margaret!"

Barbara aimed a worried look at her husband. "Donavan, perhaps I should have stayed home with the girls and let you just bring Jenny."

"It's okay, Barbara." Rebecca took her hand. "I want to be here. At least this way, Lisa and I can share your dog."

Jenny slid an arm around Rebecca's shoulders. "I'll make you a promise, Rebecca." Jenny flipped her long dark hair over her shoulder, leaned down close. "The first pile he makes off the paper, I'll let you clean it up."

"Get outta here, silly," Rebecca giggled, shrugging the arm from her shoulders.

As Sandler waved the "okay," Donavan herded them to the kennels. "This is it, everybody. Now we get to pick out our baby!" He rubbed his hands together in anticipation.

"I don't know who's the most excited," Barbara slipped her arm around Jack's waist as they continued up the path, "Donavan or Jenny."

"He won't be so excited when he starts totalin' up the food bill for one of these little giants."

Sandler opened the door to the kennel, then stood back out of the way.

"Now," Donavan said, squatting down a short way beyond the door, "here's how you find out which pup you should take. What you do is you let the pup choose you. Whichever one comes over to you, he's the one." He slid all the way to the ground, his legs spread wide, laughing as everyone, except Barbara and Jack, followed his example.

As they watched, eight fat puppies waddled through the door and straight onto Donavan's lap.

"There you go, partner." Jack leaned on the side of the kennel. "Write the man out a check for forty-eight-hundred, and you're set!"

"Sold," Sandler smacked a fist into the palm of his hand, "to the one and only bidder!"

"Don't know why it didn't work." He scratched the wide bald spot on top of his head, gently pushed the pups off his lap. "I always knew that theory to be foolproof."

"Maybe if you weren't sitting right in front of the door?" Barbara ventured a guess trying to keep a straight face.

"That's it!" Donavan pushed the pups away to get to his

feet. "Everyone spread out, then sit down." He shooed them further away, plopped back down on the ground. "I know it'll work this time." He grinned over at Barbara as she stood watching him.

Jack fished a cigarette out of his shirt pocket. "This could take a while."

To Donavan's surprise, all the pups went in different directions to crawl onto a waiting lap. Everyone's except his. "Well...what the hell's going on? This isn't how it's supposed to happen!"

He placed a hand on the ground to push himself upright when he spied one puppy waddling towards him. He lowered his body back down and shooting Barbara and Jack an I-told-you-so look prepared to wait. He let the pup crawl all the way onto his lap before making his move. "I knew it would work! I told you it would work!" he shouted, drawing a gentle hand down the dog's sleek fur, then grabbed the pup off his lap, a strange look covering his face.

"Donavan, what happened?" Barbara moved forward.

"Little bugger just peed all over my pants!" Donavan said, setting the pup back down on the ground.

"I gotta admit, your theory proved to be right," Jack told him with all the seriousness he could muster.

"In a pig's ass!" Donavan growled, pulling a handkerchief from his back pocket and dabbing at a wet spot soaking into his crotch. "The theory never said anything about this."

"Sure it did, Donavan. You said, the dog's supposed to pick you. Right? Well...he did. He just took it a step further and made sure by markin' his territory."

Donavan thought for a moment, then laughed. Cramming the handkerchief back in his pocket, he picked up the pup. "I guess you're the one then." He nuzzled his nose in the thick fur. "Come on, girls, we got our puppy!"

"Donavan, don't you think you should be sure before I write out the check?" Barbara took the pup from Donavan's arms, lifted it into the air.

"What's to think about, Barb? The theory proved right.

The pup picked me; now let's go pay Sandler so we can take him home."

"There's just one problem, Donavan." She smiled over at him. "It's not a he. It's a she."

This time, Jack didn't even try to contain his laugher.

"Go over and select a male," Barbara told him, setting the pup back down on the ground and shooting Jack a warning glare.

The puppy ran over to Donavan, plopped her round bottom on the ground, and, looking up at him, whined her plea.

Donavan scooped her into his arms. "Pay the man, Barb. Come on, kids, we're going home."

After the girls were settled in the backseat, Donavan placed the puppy in Rebecca's arms. "You can hold her on the way home, sweetheart." He shook his head as Jenny started to protest. "Everyone will get their turn."

As soon as they walked into the house, Jack went straight to the refrigerator.

"Barb, why don't you take Jenny, Lisa and the pup out in the backyard for a while, so she can start getting used to the area?"

"Can't I go, too, Donavan?" Rebecca asked a slight niggling of fear in the pit of her stomach.

"Not right now, Rebecca. I want to talk to you about something."

Sure now she had guessed right, she drug her feet behind Donavan and Jack as they made their way into the living room.

Dropping into a chair, she crossed her arms over her small chest. "I told you, Lisa made up that story about the ugly girl."

Donavan glanced at her, surprised at her insight. "I know what you told me, Rebecca, but for some reason, I don't think you told me the whole truth."

"I don't like talking about that house. It's scary."

"What's scary about it, Rebecca?" Donavan asked, ignoring the look Jack shot his way.

"I always had the feeling someone watched us." Her voice lowered as she wrapped her arms around her shoulders; ran her hands up and down her arms. "At night, after we were in bed, the lights would go off and on all by themselves."

"Did you tell your parents about the lights going off and on?"

"Yes, Margaret and I both did, but they didn't believe us." Rebecca swiped at the tears running down her cheeks. "I don't like it there."

I know you don't, sweetheart, but you're safe here with Jack and me. Tell us about the girl. When did you first see her, and what did she look like?"

Jack took a long pull off his bottle of beer, trying to keep his anger, at Donavan's relentless questioning of a child, under wraps.

"We were out playing with our dolls by the big maple," Rebecca told him, her voice taking on a defensive tone.

"By "we," you mean all three of you?"

"Yes. Margaret, Lisa and me."

"Then what happened?" Donavan prompted her.

"Lisa started waving at someone. When Margaret asked who she kept waving at, she said, "the girl.""

"Did you see the girl, too?" Donavan asked.

"No. Now can I go outside?" She scooted forward.

"Not just yet, Rebecca." Donavan halted her.

"Oh, for Christ's sake, Donavan, let her go play," Jack spoke up on Rebecca's behalf.

"I said not yet, Jack."

Jack finished his beer, swung himself to his feet.

Donavan ignored him as he stomped past them on his way to the kitchen. As he heard the refrigerator door open, then close with a bang, he went back to questioning Rebecca. "Now, what you're saying is, Lisa could see the girl, but you and Margaret couldn't. Is that right?"

Rebecca nodded, staring at the floor.

"Did *you* see the girl at any time?" Donavan asked, keeping his voice low and gentle.

Jack plopped back down on the couch, kicked off his shoes to plop his feet up on the coffee table and brought the bottle of beer to his lips.

"Yes," she whispered.

The drink of beer Jack had been swallowing spewed out over the couch. Grabbing a handful of tissue from the box sitting on the end table, he wiped his mouth then blew his nose. "Wait a minute!" His feet hit the floor. "*You* saw the girl, too?" Rebecca nodded again, her eyes filling with tears.

"Take it easy, sweetheart. You're safe. No one's going to hurt you," Donavan hastened to assure her.

Jack set his bottle of beer down on the table, tossed the used tissue into the trash basket on his way over to Rebecca. Seating himself on the arm of the chair, Jack put a comforting arm around Rebecca's shoulders, his heart turning over in his chest as she leaned into him. "Like Donavan said, honey, you're safe with us. Now tell us about the little girl."

"She would come into our room at night after Mama and Daddy were in bed."

"Did she ever say anything to you?" Jack ran a comforting hand up and down her arm.

Rebecca shook her head back and forth. "No, but the room would get real cold, and she would cry."

"Why did Lisa call her ugly?" Donovan asked, afraid he already knew what she would say.

Rebecca shivered, leaned in closer to Jack. "Because she had blood all over her, too."

Jack's heart jumped into high gear as he sat up straight on the arm of the chair to stare down at her. "What do you mean, "too"? There were others?"

Rebecca cried harder now, making her words difficult to understand. "A whole family," she pulled the words from her throat. "All...bloody and their bodies...real swollen, like...like... they had drunk too much water."

Donavan and Jack looked at each other over the top of Rebecca's bowed head, trying to sort out what they were hearing.

"But the little girl never said anything. She just cried. Is that right, Rebecca?" Donovan caressed her name with feeling.

"She couldn't say anything." Rebecca looked up at them.

"Why do you say that, sweetheart?" Jack ran both hands

over her hair, cupped her small face.

"She couldn't talk because…" she gulped, tried again, "because she didn't have any throat! Something had torn it all away. That's why…she had…all that blood on…her." Rebecca sobbed the words, falling into Jack's waiting arms.

***

That night, after Barbara and the girls were in bed, Donavan sat up with Jack talking about what they had learned. "What do you think now, Jack?"

"I think you could be right 'bout thinkin' there's more goin' on out there than any of us know."

"You think the girl they saw is the Rawlins kid?" Jack blew a long breath from his lungs, stared over at Donavan.

"Don't you?"

"Tell you the truth; I don't know what the hell to think anymore."

"Then too, it could be any little girl who's been killed out there. I wouldn't be surprised if we learn this has been going on for years." Donavan rose to his feet to replenish their beer.

Jack took a long pull off the bottle he already held in his hand and waited for the alcohol to calm his frazzled nerves.

Chapter Eighteen

Barbara took advantage of the children playing outside with Brandy, the new pup named after Donavan's favorite liquor, to put her feet up and tune into her favorite daytime talk show, "Saint Anthony Parish Today." The show covered different topics of interest in and around the parish, and people could call in and speak with the show's current guest.

Barbara hit the info button on the remote to see about today's show. When it said the host would be talking with a psychic about the paranormal, she almost switched the channel. Then, as she read a little further, the topic caught her interest, and she changed her mind, deciding to give the show a chance.

"Today, we will be talking with Seelah Stanford, a well-known psychic, who resides right here in Saint Anthony Parish," the show's host, Ronald Jonston, told his audience.

The girl on the screen didn't look like a psychic, Barbara thought, taking a drink of her coffee. In fact, she looked quite harmless, with her wild disarray of dark brown curls framing her small, heart-shaped face. Dressed in a pair of stylish jeans, the hem falling just over the tops of her brown leather, lace-up shoes, a cream-colored top and dark brown suit jacket, Barbara decided she looked more like a young college student.

"At least she isn't wearing a turban with ten pounds of junk jewelry hanging around her neck," Barbara mimicked Donavan's deep voice, knowing those would be his exact words if he were watching the show with her.

As the show cut to a commercial, she hopped to her feet to refill her cup and take a quick peek out the window to see the girls still playing with Brandy.

Sitting back down, she heard Jonston say something that made her sit up straight in her chair and give him her complete attention.

"Seelah, as someone who lives in Saint Anthony Parish and is familiar with the goings on in our fair city, what is your take on all the rumors surrounding one of our oldest and most prestigious homes? I'm sure you know I'm talking about the Hindel Mansion."

"Yes, Ronald, I do know what house you're talking about. And to answer your question concerning the rumors, the one thing I can tell you for sure is, they aren't rumors."

Jonston looked at her, the smug smile on his face saying it all.

"Am I to assume, by the look on your face, you disagree with me?" Her soft voice flowed over him.

"Well, you tell me, Seelah." He allowed himself a loud laugh. "After all, you're the psychic. Right?"

Seelah reached out, picked up a mug of coffee from the small table, and, as though she had all the time she needed, instead of the mere ten minutes allotted as one of three guests on the show, sipped from her cup.

"Uh-oh." Ronald smiled into the camera. "Do I detect a bit of hostility here, folks?" He placed a hand on Seelah's shoulder, giving it a light squeeze. "Come on now, Seelah, let's be friends." He made a great show of cupping his hand alongside his cheek as he motioned the camera closer. "I want to keep her happy, in case she *is* a psychic!" he whispered in a loud voice, enjoying the applause of the audience.

Seelah set her cup down on the table, then turned to look into his eyes. "Tell me, Ronald. Have you ever been afraid of anything?"

Ronald swallowed as a warm flush crept upward to cover his face, not sure where the conversation had taken a wrong turn. "I'm sure I've been uncomfortable at some point in my life." He felt the tight rein on his anger slip as she refused to drop her gaze. "After all, I know *I* am human, unlike some of us who profess to be otherwise."

The audience remained silent, ignoring Ronald's little sting, making him fidget in his chair.

"Oh, I assure you, Ronald, I am quite human." Seelah emitted a warm laugh. "It's just that…as a psychic, I tend to look at the world in a different light than most people.

"And in that little mind of yours, I'm sure you see a lot the rest of us 'mortals'," he veed his fingers, wiggled them to give emphasis to his point, "can merely dream about. In any case, Seelah, we have enjoyed having you on the show." He rushed to be rid of her. "Maybe someday we'll call you to be a guest on the show, again." Ronald stared into the camera, a disdainful look on his face, making sure everyone knew he had no intentions of inviting her back.

"Now our next guest…" Ronald stopped as Seelah leaned in close.

"You never gave me a chance to finish, Ronald. As the host of Saint Anthony Parish Today, I'm sure you would never be," she veed her fingers in imitation of his earlier dramatics, "'rude' to a guest. Not good for ratings, Ronald," she whispered in a loud voice. Smiling as a ripple of laughter echoed through the audience.

She's a spunky little person! Barbara thought to herself. "Good one, Seelah!" She raised her cup in a salute.

"I'm…sorry," Jonston stammered, uncomfortable with finding *himself* dangling on the brunt end of the snide remark stick.

"We are all well-aware of that fact, Ronald. To be sure." Seelah gave his hand a quick squeeze. "Now, getting back to our conversation, I asked if you have ever been afraid of anything."

"And I told you I am sure I have had some unease at some point in my life!" The mask he had taken such pains to arrange disappeared, allowing his words to spew forth with naked bitterness.

"No, no, Ronald," her sweeter-than-sweet tone slid over him, "I'm not talking about unease. In fact, I'm talking about quite the contrary. I'm talking about out and out terror!" She held onto his hand, her dark brown gaze daring him to try and snatch it away.

Ronald could feel sweat running down his face and knew his makeup had to be running right along with it. "I have never been afraid of anything in my life! And that goes double for now. Because, Ms. Stanford, unlike you, I am a born-again Christian who has welcomed our Lord Jesus Christ into my heart!" His pompous voice rose with passion. "Therefore, I don't need to worry about the evils of this world because I am saved and protected!"

A complete hush fell over the audience as they waited to see what would happen next.

"Very good, Ronald. I applaud your faith." She clapped her hands, then became serious. "In all honesty, I wish it could be that simple, for all our sakes. For you see, I love our Lord, too. But, the dark forces in this world are much stronger than most of the people on this earth could ever begin to realize. Because of that strength, they cannot be ignored. With that said, though, I want to make you a challenge. Since, according to you, there is no such thing as a true psychic. And, according to you, since you have been saved and have nothing to fear from the dark side, I challenge you to spend a night alone on the Hindel Estate. What do you say, folks?" Seelah applauded, urging the audience to do the same. "Is Ronald Jonston a true martyr, or just a redheaded, freckle-face-bag-of-wind? He has to decide. Right?" She turned to her ashen-faced host and, amid thunderous applause, placed her mouth close to his ear. "So, what's it going to be, hotshot? Are you going to accept my challenge? Or back down, and let everyone in Saint Anthony Parish know the real you? A once-a-week-Christian who goes to church to keep in the good graces of the real Christians of this town."

For the first time in his life, the host of "Saint Anthony Parish Today" found himself speechless. Seelah turned to the cameras, a wide smile splitting the corners of her full mouth. "This is Seelah Stanford sitting in for Ronald Jonston of Saint Anthony Parish Today, and we'll be right back following this short commercial message."

***

"She did what?" Donavan roared after Barbara filled him in on what happened on the "Saint Anthony Parish Today" show.

"You heard me, Donovan; she challenged Ronald Jonston to spend the night alone in the Hindel Mansion."

"As if I don't have enough goddamn problems, now I got a madwoman challenging people to commit suicide!" Donavan punched a number into the phone, listened, then spoke into the receiver. "Jack, what are you doing right now?"

"Just got outta the shower and settlin' in to watch a good western. Why, what's up?"

"Get dressed! I'll be over to pick you up in a few minutes. You're not going to believe this!" He hung up the phone.

"Donavan, do you think that's fair? Jack can't be at your beck and call twenty-four seven. He has a business, not to mention a life. Remember, you get paid for working on this case. Jack, on the other hand, doesn't. Why don't you just get him back on the force?" Barbara said, hot anger showing in her dark eyes.

"For your information, Mrs. Protect Everyone, I'm already working on that angle as we speak. Don't say anything to Jack, though. It's not for sure, yet, if I can pull it off."

"Don't you think you're taking a lot for granted here? Jack has a business to run. Maybe he doesn't want back on the force."

"Would you do us both a favor, Barb? Bitch in one direction or the other." He gazed at her. "I know he wants back on the force because there's no better crime solvers in the world than me and Jack when we put our heads together about a case!" He dropped a kiss on her open mouth, walked out the door.

Jack stood waiting at the curb when Donavan rolled up. "What's goin' on in Dodge this time, Tex?" He bowed his legs, sauntered over to the jeep.

"Are you sure you wouldn't rather saddle up your horse?" Donavan laughed as Jack pulled open the door, stepped inside.

"Nope." Jack crossed his eyes, affected a slow Texas drawl. "I already put Ole Balls-A-Draggin' in the barn for the night. He gets real testy when I wake him." Jack wiggled his brows.

"Do you want to know what's going on, or don't you?"

Donavan slipped him a sideways glance.

"Okie dokie," Jack slapped the side of his head, uncrossed his eyes. "What's goin' on you need my help?"

"I'm betting you didn't catch the Saint Anthony Parish Today show this afternoon."

"No, I didn't. Believe it or not, I had a client. Why, who was on?"

"A psychic."

Jack felt his stomach plunge. "Oh, Jesus Christ, don't tell me." He ran a cupped hand down his face, leaned his head back against the car seat. "Chandra! Right?"

"No. Although if it had been, I'm sure the outcome would have been the same. A nut is still a nut no matter what she calls herself."

"Are you going to tell me what happened or not?" Jack felt a trickle of relief now that he knew they could omit Chandra, but his nerves remained on overload.

"Some crazy bitch, claiming to be a psychic, challenged the host of the show to spend the night alone in the Hindel Mansion."

Jack thought about what Donavan said, then laughed, "Too bad we can't let him do it. He's a real prick. Right up there with Quigly."

"Speaking of Quigly, I guess he didn't mean it about pressing a lawsuit against us. He's been out for weeks now, and so far, nothing has come of it. But getting back to Jonston, he isn't worth putting our men in danger trying to save his dumb ass. And if he went out there, that's what would end up happening."

"Then you're going to help him save face by refusing to let him go. God! I hate that!" Jack turned in the seat, giving Donavan his full attention.

"I don't have any choice, Jack. You know the department would never go for something like that." He tapped his fingers on the steering wheel as they waited for a light. "Unless you can come up with a way they would." Donavan agreed with Jack in his dislike of the man. He had caught some of the shows and seen Jonston in action.

"How long do I have to think about it?"

Donavan checked his watch. "About ten minutes. That's how long it will take me to drive to the television station to talk to the producer."

***

Barbara still felt angry with Donavan over calling Jack every time he needed help. She almost wished now she hadn't told him about the psychic's challenge to Jonston to spend the night in the mansion. But of course, she knew something that important could not be kept secret.

Barbara could hear the kids playing upstairs with the new dog, and when she heard their loud squeals of laughter, she smiled, glad Rebecca and Lisa could find some happiness.

She poured herself some coffee taking it into the living room. As she sat back enjoying her moment of peace, she thought about what Donavan had told her of the "ugly girl," and her heart filled with fear as she tried to imagine what the children had gone through at seeing something that frightening.

"I wonder if it was the Rawlins girl they saw?" She mused aloud into the silence. "I wish there was a way to find out about hauntings." She sipped her coffee, thinking about her problem.

The face of the girl on the talk show flashed into her mind. "I bet she would know. She sounded like she already knew a good bit about the place."

Barbara set her coffee cup down on the end table, and leaning forward in her chair, reached into the magazine rack for the phone book. She ran her finger down the list of names beginning with the letter "S."

"Here it is!" She closed the book. "What am I thinking? I can't call this person out of the blue. She'll think I'm nuts!" She leaned her forehead into one hand, grinning as a thought crossed her mind. "According to Donavan, she's the nut, so what do I have to lose?" Before she talked herself out of it, Barbara pressed in each number with one long fingernail, then waited.

"Hello," said the same low voice she had heard on the talk show.

"Yes, hello," Barbara spoke up.

"Can I help you?"

For some strange reason, those few words seemed to give Barbara the added courage she needed. "Yes. At least, I hope you can."

***

Donavan and Jack stood waiting for the show's producer to see them in his office. "Not too shabby a place," Donavan said, looking around the plush studio with all the overhead lights and the comfortable-looking chairs placed close together on a large stage.

"Yeah, wonder how the asshole got such a cushy job?" Jack asked.

"He's the largest shareholder," replied a soft, feminine voice behind them.

Both men spun around to see a young woman leaning on the desk, smiling at them. "I'm Joan Woods, Public Relations Director for Saint Anthony Parish Today." She held out a slender hand.

Donavan took her hand in his to give it a light shake. "Glad to meet you, Ms. Woods. I'm Lieutenant Hays of the Saint Anthony Parish Sheriff's Department. Sorry about what you just heard."

"Please, call me Joan and don't let it bother you." She waved his apology away with a flick of her hand. "We call him a lot worse than that here at the studio."

Her dark blue eyes lingered on Jack. "And who might you be?" Joan smiled her most professional smile, showing beautiful white teeth.

"Oh yeah." Jack grabbed her hand, pumped it up and down, all the while wondering if the bright blue orbs smiling back at him could be that blue or if they were the product of expensive contact lenses. "I'm Jack Olivier'. I'm a Private Investigator," he told her, a lop-sided grin spreading across his face.

"Well, P.I. Olivier', I'm glad to meet you." With reluctance, she pulled her hand away. "What can I do for you guys?"

"We're here to talk to the producer about the challenge one of the guests threw out to your star attraction today," Donavan told her.

"Ah yes." Joan laughed, making her dark eyes sparkle. "I hope you're not going to talk him into letting Jonston off the hook."

"If I thought I could get away with letting him spend the night out there, believe me, I would, but I can't put my men in danger because of one goofball."

"Pity. He does deserve to have the crap scared out of him. He's insulted every guest we've had on the show, and I, for one, would love to see him get his. Just once."

"Donavan, why don't you put this off for a day or two while Joan and I try to come up with a way to let Jonston suffer a little?" Jack took Joan's hand in his, leaned in close. "What is the name of that wonderful smellin' perfume you're wearin'?" Jack sniffed, gazed into her eyes. "It's makin' my head spin."

"Here we go again," Donavan muttered under his breath, following a few steps behind the young couple as they walked to the door.

"You're quite a lover. You know that?" Donavan glanced over at Jack as they sped down the highway.

"Well...thanks, cutie." Jack scooted over a little closer to Donavan, placed a hand on his shoulder, his voice deepening with feigned feeling. "I been wonderin' when you'd...get around to...acknowledgin' that fact."

"You're also a crazy fucker! Move!" Donavan laughed over at him. "So when are you going to see her again?"

"Tomorrow night. We're havin' dinner at that new seafood place that just opened up. Goddamn, is she a looker, or what?"

"She sure as hell isn't an 'or what.'"

"Five-foot-four, blond hair, blue eyes and I'd guess, 110 luscious pounds! What a neat little package!" Jack rubbed his fingers against his thumbs. "I can't wait to pluck it all open! Jesus Christ! I think I'm in love again!"

"Ah, to be young and dumb just one more time," Donavan chuckled, shaking his head.

"Shit! You couldn't live without Barb and Jenny, and you know it!"

"Yeah, I do know it! But it doesn't hurt to fantasize every

now and then. Yep, I got the best, no doubt about that. Barb has never given me a reason to worry. I can go home after a hard day and know without a doubt, she'll relax all my worries away."

"You know, it's funny. Here you are envyin' me my freedom, and I find myself envyin' you the relationship you have with Barb and Jenny."

"That happens when you get older. But getting back to the luscious Joan, how are you fixed for cash?"

"Short."

"Before I drop you off, remind me to remedy that. And, while we're on the subject of earning a living, have you given any thought to trying to get back on the force?" Donavan glanced at him out of the corner of his eye, trying to gauge his reaction.

"I think about it sometimes. Why?"

"Let's just say if you could get back on, would you?"

"You been talkin' to somebody, haven't you?" Jack grabbed his arm.

"Yeah, and it looks pretty good. So would you take it or not?"

"Hell, yes, I'd take it! These last few months have been a real wake-up call as far as money's concerned!"

Donavan grinned. "Let me do a little more finessing, then you can go in and do your own talking. I think it'll work. You don't want to go back to your apartment, do you?"

"No, but Barb's gonna think you and me really do have a thing goin' if I don't stop spendin' the night."

"Barb loves you, you know that." He ignored the street leading to Jack's apartment. "You'll always be welcome at our house. Yep!" He smacked a hand against the wheel. "I'm one lucky man, Jack."

***

Now that she had the woman on the phone, Barbara searched her mind to think what she wanted to say. "Ms. Stanford, my name is Barbara Hays. I saw you on the Saint Anthony Parish Today show, and I wanted to tell you how much I enjoyed watching you."

"Barbara, and please call me Seelah. Why don't you just

cut to the chase about why you're calling?"

"All right." Barbara could feel herself getting a little anxious. The girl didn't believe in wasting words. "The reason I'm calling is to talk to you about the Hindel Mansion."

"Ah ha! And what is it about the mansion you want to talk about?"

"Seelah, can I trust you?" Barbara crossed her fingers.

"Yes, Barbara, you can. My reputation as a professional psychic is built on the trust of my clients. Now, what's this all about?"

Hearing the car doors slam in the driveway, Barbara ended the conversation. "Seelah, my husband just got home, so I'll have to call you back tomorrow. Is that all right?" her voice became a whispered plea.

"Of course. I'll be in all day tomorrow. And, Barbara, please think long and hard about anything you want to do concerning that house. It isn't something to play with." With that, she hung up the phone, leaving Barbara to wonder if she might be courting future regrets.

Chapter Nineteen

As soon as Donavan and Jack had left for the day and the girls had been fed and sent outside to play in the summer sunshine, Barbara reached for the phone. She had thought of nothing else all morning. As she listened for her call to be answered, she felt a twinge of guilt, recalling how dismissive she had been to Jack earlier as he tried to tell her about a new woman he had met and his chance to get back on the force.

Maybe I can make it up by inviting him and his new friend over to the house for dinner some night, she thought to herself, then stiffened as she heard the call pick up.

"Hello, Barbara."

Barbara felt her stomach jump. "How did you know it was me?"

The woman on the other line laughed then became serious. "I had a little help from my Caller I.D..."

"Oh, well…of course. I have Caller I.D., too," Barbara said in a rush.

"Listen, why don't you take a deep breath, let it out, then, when you're more relaxed, you can tell me what's on your mind."

Barbara did as the woman suggested and felt somewhat calmer. "I guess I did sound a little dramatic, but you being psychic and all, I just assumed you could see who it is calling."

"I said I have Caller I.D., I didn't say anything about having Telephone Imaging. Now, what did you want to say about the Hindel Mansion?"

"Can you see ghosts?" The words flew out of her mouth before she could silence them.

"Yes, as a matter of fact, I can. Earthbounds in particular," Seelah said as easy as though they discussed the weather.

"What's an earthbound?"

"An earthbound, Barbara, is a ghost that has not gone on to another realm." When Barbara remained silent, Seelah explained a little more of what she meant. "You hear people, people who have a strong religious nature, talk about when they die they want to go to heaven, but in reality, heaven, the other side, going through the light, etc., is all the same thing. They are all talking about another realm, just using different names to describe it. An earthbound is a soul that does not transcend, but remains on earth for whatever reason."

"Why are these, earth bounds, easy for you to see? As a psychic, can't you see all ghosts?"

"Yes, but there's a difference between an earthbound and a spirit."

"And that difference is?" Barbara stretched the phone cord enough to see out the window, satisfying herself the girls were all right.

"A spirit is a soul that has already passed on to the other side. They can come back to visit loved ones on earth, but because they have passed on to another realm, their souls take on a higher vibration than a soul who has not gone on. For example, you know when you turn a fan on low, how you can still see the blades turn?"

"Yes," Barbara said, not sure what a fan had to do with what they were talking about.

"All right, now, substitute a ghost for the slow blade. You can see it, not real plain, but you *can* see it. Now, picture that fan turned on a little higher. The blades become blurred, and you can't make out the shape of them anymore, can you?"

"No, you can't."

"That's one of the ways a psychic can differentiate between a ghost and a spirit. That is if that psychic is also a psychic medium, which I am."

"Wow, this is interesting. How long have you been able to do all this?"

"Almost all my life," Seelah said. "All right, I've answered your question about being able to see ghosts. Now my question to you, of course, is why do you ask?"

"Remember, you said everything I tell you is confidential. Right?"

"You have my word on it, Barbara."

"All right then. The reason I'm calling is to ask for your help in finding out what is going on in the Hindel Mansion."

"First, let me ask you this. Is your reason for wanting to know out of curiosity, or do you have another reason for needing to know?"

"My reason for asking for your help doesn't stem from morbid curiosity, I can assure you."

"Then what is it?"

"My husband is Lieutenant Donavan Hays of the Saint Anthony Parish Sheriff's Department. He's working on the case involving the little Stewart girl. She's the one they found murdered on the estate?"

"Oh yes, I remember hearing about that." Seelah gave Barbara her full attention now. "I understand it was a very gruesome murder."

"From the description my husband gave, yes." Barbara felt her stomach tighten as she recalled the look on Donavan's face when he came home that night. "But the story gets even worse."

Seelah remained quiet, letting Barbara tell her what she needed to say in her own way.

"The parents were unable to cope with their daughter's death. Right now, they are in the hospital on the brink of a nervous breakdown."

"Those poor, poor people," Seelah murmured. "Didn't the paper mention they had two more children?"

"Yes, two little girls, whom, by the way, are living with us right now. And they've been saying some pretty strange things about that house."

"Stop right there," Seelah told her. "I don't want to hear anything more. If I understand you right, Barbara, you're asking me to do a psychic reading on the Hindel Mansion. Am I correct?"

"What do you mean by a psychic reading?"

"A psychic reading, at least the way I work, is where you bring me something that has been in that house, and I will try to tune in to its energy. It's called psychometry."

"I have some of the children's clothing. Would that be enough?"

"Perhaps."

"I think I'd better find out first how much you charge to do a reading. I might not be able to afford what you ask. I'm not saying we're poor because we're not. But Donavan gives me just so much money to spend on foolishness, and it might not be enough," Barbara told her, then realized what she had said and how it must sound to the person on the other line. "Seelah, I don't think that came out quite the way I meant it to. Let me try again. Alright?"

"Don't worry about it, Barbara." Seelah laughed. I get a lot worse than that. As far as the reading fee is concerned, I think I will do this one just for the chance to meet a new friend. How does that sound?"

"Are you sure? I mean, isn't this what you do for a living?"

"Yes, and I also do oil paintings. At the moment, I'm happy to say they are selling quite well. And, if the truth be known, I've always had quite an interest in the mansion, myself."

"Would you like to go see it?" Barbara could feel herself getting excited now. "I have the key hanging up right here.

Seelah felt a cold shadow pass over her. For no apparent reason, she found it hard to catch her breath, almost as though someone or something had placed a smothering hand over her nose and mouth, cutting off her air.

"Seelah, are you there?"

"Yes, Barbara, I'm here." She breathed in a deep breath against the waves of darkness trying to overpower her.

"I thought for a moment we had been cut off. So, do you want to go see the mansion? It might be the one time you will be able to."

"No. But when you come for your reading, the key would be a good thing to bring. Barbara, I think we had better end our conversation for now. I don't mean to be rude, but I do have some things I need to get done today. Would this Friday morning, say around ten, be soon enough for you to come over?"

"Yes, Friday will be fine."

"My address is in the book, so you shouldn't have any problem finding me. My house is gray, trimmed in blue, and the last one on the block on the right. Until Friday then?"

"Yes, I'll see you then, Seelah. And thanks for talking with me.

"You're very welcome, Barbara. Goodbye."

Barbara hung up the phone then walked to the window to check on the girls. As she stood looking out onto the backyard, she couldn't help wondering what it would be like to know things others didn't. To be able to tune into an object and tell, just by holding it in your hands, who might have owned it or even see the face of the owner herself. Then she thought about what Seelah said about being able to see ghosts and spirits, and the idea of being psychic didn't sound so inviting.

She thought about telling Donovan what she planned to do, but something told her she better keep her Friday appointment to herself. Donavan could be funny about things he didn't understand. And, as for allowing her to go to the mansion, she knew that would be out of the question. Besides, Seelah said she didn't want to go see the house all of Saint Anthony Parish has talked about for years.

Rebecca threw the small ball across the yard, laughing and clapping her hands as Brandy waddled on her short legs after it.

Barbara smiled to herself as she stood watching the girls play. After all they had been through in the last few months, they deserved to have some fun.

The phone rang, snapping Barbara from her thoughts. "Hello."

"Hi, sweetheart," Donavan's deep voice came back to her. "Thought I'd call and make sure you don't need anything before I head home."

"Having a short day, are we?" She heard him laugh on the other end.

"There's not much going on, and besides, Jack is getting the ball rolling on getting back on the force. You know, get all the paperwork out of the way, so I thought I'd just come on home."

"Then I'll see you soon." She smiled and hung up the phone.

***

Friday dawned with a storm. Almost like an omen, Barbara thought as she showered and dressed in a comfortable pair of jeans and a black, cupped-sleeve top for her reading with Seelah. The jeans hugged her slender figure, and the lightweight jersey top, ending just at the waistline of her jeans, showing off her golden tan. After running a brush through her mop of blond curls, she dabbed on a pale pink lip-gloss and called it good. Walking into the bedroom, she stood looking around, then, leaning down, pulled her favorite black leather sandals from beneath the end of the bed. She slipped her feet into the shoes, pulled the straps up on her heels then, walked out of the room amid a cloud of her favorite cologne. She felt almost guilty asking Donavan to take the girls for a few hours on a workday, but he seemed to have no problem with it.

"Now, if I had someone to watch you for a few hours," she told the little dog, who at that moment, climbed over her feet as she lifted the key to the mansion off the hook to drop it into her over-size denim purse. "I hate to leave you locked inside. She chewed her lower lip, trying to decide what to do. "Seelah sounded like a nice person, so she shouldn't mind a small tagalong. She leaned down, scooping the pup into her arms. "You have to promise not to tell anything you hear, though."

As soon as she got behind the wheel of the car, Brandy crawled into her lap to lay still.

"Fine, you can stay there, but if you start moving around, I'll have to put you in the backseat. The dog licked her arm then settled back down across her lap.

When Barbara pulled into Seelah's driveway, she felt surprised to see such a small house. She thought someone making good money would live in a house at least the size of hers. Strolling up the walk, with Brandy in her arms and unmindful of the black and silver dog hairs sticking to her top, she admired the well-trimmed lawn with small pansies lining both sides of the walkway.

"Now, for both our sakes, I want you to behave. This girl's a stranger and may not like a visit from a puppy." She punched the doorbell, leaned in to sniff the red roses trailing over a small trellis situated above the door.

Seelah opened the door right away. "Hello, Barbara. And who do we have here?" She reached out her arms for Brandy.

The dog wiggled as Seelah took her, spreading warm, wet kisses across her face.

"Oh, Barbara, she's beautiful! I want one!" she laughed as the pup leaned back in her arms, batting at her dangling earrings, sharp yips spilling from her throat.

"If you're serious, I can tell you where we got her. She's registered and has a great pedigree. I debated about leaving her at home, but everyone's out of the house today, and I didn't have the heart to leave her locked inside."

"Don't worry about it. I love dogs. And German Shepherds are my favorite. Let's go inside."

The moment she stepped through the door, Barbara felt captivated. The house looked like a miniature fantasyland. An overstuffed couch and matching chairs were covered in dark olive and light green ivy-print with large pillows of off-white edged in old lace. Beautiful oil paintings of quaint little cottages surrounded with thick, wooden frames graced the walls, and everywhere she looked, she saw fairies. "I love your house!" Barbara gushed, spinning around as she tried to look everywhere at once.

"I take it you like fairies, too." Seelah could tell by the look on Barbara's face, she had guessed right. "Come here. I want to show you something." She set Brandy down on the floor.

"Seelah, I don't think we should let her run around. I mean your floors, I wouldn't want her to stain them."

"If she piddles, I'll wipe it up. Besides, how's she going to hurt aged and weatherworn pine floors? Now come over here."

Still leery, Barbara walked across the room to where Seelah

stood beside a well-polished cherry wood end table.

"Look down through the glass."

When Barbara leaned over, she could see fairies perched on little wooden chairs sitting around small, mounded stones complete with a log in the middle. In their hands were little sticks with a marshmallow stuck on each end.

"Watch." Seelah reached down and flicked a small switch. The rocks lit up with a red glow, giving the appearance of a small campfire.

"Seelah, that is so cute! Wherever did you find it?"

"My husband made it for me." She turned off the light. "He could be very talented. Come on, I'll pour us some coffee, and we'll get started on your reading."

Walking behind her into the kitchen, Barbara trailed her fingers over small, rectangular lamps. The lamps were black trimmed in gold, with little flues on top, a small base on the bottom, and glass windows on the sides. As she looked through the glass, she saw a small, white candle sitting inside.

Without turning, Seelah told her, "If you notice, there's a handle on each of the lamps. When my husband thought he would be late coming home, I would light the candle then hang the lamp outside the front door to welcome him back."

"What a sweet idea. Does your husband work out of town often?"

"No." Seelah bit her lower lip. "He died in an auto accident almost two years ago. Needless to say, I don't hang the lamps out as welcome anymore."

"I'm sorry, Seelah."

"Life goes on, Barbara. The weak are the ones who refuse to get back up. Now, have a seat, and I'll get us some coffee." Seelah waved her towards a round, wooden table complete with a three-tiered base and four legs, with each leg ending in the paw of a large lion and covered with an aqua blue tablecloth.

Barbara watched her as she moved around the kitchen. Dressed in a pair of jeans and an oversized, white T-shirt, her face scrubbed clean of any makeup, and her long, dark hair pulled high in a ponytail, Seelah looked even younger than she did on the talk show. Much too young to have experienced such a devastating loss, Barbara thought, as she picked up a pair of salt and pepper shakers. One in the shape of a black cauldron, the other in the shape of a long black spoon.

Turning the shakers around in her hand, she wondered what she would do if she ever lost Donavan. They met in their last year of college. She had already turned twenty-two and stayed focused studying Accounting, and Donavan had passed his thirty-third birthday and studied law. A year later, they married, and almost two years to the day of the wedding, they had Jenny. In all those years, she had never given a thought to using her degree to work outside the home. Choosing instead to have a lifetime career as a wife and mother. She never regretted her decision. "You have a very unique house, Seelah." Barbara pushed the shakers back to the middle of the table.

"It suits me." Seelah set two cups of coffee down on the table. "Now, did you remember to bring the key with you?"

"Yes, I have it right here." Barbara withdrew the key from her purse.

"Could you pass it to me, please?" Seelah settled herself in a chair at the end of the table, placed her bare feet flat on the floor, rubbed both hands together, then reached out for the key. With the key held in her hands, she closed her eyes and breathed in deeply through her nose.

Barbara watched her, trying not to feel uneasy.

"This house is much older than I thought. By this, I mean it has stood for well over two hundred years. There are a lot of earthbounds roaming this house. Many, many more than just the Rawlins family. This is a house of darkest evil."

"Can I ask you a question?" she asked, not sure if she should interrupt.

"Yes." Seelah's eyes remained closed, her fingers running over the key.

"Something attacked one of my husband's deputies. Can you tell what it might have been?"

Seelah remained silent for a moment. "For some reason, I'm being blocked from seeing what it could have been. All I can see is a large dark shape." She opened her eyes. "I've never had this happen before. It's almost like someone knows what I'm trying to see and is blocking me."

"Seelah," Barbara took hold of her hand, "do you think you could tell more if we went to the house?"

"When?"

"Now. I mean, it's daylight. Aren't bad things supposed to happen at night?" She laughed a nervous little laugh.

"Not always, Barbara. But yes, I guess we could go see what we could find out." Seelah pushed back her chair, picked up her brown leather sandals sitting in the corner. "Besides, like you said, this might be the one time we have the key."

"Come on then. We'll take my car." Barbara scooped Brandy into her arms as they headed for the door. "If anything comes after us, we'll just sic our trusty guard-dog on them."

Barbara put Brandy into the back seat then got behind the wheel. "God!" She pulled the seatbelt over her shoulder. "I need to get a life. I haven't been this excited in years." She turned the key, slid the gearshift into reverse, spared a glance behind her, and backed out of the driveway.

Seelah sat looking at her. She liked this woman with her warm smile and easy friendship. Still, she felt she had to warn her about the dangers of going to the Hindel Mansion. "Barbara, I want you to know something."

Barbara glanced over at her. "What?"

"I meant what I said about the Hindel Mansion being evil. I know you told me the parents of the murdered child are in the hospital, but that house isn't empty. Someone, or maybe I should say something, is still living there."

"Yeah, the caretaker lives on the estate, but he has his own house. Maybe you're picking up his energy. Wow! I'm already getting into the lingo." Seelah looked at her. "Okay, if it isn't Quigly, then whatever it is must be well-hidden because Donavan and his men have been all over the estate."

"It's hidden. I'm hopeful, while we're in the house, I'll be able to figure out where. I'm sure your husband could use that information."

At the thought of telling Donavan about her going to the mansion, Barbara felt her heart speed up with unease. "When I tell Donavan I went to that house, he's going to hit the roof." She thought about that for a moment, but the lure of an adventure proved too much to give up. "I don't care, though. I haven't had this much fun in years. Who knows, maybe you'll come up with something to crack the case, then it'll all be worth getting my ass chewed!"

"I hope that's all it amounts to, Barbara," she told her, then fell silent to prepare herself for what might lay ahead for them at the mansion.

Barbara pulled up close to the wrought-iron gate and started to get out of the car when Seelah held out her hand. "I'll get it." She already had the door pushed open.

Barbara drove through the gate then stopped to allow Seelah to get back into the car. Barbara glanced at her. "Don't you think we should lock the gate?"

"I just had a warning not to. We might need to get out of here fast."

Barbara moved up the driveway. "What kind of warning? I mean, did you hear an actual voice?"

"Yes, and I saw the person who gave me the warning. Her name is Chandra. She's a quadroon who lives in the bayous."

Barbara almost slammed on the brakes. "She's the woman our friend Jack dated awhile back."

"Chandra is a powerful psychic. She's also a voodoo high priestess. If anyone could tell we are here, she could."

In front of the house, Barbara turned off the car. "You know her? Tell me, what do you think of her? Is she evil?"

Seelah drew back, trying not to laugh as Barbara's questions tumbled, one after the other, from her mouth. "Yes, I know, Chandra. She's very old, but I don't think she's evil. At least, not anymore."

"Oh, I think we're talking about two different women. The woman Jack saw is young. No more than thirty-eight…forty…at the most."

"No, we're talking about the same woman. Believe me,

there is but one Chandra. How long did Jack go with her?"

"About two years or so. One day," Barbara shrugged her slim shoulders, "she just up and dumped him for no reason. He lost his job on the police force and almost lost his mind over her. You may think she's not evil anymore, but I sure do!"

"Then... he's the one who changed her," Seelah breathed. "I always wondered who he could be."

"Well anyway, enough about them," Barbara said, anxious to get inside and look around. "Since we're already here, are we going to listen to common sense or toss it to the wind and go inside?"

"What do you want to do? If you feel like we shouldn't, then we'll turn around and leave. I will say this, though. I have a strong feeling I can find out something that will help your husband."

"That's all I needed to hear." Barbara reached over the seat for Brandy. "Let's go."

As soon as her feet touched the driveway, Seelah could feel the coldness emanating from the house. "Do you have the key ready?"

"Right here in my hand." Barbara walked up the front steps and, after handing Brandy over to Seelah, stuck the key in the lock. A loud "click" resounded as the lock turned over. "After you," Barbara smiled a nervous smile as she turned the knob, pushed open the door.

"Thanks." As Seelah walked ahead of her into the house, she found herself surrounded by the souls of those who had chosen to remain in the house or been kept from passing over into the light. "This house is filled with earthbounds."

"You can see them?" Barbara peered around the room. Her grip tightened on Brandy as she wiggled and whined.

Seelah nodded, petting the pup's head. "Brandy can see them, too. Can't you, girl?" She turned away. "Now, let's see if we can send them home." Seelah took a few deep breaths then said in a clear, calm voice, "You can stop calling now; I can see you and hear you." She smiled as they quieted.

"What are they doing?" Barbara came up close to her.

"Nothing. They're in shock someone can see and hear them." Seelah stared out over the crowd of shimmering souls gazing at her, their arms outstretched towards her. "I want you all to listen to me now. If you will do what I tell you, some of you will be able to leave here."

"Seelah, this is spooky. I'm going to do some exploring while you tend to this," Barbara said, starting to walk away.

Seelah reached out, halting her. "Are you sure you want to go off on your own?"

"Why not? All the ghosts are here with you."

"You have a point. I'll be along as soon as I finish here."

Barbara nodded, pulling Brandy close against her, the feel of her small, warm body making Barbara feel a little less apprehensive.

Not willing to waste any time, Seelah spoke in a soft, clear voice. "All of you have one thing in common, and that is, none of you realize you are dead." Seelah watched as they ran their hands up and down their arms.

A very large man stepped forward. "Why do you say we're dead? I can see my body. I can even feel my body. So I can't be dead." He glanced at the others, who nodded their agreement.

"I know you can see and feel your bodies, but the fact remains your souls have left your body. Now you are energy. This is why no one else has been able to see or hear you until I came. Think about what I am telling you. Haven't you all tried to speak to the families who have lived here? And haven't they all ignored you? All of them except me?"

"How come you can see us, and none of the others could?" he asked her.

"I can see you because God gave me a special gift to see the energy left behind after a soul has left its earthly body. I'm not here to hurt you. I'm here to send you on your way to where your family and loved ones are waiting for you.

She could see a ray of hope coming into their faces, and her heart went out to them. "I want you to look around for a very bright light. Can any of you see the light I'm talking about?"

All remained silent for a moment then a chorus of voices

rang out through the crowd. "See! I told you. If I'm telling the truth about the light, then trust me about what else I'm telling you." Seelah sighed a grateful sigh as three white spirits, dressed in white robes, stepped forth from the light.

"Now, and this is very important, I have called on white spirits to come and take you home. All you have to do is, one at a time, follow these spirits into the light. They will lead you to the other side and home.

As Seelah watched, they all began walking towards a beautiful bright light and, as they moved through it, disappeared from her sight. All except one. A small girl stood watching her. "What is your name, little one, and why didn't you follow the others into the light?"

"My name is Peggy Rawlins."

"Hello, Peggy. My name is Seelah Stanford. I'm glad to meet you."

The child almost smiled, but the fear she had felt for so long pushed it back, leaving her looking sad and forlorn.

"Why didn't you go to the light, Peggy?"

"I can't. The man who lives here let Margaret go, but he said I have to stay."

"Who is Margaret?"

"Margaret is the girl who lived here."

"And the man? Can you tell me his name?" Seelah moved toward the child she wanted so much to help, but the little girl moved back, beginning to fade from her sight.

"I have to go now," she cried, her voice getting dimmer and dimmer until Seelah could no longer hear her.

"No! Peggy, come back!" Seelah tried to reach her, but the child had already disappeared.

Well, at least I got to send the others on their way, she consoled herself. She could hear Chandra urging her to leave, and she called out into the silence. "Barbara, where are you?"

"I'm down here, in the basement," Barbara answered her. "It's the open door to the left of the back door."

"I see it." Seelah walked down the steps. At the bottom, she looked around. "Sure is a lot of wasted space here, isn't there?"

"That's what I thought. All I could find is this washer and dryer and these shelves. This would be a great place to store winter vegetables, don't you think?"

"Sure would and canned goods, too. My, you're having a good time, Brandy." She leaned down, ruffling the pup's back. "What is it girl, did you find something to interest you?" she laughed as she watched the pup dig and sniff at the shelves.

"Could be a mouse. I hear even the best homes have them."

Seelah reached out, running her hand down the shelves, then jumped away. Her dark eyes alive with fear.

Barbara glanced at her. "What's the matter? Did something bite you?"

"Yeah, could have been a spider." Seelah gave her a strained smile. "I hear even the best homes have them, too. Come on, Barbara," she stooped down, picking up Brandy in her arms, "I think it's time we left." Seelah forced her legs to move towards the stairs.

"Oh, but I've just seen the first floor and the basement. I haven't even seen the upstairs yet," Barbara said as they climbed their way up out of the basement. "It will just take a few minutes." She clicked off the light, shut the door.

"Now, Barbara!" Seelah told her, the tone in her voice leaving no room for argument.

Without a word, Barbara followed her outside, stopping long enough to lock the door. As soon as she slid behind the wheel, Seelah turned to her.

"Get us the hell out of here!" Seelah told her, her face pale beneath her normal olive complexion. "And don't ask any questions until we're well on our way!"

Both women jumped as someone walked up to the window.

"Didn't mean to startle you ladies," said a soft, effeminate voice. "I'm Mr. Quigly, the caretaker. May I ask what you're doing here?"

Seelah thought fast. "I'm Jeannette Lobie, and this is my friend, Mary Ellen Bowen. We're both nurses at the hospital, and the Stewarts asked if we would stop by the house and make sure everything is all right." She pasted a smile on her face, forced herself to look up at him and not to turn away as his fetid breath blew past her into the car.

"Why would they do that? They don't even live here anymore." Quigly's hands rested on the rolled down window, his face mere inches from Sellah's.

"Oh, haven't you heard?" Barbara spoke up, leaning forward in her seat to look at Quigly. "They're getting out of the hospital in a few days, and they plan to return."

"With the children?" Quigly asked an anxious note sounding in his voice.

"Oh yes!" Seelah said. "You know they won't go anywhere without the little ones if they can help it."

"It's news to me, but you ladies being nurses and all, I guess you'd know more about their plans than me." He stood up straight, moved away from the car. "I won't keep you any longer, then." He waved them off. "Drive safely."

Seelah rolled up her window. "Drive slow until we're outside that gate, then step on the gas!"

Barbara stopped a short ways outside the gate and, as Seelah remained seated, jumped out to close and lock the gate. She got back in the car, slammed the door, and reached up to buckle her seatbelt. "What were you so afraid of back there?"

"Drive, Barbara!"

Barbara looked at her for a moment, then put the car in gear.

When they were far enough away from the mansion, Seelah felt safe she turned in her seat. "Barbara, there's a secret passageway behind that shelf."

"Well...why didn't you tell me!?" Barbara slowed the car, anger flashing in her brown eyes. "We could have checked it out!"

Seelah looked at her as if she had lost her senses. "Don't slow down!" She flipped her hands, urging her to go faster. "I couldn't take the time to tell you about the secret passageway because I knew we had to get out of that house! Barbara, there was a man standing behind that wall. I felt his presence when I ran my hand over the shelves. Brandy felt him too. That's why she kept digging."

"My god!" Barbara breathed, her hands beginning to shake on the wheel. "Sorry for snapping at you. I guess I tend to get a little carried away sometimes with my love of adventure," she apologized, then swerved the car off the side of the road, and slammed on the brakes. "Oh shit!" Barbara rocked back in her seat as the car came to an abrupt standstill. "I've seen the way those secret passages work! He could have pushed a button, and when the shelves turned around, he would have been standing right in front of us!"

"You've been in a house with a secret passage?" Seelah secured her seatbelt.

"No! But I've watched enough horror movies to know how they work!" Barbara pulled the car back onto the road.

In spite of herself, Seelah laughed. "Girl, you are too much!" She blew out a long breath, feeling somewhat calmer now.

"So, who do you think it could be?" Just the mere thought of someone being that close set her heart to trip-hammering again.

"Jonathan Hindel would be my best bet."

"I thought he lived in England. At least…that's what Quigly told Donavan and Jack."

"Barbara, I know you're not going to want to do this, but instead of taking me home, I want you to take us to your house to tell your husband what we know." She started to feel uneasy again.

"You're right; I don't want to do this. Although, if you think we should, then we will. We'll have to wait around for him to get there. I told him I had some errands to run, so he took the kids to the station for a few hours."

"That's fine. I could use some quiet time before we get into it all." Barbara's outburst of fear, at how close they had come to meeting the man standing on the other side of the wall, beginning to transfer itself to her.

"Seelah, I just had a thought. It could have been Quigly standing back there. He walked up to the car right after we got in, and I don't recall seeing him when we walked outside."

"No, not Quigly. Compared to the man behind the wall, Quigly is way too small. The black shape she had seen while doing the reading flashed into her mind. She gulped, trying to get enough air into her lungs to breathe. The suffocating feeling she had felt when first talking to Barbara about the house had returned in full force against what she now knew. "Barbara, the man standing almost in front of us is the same man who attacked the police officer and the others!"

CHAPTER TWENTY

Chandra stood on her porch looking out over the water, her thoughts lingering on the two women as they made their way away from the mansion. Thankfully the spirits had given her a heads up about the danger they were walking into. She knew the woman named Barbara to be the wife of Jack's best friend, Donavan Hays. Although she didn't care for Donavan, she couldn't let his wife walk into such a terrible situation with no warning. Most of all, she protected her because she knew the love Jack held in his heart for her.

She had thought a lot about Jack since he walked away from her that day at the hospital. She kept her energy tuned to his to see what might be happening in his life. What she saw caused her both pain and comfort. A new life would be opening up for Jack soon. He would be back working on the sheriff's department, earning a good salary, and getting on with everyday living. Ridding himself of all the pain and anguish knowing her had brought to his life.

Sharp glimpses of their life together sliced her without mercy. Their love had been but a few short moments stolen from time. Now those moments were over. Someone new would enter his life. Someone right for him. Chandra knew that all she could do now is step back and allow it to happen.

She could see the one coming into his life in her mind, and she approved of her. The woman possessed a clean spirit, a beautiful face and body and a heart filled with compassion for others. The kind of woman Jack needed to make his world complete. And, she would make Jack forget all about her and the love they had shared.

Chandra jerked her thoughts back from the pain; cleared her mind of the pictures running through it. Pictures she thought she had wanted to see.

A man's face slid into her mind. He smiled, but the smile held no warmth. Chandra waited to see what he wanted. Afraid she already knew.

"Chandra." Jonathan's smooth voice slid over her. "You will come to me by way of the outside entrance. Do not hesitate to obey me, for if you do, I will not hesitate." He left the threat suspended between them.

Anger shot through her, and without stopping to think, she answered him, "Jack Olivier' is no longer of any importance to me, Jonathan. Do with him what you will!" She visualized a thick white cloud forming around her. Its protective wall would shield her from outside forces.

Jonathan slithered through the mist before it could be formed. "You say this with your mind." His deep laugh warned her of the danger of trying to outsmart him. "I can look inside your mind and your heart, Chandra! You cannot hide from me!"

Unwilling to risk something happening to Jack, she dissolved the shield. "I will come, Jonathan."

***

Chandra stood up inside the cave, pushing her wet hair back from her face. To her surprise, she found Quigly waiting for her. "Where is Jonathan?" Her skin crawled with unease as it always did in the presence of this evil man.

"Waiting for you." He grinned, holding out a fresh towel for her and reaching with his other hand to direct her through the cave.

Chandra drew back, a repulsive shutter passing over her. "I can find my way," she told him, not bothering to hide her feelings.

"I am here to service you." His high-pitched, girlish laugh hinted at the perverse meaning hidden within his words.

Chandra whirled to face him. "You will never speak to me again unless it is necessary," Chandra hissed the words at him.

"If you do, I will kill you."

Quigly stepped back, glaring at her. "Jonathan will hear of this. You know you are forbidden to speak to me in this way."

Chandra stopped walking. Without turning, she addressed him. "Are you speaking to me?"

Quigly remained silent, following at a safe distance as she continued on her way through the cave.

Jonathan looked up from where he relaxed on the couch as she came into view. "I have asked Mr. Quigly to be present while I discuss something with you. I hope this will not inconvenience you."

"As long as he remains silent, he will be safe." She shot a warning glance across the cave to where Quigly now sat in a chair he had pulled up close to the couch.

The smug smile Quigly aimed at her dared her to harm him in the presence of Jonathan. "I think it is time our Chandra had a good lesson to remind her who is in charge here." He looked at Jonathan as he spoke.

Jonathan nodded, waiting to hear Chandra's views on this idea.

Quigly crossed his thin ankles, reclined to a more comfortable position in the chair. A slight movement caught his attention, making him glance down at his feet. His breath froze in horror as he watched a large, king cobra slither its way up his legs. Paralyzed with fear, Quigly fought to silence the scream crawling into his throat. The snake curled itself in his lap, his long, thick neck beginning to hood. Black eyes stared out at him as its great head swayed, weaving and dipping, in a lethal dance within inches of Quigly's face.

Jonathan stared over at the man, trying to see what had him so mesmerized. Then he turned toward Chandra as she stood transfixed, her dark green stare never wavering from the man sitting in front of her. He relaxed his mind, tuned into her energy. His breath shot forward at the sight creeping into his mind. "Enough!" Jonathan roared.

In an instant, the snake vanished. Quigly sank down in the chair, his face and body covered in sweat. "She could have killed me," he whispered. The terror he had been enduring still very much alive.

"The next time you come near me, it will not be a hallucination," Chandra promised him. "The next time, it will be real."

"I said, enough!" Jonathan looked at her.

Chandra's proud head lifted as she stared him down. "I will not cower before you any longer, Jonathan. You hold no power over me. You will do what you will do. I don't care anymore."

Jonathan sat up straighter on the couch. "You dare to defy me?"

"I dare to match my power with yours." Chandra glared at him. "Your strength is in evil, Jonathan. Whereas mine has evolved into something far greater than you. Through the years, that strength has grown, become more powerful. Did you think I would allow you to dominate my life forever?" Chandra watched and waited for him to make his move.

Jonathan remained seated, a knowing smile teasing the corners of his mouth. "Am I to understand you no longer care about your lover? The man you allowed to turn you into a weak, pathetic shell of the woman I created?" He waited for the fear to leap into her eyes at his mention of the man she had taken to her heart. When it didn't, he sat up, placing his feet flat on the floor to rise from the couch.

"Jack holds no interest for me." She forced herself to say his name, knowing Jonathan would be waiting to see if she could. "You are out of touch." She could feel him pushing on the barrier she had placed between them in her mind. "You will never walk into my mind again, Jonathan."

"I will destroy you!" Jonathan walked towards her.

Chandra forced herself to stand quiet. When he placed his hands around her throat, she but looked at him, watching as anger boiled up then spilled over in out and out fury as he tried to squeeze the life from her body.

Jonathan could feel the strength draining from his hands, feel them tremble beneath their useless power before dropping back to his sides. A scream ripped from the very depths of his dark soul, splitting the silence as he lunged for her.

With just her mind, Chandra lifted his body into the air to throw him crashing into the wall of the cave. As she turned, she caught a movement. She whirled as Quigly came at her from behind, a piece of thick wood raised over his head. Chandra stood still, glaring at him as he lowered the wood to the floor. "Go and see to your master," she told him, then walked across the floor to seat herself in the chair Quigly had vacated.

Dazed, Jonathan got to his feet, shoving Quigly out of his way with a vicious snarl. He looked at Chandra as he lowered himself down onto the couch. "I underestimated you, Chandra."

"Yes, Jonathan, you did. Your evil will never touch me again. Your power over me is dead. Never again will I bring young girls to feed your filthy appetite."

At her words, Jonathan's head snapped up. "I will not allow you to do this!" he growled, beginning to move from the couch.

Chandra watched him, her dark stare warning him away.

With all the strength he could call on to keep his anger at bay, Jonathan pushed himself back further onto the couch. "I cannot live without seeing Angelia. You know this."

"Angelia is dead, Jonathan. Killed by your own hand. Let her rest."

"I can't!" he cried into the silence. All the anger gone now from his face and voice.

"Without my help, you have no choice. It is time to stop the evil."

"It is much too late for that. I am what I am, and nothing you or I can do will change that."

"Let me end your suffering, Jonathan. Then you can be with Angelia forever. Don't you want that?" Chandra held her breath, waiting for his answer.

"You cannot help me. The evil is much too deep. Why do you torture me with things that cannot be?"

"I can help you, Jonathan. All you have to do is renounce the evil and turn your face back to God. He will not deny you."

"Jonathan would never do that." Quigly's soft voice came to her from where he sat on the arm of the couch. "Jonathan knows his soul is doomed just as mine is and yours too, Chandra."

"You are so wrong, Quigly. If we chose to turn away from the evil, God will welcome us home. But you don't want that. Do you?" She turned in her chair, giving the man her full attention. "Your very essence feeds on the misery of others." Chandra heard laughter bubble up in his throat to spill out into the silence.

"Come back to us, Chandra. Come back where you belong. No one can hurt us." Quigly left his chair to walk towards her.

Jonathan watched her, and what he saw made up his mind. "Sit down! I still have need of you, and if you continue to bait her she will destroy you."

Quigly licked his lips, recalling flashes of days gone by when he had enjoyed this woman threatening his existence. Then his watery eyes fell on Jonathan, and he turned back to the couch.

"I want you to tell me about the two women who were here earlier today." Jonathan paid close attention to her demeanor. "Don't bother to lie to me, Chandra. I know you warned them to leave. As I came downstairs, I heard someone pull up outside. I almost didn't have time to get to the basement before they let themselves in."

"Yes, I warned them." Chandra looked into his watchful gaze. "Would you rather I hadn't and allow them to walk in on you?"

"How did you know they were here?" Jonathan smiled over at her.

"You know I keep my energy tuned into yours just for this reason."

"You're not telling me everything, Chandra."

She knew it would do no good to keep stalling, so she gave him just enough to satisfy him. "They did not deserve to be harmed. And their coming here did a lot of good. One of the women is psychic. She sent the trapped souls in the house on to the other side."

"But not all of them," Jonathan laughed deep in his throat.

"No, the child you keep trapped here is left to continue

her suffering. Why don't you release her, Jonathan? She is but a child."

"I still have need of her. When I am through with her, then she can leave, but until then, she will remain."

"You are right, Jonathan. Your soul is too steeped in evil to think about trying to change." Chandra breathed a deep breath against all the negativity surrounding her. "Most of all, you have no intention of changing. You like inflicting pain on others."

"Tell me about the other woman, Chandra." Jonathan ignored her, choosing instead to address the subject uppermost on his mind. "Why did you want to protect her?" He reclined to a more comfortable position.

"I have never met her before."

Jonathan knew she continued to hide something from him. "You are not answering my question, Chandra." Jonathan relaxed his elbow on the armrest of the couch, tapped the side of his nose with his forefinger. "From your actions, I can tell this woman has some special meaning to you."

"They said they were friends of the Stewarts," Quigly spoke up.

"You talked to them?" Jonathan turned to stare at him. "You knew they were in the house?"

Quigly felt uneasy. "I didn't hear them drive up." He tried to defend himself. "I talked to them after they got in the car. I asked what they wanted, and they said the Stewarts were planning to return to the mansion."

"The Stewarts do not live here anymore, you fool!" Jonathan got to his feet. "They do not have a key! Where did they get a key?!"

Quigly felt cold sweat trickling down his face, but he made no move to wipe it away. "They said the Stewarts gave it to them," he whispered, trying to still his shaking.

"Are those their words? Or yours?" Jonathan took a menacing step towards him.

"Why...I assumed that's where they got it. They said they were planning..."

His words were silenced as Jonathan grabbed him by the

throat, lifting him from the arm of the couch. "You fool! You stupid, ignorant fool! Who had the key?"

Quigly tried to speak, but Jonathan refused to release him, making any speech impossible.

At last, Jonathan flung him back with great force against the couch.

"Who…had…the…key?" he demanded, his voice low and forceful.

"Lieutenant Hays had the key," Quigly gasped the words.

Jonathan swung around, looking at Chandra. "Then one of the women had to be Hays' wife." A surge of pure energy shot through Jonathan as he stood staring at her, and at that moment, saw the truth. "You protected her because she is the wife of your lover's best friend." He threw back his head, his deep laughter filling the cave. "You almost had me convinced you no longer cared for him."

Chandra tried to get back her control. "I protected them because they are good people. As I said, I have never met the woman."

"No, but she is a friend of Jack Olivier,' and that is the reason you came to her rescue."

"Kill her, Jonathan. She betrayed you and brought danger here because she broke one of your strongest rules!" Quigly sat rubbing his throat, his evil stare riveted on Chandra.

"What are you talking about?"

"The women had a dog. If they took the dog with them, down in the basement, it could have sniffed out the passageway."

"Do you know for sure if they took the dog into the basement?" His voice became low and menacing now. "Have you gone down and checked for any sign of a dog?"

Quigly shook his head, his fear of the man looming before him silencing his words.

"Then do it! Now!" he snarled as Quigly scrambled to his feet. "Come back here as soon as you know. We will be here waiting for you. Chandra and I aren't finished talking yet. Are we Chandra?" His angry glare turned on her, now waiting to hear what excuses she would offer him for putting them all in needless danger."

"I already told you, Jonathan, I will not be dominated by you any longer. There is nothing you can do to make me help you." Her head came up as she looked at him.

"Oh, but there is, Chandra. I can see your weakness. I can see where it lay hidden. But no longer. Now, it is out in the open. You did not worry for my safety or even your own. You have feelings for these people and all because they are friends of the man you still hunger for." Jonathan reached out, tipping her face up to his. "We are not finished, you and I." he smiled into her pale face.

Chandra made no move to contradict him, for they both knew he had gleaned the truth.

CHAPTER TWENTY-ONE

Barbara breathed a sigh of relief when she didn't see Donavan's jeep parked in the driveway. "They aren't back yet." She unhooked her seatbelt, leaned over the seat for Brandy.

"Good. Maybe we can think how to tell him about all this without your getting into trouble." Seelah opened the car door on her side.

"Give up on that hope because, as the wily spider said to the poor grasshopper who pleaded to be set free from her web, it ain't gonna happen!"

"Hmm." Seelah thought about this as they made their way up the walk. "I never heard that one before."

"Once you start having kids, you'll hear a lot of things you never heard before." Barbara opened the back gate, set Brandy inside, then pulled it closed. "I don't know about you, but I'm hungry."

"Frayed nerves will do that to some people. What works best for me is chocolate."

"Boy, did you come to the right place. Soon as we get inside, I'll make us one of my surefire pick me ups."

"Which is?"

"A big slice of chocolate cake with chocolate frosting, heaped high with chocolate ice cream and smothered in Hershey's chocolate syrup." Barbara grinned over at Seelah. "Complete with whipped cream and a cherry."

"All I can say is, I hope your husband doesn't get too angry because, after eating all that, if we do have to run, we're going to have about as much chance of getting away as that poor grasshopper!"

After they had finished their ice cream and cake, Seelah went out back to check on Brandy, and Barbara rinsed off their dishes, then bent over to put them into the dishwasher. A noise at the front door brought her bolt upright. Running her hands down the sides of her jeans, she walked towards the door. She reached for the knob, then stepped back as she saw the door being shoved open. With a loud squeal, she slammed the door and secured the deadbolt.

"What the hell are you doin', Barb?" came a familiar voice from the other side.

Barbara jerked open the door. "I'm sorry, Jack. You should have called out."

"Who the hell else walks into your house, unannounced?" He rubbed his forehead where the door had smacked him. "If you don't want me comin' 'round, just say so, don't knock my goddamn head off."

Her jagged nerves calmed somewhat as she looked up to see an angry red welt spreading across his forehead. Instead of giving him the sympathy he deserved, she laughed.

"What's so funny?" Jack glared over at her.

"Go look in the mirror." Barbara put her hands on his shoulders, turned him in the direction of the first bathroom.

"Ah, shit! And I gotta date tonight!" He put his face close to the mirror over the sink. "I can't go out lookin' like this!" he growled as he saw the mark on his head swell and take on a rainbow of colors. "Quit laughin' goddamn it! It ain't funny."

"Let me put some ice on it before it gets any worse." Barbara tried to control her mirth, but the look on Jack's face, as he watched the lump double in size, robbed her of all control.

"You're sadistic, you know that?" He glowered at her in the mirror. "Does Donavan know what a sick woman he fathered a child with?"

"If you don't stop standing here talking, that lump is going to be the size of a golf ball."

"If you'll give me a few minutes to take care of another problem, I'll come out and let you doctor me." He shot her a look over his shoulder, his brows raised with forced patience.

"I'll get the ice ready." Barbara closed the door.

Jack could hear her laughter echoing all the way down the hall. As soon as he could, he wet a washrag in cold water to hold it against his, by now, throbbing head. With the cloth pressed against his forehead, he opened the door and ran smack into someone standing just outside. Spying the dark hair, he pulled her close to his chest. "I'm sorry, sweetheart. I didn't know you were there."

"I'm not your sweetheart, and you can let go of me before I inflict another wound on your person you won't want seen!" Seelah told him.

Jack stepped back. "I'm sorry, little one. I thought you were Jenny."

"Right," she breathed, brushing past him to shut the door in his face.

When he walked into the kitchen, Barbara already had a chair pulled away from the table and an icepack waiting. He sat down in the chair to press the ice against his head.

"I heard a commotion." Barbara wrapped a towel around his shoulders. "Did you run into Seelah?"

"I ran into someone standin' right outside the door. From the poor lighting in the hall, I just saw dark hair, so I thought Jenny already came home. I'm not tryin' to tell you how to raise your kid, but her friend's got a real smart mouth on her. Appears to me Jenny could do a lot better in her choice of playmates."

Barbara looked up to see Seelah standing in the archway. She had to admit with her diminutive size and no makeup, she could pass for a child. "Seelah, I'd like you to meet our friend, Jack Olivier'."

Seelah walked over to the table, and as Jack lowered the icepack, she held out her hand. "I guess this just isn't your day, Jack. First Barbara clobbers you with the door for trying to break into her house, then I almost knee you in the crotch for trying to molest me." She gave him her brightest smile.

"Jack, this is *my* friend, Seelah Stanford." Barbara watched him swallow before holding out his hand.

"Sorry 'bout grabbin' you." Jack glanced up at her, plopped the icepack back against his head, winced. "I thought you were Jenny."

"No harm done." Seelah took his hand in hers, then pulled away as a warm zing of electricity shot up her arm. "If you like, I might be able to help you minimize that swelling." Her voice had lost its biting tone now as she moved closer to the table to pull the icepack away from his head.

"Oh, I'm sorry. I didn't realize you were a doctor." Jack didn't bother to look up as he delivered his rude sting. For some reason, he felt uneasy with this girl. Her next statement didn't do anything to help change his mind.

"Barbara, do you have any Preparation H?"

Both their heads snapped up to stare at her. Jack came to his senses first.

"Does this look like a hemorrhoid to you?" he growled, lifting the icepack away from his head.

"No," Seelah delivered, "although you are behaving like an ass." She waited a moment, then burst out laughing as she took pity on him. "All jokes aside, Preparation H has been known to help bring down swelling." She turned to Barbara. "Do you have any?"

"I think Donavan has some in the medicine cabinet. I'll go check." Barbara walked away, shaking her head.

"So, tell me...what is your name again?" Jack looked up at her.

"Seelah. It's Greek."

"Oh...well...anyway, what do you do when you're not prescribing outrageous medical treatments for total strangers, Seelah?" Jack grinned over at her as she seated herself in the chair next to his.

The words, to tell him about being psychic, already perched on her tongue, but she swallowed them. Instead, she replied, "I do oil paintings."

"And do you make a good enough livin' at that?"

"I do all right."

"More like a side-line? At your age, I'm sure you're still

livin' at home with your folks." He pressed the icepack back to his forehead.

"I live alone. These days I guess a lot of girls right out of high school do. We can't wait to try out our wings."

"Yep. I can identify with that." Jack nodded with understanding. "But, take it from me, Seelah; don't be in a rush to grow up. Old age will find you soon enough without your reachin' for it."

"You mean like you." Seelah tried to keep the seriousness pasted to her face.

He glanced up at her. When she continued to stare at him, her dark eyes wide with innocence, he answered her. "I wouldn't say I'm old. Older than you by a long shot, but I still consider myself on this side of the hill."

What are you, Jack? Thirty-five… thirty-six maybe." Her clear, brown eyes rounded as the numbers rolled off her tongue.

"I'm thirty-eight. So, like I said, while I couldn't by any means be considered old, I am older than you by at least twenty years."

Barbara came back into the room carrying the tube of medicine, gauze, a roll of tape, and a pair of scissors. "I hope this is all you need." She placed everything down on the table.

Jack leaned back, shaking his head, and staring at the half-rolled tube of ointment. "Ah no! You're not puttin' somethin' on *my* head Donavan's had up his ass!"

"Oh, for goodness sake. You don't put the medication on the swelling. You put it on a piece of gauze. Now lean back so we can see what we're doing." Barbara pulled his head into a comfortable position.

Seelah squirted some of the ointment onto a piece of gauze, then cut two strips of tape, sticking one end of both pieces onto the edge of the table. She dried his forehead then laid the medicated gauze across the swelling to attach it with the tape. "There you go, old man. All done." Then, surprising even herself, she leaned down, placing a kiss beside the bandage. "That should make it feel better."

Barbara watched her, a feeling of excitement running over

her. She had always wanted Jack to meet a good woman and settle down. Now at long last, she had someone to work with.

A vehicle pulling into the driveway drew their attention. Jack scooped the tube of medicine and everything else they had used into his hands. Pushing back his chair, he jumped to his feet. "I'll take all this back to the bathroom. Where does it go?"

"The Preparation H goes in the medicine cabinet, and the rest goes into the first drawer beside the sink. Oh, just give it to me. I'll take it back. I know where everything goes." She whipped the towel from around his shoulders, draped it lengthwise across her hands, then brought her hands together, enabling the thick towel to sag in the middle. "Scoop everything in here."

"Not one word 'bout puttin' that shit on my head. You both got that?" Jack gave them a warning look.

"Yes sir!" Seelah flipped him a quick salute before turning to follow Barbara out of the room. Nerves tightened her stomach as she thought about what lay in store for the both of them.

Barbara pulled her into the bathroom, closing the door behind them. "Oh, god, I'm so scared I don't think I can do this. Donavan is going to skin me alive." Barbara's hands shook as she splashed cold water onto her face.

"Are you saying your husband beats you?" Seelah pulled her hands away from her face.

"What?" Barbara gazed at her for a moment until Seelah's words sank into her worried mind. "No! Donavan would never raise his hand to Jenny or me." She pressed a hand against her stomach in an attempt to quiet its wild churning. "Although he will do a lot of yelling that I can promise you! But all his anger and yelling will be from his fear for my safety."

"Then let's go get it over with. The sooner everything is out in the open, the sooner you'll feel better. And me too," she whispered, pulling open the door.

They found Donavan in the kitchen, twisting the cap off a bottle of Brandy. When he saw them, he took down another glass. "Hi, love." Donavan pulled her against him, dropped a quick kiss on her forehead. "We have company, I see." He held out his hand. "Are you a friend of Jenny's?"

Barbara shot Seelah an "I'm-sorry look," then turned her attention back to Donavan. "Donavan, I'm going to send the kids out back to play with Brandy. My friend," she slipped her arm around Seelah's waist, "and I have something we need to talk with you and Jack about."

"Sounds real serious." Donavan smiled at the two women as they stood watching him. "Where do we want to sit in the living room or at the kitchen table?"

"The table will be fine." Barbara left to get the girls to send them outside.

Seelah watched Donavan trying to gauge what kind of man Barbara had married. As he picked up the glasses of Brandy, he smiled down at her, then waited for her to go ahead of him.

"Barb forgot to introduce us. My name's Donavan. And yours?"

"I...think I'll wait and let Barbara do the honors when she comes back," Seelah said, not sure if he would recognize her name and put two and two together.

"All right, in the meantime, have a seat while we wait for her. He held her gaze a moment longer, then turned away. "Jack, are you going to join us? Barbara said she wanted to talk to both of us."

"Sure, why not?" Jack walked over to take a seat at the end of the table.

"What happened?" Donavan peered at his bandaged head.

"Just a little mishap." He shot a warning glance over at Seelah. "I'll tell you 'bout it later.

"Lot of secrets floating around today, aren't there?" He took a sip of Brandy. "So, Jack, what did you find out at the station about getting back on the force? You were already gone when the girls and I came back from lunch."

A wide grin spread across Jack's face. "We're a team again, partner!" His hand shot out as Donavan leaned forward.

"I knew you could do it! Ah shit! This calls for a celebration! Have you told Barb yet?"

"No, not yet. I got a little distracted. But what the hell, now we can tell her together."

"Tell me what?" Barbara walked over to take a seat beside Donavan.

"I got back on the force, Barb!" He threw his arms wide.

"Jack, that's wonderful!" she squealed as he enclosed her in his open arms.

Seelah sat back, watching this show of love, and realized how desolate her life had become. Since her husband died, she had cut off all outside interests. Now her life centered on her readings and her paintings. So far, they had been enough. Now, since she had met Barbara, she realized they weren't enough. She missed having female companionship. Someone to laugh with, and, after what happened today, someone to be afraid with.

She felt Donavan nudging her from her thoughts. "You don't need to be left out of this. As Barb's friend, you're welcome to join us. By the way, Barb," Donavan looked at his wife, "you forgot to introduce me to this young lady."

The tightness in Barbara's stomach became sharper, knowing the happy moments were about to come to an abrupt end. "I'm sorry; I guess I did at that. Donavan, I'd like you to meet a new friend of mine, Seelah Stanford."

Donavan took the small hand Seelah held out to him, a puzzled frown pinching his brow. "Seelah Stanford." He repeated the name. "Why does that name sound so familiar to me? Have we met?" He continued to hold her hand.

"No, we haven't. But, I can tell you why it sounds so familiar." She pulled her hand back.

"Please do." Donavan watched her, an uneasy feeling creeping up his neck.

"The other day, I had the privilege of being a guest on the Saint Anthony Parish Today show. I'm a psychic, Donavan."

Donavan straightened up to put some distance between them. "I see, and how did you come to meet my wife?"

"I'll answer that, Donavan," Barbara spoke up.

"I wish you would, and please don't leave anything out in the telling." His voice had taken on a deeper tone, one he used while interrogating suspects.

"As I told you, I watched Saint Anthony Parish Today

and saw Seelah challenge Jonston to spend the night alone on the Hindel estate." She shot a quick look past Donavan to where Seelah sat watching her. "I wondered if she could tell me what might be going on out there."

"By goin' on, you mean, tell you what's been attackin' people?" Jack took up the conversation. His voice gentle as he spoke to her.

"Yes," she nodded, leaning towards Jack. "Seelah asked if I wanted to come for a psychic reading. She said she would do it for free, and I thought, what did I have to lose? So, today I took Brandy, and we went over to Seelah's house."

"And what did you tell her about the house, Seelah?" Jack asked, turning his attention on the woman looking at him.

"I told her the truth as far as I could see it," Seelah answered his question, looking straight into his eyes.

"What did you say?" Donavan interrupted, his voice cold with a hostile bite.

"As I said, I told her the truth as I saw it. The house is much older than I had thought. Built some two hundred years ago. When I tried to see what is living there and make no mistake, there is something still living there. Someone blocked me from seeing what it could be."

"What do you mean blocked you?" Jack asked, his own stomach starting to pitch and roll.

"Someone kept me from seeing what has been attacking people. All I could see is a large dark shape..." Her voice trailed off.

"There's more to this, isn't there?" Donavan turned back to Barbara. "Do you want to fill us in on the rest of it?"

"As soon as I go check on the kids, yes. Because you need to hear the rest of it." She scooted out of her chair.

"While we're waiting on Barbara, I want to ask you a question, Seelah," Donavan said.

"I gave Jonston that challenge because he needed to be taken down a notch. I knew he wouldn't be allowed to go out there alone. But I wanted him to feel the fear of the possibility of going out there," she answered his question, knowing what he wanted to hear about. As he continued to stare at her, she chuckled. "It doesn't always take a psychic to know what is on someone's mind, Donavan."

Barbara sat back down and after taking a deep breath to settle her nerves, she continued, "What I'm about to tell you is going to make you very angry, Donavan, but you have to know, so here goes. When Seelah told me about being blocked, I suggested, since we already had the key, we go to the mansion and try to see what she could find out. And that's what we did."

Silence engulfed those seated around the table as Donavan and Jack looked at each other. Their fear was so strong; neither could find the words to describe his terror. At the same time, they reached out to Barbara and, without a word, gathered her into their arms.

Seelah watched them spread a wall of love around Barbara, trying to protect her from something already past but still so menacing that all they could do is enclose her in their love.

"As much as I hate to bring this up, there's more to this story you both need to hear," Seelah told them.

Jack straightened up to sit back in his chair. "I hope, for your sake, you didn't put Barb's life in more danger just so you could pretend to be something you're not." His voice rose with anger. "'Cause I've had about all I can take of people who make their livin' from evil."

That stung, and Seelah could not let it pass. "Chandra is not evil, and neither am I, Jack," she told him, knowing to whom he referred.

"You will not bring that bitch's name up in this house!" Jack slammed his fist down hard on the table, making Barbara and Donavan jump.

"Stop acting like a spoiled child, Jack. We have work to do." She ignored his outburst.

"Donavan, you better throw this crazy bitch out 'fore I do somethin' we'll both regret!" Jack jumped up.

"Just who are you calling a crazy bitch?" Seelah jumped to her feet, coming forward and looking him right in his eyes. "You think that badge, you just won back, scares me? You got another thought coming, hotshot!"

The idea of this tiny girl going head to head with him almost made him laugh, but the stakes were too high, right at the moment, for any feeling except anger.

Donavan sat watching this duel of anger and found himself impressed with Seelah's spunk. "We haven't heard everything yet, Jack, so if you could, try and control yourself." Donavan motioned him with a nod of his head back to his chair. "You too, Seelah. If you don't mind." For some reason, the girl's angry stance against Jack seemed to take some of the edge off his ire. But all too soon, it pushed its way back beneath a cloud of unease. "What happened when you went to the mansion?"

"The first thing to happen is Seelah sent all the earthbounds on to the other side."

"Not all, Barbara. One child remained," Seelah spoke up.

"First of all, explain what you mean by earthbounds. Are you talking about ghosts?"

"Yes. Earthbounds are ghosts; spirits are souls who have gone on to the other side."

"I feel like I'm stuck smack in the middle of a psycho ward." Jack languished back in his chair to stare up at the ceiling.

Seelah spared him a brief glance before continuing with what she wanted to say. "I sent all but Peggy Rawlins on to the other side. She told me the man who lived there said she had to remain in the house."

Donavan's hand shot out, silencing Jack as he leaned forward in his chair. "Did she say anything about another little girl?"

"Yes, a girl named Margaret. She said the man had let her go on."

"Did she tell you this man's name?" Donavan held his breath, hoping against hope she had.

"I asked, but she wouldn't tell me."

Donavan nodded. "Then what happened?"

"I could hear Chandra urging us to get out of there, so I went in search of Barbara. She and Brandy were in the basement."

The thought of Barbara wandering alone through the

mansion set Donavan's skin to crawling again, but he fought it off, knowing he had to hear everything. "Go on."

"I went down the basement, and all I could see is a washer and dryer and some shelves over by a wall. I noticed Brandy sniffing at the shelves and digging, so I ran a hand down the shelves to try and find out what she smelled."

"And?!" Jack sat perched on the edge of his seat.

"And, that's when I discovered the secret passageway. It's behind the shelves."

"That explains why we never found it!" The words shot from Jack's mouth before he could stop them. "I thought it'd be upstairs."

"Tell them the rest of what you discovered, Seelah," Barbara whispered, leaning into Donavan's arms.

"You mean there's more?" Jack slumped back in his chair.

"Oh yes!" Seelah said, her words taking on a breathless tone. "A man stood behind that wall. That's why Brandy wouldn't stop her sniffing and digging. She could smell him."

"Jesus…jumpin'…up…Christ!" Jack shouted into the air.

"Any idea who he could be?" Donavan asked.

"My best bet is Jonathan Hindel. I reached down and picked up Brandy, and without being obvious, told Barbara we needed to leave. We were already in the car preparing to go when a man, who gave his name as Mr. Quigly, walked up to the car."

"What did he say? Did he try to detain you?" Donavan felt his anger rising against the man whose very name could send him into a stomach-tightening fit of loathing.

"He asked what we were doing there, and we made up a story about being nurses from the hospital who were there because the Stewarts asked us to stop by and check out the house."

"Did he believe you?" Jack jumped into the conversation.

"Not at first. He said the Stewarts didn't live there anymore, so there shouldn't be any reason why they would send someone out to check on the house."

"What did you say to that?" Donavan asked.

"I told him what he didn't know is the Stewarts planned

on coming back to the mansion," Barbara said. "Then he did a very strange thing. He asked if the children were going to return with them. He sounded quite anxious when he said it. Seelah told them they were, and he seemed content with that. Anyway, he said he wouldn't keep us any longer, and we left."

"And that's everything from start to finish. You haven't left anything out?" Donavan asked, making sure he knew all that had happened.

"That's it," Barbara glanced over at Seelah, who nodded in agreement.

Donavan turned Barbara around to face him. As though he spoke with Jenny, instead of his wife, he told her, "You are never, and I repeat never, to go to that house again. Have I made myself clear on that?"

"Yes, Donavan," Barbara nodded. "I have no desire to ever go back there, so you don't have to worry about that."

"Seelah, you are never to go back to that house, either. Is that understood?" Donavan watched to make sure she would comply. "That place is off limits to everyone, except those who are authorized to be there."

"I have no desire to go back there, either," she told him. "I've done all I can do there anyway."

"Seelah," Jack spoke up, leaning across the small space separating them. "I want to apologize for callin' you a bitch earlier. I'm sorry. I realize you're just a kid and weren't thinkin' clear." He placed the palm of his hand against her mouth when she drew in a sharp breath to speak. "Too, if you're friends with Chandra, I can see why your head's filled with all this hocus-pocus nonsense. But for your own good, don't go back to that house. Please?" He gathered both her hands in his.

"I won't, Jack," she told him, leaning further across the table, touched by his concern. "There is still one thing I think you should know, though."

"What?" Jack asked as both he and Donavan looked at her.

"I'm not a kid. I'm a twenty-eight-year-old woman."

He felt so relieved her words had nothing to do with the mansion, he found himself relaxing with her. "Is that right?" Jack leaned in close, smiled. "That case, maybe you should try wearin' some makeup," he lifted her long ponytail into the air, letting its silkiness flow through his hand, "and doin' somethin' with your hair so men like me won't mistake you for a teenager."

Seelah moved within an inch of his mouth and, running a moist tongue over her full lips, whispered, so only he could hear, "It's because of men like you, I don't wear makeup and fix my hair, Jack."

"Smart girl," Jack allowed. "Well, listen, I hate to call a halt to all this, but I gotta date tonight, so, I better be gettin' home."

"Are you sure you still want to go out tonight?" Barbara asked him.

"Barb, I enjoy everyone's company, but yes, I do." He shaped an hourglass figure into the air, laughed.

"Have you looked in the mirror of late?" Barbara smiled over at him.

"Oh shit." His hand shot up to his forehead. "I forgot all 'bout that."

"I'm sure she won't mind your going on a date with Preparation H smeared across your head." Barbara winked at Seelah. "So have a good time."

"Preparation H? What the hell are you talking about?" Donavan gave her a puzzled look. "Jack..." he swung his head around, "why would you have Preparation H on your forehead? That's a little strange, even for you."

Jack could feel a hot flush creeping up his neck to his face. "Ask your wife!" he advised through clenched teeth.

Donavan turned his attention back to Barbara as she struggled to control her laughter. "I still felt jumpy after we came back to the house, so when I heard a noise at the door, then saw it being pushed open, I panicked. I slammed the door shut, and Jack's head took the brunt of the slam."

"But...where does the Preparation H come into play?" Donavan asked, still trying to make sense of everything.

Seelah spoke up. "I've heard it can bring down swelling, so we put some on Jack to find out if what I'd heard could be true. Which reminds me, Jack, let's take off the bandage and check it.

Who knows, maybe it's gone down enough you won't need a bandage."

Barbara crossed her fingers behind her back the lump remained prominent.

"That's a good idea, but I'll check it out. You don't need to bother." He walked to the bathroom with Donavan close on his heels. With much caution, he pulled the bandage off to peer into the mirror. Although the swelling had shrunk, it had not shrunk enough for him to feel comfortable going out. "At least it's better."

"Next time you accuse me of having *my head* up *my ass*, remember this." Donavan poked a finger against Jack's chest.

"You tell anyone 'bout this, Donavan, I swear to Christ, you can kiss our friendship goodbye!"

"Instead of throwing out idle threats, you should be on the phone canceling that date. With your gift of gab, it shouldn't be a problem."

"Yeah, shit, I guess you're right." He turned to leave.

"You can sleep on the couch. I'm going to tell Barb to talk Seelah into spending the night, too."

Jack whirled as Donavan started to walk out of the bathroom. "Don't, man! No." Jack held up his hand. "I like my women with curves. That pathetic little waif sittin' out there," he jabbed a thumb in the direction of the kitchen, "couldn't heat me up if she stood on her head with her thatch ignited!"

Donavan gazed at him long and hard. "You should have been a poet, Jack. Yep," he nodded with conviction, "a real silver-tongued rogue you are! And, although that would be a hell of a sight to see, I doubt if she would go to those lengths to get your attention. Seelah Stanford doesn't strike me as being any more interested in you than you are in her. So the two of you, spending the night in the same house, shouldn't pose a problem. I got the feeling she lives alone, and that isn't where she needs to be in case Hindel or Quigly get any ideas about paying her a surprise visit. If she's here, we can keep an eye on her."

"Why do you need me? You'll be here, won't you?" Anger at having to call off his evening with Joan, creeping into his voice.

"Of course, but Seelah and Barbara went to the mansion together. Remember? He could come stalking around here, and if that happens, I'm going to need your help."

"I guess, since you put it that way, I'll be stayin'."

Although she didn't feel any danger, Seelah allowed herself to be talked into spending the rest of that day and night. Telling herself simply because *she* didn't feel any danger didn't mean it didn't exist. She had been given her gift to help others. It is a rarity for a psychic to be psychic about herself.

CHAPTER TWENTY-TWO

The new moon cast its glow over the surrounding area, aiding the one who made his way to the back of the small house. The one sitting alone surrounded by tall trees and low hanging moss stirring in the night breeze. Excitement flowed through his veins as he raised his head to sniff the wind trying to catch the scent of her. She would feed the terrible hunger pounding through his loins, feed the blood lust that only the sweet taste of warm flesh could satisfy. In his need, he traded quiet for haste, ripping the screen door from its hinges, pitting his vast strength against the aged door to send it flying backward. She could not escape him. His need raged too strong. He loped through the rooms in search of her, throwing furniture out of his way, ripping pictures off the wall, alert to hear her screams that didn't come. His breath quickened, echoing in the silence. He stood in her bedroom, now the room where his senses picked up her smell the strongest. Where could she be? His yellow eyes searched the room, darting here and there in a crazed frenzy. She had to be here. He needed her too much for her to have run from him! In his fury, he raked the mattress, his sharp claws ripping and shredding.

He turned, racing from the room and out into the night air. His need for blood tormenting him without mercy. For a brief moment, he stopped running, needing to collect his thoughts. A movement caught his eye, and he stepped back behind one of the trees to wait.

An old woman pushed a mewing cat out the door with her foot, but when he remained on the back stoop, staring up at her, she walked outside. "Go on now," she told him, nudging him off the porch. "Get on out there and do your business so I can get to bed."

The cat padded off toward the trees, stopping every few moments to look back, then moving on again.

"Go on!" She shooed him with her hands, anxious to get back inside. For some reason, she felt uneasy tonight. Almost as though something bad lingered in the wind.

The cat hissed, arching its back at something over by one of the trees in the next yard.

"Patches, get back here!" she ordered, stepping with some difficulty off the stoop and walking a short way out into the yard. "You're not going to keep me up all night tomcatting!"

She reached down to pick up the cat, but it hissed at her, backing away. "Have it your way, but don't expect me to get up and let you in later." She turned to go back inside, then stopped as something stepped from the trees.

"Who's there?" she called out into the darkness. "You better show yourself before I scream!" She edged toward her house and safety, but the one moving from the shadows had a more sinister plan. She had but a glimpse of madness before slipping to the ground.

He moved towards her and, bending down, lifted her unconscious body into his arms. As he loped away, in the direction of the small house, he could hear the old cat yowling after him.

He laid her body on the ripped bed, feeling his excitement leap as she moaned then tried to sit up. He could smell her terror. The odor pumped excitement faster through his veins. The moonlight shining through the curtains bathed her face letting him see the stark terror staring back at him.

The woman drew in her breath to scream. He lashed out, slashing her face open to the bone. In paralyzing fear, she stared up at him, trying to make sense of what she knew could not be happening. She watched him tear away the thin gown, his breath coming faster, harsher. He ran his hands over her nakedness, then, reached out pulling her legs wide apart to lower himself over her body. She felt a sharp stab of pain between her thighs as he rammed himself inside her. She could hear his loud grunts and growls as he pumped his body back and forth. Screams scurried from her throat in pitiful moans whispering in the stillness.

He threw back his huge head and, with a loud snarl, pumped his body back and forth...then stopped. He slumped over her, his foul breath hot on her throat.

She felt him withdraw from her body, felt his heavy weight lift. Her heart jumped as he jerked her upward to lick the open wound on her face.

He hungered now for the taste of human flesh, and he knew he could take his time in sating that hunger. He watched her fear grow moment by desperate moment. He waited until he knew the fear pumped enough blood through the veins to give it that wild taste he so desired. A taste he knew he would never tire of.

Unable to halt the hunger growing inside him, he lunged, sinking his teeth into the warm throat, tasting, at last, the hot sweet blood as it gushed forth into his waiting mouth.

When he left the small house in the predawn hours, all remained quiet. The people, sleeping in nearby houses, had no idea how close the evil passed within their midst, and they had not even been aware of its existence. One old cat, sitting in the tall tree, remained alert to the danger, his sorrowful cries going unanswered in the early-morning stillness.

***

Jack sat up, the blanket slipping from his bared chest to his waist, as he heard soft footfalls coming down the hallway. A faint glow coming from the kitchen had him all the way on his feet. Without making a sound, he padded towards the light, stopping as he saw a small bottom sticking out of the refrigerator. "I wonder if Barb and Donavan know they have an elf with the munchies raidin' their leftovers." He leaned against the wall, arms crossed over his chest as she turned to face him, holding a plate of cherry pie.

"Jack! You scared the life out of me!" Seelah said, trying to keep her eyes off his bared chest. "So...what...are you going to rat on me?"

"Not if you plan on sharin'." He walked over to take two forks from the silverware drawer. "Do you want a glass of milk to go with that?"

"Of course." Seelah's eyes skimmed with appreciation over his wide shoulders and bared back, coming to rest on his lean hips outlined beneath tight-fitting jeans as he leaned over to take a jug of milk from the fridge.

He held out the forks then opened the cupboard to fetch the glasses. "You take the pie. I'll bring the milk."

Seating herself in the chair closest to the couch, she switched the small lamp on low, then turned her attention to the pie.

"You coulda waited. Now I'll be lucky if there's any left."

"I saved you a bite." She took the glass of milk from his hand to set it down on the end table.

Jack scooped up a large bite, closed his lips over the fork, and pulled the pie into his mouth. "Barb is one hell of a pie maker." He smiled, smacking his lips.

"That she is." Seelah helped herself to another mouthful.

"Do you always get hungry in the middle of the night?"

"Yep." She flicked her tongue, retrieving a small dab of cherry-filling sticking to the side of her mouth.

Jack watched her with growing interest.

"How's your head?"

"Excuse...me?" His fork clanged onto the plate.

"Your head?" She tapped her fork against her brow.

"Oh, that head." He gulped, swallowing the rest of his pie. "It don't hurt anymore, so I guess that's a good sign. Donavan thinks you live alone." The words flew out of his mouth.

"Yes, I have for two years. I told you I had my own place when we were talking earlier."

"That's right. You gotta remember, at the time, I thought you could be Jenny's little friend. So what you told me didn't get a lot of my attention." He picked up his glass of milk.

She smiled then became serious. "I don't mind living alone. My life is filled with my clients and my paintings."

"What kind of paintings?" Jack retrieved his fork, dug in

for another helping.

"I do oil paintings of cottages. Sometimes I do portraits. Whatever moves me at the time I'm behind the easel."

"Never wanted to take the big step, huh?" Jack watched her.

"I'm not following you." Seelah sipped at her milk.

"You never wanted to be married, have a family?"

"I had a husband, Jack." She set the glass of milk down on the table.

"It didn't work out or what?"

"I had a great marriage right up until the night I received the call he'd been killed in an auto accident." She pushed the rest of the pie across the coffee table.

"I'm sorry, Seelah."

"It's been almost two years now." She stared off into the stillness. "I don't know what I would have done, though, without Chandra. The pain...it got so...overpowering...I couldn't seem to get above it. She would talk with me, and when she knew I needed it, she would be quiet and listen. As far as I'm concerned, she saved my life." She picked up her glass of milk.

"It's ironic you say that 'cause with me, she did just the opposite." He could feel the dull ache, like a forgotten foe, moving inward to squeeze his heart in a painful reminder of what used to be. "She all but destroyed my life."

"I'm sorry, Jack. I shouldn't have brought up her name. From the anger you displayed earlier, when I mentioned her, I should have known you don't like talking about her."

"Somehow, sitting here with you, it don't bother me as much." The ache loosened its grip, and Jack breathed deep against its waning. "Chandra and I saw each other for a little over two years. I loved her with everything I had." He allowed himself a fleeting glance into the memory. "I thought she felt the same way 'bout me. I guessed wrong. One day outta the blue, she left no doubt in my mind 'bout that." He inhaled another deep breath, let it out. "Seelah, I know you might find this hard to believe, but...when she left me...I felt like my heart split in two."

"No, Jack, I believe you. When Ron, my husband, died,

I felt the same way. Death doesn't always involve an actual passing of the soul. Although, it always touches the soul. The ones left behind suffer the same devastating pain. In an odd way, I think the breakup of a relationship can be harder to get over than losing someone to death."

"Why do you say that?" He turned towards her.

"When someone dies, you know that's it," Seelah told him, comforting him with her voice the way she longed to comfort him with her arms. "You know you'll never see that person again until you pass on to the other side where they're waiting for you. In time your mind accepts that. Then, when you're able, you get up and go on with your life. When someone loses a loved one through the breakup of a relationship, they still hold onto the hope of seeing that person. And when they do, the heart again feels that same heart-slashing pain. Unless they go away for a long period of time, the mind doesn't accept that it's over, and as long as it doesn't, the mind and heart will never have closure."

"In all my thirty-eight years of livin' on this earth, I've never had anyone explain the pain of loss in such a down to earth, logical way before, Seelah. Only someone with a good heart could come up with such logic as that." He clasped her hand.

"Thank you, Jack. But those aren't my words. They were given to me by an old and dear friend."

Jack withdrew his hand, sitting in the quiet, afraid to hear the name of the person she referred to. He bent forward, shaking a cigarette from the open pack lying on the table.

"Sorry you had to be a babysitter tonight. I know how much you wanted to keep your date with..." she drew an hourglass figure in the air. Mimicking *his* detailed description.

He laughed in spite of himself, glad she decided to lighten the mood. "Yeah, she's somethin'. Oh well, we woulda just gone out to a nice restaurant, had a few drinks, then gone back to her place for a while. No big loss." He grinned over at her. "Then, too, there's the flip side. If I'd gone out, I would of missed havin' cherry pie and milk in the middle of the night with you." Jack flicked his lighter inhaling the nicotine deep into his lungs.

She drew back, her brows raised in sincerity. "Hey, I don't

share my cherry pie with just any..." She inhaled a sharp breath as a feeling of unease shot through her stomach. "We've got company, Jack." She untangled the long robe, withdrew her feet from beneath her.

"What kinda company?" Jack reached out to switch off the lamp then thought better of it, knowing, when dealing with a possible prowler, it's always best to leave everything as is.

"The kind I think you better wake Donavan about, and fast!"

Jack stubbed out his cigarette, reached beneath the couch for his .38. "Come on, I'm not leavin' you out here alone."

With her hand in his, they made their way down the dark hallway. Jack tapped on Donavan's door then pushed it open. "Wake up, Donavan," he whispered

"What's going on?" Donavan reached for the bedside lamp.

"Don't turn on the light," Jack cautioned him. "Seelah thinks we got company. The way my guts are churnin', I tend to believe she's right."

Donavan threw back the covers, slid his feet to the floor. "Wake up, Barb." He shook her.

"Is something wrong with one of the kids?" Barbara said, still half-asleep.

"I think we got someone prowling around outside. I want you and Seelah to get upstairs with the girls. If you can keep from it, don't wake them." Donavan opened the nightstand drawer, withdrew his gun.

"Hurry!" Seelah whispered into the darkness. "He's right outside."

Donavan yanked on his pants as Barbara left their bed, pulling a robe on over her gown as she moved across the floor. "Come on, hold onto me." She gripped Seelah's shaking hand.

As the women made their way upstairs, Jack and Donavan crept out into the hall, their guns cocked and ready. A large shadow blocked the small window in the front door.

Jack's hand shot out, halting Donavan. "Do you see what I see?"

"Arrogant bastard's trying to come right through the front door."

They both took aim as a loud thud sounded on the heavy oak door!

Jack ran forward as a hand smashed through the window next to the door. He fired off two shots right through the broken window, then stepped back behind the curtain to wait.

Heavy footfalls sounded on the paved driveway, followed by a loud crash as though someone tripped over something in their way.

"I'll go out the front. You take the back, Jack!" Donavan yelled, already heading out the door.

"Fuck that! If it's Hindel, these guns ain't gonna stop him!"

"Shit!" Donavan retraced his steps, slammed the door, and flicked the deadbolt. "I forgot what the hell we're dealing with here!"

"I'll call for backup. Good bet he's gone by now, but there's no sense taking chances!" Jack jumped as Seelah walked up behind him. "Jesus Christ, what are you tryin' to do, woman? Get your ass shot?"

"He's gone, Jack. I saw him going through the back fence."

"You got a look at him?" He held up his hand as dispatch answered on the other line. "Yeah, this is Olivier'," he spoke into the phone. "Get two patrol cars complete with K9s over to Lieutenant Hay's house. Now!" He hung up. "Just what did you see?"

"It didn't look human, Jack. I could see him in the security light, he…" Her body pitched forward.

Jack's arms shot out, catching her against him, then lifted her into his arms to carry her to the couch. Instead of placing her on the sofa, he lowered himself down onto the cushions holding her cradled in his arms. For some reason, he didn't want to let go of her. "Okay, baby. I got you. You're safe," he whispered into her dark hair.

"Is she all right?" Donavan walked over to stand beside the couch, reaching an arm around Barbara's waist and pulling her in tight against his hip.

"Yeah, she'll be fine in a minute or two. I think seein' Hindel in full makeup turned out to be a little more'n she could handle."

"Christ!" Donavan blew out his breath. "Seeing that loping across the yard would make me feel a little woozy!"

Seelah squirmed in Jack's arms. "I think you can put me down, Jack. I'm better now."

"Are you sure? You're no burden."

"I'll fix you a drink, Seelah. In fact, I'll fix us all a drink," Barbara said, flicking on the kitchen light.

"Just some coffee for me, hon," Donavan told her. "I think everyone can use a cup of coffee."

"I just thought with the shock and all we could use one." She flipped the switch on the coffeemaker.

"Barb, are you okay?" Donavan turned her around to face him.

"I saw it too, Donavan." She put her arms around his waist, laid her head against his broad chest. "Oh god, when I think how close it got to us today...." She wrapped her arms tighter around him.

"Don't remind me." His breath shuddered as he held her.

"Backup's here, Donavan," Jack said, going to the door.

"Be right there." He cupped her face in his hands. "Better get some more cups."

Seelah passed by Donavan as he walked to the door, smiled up at him as he gave her arm a reassuring squeeze. Wrapping the robe Barbara had loaned her around her small body, she pulled a chair back from the table.

"Barb, I just had a thought."

"What's that?"

"How did he know where to come? I mean, he couldn't have known who went to the mansion yesterday."

"Chandra knew we went there. Maybe she told him. I'm trying to tell you, Seelah, the woman's evil."

"No." Seelah shook her head. "You're wrong. She's not evil. She was, but after meeting Jack, she changed."

"You like Jack, don't you?" Barbara filled each cup with

coffee, bringing theirs with her to the table.

"Yes," Seelah told her, a crooked smile lighting up her face. "He's a good man even though he tries to come off as a hard-ass sometimes."

"We love Jack a lot. He went through hell when Chandra dropped him. I know because Donavan and I picked up the pieces. She shattered him." Barbara took a seat at the end of the table.

"He's going to be leery of starting a new relationship any time soon. It takes time to heal the pain of loss."

Barbara covered her hand. "You're talking about your pain now, aren't you?"

"When I lost Ron, I thought I could never get up from the pain. It seemed to weigh me down until I felt buried beneath it. Then I found someone to talk with, and she led me back into the light. If not for her, I think I would have laid down and pulled the blankets over my head."

"Are you talking about Chandra?" Barbara drew back, staring at her.

"Yes." Seelah turned in her chair to look at her. "She turned out to be my lifeline."

Donavan walked into the room with the deputies. "Grab some coffee, then get the dogs on the scent. Since we already know where you'll end up, Jack and I will meet you at the mansion. Jamison," Donavan turned to the deputy standing the closest, "order more backup. Tell them where to meet us."

"Right, Lieutenant." Jamison pulled his radio into position.

"I think I better get showered and dressed. Donavan, do you think you could spare one of your men to take me home?" Seelah pushed back her chair.

"Whoa, hold on a minute." Jack walked over to her. "You're not goin' anywhere. If he came here, who's to say he didn't drop by your house first?"

"Jack, I have things to do today. I have a business to run."

"That's gonna have to wait. You're not leavin' here 'til we're sure everything's safe. Now sit back down and finish your coffee." He turned to leave.

"I am not a child!" Seelah stamped her foot in anger. "I will not be dictated to."

"Do you want me to tie you up?" Jack pushed her back down in the chair.

"You'd enjoy that, wouldn't you?" She tossed him a saucy grin.

Her cheekiness caught him off guard for a moment. "Maybe after we get this cleared up, we can discuss it." He winked at her, a broad grin splitting his generous mouth. "Barb, I'm gonna leave her in your hands. Don't let me down."

Light already filtered through the gloom of darkness when Donavan and Jack pulled up in front of Seelah's house. "Looks quite enough," Donavan said, shutting off the engine.

"Yeah," Jack growled, opening his door. "Let's go in and see if we were worrin' 'bout nothin'."

"Right behind you, partner," Donavan laughed. "Damn, that sounds good now that it's for real. Don't it?"

Jack grinned over his shoulder as he made his way up the walk. Putting the key in the lock, he turned it, then pushed open the door. "Son...of...a...bitch!" he dropped the words on a long, drawn-out breath, his eyes sliding over the chaos staring out at him. "Thank God I listened to you, buddy."

Donavan nodded as he looked over the room. "Come on; let's see what else he's destroyed."

They made their way down the hall, taking in the neatness of two small bedrooms and a bath.

Jack could see so much of Seelah in the house. All tiny, warm, and welcoming. He whirled as Donavan let out a curse. Making his way to a third bedroom, he walked in then stopped, covering his mouth.

The woman on the blood-soaked bed was so ripped and torn she didn't look human.

"Her throat's been ripped out just like the Stewart girl. And," his eyes moved down over her naked body, glimpsing the dried blood clinging to her thighs, "it's pretty obvious she's been raped," Donavan said. "I'll go call it in."

Jack backed out of the room, trying to close his mind to the disgusting scene before him. Seelah's childlike face jumped into his mind, and he began to shake. "Lord Jesus," he turned, walking down the hall, "it coulda been her on that bed! He remembered how trusting she had been when he held her in his arms, and without warning, an overpowering feeling of anger pushed its way past the sickness churning in his stomach. "You better get ready, you sick son of a bitch, 'cause I'm comin' for you!"

CHAPTER TWENTY-THREE

Jonathan dropped down on the floor of the cave, welcoming the darkness as his exhausted body waited to change. He forced himself to remain still, not to fight against the pain and feelings of suffocation as the skin and hair covering his body putrefied into a thick mass that seeped into his mouth and nose. When his body completed the change, he moved back into the water.

Later, after he finished lighting the torches, he dressed himself, thinking all the while on the problems mounting before him. Seated in his chair, he tried to plan what to do.

When Quigly came back after checking in front of the shelves to see if the dog had been anywhere near them, his worst fears became a reality. Small scratch marks at the base of the shelves showed the dog sensed something and tried to dig beneath the wood.

His anger continued to burn bright at not being able to get to the women who knew of his secret. He knew Hays and his men would be coming soon to find out for themselves if the woman told the truth. She had to be made to look the fool, and at the same time, he must safeguard his privacy.

Unwilling to trust such an important task to Quigly, Jonathan removed the small release mechanism beneath the third shelf himself, being careful to remove any sign of its ever having been there. The mechanism sported a button that, when pushed, made the shelves swing outward, allowing easy access to the cave.

The problem with the shelves being all one structure and attached to the wall could now be done away with. He rationalized, without the mechanism to activate the door, anyone looking for a secret passageway would be left with the obvious conclusion. Such a place as this could only exist in the mind of one with an overactive imagination.

His head came up as someone walked into the cave. "I came to tell you the police are on their way." Quigly lifted a towel from the shelf, dried his face.

"Are you sure they didn't see you slip into the water?" Jonathan felt his anger rise as it always did in the company of this foul creature. If his needs were not so dependent on the man, he would have destroyed him years ago. At present, he served too great a purpose.

So many times, Jonathan had entertained the idea of having Chandra move into the mansion to see to his needs. He always set the thought aside for the same reason. He could not have strangers coming and going on the estate unless they were there for his purpose. As high priestess, others needed Chandra far too much. So down through the years, he had made do with the ineptness of a man whose very presence filled him with disgust.

"I'm sure, Jonathan. They were still coming up the lane when I left the grounds." He hung up the towel, walked over to sit on the floor. "Our Chandra has not been wise in her choice of friends. With her simple woman's mind, she has put both of us in needless danger." He waited to see what his reminder of their peril would bring down on the woman he both hated and lusted after.

Jonathan's head turned in Quigly's direction. "You would do well to remember your own part in this." The anger mounted in his mind until it became all but palpable. "I allow you to stay here as long as I have need of you. You have disappointed me, Mr. Quigly."

Quigly hastened to defend himself. "I didn't hear them drive up. I thought since no one had a key, I could finish my mowing. The acreage is so vast it takes me a long time to cover it all."

"Except someone does have a key, don't they, Mr. Quigly?"

The smile on Jonathan's face held no favor.

Quigly could see the anger glittering behind the cold gray eyes and knew he had made a grievous mistake. "What can I do to make it up to you, Jonathan? Just say the word, and I will do whatever you say." His silly, girlish voice whined.

The sound always reminded Jonathan of a beaten down dog. It made him want to kick him away from him. Without warning, another thought slammed into his mind bringing him straight up in his chair. "You stupid fool!"

Quigly scrambled to his feet, backing away from the killing rage in Jonathan's face. Rage that very soon could be directed at him.

"You should not have come here! They will be looking for you! Your car is in the garage! Where will you say you have been?"

"Why...why...I..." he stammered, trying to think of a plausible answer. An answer that would halt the killing anger staring out at him.

"The answer you are searching for is...you did not think!!"

Quigly bowed his head waiting for the painful blows to begin raining down on him. When they didn't, he looked up. "What should I do, Jonathan?"

"You will leave here after dark and swim far downstream before coming into shore." Jonathan rubbed a tired hand over his brow. "If anyone asks you later where you were, tell them you were out searching the banks for ginseng." He watched as Quigly shook his head, warming to the idea. "For now, you will remove yourself from my sight. I have a lot to think about."

Without question, Quigly did as told, walking to the far end of the cave. Glad he had escaped Jonathan's wrath with just angry words.

Jonathan stood watching him slink away, and his disgust for the man's weakness tore at him. Of all the characteristics in the human psyche, weakness had to be the one he loathed most. He sat down on the couch trying to relax, but the thought of Hays and his men going through his house, touching his personal property, ate at him. Would Chandra's lover be among the men invading his privacy? The thought brought new anger spewing forth. Would idiots surround him the rest of his life? Jonathan tried to quiet his mind, tried to push the anger away from him. Without calling it forth, a painful memory crept into his thoughts. Needing to escape the rage all but consuming him, he allowed the memory to take root and flow through his mind.

Angelia had lived in the big house near the bayous for almost a year now. Each moment of that year, she had withdrawn further and further into her own world, although Jonathan had tried everything he could think of to win back her love.

He walked up to her now as she sat in the garden staring out over the explosion of blooms he had had planted for her pleasure. She didn't acknowledge him or give any sign she knew he stood beside the bench.

"Angelia," he pushed her pale-blue muslin gown to one side then sat down beside her on the white, wrought-iron bench to take her small hands in his, "I am glad to see you are out in the fresh air enjoying the beauty of your garden."

She pulled her cold hands away from him, folded them in her lap. "I go where I am told to go."

"Who told you to come here?" He kept his anger at bay.

"Sarah. She said I would feel better in the fresh air than sitting in the house."

"And she's right." The anger drained from him. "The sunlight is good for you. It will put some color back in your cheeks."

"Why do you keep me here?"

Jonathan drew in his breath then reached out, taking her by her shoulders to turn her around. "Because I love you. You are my wife, Angelia. Everything I do is done to make you happy."

"No, Jonathan." Her beautiful green eyes filled with tears, bringing fresh pain to his already suffering heart. "If you loved me, you would let me go. The love I felt for you is dead. Slain by your own hand."

Jonathan leaped to his feet. "You will never leave me, Angelia! If I can't have your love, then I will have to be content with your hatred, but no matter what emotion you see fit to give me, it will be given in my home, in my bed, with you as my wife!"

"I wish to go back inside now." She rose to her feet.

Jonathan remained seated watching her walk away from him, and in that moment, made up his mind to have her in every way a man could have the woman he lusted for.

He could see Angelia seated at the table when he came downstairs that evening for dinner. "I won't need you anymore this evening, Sarah. I will serve our dinner. My wife and I wish to be alone."

The older woman nodded, her dark face betraying none of her feelings. "As you wish, Monsieur. Do you want I should pour the wine before I leave?"

"No. That will be all, Sarah."

She lingered for a moment, her dark eyes skimming over the young girl seated at the table.

"Leave us!" Jonathan told her without looking up.

The woman turned and, without a backward glance, walked from the room.

"You will excuse me for a moment, Angelia." Jonathan pushed back his chair to walk into the kitchen. Taking the wine from where it sat, already open on the counter, he walked back into the dining room. With deliberate ease, he picked up the wineglass placed to the side of her plate. "You will dine with me tonight, Angelia, and you will drink with me."

"I do not wish to drink with you, Jonathan."

"Whether you wish it or not, you will do as I ask."

He turned his back to her as he poured the wine into her glass then reached into his pocket, withdrawing a small packet of powder, which he sprinkled into the wine. "You said earlier you do not wish to stay here anymore. I have been thinking about what you said, and I have arrived at a working compromise." He poured his own glass full.

"Please take away the wine. I do not want it."

"No, but tonight you will humor me and join me in celebrating, what well may be, your yearned-for freedom."

Angelia looked at him, her eyes filled with hope. "What are you talking about, Jonathan?"

"First, we will dine, then we will toast your freedom." He took his seat and, after placing a slice of roast beef on his plate, passed her the platter. "I am trying my best to be civil, Angelia. You are not helping me by refusing to eat."

In silence, she placed a small piece of the meat on her plate and, without thinking, followed it with a helping of each of the dishes Jonathan passed to her. "I pray you are not giving me false hope, Jonathan."

"Quite the contrary. I am offering you something that will benefit us both, my beautiful wife. After tonight you will see me when you desire to see me. I will never force you to come to me unless you wish me to."

Angelia picked up her knife and fork, cutting her meat into small bite-size portions. "Can I trust you?"

Jonathan almost laughed at her innocence. "You have my word, Angelia. After tonight, the times I will even acknowledge you are when you yourself want me to."

Happy now she joined him in their first relaxing meal together in almost a year.

Jonathan almost felt sorry about tricking her as he watched her enjoying her food. Then he remembered all the times he had come to her bed just to be turned away, and his guilty feelings dissolved. As his wife, she needed to realize what he expected from her.

When their plates were empty, Jonathan wiped his mouth on a white linen napkin. Taking up his glass of wine, he held it out to touch hers as she raised it towards him. "To fulfilled desires."

Angelia smiled as the sweet red wine slipped down her throat. "To kept promises," she whispered, her eyes holding his.

Jonathan nodded, watching her over the rim of his glass. Spying her empty glass, he picked up the wine bottle to replenish both their drinks.

Very soon, Angelia found herself laughing at everything Jonathan said. Her mood had a lightness, and she sang songs she had not recalled since being a very young girl.

Jonathan enjoyed this happy, carefree Angelia. The color

staining her cheeks gave her a healthy glow. Time after time, she held out her glass to be refilled, and Jonathan obliged her. He did not refill his own, however. He wanted to keep a clear mind for the night ahead.

Angelia danced her way into the other room, and as Jonathan came after her, she held out her arms to him, welcoming his embrace. She tipped back her head, staring up at him, her full mouth inviting and wet with wine.

Jonathan crushed her against him, then pulled back her head, running his wet mouth over her throat. His desire for her mounted as he heard her laughter. Unable to wait any longer, he scooped her unresisting body up in his strong arms, walking toward the winding staircase.

Angelia wrapped her arms around his neck, the wineglass dangling from her fingers. She wondered at her happiness then put the question from her mind as Jonathan continued to climb the stairs with her held in his arms.

She made no protest when Jonathan walked past her room to carry her into his. He placed her on the bed then stood back watching her. "Don't you think it is time you disrobed, Angelia?"

With a wry smile, she propped herself up on her elbows. "No!" She kicked out her legs, the movement lifting her gown away from her ankles. "You may undress me, Jonathan."

He moved forward, rolling her over on her stomach and undoing the back of her gown. With no respect for the gown's worth, he pulled it from her body, throwing it over his head where it landed in a heap on the floor. Caught up in the frenzy of her wine-induced mood Jonathan ripped the flimsy undergarments from her body, bringing a trill of laughter from her.

Jonathan stood back, jerking the clothes from his body in his haste to be inside her. He dropped down on the soft bed pulling her into his arms, his body on fire with his need.

Angelia pushed at him trying to sit up. But he would not allow her to pull away from him. He had waited too long to have her like this.

"Jonathan, let me go!" she screamed out her demand. "I cannot breathe!"

He drew back, staring at her. "What is it? What is wrong?" His words came in breathless pants.

"I am too hot! I must have air," she told him, scrambling off the bed and running from the room.

In an instant, Jonathan sprinted after her. Together they raced outside unmindful of their nakedness to sprawl headlong onto the soft grass. He rolled atop her, panting aloud as she spread her long legs wide.

"Take me, Jonathan!" she cried out her need. Her long nails trailing a bloody path down his naked back. As he rammed into her, she wrapped her legs around his waist, drawing him deep inside her.

Angelia screamed, her hot cries splitting the silence as she rained kisses over his chest, suckling his nipples and driving him mad with desire. He raised his hips then slammed them downward in complete abandonment. He no longer cared about the small girl trapped beneath him. He cared about the hot cravings driving his body to reach more extreme heights until, at last, the hot juices spewed from his body, giving him the release he so longed for. Exhausted, he slumped forward.

Angelia beat at him with her small fists. Her body squirming beneath him.

When he could, Jonathan raised up to stare down at her. "What is it, my love?"

"You have not stilled the hunger in my body, Jonathan. I demand you end this pain!" Her long legs swung out, gripping him.

"Angelia," he panted, dropping back down on her. "You must give me time to regain my strength."

"Now, Jonathan!" She beat at him. "You will satisfy me now!"

In a fury, Jonathan unwrapped her body from his to get to his feet. "You are very demanding for a woman who never wanted me to touch her before." He walked a short distance away, relishing the cool breeze blowing across his hot body.

"That does not matter!" she told him, coming to stand before him. She filled her hands with his thick black hair. "I want you to touch me! Now!"

At her closeness, Jonathan could feel his body beginning to respond. He rubbed his loins against her, laughing deep in his throat as he heard her sharp intake of breath.

Angelia jumped into his arms then screamed as Jonathan grabbed her hips, entering her and yanking her legs around his waist. He held onto her as she ground her small hips against him, then cried out, her body going slack in his arms. As he felt himself shrink inside her, he withdrew from her, but instead of standing her on her feet, he threw her small body over his shoulder to walk down the hill and into the cool, clear water.

Angelia squealed as the water touched her hot body. She wrapped her arms around Jonathan's neck as he moved them further and further out.

Jonathan laughed, happy to have his woman in his arms where she belonged and knowing now, she would never want to leave him. Jonathan leaned in, taking her full mouth with his. Angelia threw out her arms, arching her back to bring her full, pink-tipped breasts within easy reach of his hungry mouth. He did not disappoint her.

As dawn crept over the estate, he carried her back inside and up to his room. Wrapped in his arms, she fell into a deep and satisfying sleep. When they woke hours later, she turned to him, welcoming him into her body and basking in the pleasures he brought to the both of them.

With the added help of a desire-inducing powder called Cantharis, their life together continued to be good. But little by little, against the advice of the one who supplied him with the strong aphrodisiac, Jonathan laced her food and drink more and more, and as her hunger mounted, he introduced her to the dark side of his life. However, he never let her know the full extent of his secrets.

On the nights when his body cried out in hunger for the taste of blood and human flesh, he would leave her, returning when his jaded appetites had been satisfied and when he knew the putrid stench of decomposition no longer lingered upon his skin.

Angelia refused to acknowledge what she had seen that night long ago when she had returned to find Jonathan standing over her mother's body. Telling herself it couldn't have been Jonathan. She saw a beast. Jonathan convinced her she had been in shock and only imagined what she saw. By now, she needed him so much she would believe anything he said, as long as he didn't send her away.

One night, unable to sleep, she left their bed to go out for a walk on the grounds. The full moon guided her steps. She heard a noise over near the trees. It sounded like someone moaning in pain, and she hastened her steps to find out who might be in need of her help. When she got closer, she saw a young girl sprawled on the ground, her nude body covered in blood. Angelia knelt down, trying to find out what had happened. Then she saw him. Her mind flashed back to that night long past when she had seen the same horrible figure standing over her own mother.

She got to her feet.

The figure watched her and, smelling her fear, came closer, his need for blood still strong.

Angelia screamed and turned to run, and in her scream, he recognized the woman he loved. He stepped back, preparing to run.

"Jonathan!" his name spilled from her lips as she came forward. "No! Don't run from me, Jonathan. I know it is you. And now I know it was you I saw all those years ago." The sharp pain stabbing into her heart tore at her without mercy.

Jonathan stared at her, his large yellow eyes taking in her pain. He tried to draw her to him, but she backed away out of his reach.

"No! Don't touch me! I can never bear for you to touch me again!" She grew more hysterical in her fear and pain.

Jonathan grabbed her, trying to shake her into staying with him. Then it seemed as though he slipped out of control. He could hear her screams telling him how much she hated him for killing her mother and for destroying their life together. At last, he realized her screams no longer tortured him, and he let her go. He watched as her small body slid to the ground. He dropped to his knees, trying to shake her awake. As his attempts to revive her remained futile, he gave up and, getting to his feet, walked away.

When he returned the next morning, he found her lifeless body still lying on the ground, and he screamed out his agony.

And screamed and screamed until he felt someone shaking him. Jonathan opened his eyes to see Quigly standing over him.

"Jonathan, you must be quiet. The police are all over the grounds."

Jonathan threw off his hands and, grabbing the armrest, pushed himself from the couch. Sweat poured from his body. He walked to the end of the cave and, kneeling down, splashed cold water over his face. He reached out, accepting the towel Quigly held out to him. When he returned to the couch, he felt someone watching him. Looking up, he glared at the man seated in the chair next to him. But for once, Quigly refused to look away.

"I think the time has come for us to go from here, Jonathan. The danger of your being found out is too great for you to stay any longer."

Jonathan looked at him, then nodded.

CHAPTER TWENTY-FOUR

"Seelah said the passageway's hidden behind these shelves." Donavan placed one hand on the rear of the smooth sideboard, the other on the front then pulled. "They're attached to the wall. Who the hell would do that?" He moved his head, trying to see beneath the shelves. "If they aren't detachable, then there has to be some kind of button or release here somewhere." He ran his fingers along each shelf, feeling for anything out of place.

Jack was busy on the other side, running his hands down every inch of the shelves and coming up short of finding anything. "If somethin's here, I'll be damned if I can find it."

"Get the dogs down here. I want to see their reaction."

"There's just one way they could sniff anythin' out, and that's if someone's standin' on the other side. And to be honest with you, I doubt they could detect anything even then. This whole goddamn wall's made out of brick. Dogs can't smell through brick!"

"They can if the wall is raised a ways off the floor. With these shelves attached like they are, I can't tell if that's what's going on, though. The shelves are made of wood," he ran a hand over the boards, "but if I rip them out and we don't find anything behind them, then I'm liable for the damage. I'm not ready to take that chance yet."

"Hell, I'll do it!" Jack said, already starting forward.

"No! We can't destroy something until we know what we're dealing with. Seelah said Brandy dug near the bottom of the shelves." He stooped down, and as he did, saw small scratches on the edge of one of the boards. "Here they are."

"I don't know." Jack looked around the basement. "Seelah told us she felt someone standing on the other side of the wall. I still don't believe in all this psychic bullshit, even though Chandra seemed able to do a lotta strange shit. But Seelah don't strike me as a crackpot."

"All I know is there's something damn strange going on here." Donavan placed his hands on his hips, looking around the room. "The night we came out here and saw a light in one of the upstairs windows and smelled the candle, we were cold stone sober, and we didn't find jack-shit! There has to be some way he's getting in and out of this house without anyone seeing him! We just have to find out how he's doing it."

"I have a thought."

"What's that?"

"Seelah said Chandra warned her to get out of here. Right?"

"Where you going with this, Jack?"

"If Chandra knew 'bout Seelah bein' in this house, then she should be able to find out when someone else is here, don't you think?"

"What do you propose we do to find out?" Donavan waited, hoping he didn't suggest they leave to go talk to her.

"Let's call her in. Send out a couple of the boys to haul her ass down to the station and interrogate her, same as we'd do with anyone else we suspected of withholding information."

"That's not a bad idea." Donavan blew out his breath. "In fact, I think it's a damn good idea. If we can't find anything on our own, we'll bring her in. In the meantime, let's do what I suggested earlier. Get the dogs down here and see what they can find."

Alone, Donavan continued looking for something that would prove Seelah's theory about a secret passageway. He withdrew his glasses from his shirt pocket. "Now, at least I can see what the hell I'm doing." He walked back over to the shelves to run his hands back and forth beneath each board. "Hindel, you sick son of a bitch, I know you're not smarter than me, so where the hell do you have it hidden?"

Jack led the way down the basement steps. "How's the search comin'? Find anything yet?"

Donavan shook his head. "I want the dogs over here by these shelves. Also, does anyone have a flashlight?"

"Yeah, I got one right here." Jamison withdrew a flashlight from the side of his belt. "Here you go, Lieutenant."

"Thanks." Donavan took the light then walked back over to the shelves. Kneeling down on the basement floor, he shone the light over the structure then lay down all the way to shine it underneath. "Well… what…have…we…got…here?" he breathed. "Help me up, Jack."

Jack held out a hand, bracing both feet flat on the floor as he pulled Donavan to his feet. "What'd you find?"

"Looks like a long, coarse black hair." He shone the light on his open hand. "I found it stuck to the edge of the bottom board. The way it was positioned, it looks as though it could have rubbed off on the edge as someone brushed past it. But if that's the case, where the hell were they going? There's just one place to go, and that's straight ahead." He walked back over to the shelves shining the beam from top to bottom.

"Which means maybe Seelah's theory of a secret passageway ain't so far-fetched after all." Jack grinned, looking at the long hair in Donavan's hand.

"Okay, let's see what the dogs can turn up." Donavan motioned Jamison forward then stepped back out of the way.

Both dogs snarled, leaping at the shelves and whining.

"What the hell's wrong with you two? Nobody can fit behind there." Jamison pulled on the leashes, trying to settle them down.

"Accordin' to them they can, and have," Jack spoke up, patting each dog on his head. "Ok, Donavan, where do we go from here?"

"Let me think about it a moment."

"I suggest we get a wreckin' crew in here and take out this whole section." He aimed widespread hands at the wall.

"It's not that easy, Jack. First, we'd need a court order, and to get that, we have to show probable cause why we think we need one. What are we going to say? A psychic told us there's a secret passageway in Hindel's basement? Don't think it'll wash."

"Then you tell me, Lieutenant Hays, what do you suggest?" Jack said, his voice filled with impatience.

"I suggest we go talk to Quigly about all this. If we get lucky, maybe he'll let something slip we can put down on paper to get your wrecking crew out here."

"Quigly's not at his cottage, Lieutenant," one of the deputies spoke up. "We already checked. His car's there, but he's nowhere around."

"Hmmm. Wonder where the little fuck slithered off to." Jack said.

"Behind the wall, perhaps?" Donavan pulled a handkerchief from his pocket to wipe the sweat from his face. "I don't know about the rest of you, but it's too goddamn hot down here for me."

"Yeah, you'd think Hindel would have sense enough to put some windows down here." Jack turned toward the stairs.

"People can look through windows, Jack." Donavan followed behind him out of the basement. "This is a house of secrets."

"Not for long, partner, 'cause I'll let you in on a little secret of my own. I'm gonna get this sick son of a bitch if I have to blow this fuckin' place clean off its foundation!"

"That should erase any doubt some of the higher-ups might still have about reinstating you," Donavan laughed.

"Go ahead and laugh. But when it happens, don't say I didn't warn you!" Jack opened the door to walk outside. "What are you thinkin' 'bout, now?"

"Quigly not being in his cottage when his car's outside. Jamison!" he called out as the man came through the door. "Get the dogs over here."

"We'll take them down to Quigly's place; see if they can track him. I'm getting anxious to know where he is myself."

"Could be out killin' somethin' for breakfast," Jack laughed.

They stopped in front of the cottage allowing the dogs to pick up Quigly's scent, then followed behind as they took off towards the lake.

"Maybe you're right, Jack. He's down at the lake fishing."

"Not the type."

When they got to the lake, the dogs turned in circles, splashing in and out of the water.

"Must be out in a boat, Lieutenant. The tracks stop right at the water's edge. Just like they always do," Jamison said.

Donavan looked around the area. "Nobody shoved a boat off here. If they did, then they walked out to it."

"Jamison's right. Every time we get close to somethin', the trail ends right at the water's edge." Jack lit up a cigarette, handed it to Donavan before lighting another one. "The night Paulson got attacked, whatever attacked him ran off towards the swamp. Another time the tracks stopped right at the water's edge. This can't all be a coincidence." Jack motioned Donavan off to the side.

"What?"

"I just had a thought. Maybe he has more than one way in and out of that house. Could be they got somethin' goin' beneath the water. Remember, a lot of those secret passages used to hide slaves."

"Goddamn, you might have something!" Donavan could feel his excitement rising. "Seelah said this house had to be a couple hundred years old!"

"Speakin' of psychics, I still say Chandra knows a lot more 'bout this house than she's sayin'."

"Hey, I'm not arguing with you." Donavan held up his hands. "We're going to follow up on bringing her in if we need to. I also think Seelah might be able to tell us more about this place. We'll ask her about it when we get home tonight."

"Do you think she'll wanna spend the night again?"

"She sure as hell can't go back to her place for a while."

"That's right. And with Hindel still on the loose, I might just as well stay over, too. Don't you think?"

"Oh, by all means!" Donavan turned before Jack saw the

grin broadening out across his face.

"Another thing we can try is Search and Rescue. Their divers can go in where most of the tracks have been disappearin' and branch out from there. Sound like a good plan?

"Yeah…it could work."

"We won't have any problem, gettin' that okayed. There's more than enough probable cause. And if we do get a bitch 'bout the cost, we'll just give them the old "reckin' crew versus divers scenario."

"Let's go call it in." Donavan swung his arm forward, motioning the men back to the house.

While they waited for Search and Rescue to arrive, Donavan, Jack and the other deputies sat around the kitchen table eating their lunch.

"Is it just me, or does anyone else feel uneasy bein' here?" Mark Ashworth, one of the bolder deputies, spoke up.

"It's the house," Jack said, pulling the tab from a can of soda. "Place gives everyone the willies, and even more so bein' almost empty like this."

"I feel like…if I could whip around fast enough… I could catch someone standin' right in that archway." Mark motioned with a nod of his head.

Needing to get off the subject of eerie feelings, Jamison put down his ham and cheese sandwich. "Anyone heard how Paulson's doing since he got released from the hospital?"

Donavan grinned over at him then got serious. "He's doing great. Last time I talked to him," he glanced upward for a moment, "I think about four days ago, he told me he expected to be back to work in less than a week."

"That's good news," Ashworth said. "Paulson's a good man. I like workin' with him. I'm anxious to hear all about what happened to him that night." He glanced around the table at the other men.

"Whatever you hear, just be sure you keep it to yourself," Donavan warned him.

"Oh, I will, Lieutenant. That's one of the first things they taught us at the Police Academy, that whatever goes on inside the department is not to be discussed outside the department." A pleased smile spread across his handsome face as he shared this information, then disappeared. "There is one thing I'd like to know, though."

"What's that?" Donavan talked around his mouthful of chicken sandwich.

"Did a werewolf attack him?"

Donavan swallowed his food, wiped his mouth on a paper napkin. "As a matter of fact, Mark, we think it could have been a werewolf."

"Sh…it." He pushed his glasses up further on his nose, his blue eyes looking around the room and coming to rest on Jack. "What do you think, Olivier'?" His voice was much quieter now.

"Tell you the truth; I don't know what to think!" He stuffed the hamburger wrappers, used catsup and mayo packets and napkins into the empty sack, wadded the sack into a ball and, without taking aim, lobbed it into the tall wastepaper basket sitting across the kitchen. "Although I will say this. More I find out 'bout this turd-bowl, more inclined I am to keep an open mind 'bout the place.

Voices out front in the driveway brought the men to their feet. Without being told, each man gathered up his own sack and napkins to throw them into the wastebasket.

Walking outside, they waited as the men climbed out of the van. The driver got out, slamming the door behind him and holding out his hand to Donavan. "How's it goin'?"

"Meredith." Donavan shook his hand. "Didn't take you very long."

"Went off without a hitch." Vince Meredith grinned. "Captain called, said you needed a boat and divers out at the Hindel place A.S.A.P., so here we are." He glanced over as Jack walked up to them. "Glad to hear the good news, Olivier'." He slapped a lean hand down on Jack's back. "Department needs all the good men they can get."

"Thanks," Jack told him.

"So, where do you want us?"

"Hold on a minute. Ashworth," Donavan called out, "I

think we can handle it from here. You and the rest of the men can go on back to the station. Stick around there, though, case we need you."

"Are you sure, Lieutenant?" Ashworth came forward. "We don't mind hanging around." He glanced at the other men, who nodded in agreement.

"I don't want to tie you up here if you're not needed," Donavan said with regret seeing how anxious they were to stay.

"I think it'd be a good idea if they stayed," Jack said. "Things have a way of happenin' real fast in this place."

Donavan thought about what Jack said for a moment and agreed. "I guess it couldn't hurt. All right, Mark, go ahead and show Meredith where we found the prints." Donavan turned to point the way.

"You mean you want me to drive over the lawn?" Meredith looked at him to see if he'd heard right.

"I mean, I want you to drive straight over the lawn and down to the water."

"Hindel's gonna pitch a fit if his lawn gets messed up!" He spat a stream of Copenhagen off to the side, wiped his mouth on his hand.

"I don't give a shit what Hindel does. Besides, he's in England. Remember? At least, that's what everyone's supposed to think. We got an emergency here. We don't have time to call England."

"Just remember it's your ass if anything comes of this," Meredith told him as he opened the door to the van.

"That's right, and I'll be glad to take all responsibility."

While the divers suited up, Meredith backed the boat off the trailer and into the water. "How far out do you want them to go?"

"What would you say, Jack? About fifty yards?"

"That should do it. Maybe even a little less if we're usin' Quigly' as a guesstimation."

The divers climbed into the boat. When they were seated, the driver turned the key, starting up the engine. Putting the boat in reverse, he backed a little ways out, then turned, heading the boat in the direction Meredith told him to go.

"I told them to stay down twenty minutes at a time. That way, if they run into any trouble, we can move on it fast," Meredith said. "We're going to send two divers down at a time while the other two wait in the boat. Most of the time, they go in different directions so they can cover more territory, but this time I told them to stay together."

"Good idea," Donavan agreed. "This place calls for extra precaution."

"Do you think Hindel's got an underwater cave down there?"

"If he's not using another passage in through the house, then an underwater cave has to be something to think about."

"I never met Jonathan Hindel, but I've had the displeasure of meeting his son, Lawrence. Now he's a sick little son of a bitch! I went to the trial on the Rawlins' murders. I saw you there."

"Oh yeah!" Donavan removed his hat, drawing a hand back over his sweating head. "Jack had to be there too. As investigating detectives on the case, we didn't have a choice. Were you there for Hindel's big performance?"

"I missed it. I got called out, so I couldn't get back to court until the next day. I heard bits and pieces of it, but I never could get the whole story."

"I'll let Jack tell you about it," Donavan chuckled.

"Little prick's lucky I didn't put a bullet in his head that day," Jack scoffed, plopping down on the grass.

"What did he do?" Meredith dropped down beside him.

"Son of a bitch tried to kill me over my testimony." A scowl broke out across his boyish face as he recalled the incident. "I'd already stepped down to walk back to my seat when I heard a woman scream, "look out"! I looked up in time to see someone come flyin' over the bench, right at me!"

"What did you do?" Meredith leaned in close.

"After beatin' his face in?" Jack grinned over at Donavan. "I left him twitchin' and bleedin' in the aisle! The judge halted the proceedings while the bailiff got the ambulance there. They hauled his ass off to the hospital, patched him up, and the next day he showed up in court sportin' a straightjacket!"

Meredith popped the lid on a fresh can of Copenhagen to place a pinch of the smokeless tobacco behind his lower lip. "What did the judge do to you for beating up a prisoner? Everyone on the department tried to find out, but it got hushed up too quick."

"Nothin'. He saw the whole thing and knew I had to defend myself. Or at least that's the way it went down in the incident report. The judge saw the pictures taken at the scene."

"I can't believe he just got a year locked up in a nut-ward for that shit!" Vince tongued the tobacco to a more comfortable position. "How the hell did he pull it off?"

"His father paid his way out," Donavan told him. "Money talks, Meredith. If you don't believe that, go take a look at the new wing that's been added onto the mental hospital. It's real impressive."

"Yeah, but Jesus Christ! Didn't the doctors look at the crime scene pictures?"

"I'm sure they did. But money can quite a lot of guilt. I did some research after they turned Hindel loose. I found out the hospital had been trying to get the state to kick in the money they needed for another wing and a lot of expensive equipment. Jonathan Hindel turned out to be an answer to their prayers. With his money and promise Lawrence would be returned to England. What did they have to lose?"

Meredith reached for his radio as a voice came over the airway. "Yeah, go ahead."

"It's been over twenty minutes since the divers went down, Meredith. What do you want us to do now?" one of the divers who had remained in the boat asked.

"Hold on a moment," he told them, turning his attention on Donavan. "The divers aren't back yet, and it's been over the allotted time. What do you want to do?"

Donavan checked his watch. "They been down a little over twenty-six minutes. I think you better send in the other divers. Tell them to stay down no more than fifteen minutes. And if they spot a cave, they aren't to go inside. Tell them to come back up and let us know about it."

Meredith relayed Donavan's message then stood back watching as the other divers went over the side of the boat. "I got an uneasy feeling about this."

"Me too," Donavan said. "Got any suggestions, Jack?"

"Let's wait and see what the other two divers turn up. If they find a cave, then we got no choice on gettin' the wreckin' crew out here to go to work. You and I both know, Donavan, we stand a lot better chance defendin' ourselves on land than we do underwater."

Ten minutes passed while they watched and waited for the divers to come back up. Donavan paced the shoreline, his stomach getting tighter as the minutes passed.

Jack's hand shot out, pointing to the boat. "There they are!"

"Yeah, but I just see two of them. Where the hell are the other two?" Donavan breathed as the divers climbed into the boat.

The men walked down to the water as the boat made its way inland.

"What did you find?" Donavan walked forward as the men waded to shore.

"There's a cave down there all right," one of the men spoke up. "But you said not to go inside, so we didn't. We didn't see anything of the other two divers."

"Let's get back up to the jeep. I want to call this in on the cell phone," Donavan said, already walking away.

"Do you think you'll have a problem gettin' the okay for the wreckin' crew, now?" Jack fell in beside him.

"I better not," Donavan growled, worry over the lost divers making his stomach twist and turn.

When they got to the house, Donavan unlocked the jeep, reached inside for his cell phone. He punched in the numbers. "Barb, I thought I better let you know we're going to be late getting home tonight," he spoke into the phone. "We sent some divers down to see what they could find, and they found a cave."

"A cave!" Barbara echoed on the other line. "What did you find in the basement?"

"Nothing yet, but we're getting a wrecking crew out here to see what's on the other side of the wall."

"Hold on a moment, Donavan. Seelah wants to talk to you."

"Donavan?" Seelah said.

"Yeah, I'm here."

"I heard Barb say something about a cave."

"Yeah, we thought it might be a good idea to send down some divers straight out from where the footprints keep disappearing into the water. So far, two of them haven't come back up. The other two we sent down say they saw a cave."

"Donavan."

"What?"

"The other two divers you sent down were inside the cave."

"That's what I thought. I just hope we can get that wall down fast enough to get them out of there."

"I'm sorry, but there's no need for haste. The divers are already dead."

CHAPTER TWENTY-FIVE

Quigly fought his way to the top, gasping for air as his head cleared the water. "I can't breathe." He thrashed around.

"Breathe in and out. You will call attention to us splashing around like this!"

"I can't help it, Jonathan," he panted. "I can't swim that well! I thought I wouldn't reach the top!"

"You idiot! Look around you! You are safe. Chandra has the boat secreted beneath the over-hanging branches of that weeping willow tree!"

"Yes!" Quigly looked in the direction Jonathan pointed. "Yes, I see it now." He began dog paddling towards the boat.

Chandra reached down, helping each man into the boat. "We must leave here. The police are all over the grounds of the mansion."

Jonathan picked up the oars propelling the boat a short ways away from the tree but staying close to shore so as not to be seen. "They will not be looking for us outside the cave yet. We will be all right."

"Where will you go, Jonathan? The police are searching for you both."

"They will be searching even more when they enter the cave. I had to kill the two divers they sent. They won't find them for a while, though. I weighted them down and sent their bodies to the bottom of the lake."

"You didn't answer my question." She continued to watch him. "Where will you go?"

"The one place I will be safe." He smiled at her, rowing the boat out into the water.

***

Donavan continued to pace the shore as he waited for the wrecking crew to arrive. He refused to believe Seelah's warning about the two divers. However, he did find it hard to dispute the fact. If still alive, they would have surfaced by now.

"How long does it take a crew of five men to get ready?" Jack growled, dropping down on the ground. "They're gonna screw 'round and let Hindel get away."

"How the hell is he going to get away? We can see all the way out across the lake."

"It's a big lake, Donavan! He can swim downstream then come in to shore."

Donavan keyed the mike on his radio. "This is Hays; I need you to position men up and down the shoreline starting a few yards from the mansion. Also, alert all cab companies to be on the lookout for anyone matching the descriptions of Jonathan Hindel, Lawrence Hindel or Quigly."

"You better put a man at the bus depots and the airport too, Donavan."

"Good idea!" He keyed the mike again.

Jack leaped to his feet, an angry scowl spreading across his face. "What the hell are they doin' here?"

Donavan spun around to see Barbara and Seelah making their way down the hill towards them. In quick strides, he and Jack closed the distance.

"Before you start yelling, hear us out." Barbara threw out a hand to silence them.

"It better be good!" Jack said.

"Where are the girls?" Donavan asked.

"The girls are next door with Mrs. Jennings. I told her we needed to run an errand, and she said she would keep an eye on them for me."

"Why are you here?" Jack glanced at both women, but his eyes kept returning to Seelah.

"I felt I could be of help to you," Seelah told him.

"How can you help? If they made it out of the cave

undetected, which I doubt, we've already alerted the entire sheriff's department to be on the lookout for them. You can't do any more than that!"

"They aren't in the cave, and furthermore, the sheriff's department can't see what I can, Jack." She smiled up at him.

"Can't hurt to let her try." Donavan shrugged his shoulders as Jack glanced over at him. "We need all the help we can get on this."

"The promise to keep clear of this place sure didn't last long, did it?" Jack muttered

"Let's go up to the house. I seem to work better from there. Besides, there's something I still need to do," Seelah told them, already turning in the direction of the mansion.

The others followed behind. When they got to the door, Jack halted them.

"Let me go in first. If you say they're no longer in the cave, then they could be inside, hidin' somewhere."

"They aren't here, Jack. I would have felt their presence if they were." Seelah tried to keep a straight face as Jack glared at her. "It's not my fault every guess you make is wrong."

"I hope you're not gonna start this hocus-pocus bullshit again," Jack told her. "I don't think my nerves could take it."

"Then you better go elsewhere 'cause I'm going to do something you might not want to see."

"Like what?" His voice grew angry as they walked into the house.

Seelah ignored him, turning instead in the direction of the living room. "Peggy Rawlins," she called out. "I know you're here. No one is going to hurt you, little one. The man who has kept you here is gone for the time being. Let me send you to the other side where your family and loved ones wait to welcome you home."

Silence grew in the room as everyone waited to see what would happen next. Jack could stand the silence no longer.

"What are you doin'?" Jack spread his hands wide, spinning around. "Look around you. There's no one here!"

"Be quiet, Jack. I know you don't believe in this, but right now, you can do a lot of harm. A child's soul is in jeopardy. Jonathan Hindel has kept her in this house for his own sick reasons. Now that he's gone, I can send her on. Don't make her lose this opportunity."

"What the hell is that?" Donavan whispered, drawing Barbara close against him as a small white orb shot across the room.

Jack drew his gun, looking around.

"You don't need that gun, Jack. Put it away before you frighten her," Seelah told him, her voice becoming impatient.

With reluctance, Jack stuck the.38 back in his belt.

"Tell her you mean her no harm, Jack! Do it now!" Seelah said.

"Do it, Jack, please," Barbara pleaded. "We're talking about a child."

"I'm not gonna hurt you, little girl. So, come out, come out, wherever you are."

For a moment, nothing happened then, as they stood there, the white orb took on the appearance of a young girl.

"Hello, Peggy," Seelah said, her voice soft and gentle.

"Can you help me?" the small voice asked.

"Yes, I can, Peggy. All you have to do is look around until you see a very bright light, then walk towards it."

The child held out her arms, walking forward. "Mama?" she whispered, then more excited as she started to run. "Mama!"

"Goodbye, Peggy," Seelah whispered into the quiet.

Jack stood his mouth open wide, shaking his head back and forth in rapid succession. "I don't believe what I just saw!"

"That makes two of us partner," Donavan breathed.

"Now that Peggy is gone, this house is free of any ghosts. With a good psychic cleansing, it could be a nice place again."

"I think you're forgettin' 'bout what still lives here, Seelah." Jack walked over and, putting his arms around her waist, pulled her close against him to place a light kiss on her forehead. "That's for what you did for a lost little girl." He drew back, smiling down at her. "And, you could be right. After we get rid of the rest of the riffraff, this house could be a good place to live. Who knows, maybe the next one to move in'll be a vampire."

"Seelah, you said Hindel isn't in the cave. Do you know where he might be?" Donavan spoke up.

For a long moment, she remained quiet, breathing in deep breaths. "No. I'm being blocked again."

"What do you mean you're being blocked?" Donavan asked.

"Remember? I told you about it before. If I try to see something that someone doesn't want me to see, they can block me."

"Oh yeah, I forgot. You did tell me about that." A sheepish grin spread across his face as Barbara looked over at him.

"Who would do that, though?" Jack asked, then turned away.

"Yes, it could be Chandra, but it could also be Jonathan Hindel. He is very strong in his abilities to block out what he doesn't want known. Or, put something in someone's mind that doesn't exist."

"Like…making Mrs. Stewart think her daughter's calling her back to this house," Donavan spoke up.

"He needed to get the Stewart children back here," Seelah said. "I would guess he used Peggy Rawlins to impersonate Margaret. He is a very evil man."

"Sounds like we got company." Jack peeked out the kitchen window. "Yeah, the wreckin' crew's here, Donavan."

"Go let them in the back way. We'll meet you downstairs." Donavan ushered Barbara and Seelah ahead of him.

"My heart is already racing thinking about the last time we were down here," Barbara said.

"I wish you'd stop reminding me of that, Barb." Donavan walked over to the shelves.

As Seelah started to follow, Barbara reached out, halting her. "Do you think it is Chandra who's blocking you from seeing where Hindel is?"

"Yes, but I didn't want to say anything in front of Jack."

"Why do you think she's blocking you?"

"I think she's with him."

"Come on over here, Seelah, and see what you can feel." Donavan motioned her forward.

"All I can tell you is what I've already said. Hindel's not in the cave. That and this is where the secret passageway is. It shouldn't take long to get through. The door is right on the other side of these shelves, and it's raised a few inches off the floor. That's why Brandy could smell him standing on the other side."

"Well, in a few moments, we won't have to wonder anymore. He glanced up as Jack came down the stairs with five men trailing behind him.

"Where do you want us to begin?" the lead man asked as he stepped off the stairs.

"We need you to remove these shelves. We think the passageway's right behind them," Jack spoke up.

"Step back, and we'll soon find out! Do you want us to take it easy, or do you just want them out of here?" the man with a large sledgehammer asked.

"Take the son of a bitch down any way you can!" Jack told him.

"You got it." He raised the sledgehammer over his head then lowered it back down as Donavan reached out to take hold of his arm.

"Hold on a moment. Did you bring a crowbar?"

"Yeah, got one right here."

"Let me see it." Donavan took the bar from his hands and, walking over to the side of the shelves, looked for a place to get some leverage. "Nope." He stepped back. "I thought I could get the bar back behind the shelf enough to pry it forward, but it's attached right to the wall."

"Okay, look out, we're goin' with plan "A,"" the man with the sledgehammer told them.

"Let's move over to the other side and give them some room to work." Donavan slipped his arm around Barbara's waist.

"Good idea." Jack pulled Seelah with him across the floor. "One slip of that hammer, and we could end up squirrelly as Quigly!"

"We're through!" one of the men called out.

"Well, Christ, that was quick!" Jack walked back across the floor.

"The whole wall behind the shelves is made of wood. Once we got through the shelves, we just had to bust through the wood. So, now the question is, what else do you need brought down?"

"That's it. I guess you and your crew can be on your way," Donavan told him.

Along with Mark Ashworth and two other deputies, who had remained at the mansion, Jack took Seelah's hand as they followed Donavan and Barbara into the passageway. "Looks like he had all the comforts of home in here." He looked around the cave.

"I want everyone to stay together. There's no telling what may be in here," Donavan said, continuing on through the cave. As he got to the end, he could see the way the floor sagged downward into the water. "Here's the lead-in from the lake. Be careful. It's pretty slippery here." He pushed Barbara back from the entrance.

"I think you better come over here, Donavan." Jack squatted down on the heels of his shoes.

"What did you find?" Donavan walked over, peering at a wide spot on the floor. "Could just be the glow from the torches making it appear to be blood."

Jack turned his hand over, rubbing his thumb over his fingers. "No, it's blood."

"They surprised the divers as soon as they came into the cave, would be my guess.

"Yeah, now they're gone. In order to get away like that, with the house and grounds surrounded by cops, it's almost like they had someone waiting to pick them up."

"They could have called out on a cell phone, but I don't think a cell phone would be able to get out down here. I still get piss poor reception inside my house. And I didn't see a phone cord anywhere."

"Lieutenant," Ashworth spoke up, "if you don't need us anymore, we'd like to go back outside."

"No, go on. But stay together and keep your eyes open."

The three men were already walking towards the cave opening before Donavan had finished speaking.

Jack stood up and, walking over to Seelah, watched as she ran her hands over the furniture. "What are you doin'?"

"Getting a feel for the people who have been inside the cave."

Jack turned her to face him. "Seelah, I want to ask you somethin', and I want you to tell me the truth."

"Sure." Her dark eyes met his.

"Has Chandra been inside this cave?"

"Yes, Jack, she has."

"I thought so." Jack turned away, trying to slow the thunderous pounding inside his chest. Without looking at her, he allowed the words to flow from his mouth. "Is she the one who helped Hindel get away from here?"

Seelah yanked him around to face her. "Yes, she is! She has no choice, Jack! Jonathan calls to her with his mind. He has some kind of power over her." She dropped her hands to her side as he shrugged her away from him.

"I bet she's the one who told him about you bein' in the basement the other day, too. The bitch is evil!" Jack growled low in his throat.

"No, Jack, she isn't. She has changed."

"People like her can't change! Why can't you get that through your head?"

"Jack," she led him over to the couch, "the reason I can't agree with you is because I've seen the change in Chandra. I admit I don't know everything she's involved with. I do know she's involved with voodoo. I myself have never had anything to do with the practice, so I never went to any of the rituals. But as a psychic, I have the ability to tune into a person's energy. I can tell just by being close to a person if their spirit is white or dark."

"Now you're gonna try and tell me Chandra's one of the white ones even though she's into voodoo and Christ knows what else," he laughed, beginning to rise from the couch.

Seelah yanked him back down with surprising strength.

"You know what? You're starting to piss me off here!"

Jack looked at her then threw back his head, laughing aloud into the flickering shadows.

Donavan and Barbara stood motionless across the cave, watching and listening to what transpired between the two. When Barbara started to speak, Donavan squeezed her waist, silencing her.

Jack wiped his eyes, reached for a cigarette. "The downfall with that, though, is a person your size can't do a whole lot 'bout gettin' pissed off at someone." He flicked his lighter, eyed her over the trail of smoke wafting into the air.

Seelah could feel her temper rising as Jack continued to bait her. "For your information, I know Chandra's a white spirit. I even know when she turned from gray to white."

"I'll bite. When?" Jack looked at her, all trace of humor gone now from his face.

"When she met you." Seelah refused to lower her gaze.

"I don't care to talk 'bout that if you don't mind." He flicked his cigarette ashes on the floor of the cave.

"No! No, no! You're the one who started this." She poked a finger into his chest. "Now you're going to hear me out."

"I told you, I don't care to relive those days, goddamn it!"

"I know what you told me, Jack." Seelah raised her voice to match his. "And my answer to that is who cares what you want or don't want! You put down a woman I happen to feel a great deal of respect for. Now you're going to sit here, with your mouth shut, and listen while I tell you about her."

"In a pig's ass, I am!" Jack leaped from the couch but lost his footing to tumble backward as Seelah grabbed the pocket of his jeans, giving a hard yank. Before he could gather his wits, she straddled his legs to glare down at him.

"Now you listen to me, Jack Olivier'! You say Chandra just up and dropped you out of the blue. Well, I, for one, can't accept that! I knew her before she met you, and I know her now, and something doesn't add up. For a woman to change as much as she did, she had to have strong feelings for you!"

"If she did, she had a strange way of showin' it," he

whispered, all the fight gone out of him as he stared up at her.

"If I get off your lap, are you going to stay seated and talk this out?"

"Do I have a choice?" A slight grin spread across his face.

"I'm being serious, Jack. You were hurt bad when your relationship ended, and I think I can find out why it ended if you'll trust me."

"Okay, Ms. Psychic! Let's hear what you got."

Seelah got off his lap to sit beside him on the couch, and turning to face him, waited until he gave her his full attention. "When I first met Chandra, I thought her very cold. By this, I mean she would administer to those who needed her, but she did so without caring. I heard about her voodoo; strange stories of how she would choose young black girls for the pleasures of a certain man." She nodded as Jack's brows lifted. "Yes, Jonathan Hindel is the man they whispered about. It's said, when he finished with the girl, he would return her to Chandra, and she would remove the spirit of the one thought to inhabit their bodies. It's believed while the spirit had possession of the girl's body, the chosen one would take on the characteristics of the woman Jonathan craved to be with. Also, it's been rumored he loved this woman beyond belief. That he would go to any lengths to be with her."

"I don't mean to interrupt you, Seelah, but this might explain what we encountered the morning we found a girl wandering on the grounds of the mansion, Jack." He and Barbara walked over to sit down in the chair beside the couch.

"Could be," Jack said without turning. "I'm still listenin', Seelah."

"Whether these stories are true or not, I don't know." She continued with what she was saying. "I heard them from so many different people, so there has to be some validity to them."

"I'm...still...listenin', Seelah," Jack repeated once again.

"I'm getting to it, Jack, be patient." Seelah tried to hold onto her patience as Jack continued to prod her. "The change in her began some years ago. All of a sudden, she seemed happy, and she took time with the people who came to her for a healing or a psychic reading. She listened instead of rushing them away.

People saw her laughing for no reason and even singing. She was like a different woman." Seelah enjoyed talking about the woman she had come to admire. Then her voice dropped, and the smile left her face. "As I already told you, Jack, I went to Chandra to see if she could help me work through my grief. I could see a difference in her right away. Sometimes when offering me advice, it seemed like...instead of talking about me, she talked about herself."

"What do you mean by that?" Jack asked.

"I knew she had fallen in love with someone, but I could detect a sadness creeping in for some reason. One time when she held my hand as she comforted me, I tuned in to her energy, and I saw the face of the man she had fallen in love with. I saw you, Jack."

"If she loved me...so goddamn much...why did she drop me without a word of warning?! That...is what I'm waitin' to hear! And so far, you haven't told me anything to ease my mind!"

"You still have feelings for her, don't you, Jack?" Seelah leaned towards him.

Donavan's breath caught and held as he waited to hear Jack's answer.

"In all honesty? I don't know if it's...that I still have feelin's for her or...if it's just that...I want to know what the hell happened. I don't have the feelin's I had before she dumped me if that's what you're askin'. Of that, I have no doubt. I...mean...I went through too much pain for any of those feelin's to come back to life. But...it's almost like...I feel sorry for her in a way. If that makes any sense."

"It makes perfect sense, Jack," Seelah told him. "You know, in some strange way...and don't ask me why I think this because to tell you the truth...I don't have a clue...but...I feel Jonathan Hindel had something to do with why she ended her relationship with you."

Donavan pushed himself out of the chair. "I hate to break up this little discussion about hearts gone awry, but Hindel's still out there somewhere, and I don't think we're going to find him sitting here talking about him." He reached out, pulling Barbara to her feet.

"You're right, Donavan, we're not going to find him sittin' here." Jack stood, pulling Seelah up and into his arms. "But I'll make you a promise, right here…right now. We *will* find the son of a bitch!"

CHAPTER TWENTY-SIX

When they pulled into the driveway, dusk had already settled.

"I'll go get the girls, Donavan. I'm sure Mrs. Jennings thinks I've abandoned them by now." Barbara got out of the jeep.

"Here, give her this for watching them so long." Donavan held out a twenty-dollar bill and two fives. "Maybe getting paid for her troubles will make her a little more understanding."

"I can offer it to her, but I can tell you now, she won't take it." Barbara slipped the bills into the pocket of her jeans. "You know how fond she is of Jenny."

"Yeah, she's fond of Jenny, but she just spent about three hours with three kids and an untrained pup," Donavan reminded her as she walked away. He got out of the jeep, pushed the alarm button, and when he heard the beep dropped the remote in his pocket. "Barb will be right back. She went to get the girls," Donavan said as Jack and Seelah walked up to him.

"If you don't mind, Donavan," Seelah said as she and Jack walked past him carrying sacks of food they had stopped to pick up on the way home, "I'll go ahead and get the hamburgers, and everything put onto plates for everybody."

"You go right ahead. You know where everything is. I'm going to wait out here for Barb." He chuckled as he watched them walk up the porch steps and into the house.

"Do you need some help?" Jack placed both hands on her tiny waist, lifted her off her feet as she reached into the cupboard for the plates.

"Jack put me down! I'm not that short!" she squealed.

"Uncle Jack, are you flirting with Seelah?" Jenny laughed, coming into the kitchen with Rebecca and Lisa.

"Uncle Jack has a girlfriend!" the girls sang, lacing their arms to encircle the blushing couple, giggling as Brandy ran behind them, barking and nipping at their heels.

"That's enough out of you four." Donavan laughed, scooping Brandy up in his arms and heading for the back door.

Barbara shook her head at their antics as she leaned into the refrigerator to grab a bottle of ketchup. "Lisa, will you put this on the table for me, please?" She held out the bottle as Lisa hurried over to her.

Lisa turned towards the table, squealing with glee as Barbara reached out, swinging her up in her arms and snuggling her against her chest. Her eyes misted as she wondered what she would do when the time came for the girls to return to their parents.

"Everyone, take your seat before the food gets cold." Donavan sat down at the head of the table, surprise flitting across his face as he saw Jack pull out Seelah's chair for her.

"Donavan would you pass me the salt and pepper, please?" Barbara asked, then repeated her request as Donavan sat staring across the table.

"What?" he glanced at her.

"I asked if you would pass me the salt and pepper."

"Oh, yeah, sure." He pushed the seasonings towards her, then went back to watching the busy couple laughing and eating.

"Donavan, stop staring!" Barbara hissed over at him.

Jack looked up, grinning, as Donavan bit into his hamburger.

"Will you and Jack be going out after you're finished eating?" Barbara asked him.

"Yeah." He chewed, swallowed. "I want to see what's going on with the search. I'm going to have two deputies guarding the house here while we're gone, though. Just to be on the safe side." He glanced back down to the end of the table. "Don't you think that's a good idea, Jack?"

Jack turned, a french-fried potato, Seelah had stuck in

his mouth, dribbling ketchup over his lips. "Whatever you say, Donavan." He turned his attention back to Seelah.

"'Course, if you would rather stay here, I can always take one of the deputies with me."

Jack's head snapped around. "I'm ready to go whenever you are." He wrapped his lips around the bulging hamburger, biting and chewing and swallowing until it disappeared.

Seelah sat back, watching him, her own hamburger surrounded with a napkin. "I've never seen anyone eat a burger that fast and not choke," she laughed.

"Uncle Jack does it all the time," Jenny spoke up.

"Jenny," Donavan glanced at her, "you need to pay attention to your own plate."

Jenny dropped her eyes as Rebecca giggled.

The ringing of the phone had Barbara pushing back her chair to go and answer it. "Excuse me. I'll be right back."

"Finish up, Jack," Donavan told him, wiping his mouth on his napkin. "This might be the call we've been waiting for.

Jack lifted his plate over his head as Donavan walked to the sink. "Take mine, too. Just give me five minutes, and I'll be ready to go." He got to his feet to head off down the hall.

Barbara came back into the room. "I just talked with someone from the hospital. They called to tell us your parents are being released tomorrow morning." She looked at the girls as they sat staring at her. "Isn't that good news?" Barbara tried to sound cheerful.

"Does that mean we have to go back to that awful house?" Rebecca whispered.

"No, Darling." Barbara came around the table to gather both girls into her arms. "You don't ever have to go back there again."

"We want to stay here with you and Donavan and Jenny." She started to cry, slurring her words as she tried to be brave.

"We would love to have you stay, but your parents need you to be with them right now. As soon as you get moved into a nice house, we'll all come visit you."

"Do you promise?" Rebecca sniffed, her arms tightening

around Barbara's neck.

"I promise. We all promise." Barbara found it difficult to talk as her own tears flowed unchecked down her face.

"What's goin' on?" Jack walked up to the table.

Donavan pulled him into the other room. "The hospital called to say the Stewarts' are being released in the morning. The girls and Barb aren't taking it very well."

"Oh, Christ! I hope they come out better than they went in. We got enough problems to deal with!"

"I don't think they would be releasing them if they weren't ready." Donavan tried to ease his worries.

"Yeah? That's what they said 'bout Hindel!"

"Hindel landed in a mental hospital. The Stewarts' just made it to the psyche-ward of Saint Anthony Parish General!"

"I hope for the girl's sake they got their shit together!"

"Me too." He walked back into the kitchen. "Barb," Donavan pulled her to her feet to hold her against him for a long moment, "I hate to leave when I know you're upset, but we have to get back to work." He kissed her. "Are you going to be all right?"

"Yes. I got Seelah to help me."

"I called the station, Donavan. Dispatch said they sent Bailey, but he didn't know who'd be comin' with him. Said they'd be here in a few minutes." Jack delivered in passing as he made his way over to where Seelah remained seated, still finishing her dinner.

She grinned as he snatched a fry off her plate to pop it into his mouth. "You be careful out there, hotshot." She smiled up at him. "There's a full moon tonight, and you know what that means."

"Yeah, thanks for the reminder."

"All jokes aside, it's times like this you could use Chandra's help. She's a lot more powerful than me."

The blood drained from Jack's face as he pulled her up and out of her chair. "Come with me!"

Not wanting to make a scene in front of the children, Seelah allowed herself to be pulled from the table. As soon as they were through the front door, she turned on him. "What do you think you're doing yanking me around like this?" She glared at him.

"I'm sorry. I just had a hell of a thought!"

"What?" Her voice remained tinged with anger.

"Do you suppose that's where Hindel and Quigly could be hidin' out?"

"You mean at Chandra's place in the bayous?" She turned the idea over in her mind. "I think she is the one who helped them get away from the mansion, but I never gave a thought to the possibility she could be harboring them at her house.

"I think she could! They had to leave that cave in a boat, and no one has seen them since they got out of there. We had the banks up and down the lake patrolled, the bus depots on the lookout, and the airports. We also had the cab companies alerted. No one has called saying they've been spotted. So, what does that leave? I'll tell you what it leaves! It leaves a place that can only be reached by boat!"

"But...if that's the case, then the men patrolling the banks would have spotted them."

"Not if they got away before we had a chance to sound the alert!" Jack paced back and forth around the yard. "Quick!" He spun around, grabbing hold of her arm. "Do some of your hocus-pocus shit!" He snapped his fingers.

"Who do I look like, Samantha Stevens?" Seelah yanked away from him. "If you want *me* to twitch...you're going to have to ask me a lot nicer than that!"

"All right, I'm sorry!" Jack tried to quell his impatience. "Would... you...please...help me find this son of a bitch!?"

"That's better," she pecked him on his cheek, then became serious, breathing deep breaths to relax herself and tune into Chandra's energy. "My God!" Her eyes snapped open. "He is there!"

"Thank...you...baby!" Jack pulled her into his arms to land a direct hit on her full mouth, then spun on his heel, heading for the house just as Donavan walked out the door. "I know where that miserable son of a bitch is, partner!"

Donavan looked over Jack's shoulder as a police car pulled

up alongside the house. "How the hell did you find out? They haven't even gotten out of the car yet."

"Seelah told me! I asked her to help find Hindel, and she did! He's hidin' out at Chandra's shack in the bayous!"

"That would explain why no one has spotted him!" Donavan could feel his excitement rising. A chill skittered down his back as he glanced up at the full moon. "We're going to need a lot of backup on this one."

Jack turned as two deputies walked towards them. "Paulson!" Jack came forward, pulling the man into his arms in a tight bear hug. "How the hell are you doin'? Dispatch wouldn't say who they were sendin'. You had this all planned, didn't you? You sneaky bastard!"

"Yeah, we thought we'd surprise you," he grinned, backing off somewhat. "I'm still a little sore, though, so how about we just shake hands?"

"Take it easy on him, Jack. We don't want to send him back to the hospital with his bones crushed," Donavan laughed, griping Paulson's hand. "How's it going, man? Damn good to have you back."

"It's good to be back. The doctor said I could come back to work as long as I'm on light duty. I heard you're lookin' for Hindel. Have you heard anything else about where he might be?"

Jack nodded to Bailey. "We didn't mean to ignore you. We just got a little carried away with the surprise here." He slapped Paulson on the back then dropped his hand as Paulson winced in pain. "Oops!"

"Before Jack sends you back to intensive care, I'll bring you up on the latest. We think we might have a lead on where Hindel and Quigly are hiding out."

"Oh yeah, where?" Excitement shot through his body, silencing his pain.

"We think he's holed up in the bayous. In fact, I need you to call in for backup to meet us just as highway 101 cuts in out there. We'll be there in about..." he pushed the light-up button on his watch, "fifteen minutes. I want all available men and as many boats without motors as they can come up with. I'd say it's going to take them a little while to round up the boats, so tell dispatch to have them meet us out there as soon as they can."

Paulson glanced at them. "You know…before my run-in with…whatever got hold of me, I'd be chompin' at the bit to go with you guys, but now, all I can say is good luck!" He held out his hand to both men.

"Thanks, Paulson. I got a feelin' we're gonna need it."

Ever vigilant, Jack pulled the .38 from his belt, checked his ammunition.

Bailey stepped forward. "Let me ask you something off the record."

"What's that?" Jack glanced up at him.

"You don't think ole man Hindel's a werewolf. Do you?"

"Tell you the truth," Donavan spoke up, "it's beginning to look that way. The one you should be asking is Paulson. He's still carrying the scars."

"I'm not arguing the fact something got hold of Paulson. That's more than obvious. The thing I want to know is, do you believe Jonathan Hindel changes into a werewolf during the full moon?"

At the same time, all four men looked up as storm clouds scudded across the night sky to allow the glow of the full moon to shine down on them.

"I don't believe in omens, but I'll be damned if that didn't feel like one just now." Jack shivered.

"Jack," Seelah called out to him from the front porch, "could I see you a moment, please?"

"I'll be right back," he told the men, over his shoulder, as he walked across the lawn. "What is it, Seelah?" he asked, his voice softening as he looked at her.

"I want you to be extra careful tonight, Jack." She placed her hands on his shoulders, gazed into his eyes. "I feel terrible danger around you."

"I'll be careful, don't worry. The werewolf ain't been born yet who can best me," he laughed a nervous laugh, his face taking on a look of unease. "Look at us." Jack grinned at her. "You're worryin' 'bout me, and I'm feelin' uneasy 'bout leavin' you here where I can't look after you."

"No one has looked after me in a long time, Jack. I've wanted it that way."

"Same here. But, for some reason, you're worryin' 'bout me and my worryin' 'bout you feels kinda nice all of a sudden."

"Let's go, Jack!" Donavan called to him as the jeep roared to life.

"I gotta go, baby. You stay inside while I'm gone. Promise me?"

In answer, she leaned over, placing a light kiss on his soft mouth.

"You got it, hotshot."

When he drew away, he felt a warm feeling filling him up inside, melting the cold that had lingered there for much too long. "I'll be home later. Wait up for me?" he called out, backing across the lawn, unable to look away from her.

"I'll be here," she told him, blowing a kiss from her fingers as she stepped back to go inside.

Jack's arm shot out, closing his fingers over the palm of his hand as he watched her close the door.

"I know," Donavan laughed as Jack slid inside, "you think you're in love again."

The confident braggart Donavan expected to see didn't show himself. "Tell you the truth; I don't know what I am. I've never felt this way before. Even with Chandra, it never felt like this. I feel this...overpowerin' need to protect her. Almost like... I want to put her in my pocket...for safekeepin'." Jack glanced sideways to see the sneer spreading across Donavan's face. He felt surprised when it didn't appear. "What the hell's happenin' to me, Donavan?"

"I'll let you figure it out, partner." Donavan chuckled as he aimed the jeep down the highway.

***

Seelah tried to relax as she sipped her coffee, waiting for Barbara to come back downstairs from putting the girls to bed. She thought about what had just happened between her and Jack. Could she be falling in love with him? She wondered. Ron crept into her thoughts, his sad face so clear in her mind she felt as though she could reach out and touch him. She ran trembling fingers beneath her damp eyes. Two years is a long time to cut yourself off from the world. Although, until now, she hadn't minded. Now it seemed she had come alive again. The numbness ebbed away, allowing feeling to seep back in. All of a sudden, she didn't want to be alone anymore. She wanted to cook and bake and keep house for someone. She wanted to feel again that leap of excitement when that certain someone walked in the door at night. She felt alive again. After two long years, she felt like a normal woman with a normal woman's feelings. She jumped from the couch as she saw Barbara come down the stairs.

"Barb, can I borrow your car for a little while? I won't be gone long," she told her. "I just need to get a few things from my house."

"Well...I guess it will be all right. Only, are you sure you want to go back there? I mean, Donavan said it had been cleaned up and all, but still...." Her words trailed off as Seelah ran to where she kept the car keys to snatch them from the hook.

"I'm sure, Barb. I'll be back soon. And do me a favor, if Jack should call, don't tell him I left for a few moments. Alright? He'd just worry."

"Where do you want me to tell him you are? I can't very well use the bathroom excuse for long."

"He won't call, and besides, I'll be back in just a few moments." She reached out, pulling Barbara to her for a quick hug, then took off out the front door.

Paulson came outside, his hand raised in the air as she opened the car door. "Hold up a second," he called out to her.

"What?" she hesitated.

"I don't think you should be takin' off. Lieutenant Hays and Jack said we were to keep everyone here while they were gone."

"I won't be gone long. I need to get a few things from my house."

"Do you want me to go with you?" He felt uneasy about allowing her to leave.

"No," she told him, "I'll be fine." With that said, she got behind the wheel, closed the door. She started the car, gave him a brief wave as she backed out of the driveway.

Paulson stood where she had left him, then, with a shake of his head, went back inside the house to wait for her return and hoping she would be back before Hays and Jack knew she had left.

Seelah rolled down the window, switched on the radio. She felt alive for the first time in days. The wind blowing through the open window carried the scent of rain. Her heart sped up as she thought of the impending showers. She loved a good rainstorm. It seemed like the earth came alive after a thorough drenching, almost like a house after a psychic cleansing.

She turned up the radio as one of her favorites floated on the air, joining in with Boy George as he sang "*Do You Really Want To Hurt Me?*" and drumming her fingers on the steering wheel to the beat of the rhythm. The song reminded her of Jack for some reason. Seelah laughed aloud as she thought of the scolding she would get if Jack knew she left the safety of Donavan and Barbara's house. And the thought of someone trying to dictate her movements after two years of coming and going as she pleased didn't bother her in the least. With complete calm, she pulled into her driveway and switched off the engine.

CHAPTER TWENTY-SEVEN

Guess we beat everyone here," Donavan said as they pulled off the highway to wait for backup.

"When did you tell them to meet us?" Jack put a cigarette between his lips, handed the last one to Donavan, then waded up the empty pack to toss it into the garbage bag.

"I didn't. I had Paulson call it in. They should be showing up anytime."

Jack's hand trembled as he flicked his lighter, blew a stream of blue smoke out the open window.

"You nervous about going in after Hindel?"

Jack looked at him. "Hell yes! Ain't you?"

"Yeah." He nodded, unashamed at the tremor of fear sounding in his voice. "We're dealing with the unknown here. Werewolves are supposed to stay in novels and movies. They're not allowed to jump off pages and movie screens." He inhaled, making the tip of the cigarette glow red.

"Guess someone forgot to tell this one, huh?"

Donavan snorted a contemptuous laugh. "When did you start believing Hindel could be a werewolf?"

"When Paulson got attacked and told us what he saw. That and all the crazy shit goin' on with Chandra, and now meetin' Seelah and seein' what she can do." He flicked his ashes out the window. "Christ! Do we live in a crazy, mixed-up world or what?"

"We do, and most of it passed me by for a lot of years. Before Paulson got attacked, I would have bet my last penny we dealt with nothing more than a psychotic nut or a rabid dog.

Now, I don't think anything's a sure bet."

"I guess we both feel like we've taken a sharp turn somewhere and ended up in Romania, or...wherever Lon Chaney Jr. is supposed to lurk."

"Except Chaney is acting out a role. Mother-fucker we're after is the real thing!"

Headlights shone in the back window of the jeep as police cars and three pickup trucks rolled up behind them.

"Time to go to work." Donavan got out of the jeep as the sounds of slamming doors echoed through the stillness. "I want everyone to gather 'round and listen to what I'm going to tell you." He leaned back against the bumper of the jeep, crossed his legs at the ankles. "Before I even begin, I want to say that any wise-ass remarks will not be tolerated here tonight. If I hear any, the person who made them will be written up."

Silence greeted him as he waited a moment before going on with what he had to say.

"All right, here's what we're up against. I know you're all aware of the fact Paulson came close to being killed out at the Hindel Mansion. What you might not be aware of is *how* he got injured. The night Paulson got attacked, he described a large wolf that walked upright." Donavan looked around at the faces staring out at him. "In other words, in describing what took him down, he was describing a werewolf."

Jack heard the intakes of breath as the men looked at each other, trying to understand what they had just been told. "I know how you feel," he told them. "I felt the same way. But I made all my smart-ass remarks before I got back on the force. It's too late for the rest of you. You're already sworn, badged, and delivered to the sheriff's department!"

Laughter filtered through the crowd allowing the men to release a bit of the tension trickling in as Donavan continued to explain why they were there.

"We have reason to believe Jonathan Hindel is a real live werewolf. We also have reason to believe the stories we've grown up hearing about the Hindel Mansion may not be mere stories. So, with all that in mind, our main purpose for being here tonight is to find and destroy Jonathan Hindel. Notice, I didn't say arrest Jonathan Hindel. I said, destroy."

"Lieutenant."

"Yeah." Donavan looked around, trying to see who spoke to him."

"John Hendrickson here." He stepped away from the other officers. "If what you say is true, and I have to admit I'm having one hell of a time taking it all in, but if what you say *is* true, have you looked at the moon tonight?"

"As a matter of fact, I have. And I have to admit I'm not anxious to be in on this either." Donavan glanced over at Jack.

"Also, if we're to believe Hindel's a werewolf, did anyone remember to bring along some silver bullets?"

Jack tried to stifle his laughter as he glanced over at Hendrickson. "I don't know 'bout anyone else, but I sure forgot them." Jack waited until he knew for sure he had his laughter under control, then went on with what he wanted to say. "We think Hindel's hidin' out in a shack in the bayous. Along with his caretaker, Quigly. Any of you that know Quigly know he's just an afterthought and can be arrested and brought in. Unless, of course, he opens fire. If that happens, and I'm sure Lieutenant Hays will agree with me, he's open game. Take him out any way you can!"

"I agree. He's little, but he's sneaky, so watch your backs." Donavan nodded.

"What we're gonna do is surround the banks along the shack just before daylight, then go in by boat. By the way, how many were you able to come up with on such short notice?"

Jerry Carpenter stepped forward. "All we could find is three rowboats. I hope that's gonna be enough."

"It'll have to be if that's all we got," Jack grinned. "What I find hard to believe is this's Saint Anthony Parish, Louisiana, for Christ's sake. You'd think the department would have enough sense to have, at least, more than three rowboats on hand. I bet the ones you got belong to deputies."

"You're right." Carpenter shook his blond head in agreement. "One's mine, and the other two belong to other deputies."

"Okay, we're going to drive in as far as we can, then start transporting men by boat until we're all there. Jack's going to lead the first boat because he knows the location better." Donavan looked straight ahead as he spoke, although he could feel Jack's eyes leveled on the back of his neck.

"Thanks...partner," he muttered. "The shack where we think Hindel and Quigly are hidin' belongs to a woman named Chandra. She's some kind of voodoo queen of the bayous. The access to her shack is by boat as it's situated on stilts out in the middle of the swamp." Jack stopped talking for a moment, trying to hold onto his anger, as snickers were heard filtering through the crowd. "Did I say somethin' funny?" His voice took on a sharp edge.

The grin spreading across Carpenter's handsome face disappeared. "We meant no disrespect," he hastened to explain. "It's just that... a few of us know about Chandra's powers of healing. In fact, more than a few of us have gone to her for psychic readings. The woman's for real."

The anger disappeared from his voice and his mind. "The problem we're up against with tryin' to stay outta sight 'til daylight is, as I said, her shack sits on stilts, so the way we'll have to approach is on a long, wooden walkway that leads up to the shack. I don't know 'bout you, but if Hindel comes flyin' out that door, I want more room than a wooden walkway to fight on."

"Can werewolves fight in water?" Jerry spoke up.

"Is that a smart-ass remark, Carpenter, or are you serious?" Donavan looked at him.

"I'm serious!" He glanced around, his blue eyes wide and questioning. "None of us know what the hell to expect here!"

"You have a point," Donavan said. "We *don't* know what to expect. All we have is myth and legend. So, going on those theories, the werewolf is said to be indestructible until he changes back to his normal self."

"You forgot something, Lieutenant," Carpenter informed him.

"We already mentioned the silver bullets, Jerry!"

"I'm not talking about silver bullets. According to legend, the werewolf can also be destroyed by fire."

"Are you sure?" Donavan looked over at him as Carpenter nodded.

"I seem to remember hearin' that, too!" Jack said.

"Guess we should have all got together and rented a werewolf movie before we came out on this one," Hendrickson laughed.

"Might have helped!" Jack agreed.

"If we're going to surround the shack from the banks, I don't see any need to go in until daylight," Donavan said. "If legend holds true, he can't do anything after sunup. Why put ourselves in danger by going in earlier?"

"You could be right," Jack said. "I just thought we could already be situated close to the shack when the sun came up. But, yeah...we can do it your way."

"Jack." Carpenter walked over to stand closer to the jeep. "As we said earlier, there's a full moon tonight. Hindel's going to be out looking for victims. And, while it's true none of us want to run into him when he returns to the shack before sunup, I think we should also keep in mind we don't want to lose sight of him if he decides to take off somewhere else. I think it would be a good idea to get situated on the banks while it's still dark."

"Damn good point, Carpenter! I hadn't thought of that. Another matter we need to think 'bout is Chandra's in that shack. He could go after her."

"I don't think that's an issue, Jack. If he's with Chandra, then she's already taken precautions to protect herself," Donavan told him.

"Yeah, I keep forgettin' how strong she is in her own right." He glanced around at the other men as they stood staring at him.

"What he means is, if Chandra's a voodoo queen, she should be able to hold her own against a werewolf." Donavan forced a slight laugh.

"Let's load up!" Jack said, already turning away.

***

Seelah unlocked the door then stepped inside. She felt the negative energy surrounding her. Reaching out, she turned on lamps, filling the little house with light as she made her way down the hall to her bedroom.

Except for her small dresser and matching nightstands and bed, she found the room empty. Someone had removed the mattress, leaned the brass headboard, footboard, and railings up against the wall. She glanced down at the floor, glad to see no blood staining the wood.

Without warning, the horror, taking place within the room, flashed before her. She saw the hulking shape of a beast covered in short, coarse black hair as he straddled the terrified woman on the bed. She watched as he jerked the woman upright, licking the wound on her face, then, as he threw his head back with a satisfied growl to sink his long, sharp teeth into her throat. She could hear the sounds as he ripped and tore at her helpless body. Repulsed, Seelah ordered the scenes to leave her mind.

Making her way out of the room, she walked back to the living room, taking a seat in her favorite chair. There, she worked on relaxing her mind and body. When she felt calm, she gathered what she needed for a thorough psychic cleansing of her home.

Starting with the outside of her house, she sprayed a solution made up of salt and water, directing a fine mist all around the outside perimeter, being sure to include the windows and doors. As she sprayed the solution, she invoked all negativity to leave, saying aloud, "As I release all negative energy surrounding this dwelling, I ask for the love and protection of Mother and Father God to be ever-present here." Envisioning all the while a white wall of light, starting at the ground and going straight up into the sky.

Lighting a smudge stick made of sage, she walked around the house, blowing the smoke wafting from the lit stick over every window and door, saying the same words she had said earlier. This done, she walked into the house and, lifting a window to allow all the negativity to escape, she cleansed the inside.

To complete the cleansing, she took a shower to wash away all negativity from her person and to cleanse her aura. When she finished, she sprayed the shower with bleach.

Dressed in a pair of her favorite sweat pants and matching pullover, she sat back down in the chair to wait.

He came to her, smiling and holding out his hands. "Thank you for removing the evil from our home, Seelah." He lowered himself onto the hassock close to her feet.

"I will never allow evil to dwell here if I can help it," she told him. "Before you went away, this little house breathed love and happiness."

"I knew you would come if I called you."

"I will always come to you, Ron. You are my strength." She gazed at him, her dark eyes filled with so much love he had to turn away. "Why do you turn your face from me?" She sat forward in the chair.

"You must not depend on me anymore, Seelah. A new man has come into your life." He lowered his head, gazing at her as she tried to hide her face from him. "You have no reason to be ashamed of your feelings, Seelah."

"I feel like…I've betrayed you," she cried, unable to help herself.

"My darling, darling girl," Ron smiled into her tear-stained face. "You could never betray me, just as I could never betray you. But, the time has come for me to leave you."

"No!" Seelah reached out to him. "Don't leave me, Ron! I love you. I'll never see Jack again if you'll stay."

"Don't you see, my love? I want to leave. I want to go home. My time here is done."

"You don't care about me anymore?"

"Oh, Seelah," he caressed her name. "I will always care about you. Because of you, I have stayed on this earth much longer than I should have."

"I'll be all alone if you go. Don't you see that, Ron?"

"Let Jack into your life, Seelah. He is already falling in love with you. He is a good man. I approve of him."

"It doesn't feel natural my sitting here talking with you about him." She brushed at her damp eyes.

"We have always been able to talk about any subject. Don't

let your falling in love with another man change that."

"I'm not falling in love with him. We're just friends."

"My poor, innocent darling. You've been so wrapped up in your grief over me you didn't even know when love came knocking at your heart again."

She stared at him as tears ran, unnoticed, down her face.

"Seelah, I saw how you sent the earthbounds, in the Hindel Mansion, on to the other side."

"They were so sad, Ron. I felt so sorry for them."

"If that is so, then how can you do less for me?"

"I don't understand. I would do anything for you, my darling."

"Then let me go, Seelah. Let me go home where my family and loved ones are waiting for me. I don't want to remain here where hate and evil walk the earth. I want to go where love and happiness dwell. I want to look into the beautiful faces of Mother and Father God. I need to feel their love surrounding me."

"I've been very selfish, haven't I?" She dropped her face in her hands.

"You didn't do it out of selfishness; you did it out of love."

Seelah looked up at him. "Will you still come back and see me sometimes?" Her breath caught on a sob.

"I'll make you a promise right now. If you ever need me, I'll be here for you. However, please don't call me too often. I want you to get on with your life here. I want you to call on Jack before you call on me."

"If that is what you want me to do," she whispered the words on a shaky breath.

The air in the small room grew lighter as they sat looking at each other.

"After I leave, I want you to go back to the house where Jack left you. He will need your strength very much when he returns."

"I feel so much danger around him. I try to see the outcome, but for some reason, it's being kept from me," she spoke her thoughts aloud. "I don't know what I'll do if I lose both of you."

"All you can do for him, and all the men who are fighting

against this evil tonight, is surround them with the white light of the Holy Spirit."

"I already did that, and I also asked the Holy Ones to walk beside them. And yet, I still feel so much danger."

"Jonathan Hindel is a very evil man. His soul has walked in the darkness of his own choosing for almost two centuries. He is very strong while he is on this plane."

"He isn't stronger than the Holy Ones. The one thing the dark entities of this world cannot abide is light."

"I know this, Seelah. Have you tried to call on Chandra for help?"

"I don't dare call on Chandra while Jack is so close to her. If I do, then she will be able to tune into my energy, and if that happens, she will know what he and the rest of the men have planned for tonight."

He stood and, smiling down at her, blew her a kiss. "I must leave you now, my darling. Trust in the Holy Ones. They won't let you down."

CHAPTER TWENTY-EIGHT

A light fog crept over the swamp, wafting like curling fingers towards the banks where waiting men crouched amongst the rotting flora. They tried to ignore the dampness seeping beneath their clothing, but its cloying touch added to their unease as they gazed into the humid darkness. Watching for an evil that, thus far, had only existed in their worst nightmares.

An owl screeched nearby, making every heart leap and each hand move to cover the butt of a gun still holstered but unsnapped and ready.

"What are you thinking about?" Donavan balanced his upper body on his elbows, his long legs stretched out in front of him.

"Right now, I'm thinkin' 'bout kickin' my ass for not rememberin' to bring some mosquito repellent." He slapped a hand against his face. "These damn things are gonna suck us dry 'fore Hindel even makes a showin'.

"Do you ever wonder if the Aids virus can be transmitted by insects?"

"No." Jack wiped the blood staining his hand on the leg of his jeans. "And I don't wanna think 'bout it now. Where the hell do you come up with these ideas! I'd think layin' out in the swamp waitin' for a werewolf would be scary enough without addin' Aids-infected misquotes!"

"I think about things like that sometimes." Donavan turned as someone nudged him to take the Styrofoam cups filled with coffee. "Thanks," he breathed.

"Well, do me a favor, don't think about them here." Jack

pulled a cigarette from the pack sticking out of his pocket.

"Do you think that's a good idea? Smoke carries, you know."

"We're surrounded by a stinkin' swamp." Jack looked at him in the darkness. "Who the hell's gonna smell cigarette smoke?"

Donavan sniffed the air, reached for the cigarette Jack had just lit. "Now, maybe this will be a little more tolerable." He inhaled the tobacco releasing the smoke from his lungs on a deep sigh.

"Do you ever…" Jack grew quiet as Donavan reached out, squeezing his leg. "What?"

"Someone's rowing up to the shack."

Jack raised up, trying to see over the tall foliage. "It's Chandra," he breathed as he watched her climb up the ladder leading to the walkway. "Now's our chance to go get her outta there." He stood up, but Donavan yanked him back.

"There's not enough time. She'll be inside before you row halfway across."

"Goddamn it, Donavan, I can't sit here while she may be in danger!"

"You can't believe she isn't aware of what's going on here!"

"I don't know," he pulled his gun from the back of his belt, handed it to Donavan, "but I intend to find out."

"What the hell are you planning on doing?" Donavan hissed into the stillness.

"I'm gonna swim over there and see what I can find out." He withdrew the pack of cigarettes from the pocket of his T-shirt, dropped them in Donavan's lap. "Maybe, if I can get close enough to peek in the window," he loosened his belt then unzipped his jeans, sliding his thumbs inside the waistband to push them down to his feet, "I can see who all's inside." Jack pulled his shirt up and over his head.

"And what happens if you run into Hindel?" Donavan stuffed the cigarettes back in the pocket, laid the shirt down beside him. "You won't even have your gun."

"He'll have to catch me 'fore he can do anything."

"That shouldn't be hard." Donavan rolled the .38 inside the jeans. "You meet that big son of a bitch face to face. You're going to be too busy slipping and sliding in shit to think about running!"

"Wish me luck." Jack slipped down the bank and into the water. As he moved forward, he tried not to think about what could be in the dark waters with him. His fear of snakes, such as the lethal cottonmouth, making his task all the more onerous. He dove deep, wanting to get as close to the stilts as possible before surfacing. At last, he kicked his feet, pushing his body to the top. As his head broke the surface, he grabbed hold of one of the stilts sticking out of the water, trying to get his breath. He could hear voices overhead in the shack, one he recognized as Chandra's, but he couldn't quite make out the other one.

He moved to the ladder and, gripping the sides, pulled himself out of the water. He climbed up to the walkway keeping low as he made his way up the steps to the deck.

The scream started low in his belly and picked up speed as it climbed upward to his throat to be trapped as Chandra put her hand over his mouth. "Jack, what are you doing here?" she whispered in his ear.

He yanked her hand away to pull her around to the other side of the deck. "Where the hell's Hindel? And don't bother lyin' to me, 'cause I know he's here!"

"No, Jack, he isn't." Her eyes slid down his wet chest, then back up to gaze into his eyes. "Although he could be at any moment, that's why you need to leave here!"

"You're not even gonna try and protect him?" He snorted an ugly laugh, moved away from her. "You've known all along what he is, and you never said a word!" Jack stepped out of her way as she reached out to him. "You're as evil as he is!"

"By the time I decided to stop him, I found I had waited too long. I couldn't." Chandra filled her eyes with him while her mind rushed with ways to make him leave. "Jack, please listen to me! You must leave here!" She started to go to him.

"Don't touch me," he shoved her back away from him.

"I'd rather swim in your filthy swamp with a nest of slimy water moccasins than let you put your evil hands on me again."

The hand squeezing her heart tightened its hold. "The time has come for Jonathan's reign of destruction to be over." In her old familiar way, she twined her arms around her trembling body. "However, you must allow me to be the one to end his evil."

"You think I'd trust you? After all the times you played me for a fool?" He stared at her straight back, and for some reason, her apparent strength snapped something inside him. He wanted to inflict the same suffering she had visited upon him. He wanted to see her bend beneath the pain. "You... are... nothin'... more... than... an... evil... disgustin'...bitch!"

She would not bend, nor would she cry out. Her suffering had to remain silent. To do anything less would put the man she loved, the man who stood there, his face covered with loathing, at too great a risk. Chandra pushed her pain down deep inside, then turned to face him. "You have every right to hate me, Jack, and I think you have said all there is to say to me." Not one tear seeped from beneath her dark lashes as she looked at him. "I will say this to you one time." She put up her hand as he started to turn away. "I let you say what you wanted to say to me. If for no other reason than what we once shared, won't you at least listen to what I have to say to you, Jack?"

He turned back to face her. "I'm listenin," his voice remained cold as he looked at her.

"I love you in every way a woman can love a man. Before you came into my life, I couldn't feel anything but coldness. I couldn't feel the way a normal woman could about a man, but... you changed that, Jack. You taught me about feelings. And no matter what happens now, I will always be grateful to you for that. My life had been filled with so much darkness, then you came and pulled me into the light." She brushed at the tears falling down her face. "Jonathan could not allow that. He could not allow me to be a real woman with a real woman's feelings. The way he could accomplish this is he had to use you." At last, her voice broke, and she bowed beneath her pain.

"How did he use me?" Jack reached out, tipping her face up so he could look at her.

"He used you to threaten me. The last night you were here... when I had to send you away...he showed me what he would do to you if I allowed you to stay."

Jack thought back to that night and remembered how she had changed. "What do you mean he showed you what he would do? How the hell could he show you anything? If you think back, you'll recall just you and me owned that night. He didn't make a showin'!"

"Jonathan and I can get into each other's minds. He can put scenes inside my mind of what he is thinking. That night he showed me a scene of a wolf chasing after a man; his mouth covered with blood...so close." Chandra shuddered at the memory. "That wolf is Jonathan, and the man he chased is you."

Jack stood motionless and stunned, but he forced himself to ask her the question he still needed to know. "Is Jonathan Hindel the reason you dropped me like you did?"

Chandra looked up at him, her face wet with tears. "Yes, Jack. I couldn't take the chance of him hurting you."

Without another word, Jack drew her into his arms, and as he did, all the memories of their times together came rushing back to him.

"Jack, look out!" Chandra screamed.

Without thinking, Jack flung her across the deck, then wheeled, reaching for his gun, then remembered he had left it on land.

Quigly came at him, a thick, long knife raised above his head, screaming out his hatred.

Jack sidestepped him, and as Quigly turned to come at him again, Jack swiped his legs out from under him. As he hit the deck with a loud thud, Jack picked up the fallen knife. In the flash of a moment, he drew the razor-sharp blade across Quigly's throat. With cold calmness, he hefted the dead man into his arms then over the railing. A pleased grin spread across his face as he heard a loud splash, then silence.

"That felt satisfyin'," he slapped the palms of his hands

back and forth. Now, let's see to gettin' you out of here and situated where you'll be safe." Jack slipped his arm around Chandra's waist.

Chandra turned in his arms, placing her hands on each side of his face to draw his mouth down to hers. All the feeling she had pushed deep inside came pouring forth as she held him. At last, she drew away. "It's too late for me, Jack. And...it's too late for us."

"What are you sayin'? It's never too late!" He tried to draw her back into his arms, but she stepped away out of his reach.

"Another has entered your life, Jack. Someone who is right for you. Don't push her away and lose what can be."

For a moment, she allowed Seelah's face to come into her mind, and at that moment, what she saw made her heart race with terror. "Jack!" She covered her face with her hands.

Jack pulled her hands away. "It won't work this time, Chandra. I already know what you're tryin' to do. Jonathan Hindel can't scare me anymore."

"It's not Jonathan! It's another! Seelah and the woman she came to the mansion with are in extreme danger!"

"What the hell are you talkin' 'bout? They ain't in danger. We left them with two deputies. Paulson and Bailey."

"Yes, that's the name of the man Jonathan attacked! Don't you see? Jonathan made him into a werewolf!"

"Jesus Christ!" Jack whirled, trying to decide what to do. "Come on, we've got to get to Donavan!" He pushed her ahead of him toward the stairs, but she yanked away from him.

"Go to them, Jack!"

"I can't leave you!" He tried to pull her back to him.

"Jack," Chandra backed away from him, "make your choice. You can only save one of us."

For a split second, Jack hesitated, then made up his mind as to what he must do. Quickly, he dove off the deck into the water. He swam as fast as he could across the swamp, trying not to think about the horrible danger he had left Chandra to contend with, alone.

"You're damn lucky you came back when you did."

Donavan leaned over, helping Jack out of the water. "When I heard that yelling followed by a loud splash, I already had it in my mind to row over there."

Jack bent over, bracing both hands on his knees as he tried to slow down his breathing. "Get…the…boats…ready," he panted.

"Why? Isn't Hindel coming back here?"

"I don't give…a fuck…about Hindel!" Jack drew in a deep breath, then leaned over, snatching up his clothes. "We need to get back to the house!"

"Why?" Donavan felt a shot of fear slam into his stomach.

"Chandra told me…Barb, Seelah and the kids are in danger." Jack motioned the men toward the boats.

"Oh, bullshit! We left them with Paulson and Bailey. They'll see to their safety. Unless!" He jerked Jack around to face him. "Is Hindel on his way to the house?"

"No. But he don't need to be 'cause there's already a werewolf at your house!"

"Jack, goddamn it, you're not making any sense! Who the hell are you talking about?"

"Paulson, Donavan. He's a werewolf!"

Donavan didn't wait to hear anymore as he took off running towards the boats. "We're leaving! Carpenter, you and the other deputies, get your boats ready! Three to a boat just like before. The rest of you will have to stay here until someone can come back for you."

"What's going on, Lieutenant?" Carpenter came forward.

"I just found out Paulson's a werewolf, and we left him at my house."

"Oh shit!" He hastened his steps to the boats.

As word of what happened filtered down to the other deputies who had to stay behind, they stood looking out across the water at the small shack, hoping against hope the returning deputies would be in time to save them from a fate worse than death.

The men climbed into the boats grabbing oars to place them into the oarlocks. Donavan rowed the boat away from the bank, then out into the swamp. "Why the hell didn't Seelah get a heads-up about this?" he growled, pushing his body to hurry. "She's supposed to be psychic!"

"I don't know. Chandra's a lot stronger'n Seelah, and she didn't know anything 'bout it either until just now."

"I don't even have my damn cell phone! I left it in the jeep," Donavan said.

"I got mine, Lieutenant," Carpenter spoke up, withdrawing the phone from his pocket to hand it over.

"Thank god!" Donavan took the phone, punched in his home phone number. The number continued to ring with no answer. "Where the hell can they be? Nobody's answering the phone!"

"Paulson might've cut the phone lines," Jack said, hoping he guessed right.

Donavan called the station. "This is Hays; get some deputies over to my house on the double. My family is in danger."

"We already have two deputies at your house," dispatch told him. "Are you saying you want more?"

"Yes, I'm saying I want more, goddamn it! Paulson is a threat to my family! You heard me right; I said he's a threat to my family!" Donavan came back at the man on the other line. "Paulson is a werewolf!" Dead silence flowed back on the line as Donavan tried to control his anger but lost the battle. "Listen, you inept, ignorant fuck! Get some men over to my house now, or I'll have your ass up on report by tomorrow morning!" With that said, he turned off the phone.

Up ahead, they could see the vehicles lined up alongside the highway, and they put their backs into their rowing. When they reached the bank, both men jumped out of the boat to run toward the jeep.

"Carpenter!" Jack called back over his shoulder. "Soon as you have the rest of the men, come to Hays' house!"

"We'll be there!" he called out, already turning the boat to head back the way they had come.

Donavan unlocked the door, slid across the seat to unlock the passenger's side. Jack hopped into the cab, felt the jeep jump forward as he slammed the door.

Donavan smacked his hand hard against the wheel. "Why the hell didn't any of us think about the possibility Paulson could be a werewolf? We thought of every other aspect of this screwed-up nightmare."

"It's simple. We all like Paulson. The last thing you think 'bout, when you like someone, is they can be evil." Jack lit another cigarette off the one he just put out. "Can't you make this son of a bitch go any faster?"

"I'm doing sixty now. I want to get there as fast as you do, but we got some pretty sharp curves coming up."

"I feel like we're in the middle of a goddamn horror movie!" Jack said, then lurched forward, grabbing the dash, as Donavan slammed on the brakes. "What the fuck did you do that for?"

Donavan braced for impact then breathed a sigh of relief when the men behind them swerved their vehicles to a stop. "Look," he whispered, staring into the glow of the headlights.

Ahead they could see what looked to be a large animal with black hair covering the entire length of its body. It reared up on its hind legs and, turning in the direction of the jeep, walked towards them.

"Jesus Christ!" Jack moaned through lips gone dry. "It's Hindel!" He grabbed his .38 off the seat, threw open the door to climb out of the jeep. Gripping the butt of the gun in both hands, he fired off six rounds straight at the nightmare moving towards them.

"Did you get him?" Donavan asked his voice heavy with fear.

"I think I heard impact! He started to move away from the door as he heard feet running up behind him, then stopped as he saw the beast roll over, then regain its footing. "Get back in your cars. He's still movin! Give me your gun!" he breathed as it inched towards them.

Donavan jerked the .44 Magnum from his holster, handed it across the seat. "If this don't stop him, I'm going to back up and run him over."

"Just give me time to get back in 'fore you take off!" Jack aimed then fired all six shots. "Drop...you son...of...a...bitch!" Jack snarled through clenched teeth.

The beast threw back its huge head, howling into the wind, then took off loping across the road and into the trees lining the highway.

Jack got back inside the jeep. "I can't believe anything could still be standin' after takin' twelve rounds of bullets! Six of them from a goddamn.4444 Magnum!"

"We're not dealing with a normal man, Jack. Although I have to agree with you. Too bad we didn't have time to make some of those silver bullets Hendrickson mentioned." Donavan backed up then pulled onto the highway.

"Well, we might not have killed the son of a bitch, but at least I slowed him down. It should make him a lot easier for Chandra to contend with if he returns to the shack."

"He'll go back; he doesn't have anywhere else to go."

"I hope he didn't have any great likin' for Quigly. I sent that little prick to the bottom of the swamp!"

"I know this is going to sound cold, but right now, I couldn't care less who gets killed tonight, Jack, as long as we make it in time to protect *our* loved ones."

Knowing he needed to get their minds off Donavan's family and Seelah, he told Donavan what had happened between him and Chandra.

"Do you believe her?" Donavan glanced over at him.

"Yeah, I do. When I think back to that last night we were together, I thought it strange at the time how fast she changed. Yeah, I believe her."

"If that's so, why didn't you stay and help her with Hindel?"

"Because right after she told me all that, she told me 'bout Seelah, Barb, and the kids bein' in danger from Paulson. I tried to get her to come with me, but she said she couldn't. Said I had to make a choice whether to stay with her or go to help Seelah. I made my choice."

"I know it had to be a tough one."

"Of course, but Seelah and Barb and the kids tipped the scales too."

"My god!" Donavan reached up drawing a large hand over his eyes. "If anything happens to them, I don't know what the hell I'll do!"

"We'll make it in time," Jack told him, rubbing a gentle hand over his shoulder.

"I keep praying, but I'm so numbed with fear I don't know if He's hearing me or not." His voice broke as he tried to explain.

"He hears you, Donavan. You're askin' for His help to combat darkness. God will never turn His face from that!"

"I think I'm getting an inkling of how Stewart felt that night at the motel. And I'll tell you right now, if anything happens to Barb and Jenny, I'll be in the bed right next to him."

"Nothin's gonna happen to them, Donavan. We'll get there in time," Jack told him, voicing a silent prayer for those in need.

CHAPTER TWENTY NINE

Seelah walked into the house to find Barbara sitting on the couch waiting for her. "Do you have any idea how worried I have been about you?"

"I told you I'd just be gone a few moments." Seelah set the small lamp she had in her hands down on the end table.

"What's that?" she asked, then remembered the story Seelah had told her about hanging the lamp outside at night in a welcome-home-gesture for her husband. "Is that for Jack?"

"Yeah." Seelah opened the door on the lamp to place inside a small, white candle she had brought with her. "He won't know what it's for, but I will."

"I think it's a very sweet idea. I might even adopt it myself." She got up off the couch as Seelah lit the candle to follow her outside.

"There." She hung the lamp on a hook beside the door then stood back to admire how good it looked. As she started to go back inside, she noticed Paulson standing in the yard staring at her. "What do you suppose his problem is?"

"I don't know." Barbara walked down the porch steps. "Deputy Paulson, is there something you need?" She moved towards him. He stared at her, backing away. "If you tell me what the problem is, maybe I can help you." Barbara reached out her hand, but he murmured something low in his throat, shook his head.

"Barb," Seelah came across the lawn. "Maybe we should leave him alone to do his job." She took hold of Barbara's arm, pulling her toward the house.

"I want to know what's wrong with him. He's acting strange." Barbara tried to pull away.

"Barb!" Seelah hissed in her ear. "Will you just come with me? Now!"

Barbara turned to stare at her. "What is it?"

"I'll tell you in the house. Right now, we need to get away from him!"

Both women walked to the porch. "Don't turn around," Seelah warned as Barbara slowed her steps.

When they were both inside, with the door locked and bolted, Barbara pulled back the curtain to see Paulson still standing where they had left him, gazing at her through the window.

"Is he still out there?" Seelah asked, coming to stand beside her.

"Yes." He's just standing in the yard staring at me."

"Get away from the window and help me get all the doors and windows locked," Seelah told her, turning towards the kitchen.

As Seelah locked the back door, Barbara worked on making sure all the windows were locked. "Where do you suppose Bailey is? Maybe he can do something about Paulson."

"I don't know, but I'm sure not going to go looking for him. Come on, let's get busy on making sure the upstairs windows are locked." Seelah already had her hand on the banister when Barbara pulled her back.

"I want you to tell me what's wrong, Seelah. If we're in some kind of danger, then we should be on the phone to the police."

"I don't want to scare you, but I'd be willing to bet if you try and call, you'll find the phone's dead."

Barbara glanced up the stairs where the girls were sleeping. "What's going on here, Seelah?" Her voice was low and trembling.

"I think Paulson's a werewolf."

"Seelah, be serious!" A nervous laugh escaped her throat. "I don't find your sense of humor at all funny!" When Seelah continued to stare at her, she spun around to snatch up the phone. The look on her face as she put the phone to her ear told Seelah she had been right.

"Now the question is, which one of us is going to sneak next door to call the police?"

"We can't go outside! He could be waiting for us to do just that! No, we need to stay together and go upstairs and lock all the windows. But first," she ran down the hall to the bedroom, "I need to get something." She stepped back out with a .38 in her hands.

"I'm sure being the wife of a police Lieutenant, you know how to use that." Seelah let out her breath as Barbara flipped open the chamber on her .38 to make sure it contained enough bullets, then nodded.

"Good, now let's get upstairs."

They moved from room to room, closing and locking windows being as quiet as possible, trying not to wake the girls. When they came to the window overlooking the backyard, Barbara drew back, letting the drapes fall back into place.

"What's wrong?" Seelah whispered.

"It's Bailey." Barbara motioned her forward. "He's lying on the ground."

Seelah pulled back the drapes enough to see out. In the glow of the security light, she could see a body lying face down on the ground. "Oh no!" she murmured.

The sound of breaking glass made both women whirl around. "Lord Jesus," Barbara cried into the darkness. "What are we going to do?" She ran a hand over Brandy, trying to calm her and keep her from barking. She breathed a sigh of relief as the pup laid back down beside Jenny.

"Come on, let's go back downstairs and look for Paulson."

"Shouldn't we stay upstairs with the girls?" Barbara hesitated as they walked into the hall.

"I don't know about you, but I like knowing where the enemy is. Less chance of a surprise that way." Seelah hastened her steps towards the stairs then stopped staring straight ahead.

"What?" Barbara backed up.

"It's Paulson. He must have broken the glass in the back door to get in."

Barbara edged closer, peering over the banister, then blew out her breath in spite of her fear. "Seelah, he's not a werewolf," she whispered. "Look at him." She gestured with her free hand, her other hand still clutching the .38 as she saw him standing in the middle of the living room. "There's a full moon tonight. If Paulson is a werewolf, he would already be covered in black hair!" She began to move around Seelah. "I don't know why I didn't think about that earlier when we were outside with him."

"Stay back, Barb," Seelah halted her. "You're talking about werewolves you've read about in novels or seen in the movies."

"Then why isn't he changing into one? He still looks like he did when he came here."

Paulson raised his head, looking up at them.

"Paulson has been touched by evil for a short time. He still has a choice of whether to continue into the dark world or turn back," Seelah explained, all the while holding eye contact with the man staring up at them.

"Are we safe in assuming then he's made his choice since we have a dead body lying out in our backyard?"

"Bailey may not be dead." Seelah continued to watch Paulson.

"What makes you think that?" Barbara's heart jumped as she saw Paulson take a step towards the stairs.

"I think if he meant to kill us, he would have already made his move. Barbara, I want you to do something for me and not question why I want you to do this."

Barbara nodded, afraid she already knew what would be asked of her.

"I want you to stay here at the top of the stairs, with the gun ready, while I go downstairs alone. I'm going to try and talk to him."

"Are you sure you know what you're doing? Maybe he's playing a trick on us to get you to come down to him." Barbara's eyes were wide with worry as she tried to reason out her fear.

"For some reason, I don't think so. I have a feeling he's

very frightened about what's happening to him."

"If you're sure this is what you want to do. Just be careful." Barbara sat down slowly on the top step, her legs too weak to continue standing. She continued to hold onto the butt but propped the gun up on her knees.

Seelah descended the stairs keeping her eyes focused on the man watching her from across the room. When she reached the last step, she halted. "Deputy Paulson, will you give me your promise no harm will come to me if I walk the rest of the way down these stairs to talk with you?" She remained alert for any sudden movement he might make. But he only nodded.

Seelah walked over to seat herself on the couch, and without thinking about what she could be inviting, patted the cushion beside her. "Please, come and talk with me. I feel I can help you if you will trust me."

For a moment, he remained standing across the room, then he walked forward until he stood even with the couch. He sat down on the far side but kept his face turned away from her.

Seelah sat looking at him, taking in the neat, short-trimmed black hair and tanned face. She could see his full mouth tremble as he breathed out a shaky breath. "What is your first name?" Seelah kept her voice even allowing none of the fear she had been feeling earlier to gain control. "I feel awkward calling you Deputy Paulson if we're going to be friends." She forced a laugh.

"My name is Matthew. Matt." He turned to face her. "Why do you think you can help me, Seelah?"

"I think you're in trouble, and when a person's in trouble, they need a friend to help them figure out how to make things better. If you'll let me, Matt, I'd like to be that friend."

"No one can be my friend. Not anymore." He started to rise from the couch, but Seelah reached out, placing a hand on his arm.

"Please don't go." Their eyes met and locked. "If you feel I'm not the one you need to talk with after I say what I think you should hear, then you can go, and I won't try to stop you. But at least give me a chance?"

"All right," he whispered, sitting back further on the

couch, folding his hands in his lap.

"I'm a psychic, Matt. I know what has happened to you."

At her words, his head jerked upward. "What do you know?" Fear showed in his dark blue eyes as he watched her.

"I know Jonathan Hindel attacked you. I also know Jonathan Hindel is a werewolf. Everyone thought he just clawed and mauled you, but that's not all that happened, Matt. Jonathan also bit you." Seelah ran a comforting hand over his, relieved when he didn't pull away. "Can you tell me how it began to affect you?"

"I started having nightmares... while in the hospital." The words came slow and in a halting manner at first. "I told the doctor about them...but...he said I could expect that because I had suffered so much trauma."

"What were the nightmares about, Matt?" Seelah urged him on while she visualized a dark green light of healing moving down through his crown chakra, spreading its relaxing warmth through all the other chakras of his body.

"Terrible, terrible things. It felt like...I lived it all...and yet...I felt like it had to all be a dream."

"What terrible things did you see, Matt? Can you describe them for me?" Seelah continued to move the light through his body, adding a white light now to intermingle with the green.

"I remember a middle-aged man, black hair with gray at the temples."

"What did the man do?" Seelah could see him starting to relax now.

"Laugh. That's all he would do, just...come into my mind...and...laugh."

"Do you remember how long this particular nightmare lasted before it began to change?" Seelah rubbed her hand over his, tuning into his energy.

"The first three or four days after I got attacked and got sent to the hospital. It could have been longer." He propped an elbow on his knee, rubbed his fingers against his forehead. "They had me so drugged up I can't tell for sure." He sat for a moment, trying to make his mind recall more details, but gave up.

Jonathan's laughing face leaped into her mind, and she knew what he had done. Knowing how the medication would slow Paulson's mind, he had taken advantage of that to creep into his thoughts and begin preparing him for when the hospital released him. Knowing how vulnerable the drugged mind can be and how darkness can take hold, he filled his mind with evil images and addicted him to the needs his body craved.

"I would see these horrible images of people being attacked and eaten alive. The smell of blood got stronger in my mind, and then I could taste it. I started to crave that taste until it became all I could think of. I couldn't tell the doctors about this part of it." Matt dropped his face in his hands, ashamed to look at her.

"Matt," she reached over to lift up his chin, but still, he refused to make eye contact, "Jonathan Hindel is putting these thoughts and feelings into your mind. He is addicting you to the taste of blood and making you dependent on him. He wants to make you into the same monster he is."

He looked at her, and she could see the fear taking over his mind. "But…what can I do about it? I've tried to fight these needs, but…it's like…I've lost my ability to reason. I know right from wrong, and I lose track of time… long periods of time when I can't recall what has happened, and I think I might of hurt someone…his words became disjointed as the fear grew stronger.

"Matt," Seelah pulled him back to the couch, "Do *you* want to kill people? Is that what you're trying to fight, or are you just trying to fight against the images Jonathan Hindel is placing in your mind?"

"I don't know anymore." He yanked away from her. "All I know is I have to have that taste. I have to know that sweet, sweet taste."

"Have you tasted blood before, Matt?'" Seelah knew the chance she could be taking, but she had to follow through on the idea flittering through her mind.

"Not that I can recall. Why?"

"Because if you had, then you would know it doesn't taste sweet at all; instead, it has a metallic taste. And when it gets old, it has a very bad smell almost like rotting flesh." Seelah searched her mind to make the issue of blood as revolting as she could.

"Then...why do I have this vivid taste of sweetness?" Paulson glanced at her to see if she could be trying to trick him in some way.

"The answer is quite simple. What you're being given is not the taste of blood, but the taste Jonathan Hindel is placing in your mind." Seelah reached out for the letter opener lying on the end table, and without giving herself time to think, she jabbed it into her finger. As the blood shot to the surface, she held out her hand. "I want you to take my finger into your mouth."

He drew back, staring at her. "Why would I want to do a disgusting thing like that?"

"I want you to know the real taste of blood. I want you to know I'm telling you the truth about what Jonathan Hindel is trying to do to you."

"What...what if it tastes the same? What if I like it so much I can't stop?"

"I'm asking you to trust me, Matt. Will you do that? Not for me. For yourself?"

He took her small hand in his and, lowering his head, took her bloody finger into his mouth. As soon as his tongue touched her blood, he flung her hand away from him, wiping his mouth on the sleeve of his uniform. "It tastes salty, not sweet!"

"Yes." she laughed in agreement. "All of the nightmares, tastes and pictures running through your mind have been put there by Jonathan Hindel." The happiness shining from his eyes as he looked at her made her reach out to draw him into her arms. She felt his hand slide over her face, and as she pulled away, she drew in her breath at what she saw.

The happiness, shining from his eyes moments earlier, now widened in horror as black hairs popped from the pores of his skin, and his nails grew long and thick from hands now shaped like the paws of a wolf.

"Oh...my...god! "What have I done?" She gripped the arms of the couch, pulling herself to her feet.

"Seelah! What's happening to me?" He cried out, jumping to his feet as the hideous changes continued to ravage his body.

"Can Jonathan Hindel make me think I'm changing into a werewolf?"

"No, Matt," she shook her head, backing away from him. "This time, what you're seeing is real."

"Then I have to get away from here. If I stay, I might hurt you!" Paulson turned, heading for the door. As his hand touched the knob, he looked back at her. "Seelah, will you do something for me, please?"

"If I can. Yes," she told him, trying not to let the disgust she felt at his misshapen appearance show on her face.

"Pray for me?"

"I already am, Matt," she whispered as he ran from the house.

"Seelah, are you all right?" Barbara cried, bounding down the stairs to wrap her in her arms.

"Yes." She dropped down on the couch then jumped back up. "I almost forgot." Seelah ran toward the kitchen. "We need to see to Bailey! With everything going on with Paulson, I forgot all about him!"

While Barbara stood by the open screen door, Seelah ran to the backyard, just in time to see Bailey staggering to his feet. "Are you okay?" She slipped a supporting arm around his waist.

"What happened? One moment I remember talking with Paulson, and the next thing I know, everything went black." He put a hand up to the back of his head.

"Paulson must have knocked you out," she told him, staring down at the blood covering Bailey's open hand. "Come on; let's get back inside where I can have a look at your head."

"Why the hell would Paulson knock me out? We're supposed to be on the same side." Bailey tried not to put too much of his weight on Seelah as she helped him to the house.

"I'll tell you about it after we get inside." She held onto his arm as Barbara stepped back out of the way of the door.

"He must have broken the window to get inside." Bailey glanced at the glass lying on the back porch."

"Must have," Seelah said, continuing to help him through the door. "Barb," she pulled a chair back from the table. "I'm going to need some bandages and peroxide. Can you get them for me, please?"

"Yes, and I need to get the glass from the back door cleaned up too." She turned away.

Seelah bent Bailey's head forward. "It isn't bad enough for stitches. I think after I get it cleaned and bandaged, you'll be fine."

"I still don't understand. Why would Paulson do this? I didn't smell any alcohol on his breath when I got in the car with him, so he can't use drinkin' as an excuse." Bailey winced as Seelah poured the peroxide over his wound.

"Paulson's a werewolf, Deputy Bailey," Seelah told him.

Bailey jumped to his feet. "A werewolf! Oh, Christ!" He ran his hands over his body, checking for blood. "Did he bite me?"

"No," Seelah directed him back to the chair. "In fact, I think he knocked you out so he wouldn't attack you."

"How do you know he's a werewolf? Did you see him?"

"Yes, I did. Paulson hasn't been infected long enough to be dangerous. This is the first time he's changed."

"What do you mean?" He glanced up at her.

"The first time he's changed into a werewolf." She taped the bandage to the wound. "In order for this bandage to stay in place, I'm going to have to wrap your head with gauze."

"Do whatever you need to," he told her. "Where's Paulson now?"

"When he began to change, he ran out the door. He said he couldn't stay because he didn't know what he might do."

"Have you called this in yet?" He reached out, taking the glass of water and aspirins Barbara handed to him.

"We can't. Paulson cut the phone lines. Or at least we suspect he did because the phone's dead," Barbara said.

Bailey pulled his radio into position. "This is Deputy Bailey. I need some deputies at Lieutenant Hays' house as soon as possible."

The airway crackled then the voice of the dispatcher came back to him. "What is this concerning, Deputy?"

"We have strong reason to believe Officer Paulson is not of sound mind. He attacked me and is now running loose in the neighborhood," he explained. "How long ago did he leave?" He glanced over at Seelah.

"About ten minutes ago. But you have to tell them, I don't think he's dangerous."

"He left Lieutenant Hays' house less than fifteen minutes ago. He told one of the women in the house he had to leave so he wouldn't hurt anyone, but we still have to use caution since we aren't sure what he might do in his present condition."

"Stand by, Deputy Bailey," the dispatcher told him. "Be advised we have been notified of the conditions at this residence. Lieutenant Hays is already en-route to his home."

Barbara finished dumping the last of the glass into the trash compactor then turned as headlights swung into the driveway. "They're here!" she squealed, running to the door with Seelah right on her heels.

Donavan stepped out of the jeep as Barbara threw herself into his arms. "Woman, I have been worried sick about you!" He buried his face in her hair. "Are the girls safe?"

"We're all fine, Donavan," she snuggled against him, unwilling to leave the safety of his strong arms.

Before Seelah could say anything, Jack had her wrapped in his arms, his full mouth covering hers. When he, at last, came up for air, he looked at her, a wide grin spreading across his face. "I see you kept your promise and waited up for me."

Seelah cupped his boyish face in her hands to deliver a sound kiss on his full mouth. "I'm so glad you're back. I worried myself sick about you."

"You think I didn't worry 'bout you when I heard about Paulson's bein' a werewolf?" Jack pulled her into his arms, again, afraid to let her go. "I gotta tell you though," he slipped an arm around her waist as they walked to the house, "I felt bad when I heard what had happened to him."

"He's so afraid, Jack. Before he left here, he asked me to pray for him."

Jack stopped walking. "What are you sayin'? Are you

tellin' me you talked to him?"

"Let's go inside. I'll tell you about what happened." She smiled up at him.

"What the hell happened to you?" Jack said as he spied Bailey sitting at the kitchen table, his head swathed in bandages.

"I guess Paulson decided I needed to be unconscious for a little while. He clobbered me when I turned my back on him." He picked up the aspirins, prepared to pop them into his mouth.

Jack reached out, halting him. "You can't take anything if you've been unconscious from a blow to the head. Soon as the other men get here, I'll have one of them run you up to ER to be checked out." Jack grinned as Bailey gave him a sour look. "Also, be sure and fill out an incident report on this."

"I already called in about him being on the loose," Bailey told him.

"I guess he did turn into a monster," Jack said.

"He changed, but he didn't change into a monster." Seelah's voice took on an air of sadness.

"What do you mean he didn't turn into a monster? He attacked Bailey!" Jack pulled out a chair at the end of the table.

"Let's hear what Seelah has to say before we form any opinions." Donavan seated himself at the head of the table, pulled Barbara down on his lap.

"Jack, Paulson is another of Hindel's victims; he would never be a willing participant in what happened to him. He told me how terrified he felt about what happened to him. I'm afraid it's my fault he changed into a werewolf when he did."

"Would you like to explain that?" Jack turned her around to face him.

"Matt said..." she stopped talking as Jack gave her a questioning look.

"Who the hell's Matt?"

"Matt is Paulson's first name," she told him, then continued, "Matt said he started having horrible nightmares while still in the hospital. When he told his doctor about them, the doctor just explained them away as normal due to the trauma he had suffered."

"I see, and where do you fit into all this about his changing into a werewolf?"

"I'm getting to that, Jack, if you'll be patient. Matt told me about his getting fixated on the taste of blood. That he could actually taste a sweetness. When I tuned into his energy, I knew right away Jonathan Hindel put these thoughts into his mind. So…I thought I would prove this to him by letting him see what real blood tasted like."

"And…just how did you go about that?" Jack asked, his anger mounting by the minute.

"I cut myself, then let him taste my blood."

"I don't believe I'm hearin' this." Jack looked around the table to see if anyone else felt as confused as he did. "Here's a man who's already taken out a fellow officer, and you're sittin' 'round talkin' to him like he's a long lost friend. Then, as if that ain't bad enough," he glanced over at Donavan shaking his head, "you give him some blood to whet his appetite! Knowin' he has already been attacked by a real, live, werewolf. For Christ's sake!"

"Seelah, even you have to agree this is a little strange, to say the least," Donavan spoke up.

"I gave him a taste of blood to show him it didn't taste sweet!" She could feel her own anger rising. "Jonathan Hindel planted it in his mind that blood tasted like sweet wine and made him begin to crave it much like… a heroin addict would crave heroin!"

Words he had heard some time back shot into his mind, and he tried to remember where he had heard them and who had said them. Then it came to him. "I think I know where you're comin' from on this, Seelah." Jack sat up straighter in his chair, his excitement rising. "Some months ago, I went to Chandra 'bout warnin' the Stewarts away from the mansion? We got on the subject of evil, and she told me evil is at its highest when the blood of the innocent is spilled. Then, she said somethin' bout…'he would think it sweeter than the finest wine.' I thought she meant Lawrence Hindel. Now I know she was talkin' 'bout Jonathan Hindel. And here you sit tellin' me that right after you let him taste your blood is when he began changin' into a werewolf?"

"Yes." She hung her head as shame washed over her. "I wanted to show him the difference; instead, I gave him the missing ingredient to make him change."

"Did he say where he planned on goin' when he left?"

"No, he said he had to leave because he didn't trust himself not to hurt us. Don't you see? He doesn't want to hurt anyone. There is still time for him to be saved from the evil Hindel is trying to make him into." Seelah tried to make them understand, but she could see her words fell on deaf ears. "I think he has gone to the swamp to hide out."

Donavan and Jack's eyes collided, and at the same time, the same picture shot into their minds. A picture of a beast with coarse black hair running towards the jeep. A jeep he recognized. And in that recognition, he had to know what would happen if he approached it. Jack had not shot Jonathan Hindel! He had shot Paulson. The way Paulson had known he would.

"We got some unfinished business to tend to, Jack," Donavan said, glancing out the window as he heard the sounds of vehicles stop outside the house.

"Right behind you, partner," Jack told him, following Donavan out the door and leaving the three people still sitting at the table to stare after them in open-mouth amazement.

CHAPTER THIRTY

Jonathan climbed the ladder, the boards creaking beneath his ponderous weight as he made his way up to the deck surrounding the old shack. His yellow eyes gazed into the surrounding darkness, searching out any dangers. A slight movement caught his attention, and his gaze swung to the woman sitting alone in the darkness.

"How thoughtful of you to await my return, Chandra." The thoughts traveled from his mind to hers. "It pleases me to know you miss me when I am not near." He moved towards her, watching her and trying to gauge her feelings.

"We had a visitor while you were gone," she told him aloud, not bothering to say the words in her mind since he could understand and hear her when she spoke to him.

Jonathan lifted his large head to sniff the air, his keen sense of smell picking out the scent of the man he had smelled on Chandra many times. He moved closer, his ugly face almost in hers as he sniffed her body searching for any scent of semen still clinging to her from their recent rutting, then threw back his head in anger and disappointment.

"He did not come to see me, Jonathan; he came in search of you. You and Quigly."

"What did Quigly do when he found him here? And what did you tell him?" Jonathan fired the questions at her in quick succession. His bright yellow gaze holding hers.

"Quigly tried to attack him, and Jack slit his throat then threw him into the water. I assume he is at the bottom of the swamp. And…I told him the truth." She continued to stare back at him, then left her chair, needing to distance herself from him as the reek of his wet fur made her stomach start to pitch.

"You told him about my being here?"

"I did not need to tell him. Somehow he already knew."

Chilling laughter filled her mind as Jonathan drew back his thick lips in a feral grin. "The woman he threw you aside for has taken it upon herself to tell him my secret!"

Chandra did not bother to correct him, knowing he could already see the truth of his words in her mind.

"You must remedy this problem, Chandra. I do not mean with just the woman. You will also destroy your lover. Or… should I say, ex-lover?"

"Why should I be the one to see to their destruction? You are the one they are after." She began to nudge him, trying to keep his anger high so he wouldn't think about anything else.

"You will do as I tell you, Chandra!" he ordered her, then without warning, his demeanor changed. "Or perhaps not. Perhaps I should be the one to end his life, but before I do, there is so very much I can tell him about the woman he felt such strong feelings for." His large head cocked to the side as he watched for her reaction.

"You will do what you will do, Jonathan. I have no power to stop you." She looked out toward the banks of the swamp, searching for any movement.

Jonathan watched her. However, his mind dwelled on baiting her, so he missed the way her eyes scanned the shoreline. "What do you think he would say if he knew about our son, Chandra?"

At last, Jonathan had her attention. She turned, looking at him, and before she could stop it, fear leaped into her eyes. "Why would you want to tell anyone about Lawrence, Jonathan? You promised me you would never tell anyone about him. He must never know I am the one who gave birth to him!" Chandra's voice shook with her fear, and as hard as she tried to push it away, she couldn't.

"What does it matter if Jack Olivier' knows you have a son? A son sired by me. He will never live to tell anyone." His glee at seeing the reaction he craved could not be hidden.

Hatred filled her mind for the monster standing before her. Suddenly, all the fear she had ever felt for him disappeared. With a coldness she had never known, she closed her mind against him, stopping him from even entering in to talk with her.

As she walked past him, he reached out, grabbed her arm and spun her around to face him. She could see the anger in his eyes as he glared at her.

"I have nothing more to say to you, Jonathan. And, you have nothing more I want to hear." She could feel him battering against her mind trying to gain entrance.

Chandra jerked away from him and walked into the house.

Jonathan threw back his head, howling his anger into the night.

Donavan and Jack yanked the boat up on the bank then jumped to the ground ducking out of sight as the howling split the night air.

"I guess we don't need to wonder who that is," Jack said, peering over the high foliage then pulling Donavan close, pointed to the hulking shape standing on the deck.

"I think we got here just in time." He eased his body back to a reclining position. "I didn't relish having him catch us in the water." Donavan tried to keep the fear from sounding in his voice.

"Still think we should have come out here alone?" Jack swatted away a swarm of mosquitoes then whipped the T-shirt from the waistband of his jeans to wipe the sweat from his face.

"Right now, I don't know what I think, Jack!" He dragged a shirtsleeve across his forehead. "How the hell do these people survive out here? It's so goddamn hot and muggy I can't breathe!"

"They get used to it. They don't have any choice. Most of them are so poor they consider themselves lucky just to have a place to live." He raised up, looked across the water, and breathed a sigh of relief when he saw the dark shape still standing in the faint glow of the moon. "Well, we've exhausted the subject of the swamp dwellers," Jack leaned back trying to get comfortable, "so I guess the best thing to talk 'bout is how we're gonna stay alive 'til daylight."

"It should be light in less than an hour. I think we can survive that long." Donavan withdrew a cigarette from his shirt pocket.

"I wouldn't be in an all-fired hurry to light that. I hear werewolves have a keen sense of smell."

"We're in a stinking swamp, remember? Isn't that what you told me when I cautioned you about lighting up earlier?"

"We didn't have a werewolf standin' on a deck, with the wind blowin' in his face when I lit up!" Jack reminded him, smiling as Donavan put the cigarette back in the pack.

"After this is all over, I want to get a search team together to see if we can find Paulson. His family's going to need closure, and I want his widow to receive full benefits." Donavan glanced over at Jack as he heard his shaky intake of breath.

"I feel like shit knowin' I'm the one responsible for his death." He dragged a hand through his sweaty hair.

"You had no way of knowing about Paulson. Besides that, he left us no choice."

"I appreciate the "us" Donavan. But you didn't shoot his brains out. I did!" Jack jabbed a finger against his chest.

"Just because you weren't driving." Donavan came right back at him. "If I'd been where you were, I would have shot him just as dead! So don't go taking on guilt you're not entitled to."

"He had to recognize us. Maybe not at first, but when he turned, he could see the jeep in the headlights." Jack drew back, looking at Donavan. "Do you think it's possible he wanted us to shoot him?"

"I'd say it's very possible. I don't know about you, but I sure as hell wouldn't want to live like that."

"Fuck!" Jack jerked up his legs, rolled to the side, his heart pumping with fear.

Donavan sat up cocking his gun and looking around. "What the hell's wrong?"

"Somethin' big just crawled over my legs!" he whispered, his voice shaky and breathless.

At a rustling noise sounding amongst the reeds, both men

turned, staring as something slithered into the water.

"Just a snake heading back to the water," Donavan chuckled, easing the hammer of his gun back into place. "Swamp's full of them."

"You think that's funny?" Jack looked around. "I'll tell you right goddamn now! I hate snakes! Call it a weakness...phobia... whatever! I don't give a fuck! I hate them slitherin' sonsabitches! And if another one comes even close to me," Jack poked a warning finger in Donavan's face, "you better get ready to fight, 'cause this whole goddamn place is gonna erupt in bullets!"

"Jack, you need to settle down and think about where you are and what's standing just a few yards away." Donavan tried to reason with him. "You go shooting off that gun before the sun comes up. We might just as well kiss both our asses goodbye!"

"Then as a farewell tribute, I'll kiss yours, and you can kiss mine, but I meant what I said." Jack nodded, giving emphasis to his words. "I'd rather take my chances with gettin' my throat ripped out by a werewolf than die a slow agonizin' death from bein' chewed on by a goddamn water moccasin!"

"Just try to maintain for a little while longer. It's almost daylight!" Donavan wiped a weary hand over his face. "I think when this is all over, I'm going to grab Barb and Jenny and take off for parts unknown for about a month."

"Sounds like a plan. Maybe Seelah and I can go with you." Jack grinned as he saw Donavan's head snap up then drop back to his chest.

Chandra walked across the floor to the small armoire set back against the wall. Opening the doors, she reached inside to withdraw the small gun she had kept secreted. She put the gun inside the pocket of her long dress, then turned to walk back outside.

Jonathan looked up as she approached him, a smile lighting up his dark yellow eyes. "I thought you wanted nothing more to do with me, Chandra. Could it be you've had second thoughts since Quigly is no longer here to interrupt us?" He moved, watching her reaction.

Chandra removed the barrier, allowing his words to enter

into her mind. "I want you to come inside so we can talk. I have something to show you." Chandra pulled open the screen door, waited for him to enter first. When he brushed past her, she drew the wooden door closed behind them and, with a flick of her wrist, locked them inside.

Jonathan threw back his head, and as he did, a deep growl that sounded like a laugh poured from his throat. "Do you wish to talk first or later?" The words flowed from his mind.

"First," she told him, watching as interest flowed into his eyes. "I wish to talk to you about Lawrence. You said earlier, you do not intend to honor your promise to me about not telling anyone I am his mother. Why would you do this after all these years of keeping silent?"

"It never made a difference to you before, Chandra. Yes, you cared about Lawrence's feelings on the matter, but you never cared about anyone else finding out. Then, you had never fallen in love before." Jonathan eased his body onto the floor, leaned back against the wall. "You see, Chandra, when you give your heart to someone, you become vulnerable, even weak, and when that happens, you can be…so…easy to manipulate."

"Like your weakness for Angelia." Chandra sat still and allowed the words to seep into Jonathan's mind.

For a moment, he almost lashed out at her, then realized that she wanted him to lose control and leashed his anger, turning his hostility instead into a lethal weapon with which to punish her.

Chandra remained silent, waiting for his next move.

"When you followed me back to my house that night, I offered you the gift of immortality. Did I not?"

"Yes, but…" she became silent as he gazed at her.

"I gave you a life that all women would desire to have. I told you, you could receive immortality and not have to enter into my world. When you entered into your new life, you received all of Angelia's gifts. And all I asked of you is to allow me to be with the woman I love." He grew silent for a moment, his mind dwelling on the woman he spoke of. "I told you, in your new life, you would age, but one year for every ten years you lived upon this earth."

"When you offered me that life, I had just turned sixteen years old. You know that is too young to realize…" Chandra tried to keep the tears bottled up inside. Now she could feel them trickling down her face.

"Did…you…not…accept…my…offer?" Jonathan challenged her to deny his truth.

"I did! Yes! I did! But you tricked me! You didn't tell me how I would suffer in the life you gave me!" Her anger shot to the surface, and she could do nothing to stop it.

"Are you such a child…still…you think such a gift would come easy? Immortality is a gift given from the dark side! Dark entities are the only ones who can live forever! I could bestow upon you the chance to live for hundreds of years without having to die and come back to start over."

"How is it you are able to do this, Jonathan? What did you have to give to have such power?"

"The same thing you gave to me, Chandra." Jonathan looked at her enjoying her fear as she stared into his eyes. "I gave my soul to the dark side, and in return, I received the power to bless those I chose with the gift of living for centuries."

"And between us, we condemned an innocent child to the dark side. Lawrence did not deserve to have that given to him, Jonathan." Chandra turned away.

"As my son, he could not be anything but dark. When it comes time for him to step forward, to give back all he has been given, he will do so without question!"

"You allowed him to take the blame for all your evil. You allowed him to spend time locked away in a mental institution for something you and the others of your kind did. You introduced him to your filthy appetites." She allowed her disgust to pour out of her along with all her hatred as she dragged everything she felt out into the open. To do any less would have sent her screaming from the house in shame. "What more does he have to give you, Jonathan?"

"His soul, Chandra." His voice, as he filled her mind with his thoughts, sounded proud. As though the forfeit of one's soul had to be the highest honor anyone could offer up. "Lawrence is a man. Now it is time he took his place beside me."

Knowing it would be light soon, Chandra placed her hand inside her pocket, letting her fingers trail over the cold steel. The feel of its power giving her the strength she needed to carry out her plan. As Jonathan began to change, she walked over, closing and locking the small window.

Jonathan moaned, twisting and turning as his skin rotted and pooled beneath him.

With complete calm, Chandra lit the small lamps then picked up a full can of kerosene, dousing the curtains, rug and walls. When she finished, she sat down in the chair to wait.

Jonathan remained lying on the floor until the change ran its course, then stretched out his legs, giving himself time to regain his strength before getting to his feet. "You will get the towel and soap ready for me now, Chandra," he told her, his voice deep and demanding.

"That will not be necessary, Jonathan." Chandra withdrew the gun from her pocket.

"You will not argue with me! You will do as I say! Now!" He looked over at her, willing her to obey him.

"I cannot allow you to stay on this plane any longer, Jonathan. The time has come for your evil to end."

Jonathan looked at her and, for the first time, saw the gun she held in her hands. "You dare to threaten me?" He staggered to his feet as she raised the gun towards him. "You will put down the gun. Now, Chandra. You know you cannot kill me. I have lived on this plane for almost two centuries. My strength is too powerful to be destroyed." He held out his hand, but she kept the gun aimed at him.

"That is the chance I will have to take, Jonathan."

"If you kill me, you will no longer be young and beautiful, Chandra. The gift I gave you will die with me. Think of what that means, Chandra. Are you willing to let your lover see you old and ugly? Are you willing to see the disgust that will cover his face when he looks at you?" Again he held out his hand. "I can see you don't, so now, give me the gun."

Chandra lowered the gun, her hands shaking from the weight of it, and taking careful aim, squeezed the trigger.

Jonathan felt the bullet slam into his stomach, and he fell backward. He covered the wound with his hands, trying to stanch the flow of blood. "Chandra help me," he pleaded with her, a painful smile flitting across his face as he saw her standing above him.

Chandra ignored him to aim the gun once more. This time the bullet entered his throat, a fitting wound for all the times he had inflicted the same suffering on countless others. She watched the blood flow down his chest to drip onto the floor. Without a word, she aimed and shot three more times.

Jonathan tried to crawl towards the door, but his strength continued to drain from his body. His eyes widened in horror as he saw her remove the top from the lamp then turn up the wick. As the flame shot higher, she drew back her hand then flung the lamp against the wall.

She could hear a loud pounding on the door of the shack. She ignored it to walk across the floor. Calmly she picked up the gun, and without giving herself time to think, placed the barrel inside her mouth.

Jack pulled on the door, trying to get it open, but it refused to budge. "She's got the damn thing locked!"

"This place is going to go up like a tinderbox any minute, Jack!" Donavan yelled out.

"I've got to get her outta there."

"It's too late, goddamn it! We need to go!"

They heard a gunshot, then an explosion as fire whooshed through the heat-shattered window and through the cracks of the wood.

"Oh shit!" Jack yelled, still trying to get inside.

Donavan ran up beside him, and drawing back his fist, hit Jack a solid blow to the side of his jaw. As he buckled, Donavan caught him, throwing him off the deck, then leaped in after him to swim as fast as he could away from the walkway.

When Jack came to, he looked over at Donavan. "What the hell happened? Did I get hit with a burnin' board or somethin'?"

Donavan looked at him then rolled over, getting to his feet.

Jack stood up, looking across the swamp, watching as the shack tumbled into the water. "Chandra didn't get out, did she?"

"No. To tell you the truth, the way she had that place locked and barred, I think she planned it that way." Donavan stood beside him.

"I hate to think of her sufferin' like that." Jack wiped his eyes, not bothering to hide the pain in his voice.

"I don't think she did suffer, Jack."

Jack spun around. "She just burned up in a goddamn flamin' shack, Donavan!"

"Listen to me, will you? Just for a moment?"

"What!"

"We heard five shots before that shack started to burn. Right?"

"Yeah. So?"

"Then we heard one shot just as it started to go up. I think she saved the last bullet for herself. She had all this planned right down to the last board falling into the water."

Jack remained silent, then nodded. "I think you're right. When I talked to her earlier, she said the time had come for Hindel to be brought down and that she had to be the one to do it."

"It's over, Jack. Jonathan Hindel met someone stronger than him."

"Let's go home. Right now, all I wanna do is hold Seelah in my arms and try to put this whole mess behind us."

"Right behind you, partner." Donavan draped an arm over Jack's shoulders as they walked towards the boat.

As the early morning sun crept towards the horizon, a lone female wolf howled a mournful cry into the stillness.

Within moments, her cry was answered.

ABOUT THE AUTHOR

Judith Ann McDowell is a novelist with four finished books. When not working on a manuscript, Judith, along with her husband, like to travel to different cities such as New Orleans to talk with people about voodoo and to talk with those who have experienced firsthand true hauntings.

Judith is the mother of four grown sons, Guy, David, Rhett and Nick, and lives in the Pacific Northwest with her husband Darrell and their two Pekingese Chi and Tai and three cats Isis, Lacy and Keefer.

Judith is at present working on her next novel.